MISSION BRIEFING . . .

"All right," Val said, "tell me what we do first."

"First we check out the Station. If it turns out he's still here, I take care of him and you talk real fast to keep Station security from shooting me down."

"You think they'll catch you? I thought you were good enough to get it done without anyone knowing who it was?"

"On the planet, sure, but I wasn't kidding about the kind of surveillance I'll be under here. If Radman's still here, I'll just have to wipe him out and hope the security people stop to ask a few questions before burning me down. . . ."

SHARON GREEN
has also written:

THE WARRIOR WITHIN
THE WARRIOR ENCHAINED
THE WARRIOR REARMED
THE CRYSTALS OF MIDA
AN OATH TO MIDA
CHOSEN OF MIDA
THE WILL OF THE GODS
MIND GUEST

GATEWAY TO XANADU

SHARON GREEN

A Diana Santee Spaceways Novel

DAW BOOKS, INC.
DONALD A. WOLLHEIM, PUBLISHER

1633 Broadway, New York, NY 10019

First Printing, December 1985

1 2 3 4 5 6 7 8 9

PRINTED IN THE U.S.A.

CHAPTER 1

By the time the gentle chime sounded that was obviously supposed to wake me, I was already up and dressed. I didn't have much in the room that needed putting together, and that was mostly done, too. Which was definitely a good thing, since I didn't know how to turn that gently chiming alarm off. It must have been set by Val before he left, and waking up to find him already gone had surprised me. As excited as I felt about going home, I wouldn't have believed it possible for someone to leave that room without waking me. If I'd slept alone the night before, I probably wouldn't even have slept.

I stuffed my spare ship's suit into the small monolon bag, smoothed the bag closed, then turned to look over the blue-green, brown and white room one last time. I didn't really expect to see anything I'd accidently left behind, and I didn't; I hadn't shared the room long enough with Val. The last look around was a good-bye to most of the strangeness I'd run into there in the Absari base around Tildor, a volume of space no one in my Federation knew anything about. I'd bumped into the Absari Watchers of the backward planet Tildor, had helped out with a chore on the planet, and now was heading back to my Federation with a "Hi, there, neighbor!" letter of self-introduction from the Absari upper echelon. If everyone on the Federation Council didn't faint dead away at being contacted by a previously unknown, starfaring humanoid race, their expressions would be worth seeing. At least two-thirds of the Council considered the possibility of meeting equals an amusing fictional notion, something to have fun with while watching it on tri-v, but nothing to take seriously. I couldn't wait until they got a look at Val.

Sudden inspiration hit me at thought of Val, so I went back to the low, wide couch-bed we'd shared the night before, sat down on it, then stood up again. The chiming cut off immediately, bringing me a satisfied grin. Absari ways weren't Federation ways no matter now much the Absari looked like us, but a little common sense sometimes helped bridge the gap between alien cultures. That was something I'd have to remember during the next standard year, the time period Val would be partnering with me as an agent for the Federation. A little common sense—and a lot of delicate, judicious handling—and his talent could be put to use for the benefit of the Federation.

Or, at least, one of his talents. I sat back down on the couch-bed and stretched out across it, folding my arms above my head and grinning. Val's ability to change his features and appearance to match anyone he cared to was a result of his original Absari blood; I'd have to ask him if his bed talent came from the same source. I'd miss it when his year was up and he went back home, but I'd be able to look around for an adequate replacement once I came back to the Absari Confederacy to work my own year for them. If that particular talent really was in the blood, I'd have one hell of a wild time during that—

The chiming started again so abruptly that I jumped, and

this time it wasn't as sweet and mellow as it had been the first time. I'd never before heard an annoyed alarm clock, but I knew damned well I was hearing one then. I muttered a few words describing the personal habits of that alarm as I rose from the bed, then included Val in for setting the damn thing in the first place. My eagerness to get going had gotten me up, but I could still feel the drag of minus sleep beneath that eagerness, gluing shut my eyelids and making me yawn. I hadn't slept very well in the days I'd waited for the Absari rep Phalsyn to get there, and during that time I'd kept Val on the opposite side of the room with the well-known cold shoulder—and a sincere promise to break off any extremities of his that I happened to find in grabbing distance. He'd grinned at the promise, and had told me he could wait— which he did until last night, when he made up for the wait. I couldn't honestly describe the time as wasted, but I'd needed the lost sleep more.

I yawned again and shook my head, then grabbed up the monolon bag and headed for the door. I'd get all the sleep I wanted or needed once we were on our way, and what I really needed right then was a cup of coffee. The door slid open in front of me, giving me access to the hall of the residential section, which led to the work area, which in turn led to the docking facilities. I didn't know how really early it was in the base day until I walked past the offices in the work area and found most of them empty, no more than the usual skeleton crew in the comm room. The small sounds of the base's life-support systems bracketed the whisper of my deck shoes along the corridor carpeting, and the two men in the comm room didn't even look up as I passed. I wondered if the early departure time had been Phalsyn's idea, the intent being to get rid of the alien and the guinea pig with the fewest number of people watching, keeping the gossip to a minimum. The base people would know Val and I were gone, but they would not know where, at least until the formal talks started, and maybe not even then. If you think about how long it takes most people to accept even the new family a few doors down, the idea of keeping as much as possible secret for as long as possible begins to look a lot less unreasonable.

The docking area seemed just as empty as the office area had been, until I spotted Dameron leaning against the hull of my ship, right beside the access hatch. The big man had his arms folded across the chest of his dark blue base commander's uniform, studying the floor in front of his feet, the same preoccupied air holding him that had held him the night before. Not until I stopped in front of him did his eyes rise to my face.

"You're here sooner than Valdon thought you would be," he said, his broad face showing a hint of a smile. "He only just entered the ship himself."

"Probably to double-check the work he did on it," I said, giving more in the way of a smile than I was getting. "I don't blame him for not wanting to find out if he screwed up the hard way. Why don't you come aboard and get your final good-byes said while I start the departure check?"

"They've already been said," he answered with a sigh. "All I have left are yours, along with a request or two. You don't mind a request or two from a friend, do you?"

His dark eyes were studying me in a very sober, worried way. Considering the fact that Dameron knew more about what my line of work entailed than anyone else there, his worry had to be on behalf of my new partner.

"If you don't mind, I'd like to hear what those requests are before I agree to them," I said, putting my fist on my hip. "I'm not as silly as some people, who commit themselves before they know what they're committing themselves to."

"Don't rub it in!" he growled, looking annoyed, but then he grinned and laughed softly. He'd been so eager to do me a favor that he hadn't first asked what favor I had in mind, a silliness he'd be regretting for some time to come. When you make a habit of keeping your word, you really should take a good look around before giving it.

"Okay, okay, so I deserve to have it rubbed in," he conceded, one broad hand ruefully rubbing the back of his neck. "That doesn't mean I also deserve to be haunted by this thing for the rest of my life. I'd like to know just how deep a pit I dug for Valdon—and how good his chances are of climbing out again all in one piece. He's one of the best field agents I've ever had, but I don't know if he's good enough to survive at the level you seem to operate on. I still don't understand how *you* survive."

"That's easy," I told him with a wave of my hand. "I have the worst luck you've ever seen, always picking the wrong side to bet on. Any time I'm about to get a really hairy assignment, I make sure to bet someone that I'll finally get it, so I don't. Works every time."

I grinned, but the good commander wasn't in the mood for a laugh. The look in his dark eyes hardened as he began straightening himself in annoyance, so I waved my hand at him again.

"Come on, Dameron, let's be intelligent about this," I coaxed, letting some of the tiredness I felt come into my voice. "I worked a long time at my job to get good enough to qualify for hyper-A assignments; you can't really believe they'll let Val share them just because he's giant size and has all those pretty muscles. He'll have to earn the right to put his neck on the line just like the rest of us, and by then it will probably be time for him to come home. Chances are you'll have less cause to worry about him than you would if you sent him back down to Tildor."

"But—you two are supposed to be partners," he protested, still seeming upset. "If you get one of those assignments then he'll get it, or at least he'll decide he has it. He won't sit back and let you do it all yourself, and you're crazy if you think he will.''

''Are you under the impression that I don't know what he's like?'' I asked, a bit belligerently. ''Have you forgotten all the time we spent together down on Tildor? When I want Val out of the way I'll have him out of the way, whether it makes him happy or not. On Tildor *he* had all of the advantages, but in the Federation we'll be on *my* stamping grounds. I'm even willing to bet on it.''

''I thought you always backed the losing side,'' he retorted, but a shadow of his old humor was back, along with a fading of some of the worry. ''I don't feel as much confidence as you seem to, girl, but for some reason I also don't feel as bad as I did. You're sure your people won't let him have any of these—hyper-A assignments?''

''Positive,'' I answered, grinning briefly at the way Dameron pronounced 'hyper-A'. We were speaking his base language, and there was no one-to-one translation for the phrase. ''Hyper-A is short for 'high percentage risk agent,' a nickname for Special Agents. It means that if the computers rate the possibilities of success on an assignment at 9 percent or more against, that assignment is given only to a hyper-A. We're the ones who have already proven we can survive against odds like that by doing it, and the doing takes some doing. Val won't have the necessary time—or the opportunity. For the most part I plan to use him as a distraction while I do the actual work, either with his talent in full play or just as he is. A little less masculinity to his face, and he'd be downright pretty, and I can think of a lot of ways to use something like that. I wonder if he could change himself to directions.''

''You've lost your mind, girl,'' Dameron interrupted my ranging thoughts, hauling me back to where we were standing. He was looking straight at me, and his expression couldn't be interpreted as anything but ridiculing. "I thought you said you knew Valdon," he demanded. "If you think he'll stand still for being a flower boy in the background while you run around drawing fire from the enemy, you're out of your mind! What do you think he is?"

"I *thought* he was the one you were so worried about," I retorted, staring at the base commander. "Have you suddenly changed your mind, or am I going senile in my old age? I thought you *wanted* him out of the line of fire—or haven't you decided yet what you want?"

"I do know what I want," he muttered. "But what I want isn't necessarily what he'll want. Or what either of us would consider acceptable. Maybe I don't know what I want after all." He pulled his hand through his hair with a harried gesture, then turned to me. "What exactly do you think of Valdon?"

"What's to think about him?" I asked with a shrug, privately wondering if Dameron had started to lose the marble game. "He's big, good-looking, has a talent I intend making use of— Hell, Dameron, I barely know him. The only things we've really done together so far are argue and fight. I'll be able to do a better job of giving an opinion if we ever manage to exchange more than a dozen words before the fur starts flying."

"But you've still let him bed you," the Commander pointed out, a flatness in the words. "That doesn't jibe with the lack of opinion you claim to have. Or not have. Do you make a habit of spending bed time with men you scarcely know?"

"Usually," I answered with a slow nod, now almost convinced the leash was slipping. "How many men do you think I get to know well in my line of work? And what difference can a little sex make? Just because a man's good in bed doesn't mean you'd trust your back to him. Sex is nothing more than an exercise for two—or three, or five, or however your tastes run. Haven't you learned that yet?''

"That particular outlook doesn't necessarily come about through mature experience," he said, a gentleness and something that seemed to be pain looking out of his eyes. "Some people are raised to consider it a good deal more than casual exercise, more than something to be indulged in even between virtual strangers. If you ever get to the point of gaining true mature experience, you might learn that.''

"Do you mean I'll learn that some men consider a roll in the hay the equivalent of a life commitment?'' I asked, letting most of the friendliness drain out of my tone. "I've already learned that, friend, and also learned to stay away from that sort. The only thing I'm interested in commiting to is what I've already committed to, and there's no room in that sort of life for distractions. The—'level I operate on' makes other commitments impractical, especially long-term ones. My body has certain needs, and I see to them whenever I like the looks of available partners; if you're thinking about telling me that Val has kept himself pure waiting for his one true lady love, you have a shock coming. No man ever got to his level of expertise by abstaining, and please note that we're not discussing opinion. I've had to acquire a certain level of expertise myself to satisfy certain of my job requirements, and I can assure you that I know what I'm talking about.''

"I don't doubt that," he answered, amused now. "And I didn't mean to imply that Valdon was a sheltered innocent. The reactions of the field team girls he paired with made that clear enough.''

"Then what *were* you implying?'' I asked, genuinely curious. If there was a point to the conversation I'd been a part of for the last few minutes, it would have been nice knowing what it was.

"What makes you think I was implying anything?'' he

countered, more amused, calmly folding his arms again. "I just happened to be taking the opportunity to voice a couple of my own opinions. I didn't say they had anything to do with Valdon. You'll see to it, then, that your people don't let him get in over his head?"

"Cross my heart and hope to spit wooden nickels," I promised, holding up my free hand. "Was that all you were looking for, a promise to protect your delicate little former second, and a true, unvarnished declaration on my philosophy of life? No sworn blood oaths that I return him as sweet and untarnished as I'm getting him?"

"Your penchant for sarcasm must find you almost as much trouble as your line of work," Dameron remarked, looking down at me with seeming annoyance, and then the twinkle came back. "No, I don't need an oath like that from you about Valdon; I already have one from Valdon about you. Some of us still believe in the basic premise that women are there to be looked after and protected."

I stared at him in a disbelieving way for a minute, then burst out laughing. His dark brows lowered over his eyes in a frown that showed lack of understanding, causing me to laugh even harder, then shake my head at him.

"That's a hell of a sentiment to be coming from the man who deliberately set me up to be attacked by sword-swinging baddies," I pointed out when I could, still chuckling. "Not to mention the enslavement part. Are you sure you're not talking about Val *this* time?"

"Maybe I am," he agreed very quietly, with a small, sad smile, his dark eyes now unreadable. I cursed myself for an idiot and for having such a big mouth, but the damage was already done. I'd been well-enough aware of the guilt Dameron had felt over what had happened to me down on Tildor, but I'd thought he'd managed to put it behind him. Telling him *I* didn't blame him would probably only have made it worse, but I was about to try exactly that when he threw off the dark mood and straightened again.

"At any rate," he said as if there had been no interruption, "Valdon has those papers Phalsyn told you about, and the two of you can convert the time measurement in them to something your people will understand. As a final request I'm going to ask you to try to stay out of trouble and to take care of yourself, but I have a feeling that's one request you won't grant."

"I always take care of myself," I answered, still bothered by the way I had hurt him. "There's rarely anyone else around to do the job for me. As for staying out of trouble, most of the people I know consider the accomplishment in the same category as avoiding death and taxes. Dameron. . . ."

"Don't worry, girl, I'll get it worked out after I see you safely on your way back home," he assured me with a faint smile. "I'll just remind myself that whatever trouble you find with Valdon you asked for, freely and without any pressure from me. You'd better get aboard now, so I can start evacuating the air from this dock."

"Wait a minute!" I protested as he took my arm to head me toward the airlock. "What are you talking about? What trouble with Val? I don't plan on having any trouble with Val."

"Then maybe you won't have any," Dameron said with a shrug, his hand moving me right in front of the airlock before leaving my arm. "If you're a good girl and behave yourself with him, Valdon certainly won't start any trouble. Have a good trip home, girl, and be sure to stop by if you're ever in this neighborhood again."

He patted my shoulder a couple of times before he turned and headed for the dock exit, ignoring the "Hey!" I sent after him as though I hadn't uttered a sound. I hefted the monolon bag I still carried, momentarily tempted to drop it and go after him, then said to hell with it and turned back to the airlock. I didn't know what game he was playing, but calling him on it wouldn't have accomplished anything. It was a safe bet even *he* didn't know what he was talking about, and I had better things to do with my time than waste it trying to find sense where there wasn't any.

Once I had stalked past the double open doors of the lock and hit the switch that closed them, I made my way deeper into the small ship. The two cabins, salon area, shower and exercise area, and galley were all ranged together after the airlock and before the control room, so I stopped briefly to toss my monolon bag into my cabin before continuing on to the pilot's console. I also stopped in the galley to fill a mug with coffee, but obviously made too little noise performing those chores. Val was moving around in the second cabin, probably stowing whatever he'd brought with him, and didn't even stick his nose out to see who had come in. I shrugged a little over such blind trust, still too annoyed with Dameron to be interested in making small talk with Val, and carried my coffee into the control room.

The departure check I started the computer on was longer and more detailed than your average departure check, but I wanted to be sure that everything really was on the green before I kicked off into the deep black. Dameron and Val seemed to be talented in the repairs department, but they still had been working on an alien ship with no more than alien wiring diagrams and inspired guesswork to guide them. An all-systems check is boring only when your life doesn't hinge on that check, and even so it doesn't take forever. I was just finishing up when the wide metal doors of the dock slid invitingly open, showing that Dameron had evacuated the air from the dock, giving me access to the departure tunnels. My course computer clicked contentedly as it waited with infinite

patience to be meshed into the drive unit; every light on my
board blinked green, and sets of parallel blue lines lit up
along the dock wall and extended out into the departure
tunnels. I raised the ship on secondary breaking jets, nudged
us toward the open door, then followed the pretty blue lines
until it was time to leave them and the tunnels behind. Tildor
showed briefly in my screens, barely noticed in the midst of
the departure question-and-answer routine I was involved in
with the computer, and then it was a good distance behind us,
its moons no longer even visible. I stayed at the board until
the entire solar system was behind us, then got out of the
pilot's chair to stretch. Everything from then on until
destination—barring emergencies—was automatic, and I was
free to play passenger.

I dropped off my empty mug in the galley on my way to
the salon, plopped down on the nearer of the two couches,
put my feet up as I lay back, then closed my eyes. Although
it hadn't seemed like it while it was happening, the departure
from Dameron's moon base had taken better than three hours,
including the time it took to clear the solar system. Under
normal circumstances everything after rising from the surface
of the moon would have been handled by the computer,
leaving me free to watch, worry, or even walk away, but I'd
had a private project that needed programming, that had to be
done then or not at all. I'd gone through a lot waiting for
Dameron to program my course computer, and even with
Phalsyn's papers handed over for delivery, I still hadn't been
allowed to watch the course and quadrant data being fed in.
To say I'd been annoyed would be to say the sayer didn't
know me; I usually prefer getting even to getting mad. I'd
asked the main computer to rig up a double-check tape run on
its less intelligent cousin the course computer, and had waited
and watched to see if the run did what I wanted it to. We
were just at the fringes of Tildor's system when the double-

check clicked in, running a ninety-second-lag playback of where we'd just been. I couldn't copy the set-in course without purging the entire program, but there was nothing to keep me from recording where I'd been—up to and including the time of my arrival at destination. All I'd have to do at that point would be to reverse the run tape, and the breadcrumb trail leading back to Dameron's base would be in my hot little hand. I might never need it, but it never hurts to hedge your—

"All finished with starting us on our way?" a voice asked abruptly, startling me half up off the couch before I realized it was Val, speaking the Federation Basic he'd been given, most likely for practice. I wasn't used to having company on that ship, and settling back into old habits had nearly given me heart failure at the first of his words.

"Don't do that," I grumbled at him where he stood by the second couch, about five feet away, then sank back down to sitting on my own couch. "Just until I get used to having someone else aboard, I'd appreciate it if you stomped or sang or in some other manner made your presence known before you came into a room where I was. If you don't, I'm not going to last very long."

"From the way you came up off that couch, I don't think you're the one we have to worry about," Val came back, his voice dry, his deep black eyes looking down at me where I sat. "You would have ended up facing away from me if you hadn't stopped yourself, and I have a feeling that would have been only part of the move. What comes after that?"

"Oh, just a little screaming, a little jumping, nothing very special," I answered with a gesture of dismissal, smiling some to distract him. Telling him he'd almost been the proud possessor of a reverse crescent kick followed by a roundhouse kick, both to the face and head, would have probably started another argument; Val had already run into a couple of my offensive techniques, and hadn't liked them much.

"Nothing but a couple of mild surprise reactions, is that it?" he asked, ignoring my smile as he settled himself on the neighboring couch, stretching his big body out in a relaxed sprawl. "Are you sure that's all it was?"

"What else could it have been?" I asked with mildly curious and very innocent reason, at the same time wondering if he could have found out about the double-check run. "It's embarrassing to admit, but I'm afraid I forgot you were here."

I showed my embarrassment in my smile, but he still wasn't paying any attention to it. His dark black eyes continued to stare at me out of an expressionless face under dark black hair, and he didn't seem to be as relaxed as his sprawl might suggest. He was still wearing his cobalt blue base uniform, but that wasn't a likely reason for what seemed like discomfort.

"Are you sure you *forgot* I was here?" he asked very quietly, keeping those eyes on me. "Are you sure it wasn't more a matter of remembering all too well? Didn't you see that I took the other cabin?"

"I don't understand," I told him. "Why would I say I forgot when I remembered? And what has cabins got to do with anything?"

"I'm trying to tell you that you don't have to worry about my being here," he said very gently. "Whatever happened between us at the base doesn't have to happen here, not if you don't want it to. Our being alone together doesn't mean you have to think about defending yourself from me. I won't be doing anything that needs to be defended against."

He was still staring at me, but now there was a very definite expression on his face: a sincere entreaty for belief and trust. To say I was stunned would be putting it mildly; Val thought I was afraid to be alone with him!

I leaned back against my own couch still more wide-eyed and open-mouthed than I'd been in a long time, but the reason for what he'd just said wasn't hard to figure out. Val was a man in whom the ancient male hunter could be seen by any woman he turned those eyes on, the sort of man who traditionally took whatever he wanted, most especially the use of females. Women in ancient times feared men like that, but they were also used to them; whole cities were pillaged, and rape was a natural concomitant. Modern times brought about the advent of civilization, and women weren't expected to put up with that sort of nonsense any longer—but every once in a while a hunter turned up anyway. Val had been raised to be considerate of the feelings of women, to understand how fragile and helpless they were, but the hunter still looked out of his eyes. He'd been taught to feel like hell every time a woman cringed back from his appraisal, and he'd learned to make very sure of full agreement before letting his basic nature take over. He bent over backwards to reassure the females around him, most especially at the first sign of nervousness at his presence. I didn't know if he'd been brooding over the point since he first came aboard, or if my aborted attack in self-defense had triggered the thought, but most likely a combination of the two had produced the statement of intended chastity. That he hadn't learned to know me better over the last few days was annoying, but not nearly as annoying as being lumped in the "fragile, helpless" category. I'd thought I'd taught Val the hard way just how well I liked gentlemanly condescension, but it was clear the lesson hadn't taken. It looked like it was time for another lesson.

"You really understand the way a girl feels, don't you?" I said at last feigning relieved gratitude. "I can't say how much better I feel now, to know that we'll be occupying separate cabins. You're an absolute doll, Val.''

I beamed at him as I stood up from the couch, pretending not to see the way he flinched at my complete agreement with his offer. We had a decently long trip ahead of us, and hunters don't make very successful eagle scouts. Still beaming, I kicked off the deck shoes I was wearing, then opened my ship suit and started to wriggle out of it. Those black eyes were on me instantly, sliding over every curve I had, the look in them saying they still liked what they saw, and then memory returned of what had been committed to. If it hadn't been so far from his nature, I think Val would have started blubbering then; the muscles tensed all over his body, his face went expressionless, and swallowing turned his voice hoarse.

"What are you doing?" he demanded as he looked up at me. "I don't understand what you're— Diana, you're taking your clothes off."

"Sure," I agreed with a smilingly innocent nod, tossing the ship's suit in the general direction of my cabin. "It's so warm in here you don't really *need* clothes, but I couldn't take them off until you said what you did. I never wore anything on the trip out."

Which, although calculated, was nothing but the complete truth, except for the stated reason. I wore nothing of clothing on the trip out because I was born and raised on one of the only two nudist worlds in the Federation, and I revert to going natural every time I can. Val's face had taken on an appalled, desperate look, as though he were trying to imagine living with a naked woman for two months without touching her, but I made sure not to notice that look either. I turned away from him and headed for the galley, humming happily in a soft voice.

"It's going to be great having someone to talk to," I

enthused over my shoulder as I stopped in front of the food synthesizer to refill the mug I'd left there earlier with coffee. "I enjoy my own company well enough, but there's such a thing as too much of that sort of enjoyment. How about a cup of coffee?"

Without waiting for an answer I filled a second mug, then carried them both back to the salon area. Val was still sitting on his couch, one big hand rubbing at his face, a harried expression in his eyes. He waited until I'd put the mug into the slot meant for it in the front of the couch's armrest, shifted a little on the couch, then cleared his throat.

"Diana, you're not being fair," he said, no more than a trace of the hoarseness left in his voice. "I'm trying to be considerate of you, but you're not doing the same for me. I promised I'd do nothing to make you feel it necessary to defend yourself, but I wasn't picturing you walking around like that. You have to put your clothes back on."

"Why?" I asked, sipping gingerly at the hot coffee. "It isn't as if you've never seen me naked before, Val. You've seen me naked lots of times."

"I know I have," he answered through his teeth. "I know I've seen you naked lots of times, but that was when I could— Never mind. Just get into your clothes."

"I've got a better idea," I said with sudden inspiration, laughing in delight and nearly clapping my hands. "Instead of me getting back into clothes, why don't you get out of yours? Then we'll both be naked, and you won't be bothered anymore. Come on, Val, do it!"

I was still enthusiastic as I went to my couch to put my coffee down, and by the time I turned back to him, Val was on his feet. Looking at him, it wasn't hard guessing why he'd stayed seated so long; I was considered big for a woman, but Val was big for a man. You couldn't quite make two of me out of him, but if you tried you wouldn't be short by all that much. He'd known exactly how menacing he'd look to the poor little female if he was upright, but at that point he was beyond considerations of that sort. He couldn't possibly accept what I'd just suggested, not and keep his sanity along with his word; he had to start being firm, and those black eyes said he was more than ready.

"Stop dancing around like that!" he growled, coming toward me where I stood between the two couches. "You're acting as if you *want* to be attacked, and I'm just about ready to oblige you! Get back into those clothes, or I'll . . ."

At that point he made the mistake of reaching for my left arm with his right hand, just as I knew he would. He'd done the same thing once before, reaching out to grab me in anger, but that lesson hadn't stayed with him any more than the other one had. As his hand closed around my arm just above the wrist I stepped toward him instead of away, turned my hand palm upward, and moved even closer. I slipped my left hand out of the forced looseness of his grip, continued to turn his hand to the left with the added assistance of the back of my left hand fingers pushing against the trapped fingers of his right hand, and simultaneously stepped back and twisted around. With a squawk of astonishment and some small amount of pain, the great big dangerous hunter went down flat on his back, totally helpless. Before Val knew what was happening, he had hit the carpeted deck hard, and lay there with my bare heel on his throat.

"Or you'll what?" I asked very mildly, looking down at him where he twisted a little in an attempt to ease the pressure on his arm and shoulder, his expression totally disbelieving. "The last time it was partially Bellna, but this time it's all me, which should explain why you're not hurting as much as you did then. If I shift my weight onto my heel you're a goner, friend, or I could simply kick you hard enough in the side of the head to put your lights out for a while. As I said earlier, I forgot you were here; that doesn't equate with deliberately forgetting out of desperate fear of you. If you're smart, you'll start considering being afraid of *me*. Despite many opinions to the contrary, it *is* possible to rape a man, and I know how. And I haven't given my word not to.''

I turned him loose then, taking my heel away from his throat so that I could step over him on the way to my couch. I sat down and got a cigarette out of the coucharm dispenser and lit up, then picked up my coffee mug to sip at it, only then noticing that Val was still on the deck. When he saw my eyes on him he sat up slowly, rubbing at his right arm with his left hand, a strange expression in his deep black eyes.

''I don't think I've ever been told a woman wasn't afraid of me with quite that much conviction before,'' he muttered, raising his knees so that he could hang his forearms on them. ''I assume I'm to take it that if I do something you don't like, you'll let me know about it. Do you think you can catch me with that sort of thing more than once?''

''There's a lot more where that came from,'' I snorted. He seemed to be relieved that I wasn't afraid of him after all, but he hadn't liked being roughed up in the proving of it. My previous good intentions were down the drain, but I'd had to settle the question of fear the most direct way possible. Some men turn protective around women who are afraid of things, and Val and I were slated to work together. If he did his job slap-dash because he was worrying about me, it could get us both killed.

''What happens if I do manage to get the upper hand?'' he pursued, perversely trying to dent the lack of fear he had been so relieved to see. ''Once I have you in a position where you can't do me any harm, what's to stop me from doing anything I like to you?''

''Nothing,'' I admitted calmly, exhaling smoke at him.

"You're bigger than I am, stronger than I am, and you just might manage to take me before I could finish you off. But if you did, you'd have something of a problem. You would not be able to let me go afterward, because if I ever got free I'd have your heart—and a couple or three other things to keep it company. To avoid that you'd have to finish me, and then you'd find yourself all dressed up with no place to go. At the other end of the course tape is my Federation, a volume of space you don't know your way around in. Assuming you have the proper coordinates you can always turn around and head back to Absari space, but once you got there your people would start asking about that conference they're expecting to have with my people. No matter which way you turned you'd have problems, and all because of your resentment against my harmless little demonstration. If that's the way you want it, go ahead and take your best shot."

"Harmless little demonstration," he snorted. "If that was a harmless little demonstration, I'm a—" He broke it off and stared at me for a long minute, then snorted again with something more like amusement. "You think you have it all figured out. What would happen if I did take you—and afterward you discovered you liked it? Instead of coming after me, you'd end up begging not to be turned loose."

"If you were curious to know how likely that would be, you should have checked with the Tildorani slavers before we left," I said, giving him a grin with a lot of wolf in it. "After I lost my patience with them, they couldn't hand me over to Clero fast enough. In case you hadn't noticed, I'm not very good slave material."

"That you definitely are not," he agreed with sudden pleasance, picking himself up off the deck to stretch. "And now that we have that settled, you have a choice to make, too." He stepped over my legs to sit down next to me on the couch, then looked down at me. "You can either get back into your clothes, or start showing me how much you know about raping a man. I can tell you right now that if you don't do one or the other, I won't be responsible for what happens. I've discovered that looking at you does something strange to my normal restraint, which was the reason I started this in the first place. In a situation like this, with only the two of us here and a lot of empty time ahead of us, it's best if we both know where we stand.''

"I don't think I understand you at all," I said with a good deal of confusion and total honesty. "How could you not know where we stand after all the time we spent together? We weren't playing cards or swapping jokes during that time, Val. Why would things be any different now?"

"We were in the middle of the base with a lot of other people around us then," he answered gently as he smoothed my hair with one big hand. "It so happens I was in this general situation once before, sharing a bed with a woman among other people, then suddenly being alone with her in a place where no one could interrupt us and neither of us could walk away. The first time I put my hand on her shoulder, she had hysterics.''

My first reaction was to tell him he was making that up, but one look at the flinching vexation in his eyes told me he wasn't. You hear a lot about women's traumatic experiences; it looked like some men got raked over the coals just as badly.

"She must have been a neurotic," I decided aloud, pretending I hadn't noticed the way he'd sighed. "I've never heard of anything that mindless.''

"It wasn't mindless, and she wasn't neurotic," he denied, a faint smile curving his lips as he looked down at me. "She was a seasoned fighter from one of the field teams, and hadn't gotten particularly upset even the times she'd been wounded. When I finally got her calmed down, she was

terribly embarrassed and insisted on explaining why she had
done as she had. It seems that I had the same appeal for her
that her job did, lots of excitement, lots of adventure—and
lots of danger. Being in the base had been like being part of
her team, the mere fact of their proximity enough to keep the
danger from becoming overwhelming. Once we were alone,
though— All she could think about was how 'big' and 'dangerous' I was, how I might do anything I cared to to her, and
the really horrifying possibility that she might come to like
that anything. She'd seen fully trained female slaves on Tildor,
you see, and had been just as fascinated as she'd been
repelled. Those slaves served their men's every want and
whim, and loved doing it. She was afraid *she* would love
doing it, and that I would make her love it. She found it
totally impossible to stop trembling."

"Neurotic," I repeated firmly to those very black eyes
watching me. "So that was the reason behind all those strange
suggestions of yours; you wanted to get the possibilities said
and considered before I thought of them on my own. Well,
I'm sorry to disappoint you, friend, but it's just as I mentioned earlier: as far as slavery goes, I've tried it more than
once and still don't like it. Do you think you might stop
watching for the screaming and fainting now?"

"I stopped watching for that about ten minutes ago," he
said with a stronger grin, letting his eyes move briefly over
me. "You may not be terribly impressed with my size and
abilities, Diana, but you're the only woman I ever met who
wasn't. Do you understand now why I'd like to hear from
you about where we stand?"

"Yes, I can understand it now," I agreed judiciously. "I'll
be glad to give you a statement concerning my views." I took
a final sip of my coffee before returning it to its slot, then
lifted both legs and swung them across Val's lap. "As I see
it," I told him, "I've been promised that nothing would be '

done to me that would cause me to want to defend myself. I was told that by someone who tends to keep his word, you see, which turns out to be a very good thing. Even with the master matter converter, disposing of bodies in a ship like this tends to be hard work, and I'm not in the mood for hard work.''

"What *are* you in the mood for?'' he asked, and again I was struck by the difference between the softness of his words and the look in his eyes. His big hand had raised to my hip, and now stroked slowly down my thigh and leg.

"Truthfully, the thing I could use most right now is a few hours of sleep,'' I answered, tucking my hands behind my head. "How's that for an idea?''

"Lousy,'' he said with that faint grin back again, both of his hands going to my waist to pull me more completely into his lap. "I have a much better idea.''

His hands moved over me as his lips lowered to mine, and it didn't take very long before I had a better idea, too.

CHAPTER 2

When Val and I woke up after indulging in his better idea, he brought out a pair of tight-fitting but flexible, cobalt blue exercise shorts, I guess you could call them—and then joined me in some muscle-loosening exercise of the non-horizontal variety. After that the shower washed our sweat away; the air blowers dried the shower water; and then I dialed us a couple of synthsteak sandwiches and mugs of coffee, to take care of the hollows within. My ship guest wasn't very happy with the food, which naturally led him into looking for something to complain about.

The something turned out to be the way I'd roughed him up. Accusations started flying back and forth; our words went from heated to out-and-out inflamed, and before I knew it I was being challenged to see how well *I* could take something of the same sort. Having no idea of what he was talking about I immediately accepted the challenge—and only then found out what a really stupid move that was.

From the very first time Val touched me, back in the base, I'd discovered that there didn't seem to be any way of resisting him once his hands were on me. Now, Val marched me into the salon, sat down on one of the couches and pulled me into his lap, went to work on me in his usual way, and then, when I was just about out of my mind, moved me out of his lap to sit on the deck carpeting next to his leg with orders not to move.

It took quite a few suffering, mindless minutes before I could think clearly again, and another few minutes after that before I began to understand. At first none of it made sense, but then it suddenly came to me that Val was specifically doing to me what I had done to him. I was as helpless before his expertise as he had been before mine, and rage and suffer though I might, there was nothing I could do to even the score. I'd pledged myself to do nothing in response to whatever he did to me, just as he had obviously pledged himself never to use his full strength against a woman. It was a terrible, confining feeling, a screaming that demanded satisfaction. My hands clutched his leg and my body pressed to it in dry-throated need, but I did understand what was happening.

Or, at least I thought I understood. No more than another few minutes went by before the screaming and snarling began growing higher inside me, stretching out of all proportion to what had been and was being done to me. I gritted my teeth, trying to keep it from rising even more, but it was simply no use. My usual iron-bound self-control refused to cope with the problem, and I was left with a mad that made me more and more willing to strike out at anyone handy. In desperation to keep something ugly from happening I jumped to my feet and raced into my cabin, but Val followed me in almost immediately, bringing along the problem I'd been trying to avoid.

"Diana, are you all right?" he demanded, his voice sounding upset. "What happened? Why did you run like that?"

"You might say it was a call of nature," I told him, standing with one hand against the far wall of the cabin, the

other over my eyes. I didn't want to admit it was my own
lousy nature that had called, the temper I knew I couldn't
afford to lose. "If you'll give me a minute, I'll be right back
with you."

"Don't be an idiot,"he snorted, and then he was standing
there next to me, pulling me into his arms and up against
him. My hand came away from my eyes as I stiffened
involuntarily, but I didn't realize just how I'd stiffened until I
saw the look on his face.

"Just calm down, little girl," he said in a soothing way,
his arms around me more supportive and comforting than
intimate. "Remember me? I'm the one you don't have to
defend yourself against, so just let those muscles relax. I'm
not going to hurt you, Diana, so just take it easy."

I looked down at the way I was standing, at the double
knife-hand my fingers had stiffened to, and couldn't believe
I'd actually slipped that far from control. That was when I
really understood what Val had been trying to tell me, the
message that said the sort of anger I'd bred in him got worse
with the passage of time, not better. I *hadn't* been justified in
knocking him around, and it was time I admitted it.

"I'm—not doing very well with that agreement we made,"
I got out, looking up at him with self-disgust and annoyance.
"In case you were wondering, you made your point. I guess
I'm just not built to take it as well as you did. I think I'm
going to need more than that minute before we start again."

"You don't have to worry, we won't *be* starting again,"
he said, suddenly sounding odd. "You look like you're coming face to face with an uncomfortable truth, Diana, but it's
nothing you have to be upset about. If you're having second
thoughts about the wisdom in choosing me as a partner, you
don't have to worry about hurting my feelings. It would
hardly be the first time I was told something like that."

His voice had grown very gentle and the look in his eyes

was hooded. Val had totally misinterpreted everything that had happened, and was braced to take the bad news like a trooper, leading me to wonder fleetingly just how many times he'd had to take that news. The prejudice of the unwashed herd had obviously brought him a lot of hell, and I felt a twinge inside me that was stronger than sympathy. If I tried telling him that *I* was the problem, not him, he'd never believe me.

Silently I beckoned to him to follow me, then led the way out of my cabin and back into the salon. When we reached a low, squarish utility table next to one wall, I held up my hand at Val, then continued on into the galley alone. It took no more than a minute to get what I was after, and when I came out Val was frowning in confusion. He watched me step up on the utility table, which put my head an inch or so above his, then stood there in speechless shock as I emptied the large plastic container of water I had gotten, right over his head. Once the last drop had been emptied I tossed the container away, then put my fists on my hips.

"I'm not having second thoughts about anything," I told him, watching calmly as his big hand wiped the water out of his eyes and pushed his sopping hair back. "How about you?"

He looked at me with thunder and lightning blazing in those eyes for about five seconds, and then a grin broke through.

"No, no second thoughts," he said, tossing a lock of wet hair back out of his eyes. "How could I have second thoughts when I haven't even come to terms with my first thoughts yet? I can see I'm never going to know what to expect from you, Diana, but maybe we can narrow the field a little."

I didn't know what he was talking about, and I didn't realize I was about to find out. One minute that grin was right in front of me, and the next I was off the table, turned around, and held about the waist by one of those should-be illegal arms. Five or six hard, fast smacks were delivered to my bare bottom, and then I was set back on my feet on the deck carpeting.

"First you use words alone, and then, if that doesn't work, you try something else," he lectured with one finger pointing at me while I stood in outraged speechlessness with my hands rubbing behind me. "The next time I have to tell you that, you'll spend some time standing up."

I was so mad I couldn't say a word, but having a chat wasn't what I wanted to do with him. I actually took one step toward him before I had control of myself again, and then I turned and stalked away to my cabin, slamming the heavy but well-balanced door behind me. The nerve of that jerk! Go ahead and try to help someone, and see what you get for it! I stalked back and forth across the tiny cabin, trying to calm down, but it took quite a while before I made it. No one but a backwoods hick of a second from a backwoods outpost would be stupid enough to spank a Special Agent, but that was the second time that jerk had tried it. The first time had cost him a lot of blood, but he didn't seem to learn from anything that happened to him! It was fairly clear I should have taken someone else in his place after all, but it was too late for that now. I'd just have to teach some manners to what I had, over and over again, if necessary, until the lesson stuck with him. I sat down on my bunk and drew my knees up for my chin to rest on, then began making a mental list of possible lessons.

I let a few hours go by before I left the cabin again, and when I did I made it very clear that Val had turned invisible. He was sitting on a couch reading a slim, leather-bound book when I passed him, and I paid no attention to the way he followed me with his eyes and a grin. I went into the control room and ran a quick systems and course check, made sure my double-check tape run was progressing properly, then went to the galley. A synthburger and coffee were enough to take care of what little appetite I had, and these I carried back to my cabin with me, slamming the door again behind me. When I'd come out of the galley with my food Val had been back on his couch, but it was obvious he'd left it briefly by the presence of the blanket he was wrapped in. He made sure to begin shivering violently as I passed, but he hadn't done anything about that stupid grin. I swallowed my meal with my nose stuffed into a book of my own, read for a short while after that, then declared official ship's night.

When I woke up I discovered it was past nine hundred hours Arbitrary Ship Time, but that didn't mean much. I'd started the night early when I'd gone to bed, and there wasn't anything on the ship that called for crack-of-dawn rising. I stretched hard and then lay still for a minute, grinning when I remembered the very discreet push against my cabin door the night before. I'd been lying in the dark for a while, waiting to fall asleep, when I'd heard the faint creak of the door in its frame. It had been trying to swing obligingly inward, but the lock I'd flipped on had kept it from doing so. I'd been wondering whether Val would try to catch me asleep and vulnerable, and now I knew; gentlemanly conduct goes by the boards when you've been heated up and not been given a chance to cool down. I'd had some of the same trouble myself the night before, but it was worth it if Val had suffered more.

I got up and visited the bathroom, got a cup of coffee and ran the routine control room checks, then went to start my morning loosening up. That was when Val showed up, looking well rested and fresh from the shower. His cobalt blue exercise shorts looked fresh and clean too, as though he'd been using the launderer. I still didn't need the launderer, and Val's eyes showed he was well aware of that as he sat down on a corner stool to watch me. As I've mentioned I'm consid-

ered big for a woman, but I'm also nicely well-endowed. The
Absari clinicians didn't have to touch my body when they'd
matched me to Bellna, the Tildorian princess I'd decoyed for;
that body went very well with the outstandingly beautiful face
I'd been given to play the part of Bellna, the face that was
now mine as well as hers. I still wasn't used to being a
redhead, but Val didn't seem to miss my original brown hair
and eyes. He watched closely as I twisted, bent, stretched and
jumped, saying not a single word, but as the saying goes, his
eyes spoke volumes.

When I finished the exercising, I went for a shower. I
hadn't skimped on anything I needed to keep up decent
muscle tone, but I'd intended running through a couple of the
stricter forms designed to keep your fighting muscles well
oiled and then had changed my mind. To deny that Val's
stare had gotten to me would be a waste of time; if he hadn't
been there, I would have done those forms. I slapped the
water-flow switch with more strength than was strictly necessary, absolutely disgusted with myself. So what if his stare
was pure evaluation, the owner of a breeding ranch looking
over his bloodstock, or a hungry carnivore considering the
taste of the prey he was about to pounce on? Was I a placid
broodmare or a cute little bunnyrabbit that I couldn't tell him
to go to hell and then ignore him?

I closed my eyes and let the cool water fall directly over
my face and head, something that always made me feel as
though I stood under a falls on a planet instead of in a
sub-coffin-sized shower stall on a ship using recirculated
water. I couldn't help remembering the thoughts I'd had
about how my body looked. Once, when very young, I had
gone with my mother to visit some friends of hers. The
people had been animal lovers, and they had had dogs and
cats and birds and rodents and all sorts of cute and/or cuddle-
some pets scattered about in almost every room of the house.

When my mother and her friends had begun talking business I was given the run of the house, something I wasn't reluctant to accept. The idea of all those animals living together had fascinated me, and I'd wandered from room to room, admiring the comradely peace and calm—until I came to the rule's exception. A small but beautifully colored bird was flapping around in a frenzy in its large, ornate cage, beating mindlessly against the bars and swings and perches, acting as though it were trying to get away from some horrible menace. I'd looked all around; trying to see what the menace could be, but hadn't found anything at all to explain the bird's behavior when a house servant entered the room. The bird's frenzied flapping caught his immediate attention, and with a sound of annoyance he went straight to an orange and white cat lying quietly near the cage, picked up the animal up, then left the room with it. The bird's fluttering hysterics had started quieting immediately, but I hadn't understood why. The cat hadn't been doing anything but staring at the bird . . .

I took my face out of the water so that I could sigh deeply, wondering what the hell I was going to do. The cat in question wasn't a housecat but a hunting cat, and the bird wasn't a cagebird but a mutated hunting hawk. If they ever got down to it in a serious way more than feathers and fur would fly, but the cat didn't seem prepared to back off, and the bird was beginning to feel her talons flexing in pure reflex. If something didn't happen to establish a truce between them, the upcoming months would not be at all pleasant, but the hawk didn't want a truce on the cat's terms. I damned well *couldn't* accept a truce on Val's terms, not and still look myself in the face when I brushed my hair. He could stare until he was blue in the face, but I'd be damned if I'd let it stampede me.

With which strong-minded resolve I finished my shower, let the air blowers dry me, then marched out of the shower stall. The small exercise room was empty, but when I turned the corner into the salon, I ran smack into the cause of my frenzied fluttering in the flesh.

"Hey, be careful!" Val said with touching concern, grabbing my arms to keep me from going over backward at the collision. Then he grinned faintly and observed, "Small ship, isn't it?"

"Not that small," I muttered to myself and began to step around him, but suddenly he was in my way again. I looked up at him with what must have been automatic talon flexing, and he immediately held up a conciliatory hand.

"I'm really not trying to crowd you," he said. "It's just that I have a problem, and I need your help with it."

I studied his very innocent face for a minute, knowing damned well he was trying to con me, but still said, "What problem?"

"It's right this way," he said, stepping aside and gesturing with one hand. "Come on and I'll show you."

I half expected him to lead the way to his bunk, but his actual destination turned out to be the galley. He led me up to the synthoserver, then turned and gestured at it over his shoulder.

"I can't eat what that thing puts out," he said, the distaste in his expression testifying to the truth of his words. "No matter what color or shape or texture it comes out in, it all tastes the same and I can't eat it. If that's all this ship has in the way of food, I'm not going to make it to your Federation."

He was looking down at me in a strange way, obviously not kidding about the syntho, but at the same time pleased he had found something I couldn't ignore him about. I was *that* close to telling him he'd get used to the syntho after a while and if he didn't he could starve with my blessing, when I suddenly got a better idea. The ship was, after all, a luxury yacht, and I could do with a little luxury.

"If it's fresh food you want, the dispenser's over here," I told him, pointing out the recess on the opposite side of the galley. "The ship needs about ten minutes to thaw out whatever you decide on, and operating instructions for the broiler-grill-oven are in that cabinet, right next to the seasoning, utensils and plates. If you don't like syntho, you have to cook your own. Enjoy your meal."

For the second time in five minutes I started to walk around him, but even a ten-year-old could have blocked the doorway without trying. Val, about as far as you can get from a ten-year-old, *was* trying, and what a surprise *that* turned out to be.

"I'm not very good at following instructions like that," the man who had helped rebuild my ship said in a coaxing voice, at the same time looking down at me with a smile in his dark black eyes. "Why don't you stay here and help me, and then we can both enjoy the meal."

I let myself stiffen enough for him to notice, then glared up at him.

"You don't have to rub it in!" I hissed with enough venom to widen his eyes in startlement. "If I knew how to cook, don't you think I'd be eating food instead of syntho? Don't think you can embarrass me about it, because you can't! I'm good enough at enough other things that cooking doesn't mean a thing! Not a thing! Now, get out of my way!"

He retreated in confusion at my tirade, giving me enough room to stalk out of the galley, then let me carry my coffee away to the control room without saying a word. I settled myself and the coffee in the pilot's seat, activated the forward screens, then grinned faintly as I sipped and watched our not-yet-visible progress through the deep black. Syntho might not taste very good until you got used to it, but it was more nutritionally balanced than natural food, it helped keep you in better shape physically during a dead-time trip like the one

we were currently on—and it was incredibly convenient for people like me who didn't care to be bothered with cooking. If
Val reacted to my play-acting the way I expected him to, I'd
have my choice of the syntho or an already-cooked meal of
natural food for the rest of the trip. Already-cooked by Val. If
he ever found out I cooked well enough to suit just about
anybody I'd probably have to defend myself, but life without risk is nothing more than existing. I put my heels up
on the edge of the board, sipped at my coffee, and began
thinking about how long I ought to resist being invited to
dinner.

I stayed in the control room until I finished my coffee,
went to my cabin to read and nap for a while, then returned to
the exercise area to run through those forms I hadn't gotten to
earlier. I would have thought Val had disappeared off the ship
if I hadn't heard the muted clatter and movements every time
I passed the galley; his new preoccupation was taking all of
his attention, an absolute blessing as far as I was concerned.
The change of being out from under surveillance for a while
made it more than worth it. When I finished the forms I
showered again, then sat down to read.

It was just about 1800 hours AST when I put my book
aside, too distracted to sit there any longer. I hadn't been
particularly hungry earlier that day so all I'd had was coffee,
but just then I was feeling the hollowness clear down to my
ankles. I'd been expecting Val to figure out how to use the
cooking unit, but there was always the possibility he would
turn out to be King Thumbs in anything domestic. It would be
too bad all the way around, but I could survive easily on
syntho, and Val would just have to learn to like it. I left my
cabin and went straight to the galley and the syntho server,
ignoring the galley's other occupant until my wrist was grabbed
in a big hand before I could touch the selector dial.

"You don't want any of that," I was told in very firm tones, the hand pulling me gently around and away from the server. "Don't you remember how hard it is to dispose of bodies on this ship?"

"If I don't get any of that, you'll be faced with the need to make the effort," I pointed out, moving my wrist in his hand. "I happen to be hungry, and I'd like to get something to eat."

"Then let's get you something to eat," he said with a faint grin, heading me toward the other side of the galley before turning my wrist loose. "Is there some place with more elbow room where we can set this out?"

"This" turned out to be more courses of fresh-cooked food than I ever expected to see before I got back to the Federation, all kept nice and warm behind the holder panels surrounding the cooker. I could now understand why I hadn't smelled any of his efforts, but not why he hadn't already begun digging in.

"There's a pull-out table in the salon you can use," I answered. "I'll have mine in a minute, and then I'll be out of your way."

I tried to turn away from the open holder panels, but the hand in the middle of my back wasn't allowing that. My avenue of retreat was well blocked off.

"What's the matter, are you too good to eat with me?" Val asked softly, making sure his arm stayed in my way. "Are you afraid to try it in case you like it? It takes a big person to accept a shortcoming, Diana, but I thought you were big enough to do it. Was I wrong?"

I looked up at the sober face looking down at me, silently giving E for effort to the line he'd decided on. "All right, I'll join you," I grudged, trying not to lick my lips in anticipation of what was making those delicious smells. "But only this once. It so happens I—like syntho."

"Only this once," Val agreed without hesitation, showing his grin nowhere except his eyes. "You get the pull-out table pulled out, and I'll start bringing the food."

With chore assignments made I was free to go where I liked, which was into the salon to see to the table. A pretty white cloth fluffed out once the table was locked into open position, and Val began covering it with dishes while I unracked a couple of chairs from the dining set recess, then checked the wine list to see what was available. On the trip out I'd used a heavy brandy to get stoned on once, not caring to waste anything better on the urges of deep depression. A wine drunk is murder on the constitution, and the hangover had been bad enough to keep me from doing it a second time, which left the figurative cellar almost untouched. Val had prepared a seafood appetizer, a meat soup, a meat and vegetables main dish, something with about ten million calories for dessert, and had cheese and fruit and breads scattered around. I selected one good white wine, an average rosé and a darned good red, then decided against the excellent brandy the yacht's original owner had undoubtedly laid in for himself. If I felt like sharing brandy with Val, I could always call it up later.

Once we were settled at the table, there was more plate-passing and swallowing than gabbing accomplished, the sort of silence one gives to a very creditable effort. Val's handling of the seasoning was unorthodox but interesting, and the fact that I could have done better didn't keep me from thoroughly enjoying myself. We worked our way through the first two bottles of wine along with most of the food, then sat back to sample the third.

"This is nice," Val observed, raising his glass so that the light gleamed red off its contents, then brought it to his lips again. "Have you made any plans for our first stop after we reach your Federation?"

"I certainly have," I answered with a good deal of satisfaction, noticing how close to blood color the wine was. I felt relaxed and good after that meal, and didn't mind talking about my plans. "I have some unfinished business named Radman to see to, and then I'll show you a few of the sights."

"Isn't that the name of the slaver who first put you on this ship?" Val asked, looking at me over the rim of his glass. "When Dameron first questioned you he found out you'd been after this Radman, but he never learned exactly why. What law did he break?"

"Aside from what he did to me?" I asked, remembering the way I'd felt after waking up aboard that ship, the control room in ruins, unexplored vastness all around me, my future all behind me. If I hadn't been too stubborn to give him the satisfaction, I would have gone slowly mad, locked up in a crippled hulk on my way to the far side of forever. And it was all Radman's doing, the slime who found that sort of thing more fun than a clean death, the filth who never thought I'd come back from it, the dead man who didn't yet know we had a final date penciled in on the calendar.

"Radman's a special case among slavers," I said after taking a deep, necessary swallow of my wine, only vaguely noticing that Val hadn't filled the gap between my question and the beginning of my answer to his question. "As long as he stuck to ordinary slave-trading he was none of our business—too many member planets consider slavery of one sort or another legal. Not long ago, though, he decided to branch out.

"Two Councilmen were arguing for opposite sides of an important political question, and Radman, in an effort to increase his power, approached one of them with an offer. For all I know, the Councilman may have thought he was acting in the best interests of the people; whatever it was, he made a deal with Radman and two days later the other Councilman's three children disappeared. The second Councilman was told he would see them again only if he abandoned his opposition to the first Councilman's stand."

Val was still staring at me silently, his wine glass held in both hands, his lack of expression giving me no clues as to what he was thinking. I took my eyes away from him, and went on with the story.

"Unfortunately for his children, the second Councilman was a man of honor," I continued. "He refused to desert his stand, and the kids paid for it. They were never seen at home again, but were eventually traced to the pleasure planet Xanadu, purely by accident. Radman had sold them to the Pleasure Sphere, and it was much too late to save them. The nine-year-old-girl and twelve-year-old-boy had been used to death by the patrons, and the sixteen-year-old-girl had committed suicide. It didn't take long before the Councilman went the same way his oldest daughter had gone."

"And all that because of someone's twisted desire for power," Val said very softly, so softly that I looked back at him in startlement. I'd never heard such chill menace from him before. "And you were supposed to arrest him, but instead of your getting him, he got you. Why were you sent alone? Why didn't they send a squad of peacekeepers?"

"A squad of *male* peacekeepers, you mean?" I asked with a very faint smile before sipping my wine. "We don't call them that in the Federation, but I catch your meaning. The only problem with that is Federation police can't do what I do."

"Why not?" he asked, almost in annoyance, his wine forgotten. "What makes a lone female more qualified to arrest filth like that than a squad of men?"

"Possibly the fact that there's no arrest involved," I answered, trying not to watch him closely and failing miserably. "The Council issued a death warrant on Radman to show how much they appreciated his efforts, and I'm the Special Agent they sent to serve it. If someone hadn't warned him I was coming, I would have killed him and left the body for his friends to find, as a warning against trying something like that ever again. It would hardly have been the first death warrant I ever served, Val, and if I'm very, very lucky, I'll get back to find that no one else was sent to see to it in my absence. Not even police special squads are authorized to—or capable of—executing a death warrant. I am."

I watched him absorb the news. It hadn't been necessary to tell him that with a two-month trip still in front of us, but I couldn't hold back. Val knew well enough that I'd killed on Tildor—hell, I'd almost done it to him!—but there was a big difference between killing in self-defense and killing in cold blood. That the end result was the same made no difference to most people; deliberate executions of any sort were horrifying, and the soulless, inhuman creatures capable of taking life without the mitigating emotions of rage or fear-for-self were more horrifying still. Those black eyes watched me while I watched him, the thoughts behind them totally unreadable, and abruptly I didn't care to play the game any more. I didn't give a damn how shocked he was; at least it would keep him out from under my feet from then on.

"Thanks for the meal," I said, swallowing the last of my wine before replacing the glass carefully on the table and then standing. "If you'd ever like it matched in syntho, just let me know."

I started back toward my cabin, looking forward to being alone, but Val was out of his chair so fast he practically materialized in front of me, blocking the way.

"Come on, you don't really want to put us back to where we were," he said, sounding as if that was all there was worth discussing between us. "That wine is much too good to be left after a single taste, and I really hate drinking alone. And you haven't finished telling me what we'll be doing in the Federation once we take care of that Radman garbage. Just a little while longer, and a little more of the wine— What do you say?''

"After *we* take care of Radman?'' I echoed, feeling as if I'd already had more than enough wine. I couldn't understand how he could dismiss what I'd told him so lightly, not with the way people usually took it. ''What about—what I just said. Didn't it bother you?''

"Of course it bothered me,'' he said, looking faintly startled. ''Just because you're capable of doing a tough job like that doesn't mean they had the right to send you in entirely unprotected, without any back-up. Something can slip in any dangerous situation, just the way it did in yours. Next time he'll have the two of us to contend with, and I don't think he'll do as well—no matter who warns him about what.''

"The two of us,'' I echoed again, almost in a whisper, feeling so strange that I couldn't describe it, even to myself. I'd had partners before, usually under protest and usually forgotten as soon as the assignment was over, but even when it had worked out I'd never felt so—really wanted. It was stupid, and probably a combination of imagination and too much wine, but as I looked up into those dark black eyes, it almost felt as though Val was considering me with an eye for more than what most men usually wanted. A big hand came gently to my face, and I looked up in time to see how close *his* face was. Warm lips touched mine briefly but without any doubt, and then we were heading for one of the couches, to discuss the Federation a bit more over another glass of the really good wine. When it finally came to me that what he probably wanted was nothing more than some human interaction in the midst of the ultimate isolation all around us, I was able to relax again and hold up my end of the conversation. The rest of it was just wine and imagination after all, but that strange feeling still warmed the rest of that "night."

CHAPTER 3

Life settled down into routine after that, but there wasn't much of the boredom you'd expect. Val took to joining me in morning loosening-up exercises, but he didn't know enough to join me in afternoon fighting practice and I wasn't about to teach him. In the afternoons we took turns in the exercise room, and he didn't offer to teach me what he was doing either.

I continued to eat the syntho any time I wanted a quick snack, but Val cooked every time he was hungry, which seemed more often than it should be. I know he had to keep that big body of his fueled, but how you can eat that much in such confined spaces is a complete mystery to me. We shared dinner every ship night, and I was well prepared for the time he decided to "teach me how to cook." My attitude was "gamely willing" when we started the lesson, but it didn't take long before I managed to burn myself on the cooker, in the process destroying the simple meal it was cooking. I cursed out the cooker and my own "clumsiness" without once blaming Val, and that was the end of the lessons.

There were times when we didn't say a word to each other,

but there were also times when we talked about ourselves. Val didn't say much about himself except for the fact that he'd been at Dameron's outpost for about three Absari years, had worked in the field for a while, moved into heading his own team, then accepted the job as Dameron's second. He was so vague about his family and life before that that I decided not to press him; we all have things in our past we'd rather not discuss. From other things he said I gathered his family was to some degree important on their home world, and maybe that was the trouble. If he'd done something to embarrass them he would have had to leave, and something like that was none of my business.

The trip out had been endless, but I awoke one day to discover that some time during the ship "night" we had moved into communication range—or, at least, into communication range with my department. We had barely entered the fringes of Federation space and were still a good hop, skip and a jump away from what might be considered inhabited space, but triangulation showed that one of our souped up, highly classified comm boosters wasn't too far ahead. I can't imagine what sort of thinking went into anchoring those boosters at countless points on the edges of nowhere, but I didn't have to have their raison d'être in order to use one. I sent out a pulse on my departmental frequency, established it for repeat, then went to get a cup of coffee. The relaying would take a while, but once they locked onto me we'd have a two-way with no lag.

About fifteen or twenty minutes passed before I got a double-pulse echo, and then a lock-on decrease in static. I cut my own pulse just as the double cut out, and then there was nothing but the hum of the open connect. The silence said they were waiting for me to identify myself, so I recited a string of code numbers designed to tell them who I was, then waited for a reply. It wasn't long in coming.

"Please repeat series," a familiar voice said. "Reverification necessary."

I repeated the series and added, "That's the last repeat you get, Jerry. I don't need practice in pronouncing numbers."

"Diana!" the voice exclaimed, "It *is* you! Where the hell have you been? We wrote you off two months ago."

"Thanks for the vote of confidence," I told him, stretching into long comfort in the pilot's seat. "It's only been about six months altogether."

"I should have known better." Jerry laughed. "It would take more than Radman to put you away permanently."

"Yeah, well he almost made it," I answered, no longer amused. "You'd better record if you're not doing so already. I have a report that's going to shake everyone in sight. And if you're not alone, clear everyone else out. This report goes straight to Ringer, and is guaranteed to burn anyone not authorized to hear it."

"Recording," he acknowledged, sounding curious. "Should I put my fingers in my ears?"

"It would not hurt, my boy," I laughed, "it would not hurt. Report beginning." I started from the time I woke up outward bound, continued through to the present, and finished up with, "Valdon and I have recalculated the date of the conference, and everything is ready to be turned over to whoever has to get it. I refuse to attempt any conclusions as to the Confederacy's aims, but I must point out that they would still be unknown to us if I'd had a fatal accident before I could lift off. As for Radman, I claim a priority on him. I'd like to finish my business with him before Valdon and I take on any other assignment. End of report."

There was silence on the other end of the line for a minute, then Jerry's voice came through again, sounding shaken.

"I should have taken your advice and put my fingers in my ears," he muttered. "I'll get this to Ringer, but if he's anything like me, he won't believe a word of it. I'm leaving the frequency open so Ringer can talk to you. Out for now.''

There was nothing else after that but the hum of the open connect, so I went to the galley, got another cup of coffee, then retraced my steps to the control room. Val had been puttering in the galley as usual, paying no attention to what I did in the control room, but the glance he gave me showed he knew something was up. He didn't ask any more questions about what I was up to than I'd asked about his past; when it was time for him to know, he knew I'd tell him.

As usual, Ringer didn't waste any time. Five minutes after the minimum time needed to listen to my report, his voice came through the speaker.

"Diana, are you there?" he demanded without any preamble, his voice its usual growl.

"I'm here, Ringer," I answered with a faint smile I couldn't help. If I'd never heard Ringer's voice again, I would have missed it.

"I've learned never to expect the normal from you, but this is more than ever I would have expected," he said with a grin. "Have you ever heard the ancient saying about someone who falls into an unusually filled barrel, and comes out with an improbable smell?"

"I've heard it, Ringer, but the smell hasn't been established yet," I said as I sipped at my coffee. "What do you think of their proposal?"

"I'm with you," he growled. "I'll leave the conclusion-drawing to Federation artists trained for it. As soon as I'm finished with you, I'll get through to some people I know and dump it in their laps. By the way, you didn't go into any detail about how Radman grabbed you. Did you fall asleep on the job?"

"Not bloody likely," I snorted. "How many ears are there in the room with you?"

"Just my own," he said suspiciously. "Why?"

"Because Radman was waiting for me with open arms," I told him. "What does that sound like to you?"

"It sounds like a sellout," he said after briefly cursing with feeling. "Do you have any idea who?"

"Not the slightest," I assured him. "If I did, they'd be on the top of my list instead of Radman. I hope you haven't sent anyone else after him. I'd hate to think I missed out."

"I was going to, but the Council withdrew the warrant until we could find out what happened to you," Ringer said, the faintest bit hesitant over the tone I'd used. "You know the Council doesn't believe in wasting agents. If something stopped you, they wanted to find out what it was before sending anyone else in."

"Good for them," I nodded in satisfaction. "They may be learning to use their heads. Where is he now?"

"Don't start resetting your course just yet," he ordered, with a hint of annoyance. "You've got a piece of paper for me, remember?"

"Oh, yes, that." I sighed and sat back again. "Okay, where do you want it?"

"Head for Faraway Station," he decided after a minute of silent consideration. "You can make it in a few days, and so can I. You'll give me what you're carrying, and I'll give you a couple of sets of identity papers. How do you think your new partner will work out?"

"He shouldn't be too bad at all—on the easy stuff," I answered, remembering my promise to Dameron. "You'll flip out when you see what he can do, and we can have a contest to see which of us gets to believe it first. When you leave for Faraway, bring along some essentials for me from my apartment; you know what I'll need. And make sure that warrant is back in effect, I don't want to run into any static about operating under a cancelled instrument. And when we get to Faraway, you can buy Val some clothes. If I gave you his measurements now, you'd never believe them.''

''If he put up with you for two months and is still in one piece, I already know what his measurements *have* to be,'' Ringer came back with a dig in his voice that made me grin. ''Any other orders, ma'am, any other little thing I can do for you?''

''Nothing I can think of right now,'' I drawled, knowing the drawl would irritate him. ''Didn't you miss me, Ringer?''

''I certainly did,'' he answered, and I could almost see the gleam in his eyes. ''One day soon I hope to tell you exactly how much.''

''I haven't done a damned thing you can cite me for and you know it,'' I came back with a laugh, remembering again how much I enjoyed prodding him. ''Even I can't break any regs from way out here.''

''If there's a way, you'll find it,'' he returned with the sort of dryness I seem to inspire. ''If you think of anything else I ought to know, save it until we both get to Faraway.''

''Read you ten and zero, O mighty leader,'' I acknowledged, but despite the irreverence it so happened I agreed with him completely. Not knowing where the original leak about my assignment had come from meant I couldn't leave any meaningful messages to be passed on to Ringer by anyone else. There were certain people, like Jerry and his brothers and sisters in communications, who had been rendered incapable of betraying anything that passed through their hands and minds, but voluntary conditioning of that sort wasn't required of everyone who worked for the department. Our people would find the leak eventually, but until they did I would be talking to no one but the man I worked for.

Ringer and I took turns at sign-off, then he broke the connect, which brought the static back. I flipped off the communicator and was about to get out of the pilot's seat, when a glance over my shoulder showed me an unexpected sight. Val stood leaning against the bulkhead right next to the entry, his arms folded, his ears all but flapping. It seemed the galley had at last lost its fascination, and I couldn't help but wonder at the coincidence of the timing.

"Having fun?" I asked, turning the seat around so that I could look directly at him. "Hear anything you'd like to write home to mother about?"

"I wasn't eavesdropping, if that's what you're implying," he answered, looking not the least bit ashamed or guilty. "We're supposed to be partners, and partners share things, especially contact with the home base. I assumed you simply forgot to invite me, and went ahead and invited myself."

His black eyes showed a good part of the annoyance he seemed to be feeling, an annoyance which was, by my way of looking at things, wholly unjustified.

"It won't be your home base until you get your first assignment," I pointed out, raising my mug to my lips for a sip of what was left. "Until then it's *my* home base, and I would have appreciated some privacy."

"For all the highly classified things you had to discuss," he said with a nod, prying himself off the bulkhead to walk to the co-pilot's seat and fold down into it. "Things I know nothing about, like the experience you had on Tildor, and the proposed conference between our people, and the trouble you had with Radman—and the sort of assignments I'm to be given."

So that was it. Val didn't like the idea of being given nothing but "easy ones," and that was just too bad.

"What about the assignments you'll be given?" I asked with full openness, looking at him over my mug rim. "What sort of assignments did you expect to get?"

"I expected to get what my partner got," he growled, not

about to let himself be soothed. "Is that what you'll be doing, Diana? The 'easy' ones?"

"If they come my way, you won't find me turning my nose up at them." I shrugged. "If you spend too much time with your life constantly on the line, you get to the point where you're too tired or too bored to put out maximum effort. After that you find yourself intimately involved in final sort of happenings, the kind that take you out of the game for keeps. What's your departmental rating, Val?"

"I don't understand," he said, surprised at the unexpected question. "How could I know my rating in a department I haven't even officially joined yet?"

"Well, you seemed to know what sort of assignments you should be given," I pointed out. "If you don't know what rating you are, how do you know what an 'easy' one consists of?"

His face took on a frustrated look, an awareness of the way he was being backed into a corner without knowing how to get out of it again. He shifted in annoyance in the seat, his eyes not at all pleased with me, and then he found a corner to hang argument on.

"You said you'd take the easy ones 'if' they came your way," he countered, the feral look firmly planted in his eyes. "You obviously don't expect them to come your way, but you want them to come mine."

"I've spent twelve years proving what I can do," I pointed out. "I started learning what I was up against when I was eighteen standard years old, and the twelve years show how well I learned those lessons. I'm a Special Agent, Val, and in my frame of reference 'easy' means anything that isn't automatically considered certain death. You better believe I'll take an easy one if it comes my way, but there are too many assignments that aren't easy—and not enough Special Agents to do them. If you prove to my people you can do what I do, they'll be more than happy to change your designation. Why you would want it changed I can't imagine, but you have to give them a chance to evaluate you."

His sharp, annoyed movements in the seat showed he was still struggling against the box I had him in, but sweet reason has it all over driving argument when you want to nail someone good. "They can evaluate me all they like while we're working together," he said at last, his tone announcing that that was the sole concession he was willing to make. "Partners are two people who work together, and that's the reason I came here with you: to be your partner. What's an orbital station?"

The abrupt change of subject was a lot more of a concession than the one he'd voiced, and I smiled to myself as I turned back to the controls. When the time came, Val would do what he was told to do, and in the meanwhile I was no longer the bad guy.

"An orbital station is part of the system the Federation set up to make traveling easier," I said, letting the instruments confirm my estimate that it was too soon to change my heading for Faraway. "Major spaceports started out right on the planet designated as a 'change of trains' stop, and all kinds of unexpected difficulties developed with them. If people had to wait a week or more to make connections with a ship going their way, they started wondering about what was beyond the spaceport fence. If they'd checked out local customs first, they might have been there waiting when their ship got in, but most sightseers didn't bother. They just went their merry way and found out about strange laws the hard way."

I shifted away from the controls and continued. "The Federation wasn't about to start a shooting war with half its planet even if the problem of shaking tourists loose from their grip was getting worse by the day, so some bright boy came up with the idea of orbiting stations where sightseers could wander all they liked and never get into trouble. If they want to hit dirt, they have to sit through a lecture on local behavior and pass a test before they're allowed down, so most don't bother. Those orbital stations are Federation run and have everything you can think of, but Faraway, being so far out, is a little on the rough side, just like the planet it orbits. If they didn't need it for a change-of-trains stop, the planet Faraway would have to get along with shuttles and freighters the way other young planets do. A planet doesn't get an orbital station until its rate of advancement earns it one.''

The black eyes watching me grew briefly annoyed at the statement of fact I'd made, then became amused.

"I've discovered that anything worthwhile has to be earned,'' he commented with a faint grin while I took my attention briefly away from him. When I looked up again he was standing right over me, the faint grin widened. "I've never minded having to earn things, Diana, and I've always managed to earn whatever it was I really wanted.''

"And what is it you really want this time, Val?'' I asked, for some reason feeling uncomfortable as I looked up at him. The control room was too bright for me to miss seeing any part of his expression, and the amusement he showed in both face and eyes was completely unexplained.

"This time I really want to be partners with a female who spent twelve years proving what she can do,'' he said, leaning down suddenly to lift me out of the pilot's seat. "I don't think it will take me nearly as long to prove what *I* can do.''

"Not many assignments are given out on the basis of that sort of expertise,'' I pointed out, as I moved in protest against the arms holding me. "If you're thinking about trying to match me, Val, don't waste your time. And put me down. I haven't done any loosening up yet this morning.''

"Don't you think it's about time someone did try to match you?'' he asked, looking less amused as he held me without the least effort. "There's a saying among my people that points up the lack of crowding in the highest positions."

" 'It's lonely at the top,' " I quoted without thinking, then immediately regretted saying something that mindless. "Lonely and rough, or possibly lonely because not too many people can hack it. If you're tired enough of living and want to give it a stab, why should I care?"

"That's right," he agreed very quietly, for some reason watching me as he finally put me down. "Why should you care?"

I turned away from him without adding anything to the conversation, then remembered the exercising I hadn't done. I wasn't really in the mood any longer, but went to take care of it anyway. In the past I'd cared about my partners, but only in so far as the job was concerned; what they did outside that particular frame of reference was strictly their business, and absolutely none of mine. If Val wanted to get himself killed the way so many others had, why should *I* care? It was his life, wasn't it? I stood still in the middle of the exercise area for a minute, suddenly less than pleased at being so close to home, then said to hell with it and got on with the exercising. Val was nothing but another partner, so why would I care *what* he did?

"How many times did you say you've done this sort of thing?" Val asked from the co-pilot's seat, his eyes glued to the screens. "What happens if you miss the opening?"

"I've done it at least twice, and if I miss the opening the ship will crash and explode," I muttered in answer, paying more attention to what I was doing than to Val's hysterics. Commercial liners send shuttles to all orbital stations to pick up and deliver passengers, but small private ships rarely have shuttles to send. With a ship the size of ours it was necessary to dock the ship itself, and that docking was done tail first. Just then I was edging us closer and closer to the huge globe

that was Faraway Orbital Station, aiming for the relatively
tiny docking aperture that had been assigned to us, easing
our approach by means of the ship's gentle directional jets.
The screens in front of me made it seem as if we were
moving forward, and it was necessary to consciously remember it was backward movement we wanted. Too little thrust
and the "wind" created by the massive station would send us
floating away again, too much thrust and we'd go slewing all
over the place. The littlest bear's touch was what was needed
just then, and I had no concentration to spare for a man who
didn't trust women drivers.

"That wasn't very funny," Val growled, but softly enough
to keep from distracting me. "You may have gone through
this before, but I haven't. In the Confederacy we'd land a ship
like this directly on the planet, not try putting it into a
half-inch diameter hole in an orbiting space station. If you'd
given me some warning about what had to be done, I could
have tried *my* hand at it. I probably have more experience at
precision piloting than you do."

His voice was so filled with automatic, unconscious
superiority that I nearly *was* distracted, with the urge to look
around for something to beat him over the head with, if
nothing else. Before I could give in to the urge, though, I felt
the first tentative touch of the grabber field, and then it was
locked on tight, ready to slide us automatically into the berth.
The controls went dead under my hands as the field took over
completely, the safety field that made sure no one *would* end
up smashing into the Station. I'd only had to guide the ship in
close enough to where the field could take over, but exact
positioning is a matter of contest among the people I worked
with, and I'd known Ringer would be watching. As soon as I
saw my jockeying had put us dead on I felt the usual satisfaction, but then I thought of a way to increase the feeling.

"Well, if you're so good, go right ahead and take over," I

said to Val in a huff, pulling my hands completely away from
the controls as I turned to glare at him. "Well, don't just sit
there, go ahead."

"Diana, the controls!" he shouted, reaching forward to
slap frantically at the board. "Do something, or we'll crash!"

"You should have thought of that before you opened your
big mouth." I gloated, watching him jump between the board
and the screens. "We still have about a hundred and fifty
yards to cover before we hit. Let's see some of that precision
piloting."

"How can I pilot when the controls won't respond?" he
demanded, fighting desperately to get the board to react to his
efforts, then doing a double-take when his glance showed him
the way I'd stood out of the pilot's seat to stretch. He
couldn't help but smell a rat then, especially when I smiled
sweetly at him.

"I think we can trust the grabber field to do the rest of the
docking, don't you?" I asked as he stared at me darkly. "We
should be all sealed in in no more than another couple of
minutes, so let's get our stuff and wait at the lock."

"Grabber field," he muttered as he came along behind me,
following as I led the way to the salon where we'd left the
things we were taking with us. I was dressed in a light blue
ship's suit and canvas deck shoes, and Val was wearing his
cobalt blue uniform, but the uniform looked enough like a fancy
ship's suit that it would pass any but the closest inspection.
On another orbital station I might have fretted a little; on
Faraway it was strictly no sweat.

"You might have told me the Station had automatic docking," the hovering hulk behind me growled, definitely unhappy with me. "Does seeing people having heart failure
before your very eyes make the day for you? Do you remember what I told you about using words first and only then
indulging in other tactics?"

"Stop getting so wild." I laughed over my shoulder, at the same time picking up the packet of now-translated documents Phalsyn had given us and tucking it in my bag on the side opposite my completed double-check tape. "When you learn about something in an unusual enough way, the learning sticks with you longer. Don't you want to remember what you learn, partner?"

I picked up my already-packed monolon bag and turned to look at him, giving him a grin. Val didn't seem to appreciate my sense of humor and looked about ready to make mention of the fact, but he was interrupted by the soft bump and scrape of the ship sealing in. A final clank announced it was time to leave the ship, so I turned and headed for the airlock before Val could go back to casting that feral stare; I'd already had more of it than I was interested in, and as I strode away I could hear my partner grabbing up his own bag and hurriedly following.

I'd been idly wondering just where on the Station Ringer would be waiting, but I should have known better than to waste the effort. When the double doors of the airlock slipped back to let me out of the ship, he was standing not five feet away and staring directly at me, his expression more intent than I'd ever seen it. Ringer, Chief of Agents who reported directly to the Federation Council, a Special Agent who had lived long enough to be given a position like that, wasn't terribly imposing to look at. With the enormous and nearly empty docking area behind him he looked smaller than he really was, round and harmless and neatly dressed in a green four-piece businessman's suit that suggested to the universe around him that here was a man who probably sold ladies' underwear. If his brown hair was a trifle too long for your average businessman, and his black eyes a trifle too sharp, those things were usually overlooked in favor of his pudginess— which was almost all camouflage for the muscle underneath.

Ringer wasn't a man who put other men on guard—which was probably one of the reasons he had managed to survive.

Right at that moment, however, Ringer's eyes were examining me so closely that anyone trying to sneak up on him would probably have been able to get within ten feet of him before he noticed. His sharp black eyes moved from my long red hair and blue eyes to my face, traveled quickly up and down my body, then went back to my face and started the trip all over again. I smiled faintly at the way he was trying to swallow down his disbelieving shock, and strolled over to him.

"Hi, cutey, wanta have some illegal fun?" I asked in a low, throaty voice, giving him a smile to match. The expression in his eyes flickered as he remembered the recognition signal we'd used the one time we'd worked together on an assignment, about ten or eleven years earlier, and then he grinned.

"I recognized your hand at the controls during docking, but I didn't expect that to be the only thing I'd recognize," he said in a low growl looking me over for the fifteenth time. "Being warned doesn't do a damned thing to prepare you."

"You ought to try it from the inside," I suggested, grinning. "Looking in a mirror has become a traumatic experience —but only from the neck up. From the neck down, everything's the way it used to be, I'm happy to say."

"So I noticed," he murmured, then moved his eyes to a point just behind my left shoulder. "And that can't be anyone but Valdon," he went on in a normal-toned voice, coming up with an unphonied smile of greeting as he put his hand out. "I can see why he's still in one piece after spending two months alone with you."

"She came close to changing that," Val said dryly as he stepped forward to take the hand offered him, shaking it as though he'd indulged in the gesture all his life instead of just recently having learned it from me. "She forgot to mention that Stations have grabber fields to do the docking, and simply leaned back from the controls when it looked like we were about to crash. She thought it was amusing."

"Your people would have been smarter changing her sense of humor rather than her face," Ringer observed, flexing his hand surreptitiously as he took it back. Val's grip tended to be somewhat on the firm side, and I was sure he'd toned it down more in practice with me than he had a moment earlier with Ringer. They were examining each other in a sizing-up sort of way that seemed to satisfy both of them; there was an easy, tension-free air between them that grew to the point of friendliness almost instantaneously, the way it sometimes does between two strong men who recognize each other for what they are. Being female I found the process fascinating, but I wasn't given the opportunity of studying it for very long.

"That so-called sense of humor of hers has gotten her into more hot water than you could possibly believe," Ringer went on to Val in a chummier tone than I cared for. "Some day it'll get her in so deep she'll end up boiled for supper."

"I'm surprised it hasn't already," Val answered, also chummy, while Ringer sent me a disapproving stare. "You should have seen the things she did to me on Tildor, not to mention the trip here. I think something ought to be done about it."

"If you can think of something and make it stick, you have *my* blessing," Ringer told him with a wolfish grin for me. "And I can probably also guarantee the Council's blessing, providing you don't leave too many visible marks on her. Some of them are squeamish."

"I think you just blew it, Ringer," I said with a grin I couldn't hold back on, seeing the sudden surprise that Val was registering.

"Blew what?" Ringer asked, and then he turned his head to see Val's expression. "Is something bothering you, Valdon?"

"You might say so," Val answered with a slow nod, turning those eyes on Ringer instead of me for a change. "Just what exactly did you mean about not leaving too many marks on her? What do you think I am, that I would do something like that to a woman?"

"I *thought* you were somebody who had gotten to know her," Ringer came back with a calculating look in his eyes. "As big as you are you might have an even chance against her, but not unless you're willing to use everything you've got. You don't seem to understand that it's a Special Agent we're discussing, not a woman; getting her to change her ways will take more than waving a finger in her face and lecturing her. Believe me, it's been tried before, and by experts."

"And what sort of marks did *they* leave on her?" Val asked in a too-soft voice, still looking at Ringer. "Ones they were careful not to let show?"

"They didn't get a chance to leave *any* marks on her," Ringer answered with the same unconcern he'd been showing all along, somehow missing the way Val was looking at him. "She was the one who left the marks on them, visible or otherwise. And I think I understand now; you thought I was throwing her to the wolves."

"Weren't you?" Val said without hesitation, unimpressed by Ringer's calm. "You've never seen me before, know nothing about what I'm like, and yet the first thing you do is give me a free hand with her, on the provision I don't leave any marks that can be seen. What would you call it?"

"I expected to call it sharing an inside joke," Ringer said with a sigh, on the verge of shaking his head. "Right now I think the joke's on me. Apparently you don't understand how much I do know about you."

Val opened his mouth to demand an explanation of that statement, but that wasn't the place to have a private conversation. There were no more than about a hundred people trying unsuccessfully to fill the immense docking area, but some of them had started drifting closer, attracted by the apparent argument between the two men. Waiting for a liner shuttle is boring business; a good fight livens it up any day. In view of this, I interrupted before Val could get the first word out.

"How about we find ourselves a quiet corner somewhere?" I suggested, looking first at Ringer and then at Val. "You two are starting to draw a crowd of admirers."

"She's right," Ringer agreed without looking around, smiling faintly at the sudden awareness in Val's eyes that nevertheless wasn't enough to cause him to glance around in the guilt reflex. He turned to our right and began leading the way out of the docking area, and Val and I ambled along behind him.

Faraway Orbital Station had been in service for almost ten years, but it still looked as though it had only just been unwrapped and put into service. We passed beyond the docking area into the main body of the Station, ignoring the room reservation alcoves, enjoying the appearance of new-seeming carpeting under our feet, bright drapes covering the metal of the walls, soft music playing. The saying that goes, "If you've seen one Station you've seen them all" is perfectly true, except that on Faraway you sometimes get to see an almost empty Station. Right then the volume of traffic going through was minimal.

We ignored the almost empty dining rooms for the even emptier bar, found our own fairly well lit corner, and claimed a table. Just as we were settling ourselves, a tall, thin, long-faced specimen materialized out of nowhere.

"The robot's out for servicin'," he announced in a slow drawl, his long face making the simple statement of fact a tragedy of the ages. "Ah'll have to fetch whatever it is yore drinkin'."

"I think we can survive that," Ringer answered with a glance for me, undoubtedly as amused as I was. "Make it Selesian brandy all around."

"Why, shore," the man agreed with an amiable nod, then sort of floated on his way again. It looked like it would be awhile before our drinks came, but Val didn't seem overly concerned.

"All right," he said in a soft voice, to keep from carrying his eyes on Ringer again. "You claim you know more about me than I realize; what do you think you know, and how did you gather all of this intricate knowledge?"

"You'd better watch yourself, Valdon," Ringer growled with faint but very real amusement. "Diana's sarcasm is beginning to rub off on you. What I think I know about you is pure deduction, but that deduction is based on what I know for certain about Diana. Do you believe I know Diana?"

"Considering the way she greeted you, I think that's a safe assumption," Val answered dryly with an odd glance for me. "Does she make that offer to all her old friends?"

"Only to a certain select few," Ringer said with even more amusement, glancing at me. "It brought back a lot of old memories, and let me be as sure as possible that this little girl I'm looking at is the woman I'm used to working with. Until then, I wasn't sure at all."

"That's 'young woman,' not 'little girl,' " I corrected Ringer, bringing his eyes to me. " 'Young woman' I can live with without any hassle; 'little girl' is positively out."

"Little girl," Ringer repeated very firmly, grinning widely, then turned his attention back to Val. "You just finished a two-month trip with this harmless-looking little girl, and the first thing you did after leaving the ship was complain about how she treated you. Look at her and tell me what you see."

Val blinked and looked at me, but not understanding what Ringer was talking about made it a waste of time.

"I don't see anything," Val said after that very brief hesitation, his black eyes puzzled. "What is it I'm supposed to see?"

"Just what you did see," Ringer answered, settling back comfortably in his armchair. "Nothing. Which is just what I saw, and on both of you. If Diana ever makes a mistake in character judgment and ends up alone on a long trip with someone who turns out to be the sort no gal would bring home to meet her mother, you can be damned well sure she'd do more than let herself be stretched out to dry. I remember one crumb who tried to use her to prove what a big man he was; she put him face first into a brick wall. But there was also one who got the drop on her, and I remember what *she* looked like afterward. She isn't bright when it comes to cooperating with something like that when she isn't on assignment."

"And since there wasn't a mark on either one of us, she had no trouble with me on the trip," Val summed up, understanding finally breaking through the confusion. "But what if I had—gotten the drop on her, and simply hadn't beaten up on her? How would you have been able to tell?"

"I was trying to explain how well I understood the trouble you had with her," Ringer answered, with a sigh of patience, pausing to sip at his brandy. Brandy sits best on top of an exquisitely cooked, many-coursed meal, but Ringer had ordered it as a special welcome-home for me. Selesian brandy is very expensive, well worth every credit, and my personal favorite among potables. The only other time he'd ever bought it for me was the day I finally made it out of Blue Skies, a Federation hospital, after a particularly un"easy" assignment. When I'd first been brought in there, they hadn't thought I would live.

". . . are any number of people in this Federation who have had personal experience with Diana's sense of humor, and would love to explain their view of the experience to her in detail," Ringer was continuing to Val. "Unfortunately for them, none of them can fight as well as she can, or if they can, they can't afford to have her on the sick list when there's urgent work to be done. The common daydream is to someday get even with her, even if it means leaving a mark or two. It won't ever happen, of course, but there's still the dream; I was just offering you a chance to share it."

"Why won't it ever happen?" Val asked, and I could feel his eyes on me even though most of my thoughts and attention had drifted elsewhere.

"Because most of those people believe they owe her even more than she owes them," Ringer answered lightly. "She has a habit of exercising her sense of humor any time there's a danger of the gratitude or sentimentality rising too high, and it does make a damned good distraction. She's never learned how to take a thank-you gracefully."

I made a rude noise. "At the salary I get, thank-you's become superfluous," I told them both, not liking the bright interest I saw in Val's eyes. "And my bank is fresh out of deposit forms for maudlin sentimentality. How about changing the subject to something more interesting, like where Radman might be right now?"

I hoped I'd diverted them from silliness to business, but no such luck. Instead of taking the hint, they just laughed.

"You're right, of course," Val said to Ringer, and the closeness was there again. "Most of the things she does have reasons behind them, but even if the reasons are good ones, her efforts tend to be on the excessive side. There has to be a way of breaking her of the habit."

"I told you," Ringer growled, making a face. "It's been tried more than once, and by people who were downright eager to get somewhere. Even I gave it a shot once, for all the good it did. The only thing it taught her was to keep her distance when she played games, and to stay out of my reach while I still had the urge to strangle. A few members of the Council would give me a medal if I killed her, but most of them would be annoyed. They don't like seeing agents of her caliber wasted.''

"And speaking of agents of a particular caliber," Ringer went on to Val, "I understand you have a certain talent of your own. If I'm not misinterpreting what Diana told me, you ought to find it a handy thing to have during the next year.''

"It wasn't exactly a waste during the past three years, either," Val answered with a small laugh of amusement, probably because of Ringer's expression. The man I worked for was trying very hard not to look like a hick from the sticks on his first visit to the big town, awed by all those gosh-darn *tall* buildings. Ringer wanted to know more about Val's changing talent, but obviously felt that asking straight out for a demonstration would be boorish. I could have let him continue stumbling along on his own, but soft-heartedness is a major failing of mine.

"I think he'd get a kick out of seeing that drink server again," I told Val in the trade language used at Dameron's base, then made an annoyed sound for Ringer's benefit. "Damn it, if I don't pay attention to what I'm saying, I slide right out of Federation Basic," I said to Ringer's frown in what I knew he'd take as an explanation. "What I was trying to say was, can you reach my bag? I have something I want to show you, but somehow it ended up closer to you than to me.''

Ringer grunted in what he thought was understanding and leaned over to look under the table, missing Val's grin and the way my new partner slid out of his chair. I'd pushed my monolon bag as far away as I could with my foot, mostly to give Val the time he needed, but Val didn't need much in the way of time. Even as he stood, his features were already blurring and his body was slimming; when Ringer straightened up no more than a moment later, Val even had the proper slouch.

"How 'bout a nuther round?" the waiter's voice asked a Ringer who was paying almost no attention to him after noticing that my new partner seemed to have disappeared. "Ah don' mind fetchin' it."

"Not right now, thanks," Ringer answered absently while looking around at as much of the bar as he could see. "Diana, where did Valdon go? And why didn't you go with him? He hasn't been here long enough to wander around on his own."

"For some reason, people get huffy when I tag along with those using men's rooms," I told Ringer with a faint grin, but I wasn't grinning at what he thought I was. "If you think he'll need the help I'll ignore the huffiness, but I think he can handle it on his own."

Ringer opened his mouth to growl an answer to my wise-cracking, but the "drink server" he'd already dismissed in his mind beat him to it.

"Say now, looky here," Val drawled, sitting down in his chair again and picking up his only partly tasted brandy. "This here feller din't finish his first. Guess Ah oughta do it fer 'im."

"What the hell do you think you're doing?" Ringer demanded, finally turning to watch as Val-cum-the long and lanky waiter reached the glass to his lips and took an appreciative swallow. "Get your butt out of that chair and back to where it belongs, and while you're at it you can replace that drink you just tasted—on the house. My friend isn't into sharing."

"Oh, come on, Ringer, don't be so stuffy," I put in as he

continued to glare at an innocently sipping Val. "Let the guy stay and have a drink with us. Val won't mind."

"He surely looked like a right decent feller t' me," Val agreed in the same drawl, leaning back in his armchair. "Ah don' think he'd mind neither."

Ringer opened his mouth a second time to put his annoyance into words, but this time he stopped himself. His eyes had gone from the waiter's face to the familiar blue base uniform that didn't quite go with the face, a uniform he hadn't taken the time to notice earlier, and suddenly everything clicked into place. He stared at the waiter's face again with disbelief, then shook his head.

"I'll be damned," he said very softly, taking it a lot better than I had, his stare still unmoving from Val's face. "If you'd had the time to change clothes, there's no way I would have known. I don't think I've ever seen anything like it."

"I would have had him do you, but people tend to have trouble recognizing themselves," I told Ringer. I was still being ignored because Val was blurring back to himself and filling out again, and nothing short of armed attack would have been able to draw Ringer's attention away. "If he ever manages to do reversals, we'll never need a mirror again."

"I'm sorry to spoil your good time, but I'm not a toy," Val said to me. "I came here to work, not to take the place of your vanity table."

"Well, we all have to do what we do best," I retorted. "Personally, I think you'd look cute as a vanity table."

"Personally, I have the feeling I shouldn't have had this brandy without eating first," Ringer cut in after lowering the glass he'd abruptly emptied. "I've never worried about that before, but this seems to be a day for firsts. Anybody else interested in a sobering influence?"

"Not me," I said with a shake of my head, leaning back in

my chair, swirling the brandy in my glass. "I grabbed a snack just before approach, and it'll hold me for a while."

"Syntho," Val said with a grimace, obviously deciding to drop the discussion we'd been having out of deference to Ringer's near-upset.

"Syntho has its place, but I prefer the real thing," Ringer agreed with Val's prejudice, looking around to see if he could spot the real drink-server. "Diana does too, when she isn't feeling restless—or too lazy to do her own cooking."

"What own cooking?" Val asked with a soft sound of ridicule, and suddenly the conversation took on a new interest for me. "Diana can't cook."

"Don't tell me *you* did all the cooking during those two months," Ringer growled disbelievingly at a Val who had begun to color somewhat. "Come on, Valdon, you didn't really *believe* her? Haven't you learned you can't believe a word she says if it doesn't involve an assignment?"

Without a sound Val started to get out of his chair, the fury in his eyes so strong that I got ready to drop my glass fast and kick the table into him as a delaying tactic until I could get clear of my own chair. One more inch upward and I would have done it, catching him where it hurts the most, but Ringer had moved too fast, clamping a hand around his arm and forcing him back down.

"This isn't the place to settle private disagreements," Ringer growled low to Val, tightening his grip, until Val looked away from me and focused on him. "Starting a brawl in a bar does nothing more than attract unwanted attention. And I thought you weren't the kind to beat up on women?"

"So did I," Val said, taking a deep breath. "Or, I never used to be. You can let go of my arm now. The urge to kill is passing."

"It only passes on a temporary basis," Ringer told him with a very faint smile, taking his hand back while Val ran a calming hand through his black hair. "For someone who claims to know her, you got hotter than I thought you would."

"The effect seems to be cumulative," Val answered, leaning back in his chair to glance at me with an unreadable expression. "I seem to be able to take only so much from her before the explosion comes, and finding out about the cooking thing after her vanity table comments and what she did during docking put it together too fast. I don't like being made to feel like a fool."

"Not many of us do," I put in before Ringer could comment. "That outrage of yours was spectacular, but I don't think you can justify it. Whose idea was it to start cooking in the first place? Mine? Who was the one who decided he couldn't eat syntho? Me? Who was the one who talked the other into sharing the first meal? Into continuing to share the meals? So I led you to believe I couldn't cook. At what point did I twist your arm hard enough to force you into cooking for both of us?"

"Looks like she has you there, Valdon," Ringer observed. My supposed partner was looking vexed, as though he didn't quite agree with me. "Is she telling the truth this time?"

"As far as she goes," Val grudged, shifting in annoyance in his chair. "She knew damned well I'd never sit down to a meal alone when I believed she couldn't make the same meal for herself if she wanted it. How could any man eat food, when the woman with him is forced to eat syntho?"

"Especially when he was planning on making a suggestion during that meal," I said. "Syntho doesn't set the mood very well, and it's hard to decide what wine to serve with it."

Ringer chuckled at the way Val flushed, which made Val even more uncomfortable, though why he should be uncomfortable was beyond me. Did he think Ringer believed we did nothing more than play twenty questions to while away the time of a two-month trip? If he did, I'd have to decide which bridge on Hidemite, the Federation's capital world, to sell him.

"That was a low blow, but women are famous for it," Ringer consoled Val, swallowing down the chuckling. "If you touch them even once, they can claim everything you did for them before that was with that one end in mind. She probably knows better than that, Valdon, but you'll never get her to admit it, so arguing would be a waste of breath. Finish up your brandy instead, it'll make you feel better."

"There's only one thing that would make me feel better right now, but you're right about this not being the place," Val came back with one of those glances for me before lifting his glass to swirl the liquid in it. "I think you and I are going to have to have a little talk later, Diana."

"Sounds like he has something in mind, Diana," Ringer was quick to notice. "What with the way you look now, he just might sit you on his knee to lecture you for a while, then send you to bed early without supper."

"And then jump right in after me." I laughed, finishing the last of my brandy. Then I looked at Val. "You'll have to give me a raincheck on that talk, partner. I'll reschedule with you as soon as I get back from Faraway, and while I'm gone Ringer can show you the Station. I won't be more than a couple of days."

"You thinking about dropping in on Sellers?" Ringer asked as I pushed my chair back and stood, his eyes looking up at me. "I don't think that's a very good idea."

"If this Sellers is down on that world we're orbiting, I have to agree," Val put in with a frown, his eyes joining Ringer's. "You have no business running around on a frontier world all alone."

"You think Sellers won't know me?" I asked Ringer, ignoring Val's absurdity entirely. "After the first five minutes he won't have any doubts, and I really need his spirit after two months locked in a closet. The papers you want are in that bag sitting near your left foot, and I think that takes care of everything.''

"Not quite,'' Ringer denied, with only a glance for the peculiar expression Val had developed. ''If you take two days off to hunt spirits on Faraway, you'll miss your liner shuttle, which should be docking about three and a half hours from now.''

"What liner?'' I asked, only then noticing the hidden assessment in his eyes. "Wait a minute— You've located Radman. You know where he is.''

"We've known all along where he was,'' Ringer said, watching me calmly. "We've been keeping an eye on him ever since you disappeared, and two days ago he boarded a liner for Xanadu. We don't know whether the trip is business or pleasure, but that's where he'll be for a while. Still thinking about going spirit hunting?''

"No,'' I answered, sitting down in my chair again. "I've found something better to hunt than a few harmless spirits. Is that warrant back in effect? Did you bring my knives? What about a replacement for my I.D.? Was there enough time?''

"Yes, yes, and no,'' Ringer answered, making another stab at spotting the drink server. "I have the warrant and your knives, but there wasn't enough time to culture another I.D. for you. What I do have is identity papers for you and Valdon, absolutely authentic and properly documented and sealed, but you'll have to be careful with them. The ink's still wet.''

I snorted softly in amusement as I leaned back in my chair, knowing those identity papers would be a better job than what Ringer was trying to make me believe. They would not be perfect or in any way legitimate, but they'd be more than good enough to get us to Xanadu, right on Radman's tail.

"I know I'm just a tourist around here,'' Val broke into my

thoughts and Ringer's searching, "but would one of you mind telling me what spirits are? And why the name Xanadu sounds familiar? If it isn't too much trouble."

Ringer let the heavy sarcasm roll by without comment. Val was feeling left out, and he wanted us to know it.

"Spirits are the most aggressive carnivores Faraway has," Ringer told him in the most off-hand tone he was capable of. "They're big, catlike creatures that seem to materialize out of thin air in attack, then disappear the same way, which is why they're called spirits. Anyone who has ever hunted them will swear they enjoy the hunt and there's no reason why they shouldn't. The minute you walk into their territory, your chances are no more than fifty-fifty of ever walking out again, which means they take as many trophies as we do."

"And that's what you were going to do to clear away cobwebs?" Val said to me, outraged. "I think you'd better take another look; that's not cobwebs bothering you, it's insanity."

"Some day I'll explain an old saying about meat and poison," I told him with a laugh. "Right now I'll remind you where you heard about Xanadu. It was when you asked about what Radman had done to make the Council send me after him. Xanadu is the pleasure world Radman deals with on a regular basis, and . . ."

"And is the place those children were sold into slavery," he finished for me, his face suddenly going entirely expressionless, his eyes turning colder than LOX. "And that's where we're going."

"That's where *I'm* going," I corrected gently. "I started this assignment alone, and I don't mind finishing it the same way. Ringer can show you the sights while I'm tied up, and I'll take over later. Don't think you have to come with me."

"Try and stop me," he said with a snort of scorn, abruptly going back to the brandy he'd just been holding. "Seeing that you *don't* get tied up is one of the reasons I'll be there, remember? It's time you learned how much better teamwork is than going it alone.''

Ringer glanced at me as I sat back in my chair, but he didn't say anything and neither did I. I was going to have company on my hunt, and the benefits or drawbacks of the arrangement remained to be seen. Since the most important preliminaries had been taken care of, Ringer leaned back in his chair and thrust his hand into the right side of his coat as he looked at me.

"Here are your papers, liner reservations, and credit proofs,'' he said, pulling out a double stack of the sort of official nonsense no one in the Federation could get along without. "Valdon is Valdon Carter and you're Jennifer Kent, a precaution in case Radman was also given the name of the Special Agent sent after him. The renewed warrant is in the sealed compartment of your credit proof, handy in case you have to produce it, out of the way if you don't. Just watch what you do with those credit proofs; they're hooked into our discretionary fund by way of the usual blinds, and I'll expect an accounting for every credit spent.''

"And you'll get that accounting," I agreed solemnly, quickly activating the credit proof handed to me with my thumb print in the activating square before Ringer could change his mind. "You know how creative I am. Just don't expect any miracles. We're going to Xanadu, not Faraway.''

"I know, I know," Ringer grumbled, showing Val how to activate his proof. "All I'm asking is that you don't get carried away and take an extended tour of the planet. I know you, Diana, and giving you a direct tie into departmental funds makes me nervous.''

"How many times have I offered to pay you back?" I demanded, trying not to laugh aloud. "If you were silly enough to let them set up an accounting program without provision for illegal procedures it's not *my* fault, it's yours. If I have to grease a few palms, or buy certain information, or happen to come across a special weapon that appeals to me, what am I supposed to do? Forget it?''

"You know the Council won't acknowledge illegal procedures," he growled, the sharp look back in his dark eyes. "The more I have to camouflage them as something else, the more static I get. And since that fund is strictly for departmental expenditures, you can't pay anything back without admitting you used it contra regs. I go through this with you every time I have to give you access to the fund, and I'm tired of wasting my breath. It's not as if you don't understand it as well as I do; you just enjoy giving me a hard time.''

"Me?" I protested in shocked disbelief. "*I* enjoy giving you a hard time? Ringer, how can you say that?''

"With no effort whatsoever," he replied in his continuing rumble, then looked at Val. "Do me a favor, Valdon; see if you can keep her away from her usual nonsense this time. If it isn't absolutely necessary, don't let her do anything that costs credit.''

"And I'll be sure to let him know what's absolutely necessary and what isn't," I put in, glancing at my papers and reservation slip before sliding them and the proof into a pocket of my ship's suit. If it hadn't been unwise, I would have laughed aloud.

"That's a good point," Ringer said immediately, seeing through my comment to the heart of the problem. "Valdon doesn't know enough about the Federation to get along on his own if you two get separated. I think you'd better let him learn as much as he can on the liner to Xanadu O.S., doing the ordering and paying and such. You can tell him what to expect, and by the time you get to Xanadu he'll have had enough experience to get by on.''

"The ordering and *paying* and such," I repeated with a

half-hearted grin. "Anything you say, O chief, O Fearless Leader, O Master of my Destiny. What about our clothes?"

"Yours are in your luggage waiting to be sent to the liner," he answered, giving me one of those lowered-eyebrows looks for my wise-guying. "As far as Valdon is concerned, we'll buy him what he needs here on the Station. There's just enough time to have it made up before the shuttle docks. And before you bother me about it again, here."

He reached into his jacket again, but what he came up with this time was my idea of a real welcome-home gift. It was one of the two matched, specially made throwing knives I usually carried, complete with sheath, and I took it even faster than I had activated the credit proof.

"Bless you, Ringer, you always know how to treat a girl right," I told him with a glance and a grin, easing the blade out of its sheath to check it. Six inches of razor-sharp mirroring plus hilt gleamed back at me in the glow of a nearby chandelier, a sight I'd had occasion to miss once or twice in the last few months. "The other one's in my luggage?"

"Other one?" Val asked, an interested appreciation in his eyes for the weapon I held. "You mean you have more than one like that?"

"This is one of a matched pair, and I don't lend them out," I said with finality in my voice, setting the blade back in its sheath as I looked at my partner. "If you want a set of your own, have them made the way I did."

"It doesn't much matter how many of them there are," Ringer put in while Val grinned at my possessiveness. "Those cover I.D.'s I gave you won't let you carry weapons on you down to Xanadu, Valdon, so Diana will put that one away with its mate in a place in her luggage where it won't be found. If you've got anything that will raise eyebrows in a customs check, you'd better let her put it in with the rest."

"I didn't bring any weapons with me," Val said. It wasn't

hard to see he was telling the truth—not to mention the fact that I'd checked his belongings during the trip. Val hadn't come to the Federation as a peace emissary, he'd come to work with a Special Agent; making the trip unarmed just about shouted how good he thought he was.

"I don't know about you, but I feel a good deal safer over that," I said to Ringer, only glancing at Val. "If you'd seen him using a sword on Tildor, you would not be very anxious to have him handling any other weapons."

"She means I didn't go around trying to skewer everyone in reach, unlike some people I could mention," Val came back, dryly. "If we can't carry weapons openly down to Xanadu, why wasn't that one left with its twin? Why did you have to bring it along and give it to her now?"

"They're not fussy enough on this Station to give her a hard time over it," Ringer answered with a shrug, clearly unwilling to go into details about the various usages a Special Agent put a knife to. "I knew she wouldn't care to wait until she could get to her luggage, so I brought one along for her. She always claims she feels naked without a knife."

"You spoil her like that and then complain when she gives you a hard time?" Val asked, still enough amused to cause Ringer to stiffen very slightly. "If there's something she really wants, make her behave herself before she gets it, otherwise don't let her have it. She might not like it, but she's bright enough to learn to go along with it if she has to. It should save you some headaches."

"That doesn't apply to the knife, but you may be right," Ringer said with something of a nod, letting the stiffness disappear as he turned his head to look at me. "Why don't you try making her behave herself during this assignment, and then we can talk about it. Also let me know if you figure out a way of keeping her from something she really wants; I haven't been able to come up with an answer to that one in nine years of trying.''

The look in his eyes was no more than one percent wistful as he watched me stand up to fit my knife sheath into the slot in the right side of my ship's suit, a place that put the hilt handily close to my palm. The slot was meant for a tool a lot more innocuous than a knife and was almost too narrow to take the sheath, but a moderate amount of forcing did the job and let the knife slide clear of its covering without the sheath coming with it. No one would bother me about carrying a knife on a Station that orbited a raw, young world like Faraway, and that was probably a very good thing. Val's comment had annoyed me, and the only thing that had kept me from telling him what to do with himself had been the fact that I usually made it a point not to start fights when I felt annoyed and had a weapon in handy reach. That Ringer had acknowledged his idiocy even so far as to give him a sardonic approval of whatever he came up with added to my annoyance, something Ringer could see as he followed my example and stood.

''I think we'd better get those clothes bought for you, Valdon,'' he said, sharp-eyed gaze warning me to keep on being smart and letting it lie. ''You ready, Diana?''

''Not for the heart-stopping excitement of clothes shopping, I'm not,'' I said, ignoring Val's frown as I reached down to my monolon bag. ''Now that you have room in your pocket, you can take these papers off my hands. You two have fun getting Val all decked out, and I'll meet you in the docking area about fifteen minutes before the shuttle is due in.''

I handed over the stack of Absari greetings into Ringer's willing hands and began to turn away from the table while trying to close the bag again, and suddenly found myself on the verge of running into Val. He'd gotten out of his chair at almost the same time Ringer had, and only needed a step or two to put himself directly in my path.

"You can't really have anything so urgent to do that it can't wait a few more minutes," he said, looking down at me with those eyes. "It won't take me long to decide on what I want, and then we'll all go where you want to go."

"Without making me earn the privilege first?" I asked with what was supposed to look like monumental surprise. "Shame on you. Are you trying to spoil me?"

"If I was, I'd be too late," he came back calmly. "If you're going to get mad at me again go right ahead, but at least try not to misquote me. I said you ought to be made to behave yourself before getting what you want, nothing about earning privileges. There was very little wrong with the way you behaved while we were sitting here, so there's no reason not to let you go wherever you like once those clothes are taken care of. Which, as I said, will only be a few minutes, especially if you come along and give me some advice on color and style."

"Ringer can give you whatever advice you need," I told him, having no trouble resisting what he seemed to consider irresistible bait. "Since you apparently think I ought to be denied things, you should be pleased that the first thing I'm going to deny myself is the inexpressible pleasure of your company for a while. Besides, if I came along I'd be far too tempted to make sure you looked even dowdier than Ringer will make you look. Try not to miss the shuttle, or I'll be brokenhearted."

I gave him a cheerful little wave to go along with the reassurance I'd already given him, then turned and walked away from the frustrated annoyance he was making no effort to hide. Ringer had excellent taste when it came to his private, non-business wardrobe, but after what I said Val would never be able to make himself believe it. He'd try to judge alien styles and material all by himself, unconsciously discounting whatever advice Ringer gave, and would end up looking like someone who was all opinion and no taste. Val understood the spot I'd put him on, and also understood that knowing about it would not get him off it again. He'd end up unhappy with whatever he got.

When I walked out of the bar, I paced along the corridor until I found a cluster of shops to do some browsing of my own in, but the near-emptiness of the Station was too much of a distraction to make anything appealing enough to buy. Despite Ringer's worries I wasn't in a mood to throw away departmental funds, and I didn't care for the dismissive looks I was getting from the shops' salespeople. For some reason they were writing me off as a no-sale after a single glance.

The cluster of shops included a small shop catering to junk food, and I suddenly discovered that that's what I'd missed most all those months I'd been away. My appetite did flip-flops at the first sight and smell of the mouth-watering garbage, and I spent a few minutes stuffing my face with more pleasure than I'd felt in a long while.

The immense docking area wasn't much changed from the way it had looked a few hours earlier. The right side of the Station was reserved for incoming liner shuttles, the colored lights around the bays coming on and blinking at the first approach of the shuttle and continuing on that way until it left the bay for the liner again. The left side of the Station was for private ships which, of course, included navy shuttles, which were usually as large as private ships. The lights overhead and all around were bright without glare, clearly illuminating the two blinking shuttle bays and the one new private ship that had come in. Two blinking bays out of eighteen, four private ship slips filled out of fourteen, and less than two hundred people in an area designed to hold the traffic from maximum filled shuttle and slip space. It looked like Faraway was destined to continue as a ghost station until that sector of space filled up a good deal more and the frontier moved out past it.

I continued my amble into the docking area and down the center, idly glancing at the rows of empty waiting-seats, uninterested in them despite the added weight of books in my monolon bag. I had almost reached the spot when footsteps sounded behind me, and I turned to see Val and Ringer coming up. Ringer looked just as he had a little while earlier, but Val was no longer wearing his cobalt-blue base uniform. He'd traded it for a pair of dark slacks, a blue-green wide-sleeved shirt, dark loafer-like shoes, and an expensive-looking woven-metal neck chain of gleaming, silvery stellenium. He looked a hell of a lot better than an absolute stranger had any right to look, but I made sure not to let the opinion show on my face.

"Looks like we both decided to get here a little early," I said to Ringer. "Too bad the shuttle won't do the same."

"Just be glad you timed it so well," Ringer answered, glancing around at the twenty-five or thirty people sitting in waiting-seats not too far away from us. "If you'd come in too late for this liner, you would have had to wait more than a month for the next, or you would have had to take that ship in closer to Xanadu than was smart. It wasn't hard getting the Station officials here to neglect checking the registry on your transportation, but almost anywhere else the request would have had to be through channels more public than we would have liked. We need as much quiet on this as we can manage, for as long as possible."

"Until we spot the busy little eyes and ears at work," I nodded, glancing around the way Ringer was doing, automatically checking that no one had too much interest in our conversation. "But if we were really up against it, we could always take your ship. A month off wouldn't disagree with you, would it, Ringer?''

"On Faraway Station?'' he asked with a growl of ridicule. "If I have to be stranded somewhere, it isn't going to be a place like Faraway O.S. I left that behind me a long time ago. Let's sit down for a while, or it will feel like that shuttle is never coming.''

Ringer started for an empty section of seats in his usual way, without checking to see if anyone was following, but this time I didn't get the immediate choice of joining him. A big hand took my arm before I could turn, nearly crushing my sleeve despite the lack of deliberate muscle in the grip, and I looked up to see Val's calm appraisal.

"You haven't said anything about how dowdy I look,'' he observed with a hint of amusement. "I'm sure it's as bad as you expected it to be, if not a good deal worse.''

"It was clear he knew he didn't look dowdy at all, and it was also clear he expected me to do anything but admit it.

"Why, not at all, Val,'' I protested in very sincere tones, a friendly little smile backing the words. "You look just fine, you really do, and Ringer must have been very pleased with the amount of money you saved the department. Keep it up, and you and he will get along just fine.''

"So you've decided to keep on being mad at me,'' he said, a compromise between doubt and annoyance. "How long do you intend keeping it up?''

"Oh, I never get mad at the men I partner with,'' I assured him. "We'll do just fine working together—but I hope some of those clothes you got are warmly lined. If you don't manage to score elsewhere during your off-hours, you'll need them.''

"If being an irresponsible brat is one of your criteria for being an agent, I won't be qualifying,'' Val said with a look of scorn. "If she considers you off-limits and leaves you out of it that's your good luck, but I intend getting a piece of it. When I get through with her, I'll be even more off-limits."

"She doesn't consider me off-limits," Ringer said with a frown of sudden revelation, turning his head to look at me. "She gives me the same hell she gives everyone else, but just stays out of my way a little longer. For nine years, I've been thinking of that as a compliment."

"Some compliment," Val snorted, but more in sympathy than in derision. "In case you're wondering, the footprints don't look any better on your face than they do on mine."

"If you two don't watch it, you'll be comparing scars and discussing operations next," I broke in, beginning to wish I'd left Val where I'd found him. Ringer was getting bent out of shape by his prodding, and I was getting tired of hearing that same song and dance.

"You see?" Val incited, and now both of them were looking at me. "She doesn't have any regrets over what she did, to either one of us. If something isn't done, she never will learn to behave herself."

"You know, Valdon, I have a feeling you're going to be the first to get somewhere with her," Ringer growled. "Because of that, I think I'll start you off with a little help."

Ringer may have been nine years away from the life of an active Special Agent, but his reflexes hadn't slowed enough to make that much difference. Before I could draw my legs in or unfold my arms, he had pulled my knife out of its sheath and was holding it in his right hand, too far away for my belated grab to do any good. He moved it even farther away when I tried to reach past him.

"Don't even think about trying it," he warned, his dark eyes sharp with decision. "If you wanted to keep this, you should have behaved yourself the way Valdon said. Now I'm going to give it to him, and if you want it back you'll have to square accounts with him. It just might help to teach you to be a good little girl next time."

"I am a good little girl," I told him, not amused. "Especially with knives—or aren't you remembering anything that isn't convenient? This is absolute stupidity, Ringer, and if that big jerk hadn't gotten you hot on purpose you never would have done it. If you try giving him my knife, for however long, I just may decide to let him meet its twin."

"The big jerk is willing to take that chance," Val interrupted before Ringer could answer me, just short of a chuckle despite what I'd called him. "Put it in that bag she was carrying, Ringer, and I'll take over the carrying. Just how important is it to you to get it back, Diana?"

He was really enjoying the game he was playing, even more so than Ringer, but I'd had a lot more experience at that sort of thing.

"Important's the wrong word, Val," I said with a casual shrug. "If you'll feel safer with the knife out of my hands for a while, go right ahead and carry it for me. All I ask is that you make sure not to lose it; it has great—sentimental value for me. And I'll probably need to use it again some day."

I let my eyes laugh at him, then turned away from them both with only a neutral glance for Ringer. The bossman was putting my knife in the monolon bag I'd been carrying, bracing it in and protecting the bag from it with the books I'd bought. Ringer had ignored the little speech I'd given Val, but Val couldn't ignore it. It annoyed him that I'd suggested he was afraid of me, and whether it was true or not had no bearing. Under the rules I'd forced on him, the only way he could prove it would be to return the knife.

I spent the rest of the waiting time for the liner shuttle moving calmly around the immediate area, enjoying my relaxation, but getting more impatient with every passing minute. There's nothing like the feeling of starting a new assignment and despite my personal stake in this one, I'd make sure it was handled professionally all the way. Val and Ringer spent the time chatting, and when the lights started blinking to announce the approach of the shuttle, they left their seats and came over to join me, Val carrying both his bag and mine. If I'd expected him to hand over the bag then, I would have been disappointed. He was still determined to do things his way, not yet knowing that game time ended as soon as an assignment started. I nodded pleasantly at Ringer when he told us to enjoy ourselves, then went with Val to find a place on the line that was forming.

It didn't take long to get to the liner, which was definitely a good thing. As soon as the shuttle reached the Station I'd forgotten all about the silliness that had gone on before, but our fellow passengers hadn't. The looks they gave Val were on the chilly side, and there was altogether too much whispering and sideways glances. That public notice I'd been trying to avoid hadn't been avoided, and now we were surrounded by a bunch of narrow-eyed spectators. I didn't much like the idea, but if we couldn't avoid the small horde once we boarded the liner, we'd have to stay in our cabins until we reached Xanadu.

Putting our reservation slips into the backs of the seats in front of us on the shuttle programmed the directional rods sitting in the slots to the right of each seat back. Once the shuttle had sealed into the liner we took the rods and left our jolly traveling companions without a backward look, which undoubtedly caused more comment but at least got us out of there. Ringer had reserved two single cabins for us, the sort that had a communicating door, and the corridor was empty when the directional rods blinked rapidly to show we'd reached our destination.

"If you're ever outside a cabin and want to let whoever's inside know you're there, press that tab," I told Val, indicat-

ing the door annunciator as I slid the key end of the rod into
the door lock. "The key you'll use for the rest of the trip is
inside your cabin, next to the rod-return slot. You'd better
use your rod key before it stops blinking, or you'll need the
purser to open the cabin for you."

Val nodded and went to his own door, and once he got it
open I went into my cabin, already working on a mental list
of all the things he'd have to be shown how to use or do if he
wasn't going to draw unwanted curiosity. The reality of the
project was well-nigh staggering, considering the number of
things there were for him to learn, but somehow we'd have to
get it done. It helped that he was intelligent, but we'd probably have to resort to a few dodges anyway to avoid notice.

"The cabin is open and the bags are inside," said a voice
from behind me, causing me to turn. "I only gave it a quick
glance, but I didn't see any keys or rod-return slot."

"They're here, behind the door," I answered, gesturing
Val in before swinging the door shut. "Just remember always
to look over your shoulder before saying something like that.
There are people in this Federation who have never traveled,
but you're not supposed to be one of them. If you get caught
in an awkward situation, shrug it off by saying you're more
used to traveling by private ship than liner, and can't seem to
get liner protocol straight. You may get laughed at, but that's
better than having a finger pointed at you. Take a few minutes to look around your cabin, and then we'll start teaching
you what it was you were looking at."

I turned away from him and headed for my luggage, which
was stacked to the right of the small double bed, in front of
the cabin's built-in drawers and closet. The cabin was relatively crowded, with only two soft chairs and a small square
table to the left of the cabin door, the bed to the right, and the
tiny bathroom also to the left, beyond the chairs and table.
Val's cabin was to the right of mine and was probably exactly

the same, up to and including the dark gold and deep green of the decorations. Ringer was watching the pennies again by putting us in cabins like these, but once we got to Xanadu O.S. those pennies would be gone, along with lots of their brothers and sisters. No one with money took third-class accommodations, and no one went to Xanadu without money. On Xanadu O.S. and the planet itself we'd have roles to protect, and Ringer might grumble but he'd never be able to deny it.

"I would not mind at all knowing what I was looking at," Val said slowly from his place near the door, sounding perplexed. "Are you the same female I've been traveling with for the last two months, or did somebody pull a switch while I wasn't looking?"

"What are you talking about?" I asked, looking up at him from the place I'd plunked down on my knees on the deep green carpeting, in front of the big trunk Ringer had packed for me. That trunk took some opening, and I wanted to get as close as possible to it before starting.

"I'm talking about the way you're suddenly treating me," he answered, closing the few steps between us to crouch down next to me. "No sarcasm, no put-downs, no arguments, or fancy stories or looking right through me. You actually sound as though you might be dealing with another thinking being instead of a patsy. I'm certainly not complaining, but I'd like to know what brought on the change."

"Our being on assignment brought on the change," I said, looking up into curious black eyes with none of the amusement I felt showing. "Once the flag goes down there's no more game-playing, at least not between ourselves. Unless, of course, you don't much care if you survive. If you find yourself falling into that kind of mood, let me know and I'll take it alone from there on."

"That's better," he said with a grin, reaching out to brush

some hair out of my face. "With at least the sarcasm back in place, you're recognizable again. Are you telling me that as long as we're on assignment, I don't have to keep looking around for the direction the next attack will be coming from?"

"Considering the assignment you might want to put that another way, but you've got the idea," I agreed. "Right now watch how I open this, and plan on memorizing the sequence. This luggage knows how to protect itself, and if you use the wrong sequence after I open it initially, it'll feed you an electrical charge any time you try working on it after that until I can key it again. If I don't happen to be around to do the keying, you're permanently locked out. Now, watch."

The main lock of the trunk was keyed to my brain wave pattern, and once I'd put it on passive alert I was able to open the secondary locks. The sequence wasn't something Val would learn in five minutes, but seeing it done right would help him to learn to do it on his own. The end of the sequence left nothing to do but unfold all four quarters of the trunk, and Val had to help after the way Ringer had stuffed it. He found its weight surprising when he saw the relatively small amount of clothing, then stared with sudden understanding when I thumbed back the first of the false sides.

"That's a Mark IV blaster, heavy enough to burn a hole through anything living as well as uncounted numbers of thick, inanimate surfaces," I said, pulling the blaster out of its niche to check its charge level before pressing it back in place. "That small gun next to it is a stunner, adjustable beam and adjustable level, no charge leakage and automatic shielding against backjumping. The empty space to the right used to hold a dart gun, but darters are unreliable and even the best of them will jam, usually at the worst possible time. I won't carry one again, but some people swear by them. Your best bet would be to wait and try one, then make up your own mind."

"You seem prepared for anything up to and including a major war," Val commented when I closed that compartment and opened and began explaining about the one with pinhead mines, fingernail grenades, blinding spot flashers and inward exploding stick-ons. "How much of this do you expect to be using on Xanadu?"

"If we're lucky, we won't be using any of it," I said, closing that compartment and opening the next. "Xanadu's security is fairly tight, but any security system can be breached if you go about it in the right way and you know their blind spots. We'll play it by ear until we see whether there have been any major changes since the last time the system was mapped."

"Now, that I recognize," Val said, pointing to one of the knives I'd just uncovered. "With all the rest of that stuff, you probably don't even remember I have the mate to it."

"I remember," I answered shortly, then pointed to the thick, smoky blade in the third niche. "That one is completely non-metallic and won't register on any alarm systems, and it takes and holds a better edge than steel. It's only drawback is that it can't be balanced as well as my other knives, so throwing it from farther away than six feet is a waste of effort. For six feet, you might as well keep it in your hand. That last knife there is a set-up, so don't touch it unless you need its particular quirk. If you grab it hard, as you would if you were about to bury it in someone, the blade will come back into the hilt and spread out, slicing into whatever's wrapped around the hilt. Since you want that to be someone else's hand rather than your own, don't get it mixed up with the rest of the hardware."

"I think you can take my word that I'll remember," Val said, peering closely at the knife. "What's in the last compartment?"

"Odds and ends and something you especially have to

know about," I answered, opening the last section. "That little piece of metal is a magnetic lock pick, the dark strand next to it is a strangling cord, and that shielded coil is monomolecular ambush thread. Don't ever touch it with your bare hands, or you won't have any hands left. The rest of it I can show you some other time; over here is the device you have to learn how to use."

I pulled the telelink out of its nest and handed it to Val, watching as he turned the thick black circle this way and that, trying to figure out what it was. He made no effort to touch either of the two contacts in the middle of the round face, which was commendable caution on his part.

"That device is called a telelink, and is currently used by no one but my department," I told him, settling back on my heels. "It's range under normal circumstances would be quite limited, but it doesn't operate under normal circumstances and you're not cleared for the circumstances it does operate under. The only thing you have to know is that it's your direct line to departmental headquarters."

"This?" he asked with a glance at me, a frown for the palm-sized device in his hand. "How can this possibly reach other star systems?"

"As I said, you're not cleared to know that," I said, not blaming him for not liking the answer. "Just take my word for the fact that it does. In order to open the link to headquarters, press one of the contacts; to cut the link, press the other contact. When you get through, your vid will form in the air just above the link's rim. When Ringer's on Hidemite, where our H.Q. is, the link will give you to him directly; when he's not, someone there will relay you through to him. Right now we're on our own, except in cases of extreme emergency."

"Because of that leak they haven't found yet." He nodded, handing back the telelink. "The only question I have right now is, why are you showing me all this? It's almost as though you're getting me ready to be on my own."

"In a manner of speaking, I am," I agreed, putting the telelink back where it belonged. "This assignment should be no problem at all, but I'd hate to tell you how many agents have been finished off by no problem at all. I'm the one who brought you here, and I don't want you suddenly abandoned in a strange neighborhood with no idea of which way to go. If anything slips, you'll at least be able to reach Ringer."

"If anything slips, I'll be right there next to you to catch it," he said with what was nearly an angry growl. "I appreciate the emergency training, Diana, but I don't expect to be using it. Just make sure you don't leave that trunk open, and all that stuff will be there for both of us to use."

"Under normal circumstances, it doesn't matter whether I leave it open or not," I said. "The outer security system is supposedly to protect the expensive jewelry I carry, and if a customs official wants to inspect the inside, there's no reason to stop him. He won't find anything."

"How could people not find anything?" Val demanded, pointing to the trunk. "They couldn't possibly miss all those things you just showed me."

"Is that so?" I asked with a grin, shifting over on the carpeting. "If you think there's something there besides clothes and jewelry, show it to me."

The expression he sent me was ridiculing, as though he knew I was trying to put one over on him, only he wasn't about to allow it. He moved his crouch closer to the trunk, put his hand on one of the compartment covers—and slid it back to show six lines of very expensive earrings.

"And every bit of it is real," I told him. "It has to be, or I'd have no real excuse for the elaborate security system I use. Would you like to try the other compartments?"

"Not really," he said, matching the grin I'd shown earlier.

"I'd probably find more of the same. There's a special way of opening those compartments, I take it."

"Like this," I said, closing the one he'd opened, then placing my fingers with exaggerated care. "Your index finger goes on this little star first, then you catch the slide post with your thumb. Only then do you place your smallest finger on this snowflake, making sure your other fingers aren't touching anything. Then you slide it open in the normal way."

The compartment now showed weapons again, and Val had no trouble bringing the same up on the end compartment. It was a simple little trick, but it kept snoops, official or otherwise, out of places they didn't belong. I closed my compartment again and so did Val, then I climbed to my feet.

"You'd better get your cabin closed before we go into anything else," I told him, kicking off my deck shoes and starting to open my ship's suit. "If someone walks off with my knife, I'll take it out of your hide. We'll continue with the lessons after I've had a shower."

I left the ship's suit where it fell and headed toward my bathroom, paying no attention to the way Val was looking up at me. I recognized that look from the two-month trip we'd so recently completed, but as I'd told him earlier, play time was over and business was our first concern. The bathroom was really small as far as liner accommodations go, but the shower cubicle was more than twice the size of the one I'd used so long on the ship, and it felt downright spacious. As soon as I had the door closed I turned the water bar on, and then was again standing under a falls on a planet with air and sunshine and open spaces all around.

I was just about ready to add soap to the water when the cubicle door opened, startling me. I began to turn automatically toward I-didn't-know-what, when a big, naked body squeezed its way in, pushing me toward the cubicle's far wall.

"I closed my cabin and your knife is still perfectly safe," Val said, looking down at me through the warm, streaming water. "Just to be sure, though, I brought my hide back in case you had any other use for it."

"Val, we're on assignment now," I said in exasperation, pushing my wet hair back so that I could look up at him. "From now on we have business to consider, and mixing business with pleasure is. . . ."

"One way of making business more pleasurable," he interrupted, moving even closer and putting his hands to my arms. "Have I ever told you how good you look soaking wet?"

"No, you haven't," I muttered, discovering that it was impossible to back away from those caressing palms. "As a matter of fact, I could have survived without hearing it this time. Val, you have your own shower in your own cabin, and I'd appreciate it if. . . ."

"We use that next time," he murmured, sliding his hands behind me to pull me against him. "I can't see any problem with that, but only if it's as nice as this one. This shower is so—soft."

That all depended on how you looked at it. From my particular point of view there was nothing soft at all, not the big, wet body I was pressed to, not the thick, wet arms holding me, and especially not the very evident interest that was searching me out. My hands went to those arms as my breasts pressed into wet, black chest hair, and I looked up into deep, unwavering black eyes.

"Val, we're on assignment," I nearly begged, silently damning the fact that once those hands touched me I was a goner. "You can't . . ."

"Walk away from it now," he interrupted for the third and last time, tightening the hold he had on me. "But if you want me to, I will, Diana. Tell me you want me to walk away and I'll do it."

His head came down in the pouring water, and his lips made sure I wouldn't be telling him anything for a while. I put my arms around his neck as his hands began moving all over me, the sensations I felt forcing me into demanding his lips as strongly as he was demanding mine. I knew I was a damned fool for not standing my ground, but after all, he was already there. . . .

CHAPTER 4

Our travel time to Xanadu O.S. disappeared behind hours of work getting Val prepared for what would be coming at him in the course of a normal, uneventful day. The hardest part turned out to be figuring out what he didn't know, which could be something as insignificant as how to press an annunciator tab, all the way up to handling a planet-bound or atmosphere vehicle. We took care of the driving and flying parts by deciding he was much too good to do his own menial labor, and also added him to that large group of Federation citizens who knew nothing about Federation politics and cared even less. "Why would I care?" became an integral part of his vocabulary of phrases, but that didn't cover things like making phone calls, knowing how much to tip human servants, or using public bathrooms. Everything I took for granted and did without even thinking about had to be examined, and then we ventured out of our cabins to find things we'd missed and practice ones we hadn't. By shifting our day-night schedule we avoided most of those people we'd taken the shuttle with, and thereby avoided the trouble my cute idea could have brought.

Or, at least we avoided most of it. The majority of our shuttle companions stayed with the schedule they'd been following on Faraway Station, shifting only slightly to accommodate themselves to the nearest major liner schedule. Val and I took a minor schedule, eating at the tail end of the six-hour meal slot of whatever meal we were having, and then wandering around the ship during the time Faraway people would be sleeping through their "night." During Faraway "daytime" we did our own sleeping—as well as one or two other things that my partner considered essential to his health and well-being. He laughed off my few half-hearted attempts to keep him on his own bed by saying the assignment would not really start until we reached Xanadu O.S., then distracted me with a question on something important. His casual taking over direction of my in-bed activities annoyed me, but there was no time to argue the thing through with him. We needed every minute we had for getting him acquainted with Federation ways, and I decided that once we were on Xanadu and out of each others' laps, closing the door in his face would be a lot easier. The distraction he provided bothered me, but once I began closing in on my target, no outside distractions would have a chance of getting through to me.

"That assignment is more important to me than *I* am," I said, lowering myself into a seat with my back to the man who insisted on being my partner. "Some people call it dedication, but most have trouble understanding the attitude. They've never been in the sort of situation I'm usually in, you see, where hundreds or thousands of lives can be lost if I screw up. That sort of thing makes you very dedicated very quickly, and the attitude carries over even to assignments like the one we have now. It isn't a habit I'm willing to try breaking, so if you're feeling put-upon you can ask Ringer to find you another partner. I prefer working alone anyway."

I kicked off my deck shoes and pulled my feet up into the chair, finding it just wide enough to let me sit cross-legged as I usually preferred doing. There was a thick, unresponsive silence behind me, the sort of silence my "uncaring" attitude toward my co-workers often brought me, and then Val came around to stand in front of my chair.

"Most people *don't* understand dedication," he said very quietly, drawing my eyes up to the sobriety looking down at me. "All they understand is how hard it is to live with someone who has it. And there's no question about it being hard. I'm sure you don't run into many who are willing to put up with it."

"No, you don't," I answered shortly, looking away from him again as I wondered why he needed such an elaborate preface to announcing that he'd rather partner with someone else after all.

"It sounded as though you'd made that same offer to other people at other times," he pursued, still trying to lead up to it gracefully. "Many of them take you up on it, did they?"

"Enough," I said, looking around the cabin as I began feeling bored and a little tired. It was almost our "night," and the thought of sleep was starting to be appealing.

"Enough to make you feel that working alone is the better bargain?" he asked, still relentlessly pursuing whatever point he was trying to make. "Enough to make you expect the offer to be accepted more often than it's turned down?"

"Look, Val, being one of the majority isn't something that should upset you," I said, getting abruptly out of the chair while still looking around the cabin. "I know it's shattering to the male ego to learn that a female considers other things more important than him, but you'll get over the shock faster if you admit straight out that you don't like the idea. The admission will help you to think of all sorts of more important things that *you* could be doing, and then you'll see how appealing the thought of being somewhere else is. Before you know it you'll be a lot happier than you are now, and we can both get on with what has to be done. Have a good night's sleep, and I'll see you in the morning."

I began to turn away from him, knowing he'd find his way out fast enough once there was no one in front of him to protest his changed position to, but a big hand was suddenly wrapped around my right arm. I glanced up at him, really not in the mood for any more back and forth, and was surprised to see what looked like pain in his eyes.

"I don't like the idea of you considering other things more important than I am," he said, holding both of my arms as he looked down at me. "No other woman has ever dismissed me from consideration the way you do, and I sure as *hell* don't like it. But that doesn't mean I intend walking away in disgruntlement to soothe my bruised ego, it only means I intend doing something to change the situation. Just what that something will be I don't know yet, but walking away won't be a part of it."

"If you're thinking of me as a challenge, you're out of your mind," I told him, making no effort to keep the disgust out of my voice. "There have been men who looked at me that way before, their noses out of joint because I didn't fall swooning at their feet like the rest of the female population. Their ultimate disappointment just about crushed them, but knowing it would didn't stop me from doing it anyway. Ruthless, they called it, and they were absolutely right. It's one of my better character traits. I'd like to go to bed now, so I'd appreciate your letting go of me."

"There's nothing wrong with your character that a few good, hard whackings on the backside wouldn't take care of," he said with a faint grin, keeping those hands tight around my arms. "I'm not looking at you as a challenge,

Diana; only a boy sees a woman in that light. What I'm doing right now is trying to figure you out, trying to stay in one piece while I'm doing it, and trying to decide what makes you so different. When I have a spare minute, I'm also going to see what I can do about that so-called sense of humor of yours. As a defense mechanism, it does more than you know. Ever since we first met, I've had this overwhelming urge to defend myself.''

His grin widened at that point, trying to show me he was kidding, but I couldn't seem to find the wherewithal for sharing the joke. As embarrassed and as upset as he'd felt he should have turned around and walked away, and I didn't understand why he hadn't. Without saying anything I tried to pull away from him again, but this time he drew me close and put those arms around me.

"You said you were tired and want to go to bed," he murmured, the words as soft as the way he stroked my hair. "That sounds like a good idea to me, so let's do it.''

"Not with you," I said in a whisper as I shook my head, tensing so quickly in his arms that they had to tighten to keep me near him. "Not with anyone. I want to go to bed alone.''

"Alone," he echoed with what seemed like difficulty, the pain that had earlier been in his eyes now in his voice. "You've had to do most things alone, haven't you, Diana? And for so long that it's become a way of life. Stop trying to squirm loose and push me away, you're not fighting against what you think you are. We're going to bed together, but all I'll be doing is holding you. You can be as alone as you like—as long as my arms are around you.''

He picked me up then and carried me to the bed, got us out of our clothes and under the covers, then simply put his arms around me again. It was warm and comfortable in those arms, his chest against my cheek a solid, positive presence, and once he was asleep my arm stole around him to hold him the way he held me. I couldn't say anything about what he'd done and refused to let myself think about it, but holding back that arm just then was totally beyond me.

CHAPTER 5

The rest of our travel time on the liner wasn't long, but we took a precaution we should have taken right from the start. In order to avoid any more trouble, Val changed himself to look like a very plain, nondescript individual. If I'd been used to his quick-change act I would have thought of it sooner, but I wasn't and I didn't. That time "better late than never" seemed to work; no one recognized him.

Compared to Faraway Station, Xanadu O.S. was a madhouse. Rather than the one shuttle trip from liner to Station that had been used on Faraway, Xanadu required the three that every major Station did. People left one liner shuttle and ran to a second, or took up places on a line, or sat themselves down to wait the necessary time. Some few, with longer waits ahead of them, went to have a meal on the Station or arrange for accommodations. People moved everywhere, including those who, like us, meant to stay for a short while and then go down to the planet. Lights blinked, the crowd noise pounded at us, people jostled us, and Val finally understood why we had had our last conversation with instructions in my cabin.

We fought our way through the insanity together for a while, then split up to see to the individual chores I'd assigned us. Since we were staying on the Station and then going down to the planet, our luggage had to come out of bond and be checked through customs, and that was the job I had given to Val. He had looked at me with wordless questioning in his eyes, probably wondering if I were setting him up again, and I had had to reassure his qualms. In full truth I would have preferred seeing to the luggage myself, but it would have looked odd having a grown man tagging idly along behind me while I did it all, and we couldn't afford to look odd; better to take separate directions and get it all done without any fuss.

The twelve registration alcoves still had people on line in front of them despite the fact that we'd waited for the third shuttle before coming over, so there was nothing for it but to pick one and join the crowd. My Special Agent's I.D. could have had the Station Manager doing the registering for me, but even if Radman hadn't taken it before kicking me off, I still couldn't have used it. No matter how quiet they swear to keep these things word always gets out, and I preferred standing on line to giving Radman advance notice that I was coming.

My line moved slowly forward, and everyone waiting seemed as anxious as I was to get out of the bedlam of the docking area and into the relative peace and quiet of the Station proper. I had enough time to wonder how Val was doing, then wondered if he'd gotten over his indignation yet. I'd had occasion, just before we took the shuttle, to remind Val that I outranked him on that assignment, and most of the decisions made during it would not be made by the democratic process. I let him know that if I didn't find him up in the air when I said jump, he'd have lots of time to investigate the various means Federation people use to fill free time. He didn't like the idea, didn't pretend that he did, but couldn't keep pressing his arguments when the time to leave rolled around. Val, for some reason, was very used to running things, and clearly intended extending the practice into the Federation; in case he hadn't already gotten the message, I had a surprise waiting for him.

In time all things pass, even the line you happen to be waiting on. When the man in front of me left the registration alcove I stepped inside, then went up to the computer outlet it held. Station computers run everything, regulate everything, and know about everything, a normally invisible dictatorship that's about as complete as it's possible to get. The outlet's recess took my papers with a polite purr, acknowledging my request for a suite, but instead of a key showing up in the proper slot, the outlet blinked twice in an odd sort of way, and my papers were locked tight where I'd put them. In all my years of traveling nothing like that had ever happened to me, so I stood and blinked back at the outlet, wondering if it was malfunctioning, and then a man walked into the alcove. He was tall and well dressed in an expensive way, a sleek fifty with the polish of a professional maitre d', and as soon as he opened his mouth, I found I wasn't far wrong.

"I'm the Station's hotel manager," he informed me with a calming smoothness. "Can I be of some service to you, young lady?"

I hadn't been called "young lady" in a lot of years, but I let the matter pass.

"The outlet seems to be malfunctioning," I told him, gesturing toward the machine. "It won't give me a suite, and it won't release my papers. Do you think you can shut it off?"

"It can be shut off if necessary," he answered, walking toward the rear of the machine. "Let me have a look first."

He disappeared behind the large, bulky outlet, leaving me

to wonder what was going on. I knew damned well that the papers the outlet held were no more than days old, but I would have taken long odds that whatever the problem was, it had nothing to do with the phoniness of my papers. I'd used department-issued identity papers many times over the years, and even when they'd been produced fast enough to get them to me yesterday I'd never had any trouble with them. The only way to establish their phoniness was to get in touch with the bureau of records of my supposed home planet, and computers weren't programmed to do that. The problem had to lie elsewhere, but I was hanged if I knew where.

The Station's hotel manager stayed behind the outlet longer than I expected him to, and when he finally came out he was looking thoughtful.

"Your papers show you have a traveling companion," he mused, staring at me in a strange way. "Where is he now?"

"He's seeing to the luggage," I said, returning the stare. The question seemed totally off the point, but there was no harm in answering. "Why do you ask?"

"I ask because I'm afraid we can't allow you to register," he answered, shaking his head regretfully. "You *are* familiar with our policy on minors?"

"Of course I'm familiar with it," I snapped, losing patience with the way he kept avoiding the main issue. "What does your policy of minors have to do with not letting me register?"

He looked somewhat unsure over the tone I'd used, and put his hand on the bulky machine next to him as though to gather support from it.

"The outlet's biological readout shows you to be two months and thirteen days short of seventeen standard years of age," he recited, taking refuge in unshakable facts as his eyes moved quickly over the black jumpsuit I was wearing. "I must admit you do sound and look—ah—almost adult, but we tend to be very careful with this sort of thing. I assure you there's been no mistake, unless you've forgotten to submit your majority certification form? No? Then I think it best that we wait for your traveling companion. Maybe he'll be able to register the two of you.''

The man leaned back against the machine looking satisfied, but I was numb with shock. Me, a minor? I wanted to laugh myself silly over the idea, but the hotel manager wasn't laughing and solitary amusement is too often pathetic. I thought about going to look for Val at customs, realized the computer would already have sent for him, then stood there simply waiting until he showed up, followed by a short, squat, luggage robot. The hotel manager brightened when he saw a real, live grown-up, something that sent an involuntary shudder through me.

''This is my uncle, Valdon Carter,'' I jumped in before anyone else could say a word. ''I'm sure he's old enough to register us. Can I set it up for you, uncle Val?''

There was no way Val could have had the foggiest idea of what was going on, but he didn't blink an eye. ''Sure, Jenny,'' he drawled, smiling down at me fondly. ''If you think you can do it right.''

His fatuous answer may have been just right for the situation as it stood, but he was lucky I didn't kill him on the spot. I took his papers without a word and substituted them for mine, set the registration just as I had before, but this time let Val stand in front of the scanner. The idiot outlet hummed and chuckled to itself, and seven seconds later Val had his papers back and a key to a suite in his hand.

''Welcome to Xanadu Orbital Station,'' the hotel manager beamed at Val. ''If you'll place the key in the lighted slot on the luggage robot, it will lead you to your accommodations. Have a pleasant stay.''

Val nodded in acknowledgment, thanked the manager for

his help, then gave his key to the little robot. The robot, now prepared to lead rather than follow, took off into the Station proper and toward the nearest elevator bank, carefully keeping to a pace that Val and I could match. We followed along after the thing, Val casually commenting on whatever took his eye, me not saying a word, and in just a few minutes we stood outside the door to our suite. The little robot used the key to open the door, then trundled on through the elaborate sitting room to each of the bedrooms in turn, leaving Val's bags in the room to the left and mine in the room to the right. It chuckled its contentment over a job well done as it rolled out of the suite again, and I waited just long enough for the door to close before blowing up. I cursed as I'd seldom cursed before, getting more satisfaction over volume than inventiveness, and finally turned on a puzzled, frowning Val.

"How the hell could that be?" I demanded with a snarl. "Even if those idiots back at the outpost are responsible for this insanity in some way, how could I be seventeen? What the hell is going on?"

"Now I understand," Val said with a came-the-dawn expression finally breaking through his confusion, at the same time nodding his head. "You didn't know that you'd been matched to Bellna inside as well as out, but that's the way it works. You couldn't say you'd been matched to her if you didn't have her age as well as her features."

"But Bellna was fifteen!" I all but shrieked, raising hands toward him that wanted to become claws. "How the hell does fifteen become two and a half months short of seventeen?"

"Bellna was fifteen *Tildorian* years," he answered with such calm and reason that he came close to losing his life for it. "Absari standard doesn't match Tildorian standard, and neither, obviously, does Federation standard. Fifteen on Tildor must translate to just short of seventeen here."

Just that neat and simple. Your biological age has been

changed, Diana. You're now a minor, Diana. Don't worry
about it, it isn't anything important. I must have stood there
staring at Val for a full minute, before turning away from him
to walk to a chair and collapse down into it. Part of me
wanted to rip, tear, rend and destroy, but the rest of me was
too numb to go along.

"Diana, what's wrong?" Val asked, staring at me where I
sat slumped in the chair, his voice sounding worried. "Why
do you suddenly look so strange?"

"You think I *look* strange?" I asked, still keeping my eyes
away from him. "You should feel how I feel. What the hell
am I supposed to do now?"

"I don't understand the problem," he protested, taking a
chair across from mine. "Is it part of whatever went on at the
registration desk?"

"It is *all* of what went on at the registration alcove," I
answered disgustedly, finally looking up at him. "I am now
registered as a minor, and if I try arranging for a majority
certificate, I'll probably miss Radman altogether."

I pulled a cigarette out of my jumpsuit and lit it, then
leaned back, trying to rearrange my thinking.

"I still don't understand what you're talking about," Val
broke into my distraction. What's the difference *how* old you
are?"

"There's a big difference," I said, finally noticing the
more-than-comfortable furnishings of the suite's sitting room.
"If you want all the gory details, here they are. The Federation runs these Orbital Stations not only for the safety of the
passengers; they also expect a return on their investment.
When they first started taking guests they ran into a peculiar
problem. They would register an obvious adult, and then
find out that by the standards of his home world he was a
minor and not required to pay. Then they would refuse to
register someone who seemed to be a minor, and find out that

the seeming minor was actually a well-to-do, responsible citizen. It almost drove them crazy, so they decided to make a stand. They told their member worlds that eighteen was the legal age they had decided on. If a planet allowed its minors to travel about without restrictions, that world was responsible for paying the minor's debts. If they refused, all liner service would be halted until they reconsidered. Conversely, if their citizens included people who were usually considered minors, these people would have to have certificates of majority issued to be produced on registration.''

I drew my legs up under me, and grimaced down at the nearly knee-deep carpeting.

"At any rate," I continued, almost distractedly, "the member planets screamed but eventually agreed, and the biological detectors were brought in. Now, no minor may register without one of two things: a majority certificate guaranteeing full payment for all services rendered, or an adult guardian accompanying and directing them. If I had the certificate there'd be no problem—I would be registered as an adult. Since I'm registered as a minor, I'm only allowed to move about and do things with the express permission of my guardian, and the Station computer will keep a constant watch on me to make sure I don't destroy the place. I can't order meals on my own, use the facilities on my own, can't even leave the Station on my own. I'm tied hand and foot with no immediate way out.''

"So that's what that 'uncle Val' business was about," he said slowly, staring straight at me. "I'm your guardian.''

"And I've got to figure out a way around it," I agreed, as I looked about at the white and gold walls and trimmings of the sitting room. "There's got to be an out, something I'm just not seeing, something that won't take the time getting a majority certificate would. Just give me a few minutes to think.''

My mind had already moved into high gear, checking the file drawers of memory and rummaging through the stacks of unclassified-therefore-unfiled bits and pieces of trivia I tended to accumulate, looking for even one hint that might do me some good. Val said something that didn't get through the whirling concentration, so when I pulled my mind back and looked questioningly at him, he said it again.

"Why bother?" was what he had asked, looking very comfortable in his chair. "No need to rack your brain to get around something that's already taken care of: I'm your guardian."

"And that's your idea of a solution?" I asked with all the ridicule I was feeling. "Hasn't it come through to you yet that that's the problem, not the solution? I can't walk around as a minor, legally required to ask permission for everything I do. It would be too ludicrous for words."

"Why?" he asked again, and suddenly it came to me that he looked *too* comfortable. "It's not as if I don't know what we're here for. If I have to be the one to get us where we're going instead of you, what difference does it make?"

"It makes a lot of difference," I answered in exasperation, wondering why he was looking at me in such a strange way. "You don't know much beyond the generalities of this culture; what if you get put on a spot? And what do I do once we get down to Xanadu? Wait until we happen to trip over Radman, then take you aside to ask your permission to execute the death warrant? Sorry, Val, but I don't operate like that."

"I know how you operate," he murmured, the strange look growing even stranger. "You do everything your own way, and you go over anyone who doesn't get out of the way in time. It may be an effective way of getting the job done, Diana, but one day you'll run into someone you *can't* go over, and then *you'll* be the one who's done. As I see it, you now have two choices: either forget about going after Radman until this age business is straightened out, or start practicing the way to ask nicely for things. As your guardian, I'll expect to see a lot of improvement in your manners."

"But I can't forget about Radman!" I blurted, feeling almost as shocked as I had at the registration alcove. "You know I can't just turn my back and walk away, hoping I'll catch up to him some other time! You have no idea how many lives he could ruin, even in a couple of days! And what do you mean, practice asking for things nicely? You wouldn't—"

I couldn't bring myself to finish the sentence, but I didn't have to. Val knew exactly what I meant, and his grin showed it.

"Make you behave yourself?" he asked with a chuckle, really enjoying himself. "Have you been thinking of me as the sort who would pass up an opportunity like this? Would *you* pass it up?"

I opened my mouth, started stuttering, then quickly regained control of myself. The whole thing was so ridiculous it had gotten to me for a minute, just as though he really meant what he was saying.

"Val, we're on an assignment," I said with an attempt at a smile. "If you try to play catch-up games now, you'll be putting both our necks on the line. As soon as this assignment is over you can do anything you like to get even with me, and you'll have every right, but not now, not while we're working. You can see that, can't you?"

"Of course I can see your point," he said with an agreeable nod, giving me a smile of his own. "Game-playing under fire is always a dangerous pastime, one I avoid whenever possible. But that doesn't have anything to do with our current situation. The age you register is a fact, as solid as the fact that you've already named me your guardian. What could be more natural than my making you behave yourself, just as I would if you really were not yet seventeen years old? Show me how that jeopardizes the assignment and I won't do it, but first you have to show me.''

"It jeopardizes the assignment by restricting me," I said, still refusing to believe he meant what he had said. "I have to be free to move around on Xanadu as the situation demands, following Radman's trail to wherever he is. I can't find him by tagging obediently along behind my 'uncle.' ''

"But that's exactly what you have to do," he said, his tone reasonable. "You and I may know you're not seventeen, but to everyone else around here, that's exactly what you are. How do you plan on making it *not* necessary to tag along after me? You've been declared a minor; how do you plan on getting it undeclared?''

I just sat there with my feet under me in the light-gold chair, staring at him in silence, finally knowing the meaning of the strange look he'd been giving me. It was a lot like the look I'd seen in his eyes when he'd kept me in bed during that time while the wound in my side healed, and he'd done it "for my own good." There would have been very little chance of arguing with him then even if the Bellna presence hadn't been in control; his eyes said "no" at the same time his mouth did, no uncertainty, no lack of confidence. He had decided to do that to me again, I could see, and the thought upset me more than I would have believed possible.

"Don't think you have me in a corner, because you don't,'' I said after the silence. "If I can't think my way out of this, I'll—I'll—''

"End up being a good little girl, or passing on the assignment,'' he finished for me, a thing he'd been doing a lot lately. "While you're thinking, I'll order up some lunch for us. That's just about what Station time is now, and it's been much too long since we had our last lunch on the liner. It's usually easier to think on a full stomach.''

"I'm not hungry," I told him, unfolding my feet to stand abruptly out of the chair. "And I prefer doing my thinking in private."

I turned away from him and went toward my bedroom, keeping myself from hurrying despite the weight of his eyes on my back. I entered the room and closed the door quietly behind me, walked over to the double-double bed and picked up a pillow, then threw the pillow as hard as I could toward the door to my bathroom. The room was done all in pale blue and silver, normally cool and soothing colors, but nothing short of knock-out gas could have calmed me down right then. No matter how furious the idea made me, there was no getting around it: if I *couldn't* think my way out of the box, I was smack up against the choices Val had mentioned. I turned back to the bed and threw myself down across it, then set my mind to deep-think searching.

I don't know exactly how many hours went by, but enough of them passed to allow me to know just where I stood—or, in that case, lay. Calling the situation bleak would be like calling a feather light, an unnecessary redundancy that was as angry-making as an intimate caress from a strange hand in the midst of a crowd. I'd spent some time considering whether it would be possible to do anything illegally, and had come to the reluctant decision that risking it on Xanadu wouldn't be the smartest of moves. If I really had to I could get down to the planet without Val, but Xanadu's security set-up specialized in catching those attempting to barge in without invitation. If they managed to get their hands on me, the fact that I could pay my way would not alter the fact that I'd been caught in an illegality, and was therefore, according to their laws, a criminal. Criminals on Xanadu were not treated with patience and understanding; they were very quickly tried, convicted and sentenced, the penalty involving the criminal, in various unpleasant ways, in Pleasure Sphere doings. That kind of thing would very likely get me closer to Radman, but not in a position where I would be able to do anything about him. I turned on my back in frustration, searching the blue and silver ceiling for answers, but wherever they were hiding, the ceiling wasn't it.

"Have you come up with any strokes of genius yet?" a calm, deep voice asked, drawing my eyes to the now-open door. Val stood there, in the same red-orange shirt and black pants he'd worn earlier, and he didn't seem very worried.

"I've had one or two thoughts," I agreed, determined not to let him see me squirm. "The primary point that came to me is only a belief, but it has a lot going for it. If I refuse to go along with your fun time, if I simply go ahead and do things my own way no matter what age everyone thinks I am, what can you do about it? You won't simply sit back and put your feet up, refusing to do the job, because you know as well as I do how badly it needs doing. If I had to bet on it, Val, I'd bet that you have as much of a need to get on with it as I do."

"You *are* bright," he conceded with a faint grin, leaving the doorway to come and stand over me next to the bed. He folded his arms across his chest in a casual way, and looked down at me with amusement. "The only thing you haven't taken into account is my own thinking on the subject. You're right in believing I want to see Radman get his just as much as you do, but you forget that you're the only one in the known universe who considers me helpless. If you decide you're too good to pay back some of what you owe, I'll leave you here on the Station and go after Radman alone."

I know my jaw dropped open then, but I just couldn't help it. He couldn't possibly be serious, but he did seem to be. I sat up fast, and looked up at him.

"You couldn't possibly mean that!" I got out in a rush, struggling to keep some control over myself. "You can't go after Radman alone, you don't even know what he looks like! And you don't know Xanadu! And if you think I'd stay on this Station, you're crazy!''

"I don't have to know what Radman looks like," he answered with that damnable calm he seemed to be trying to soothe me with. "There are people on Xanadu who do know what he looks like, and they should be easy to find. As far as the planet itself goes, there seem to be a lot of people who don't know it, so many that the Station has an information clip on it available for viewing. I'll have a lot of company not knowing that world." He unfolded his arms and sat down next to me, then smoothed some hair back from my eyes. "And this Station also has a special baby-sitting service, designed to take care of the minor children of those who go down to the planet. The clip explained how gently they treat the older children, especially the ones who are angry enough at being left behind to try following their parents. Maximum security detention facilities could learn something from their methods.''

I knocked his hand away from me with a snarl and turned my back on him, so furious I could barely think straight. How nice that he'd spent the past few hours so profitably, viewing clips that *I'd* taught him how to view! I hadn't known about that damned baby-sitting service, and the thought that *I* could be subject to such a thing was more than I could accept. I didn't *want* to be less than seventeen, and I wasn't!

"If you want to take over this assignment, there's a specified way to do it," I told him in a tone without inflection, still turned away. "Whether or not you like it, I do outrank you, just as I outrank everyone who isn't a Special Agent. If you want to be assignment leader, you have to face me."

He shifted silently in place for a minute, then said, "What do you mean, a specified way of taking over the assignment?

Isn't the highest ranking agent automatically the leader of an assignment?''

"No," I answered shortly, keeping my eyes on the far wall, my legs folded in front of me. "The best fighter in the group is entitled to lead it, which is only right since most teams are combat groups. The one with the highest rank is usually also the best fighter, but not always; and even if he is, any member of the group is entitled to challenge him as long as the challenge doesn't jeopardize the assignment. This room is more than big enough, so we can start any time you feel up it.''

"I get the impresion you've been challenged before," he observed, curiously. "How many times have you lost?''

"Twice in the last nine years," I answered, finally turning to look at him. "Once when I was too badly wounded to know what I was doing and needed to be challenged, and once when I went up against a brother hyper-A who happened to be better than me that day. The next time we faced each other *I* won, and after that we took turns as assignment leader when we happened to work together. And no, I haven't had that many challenges over the years. Everyone I know but you is bright enough to keep from antagonizing a Special Agent. But the fact that I *have* been beaten should give you some confidence, so let's get at it. If you want to be big boss all that badly, you just might make it.''

I started to swing my legs toward the side of the bed so that I could get to my feet, but Val's arm came up, blocking the swing. The look on his face was amused, but somehow it was different amusement than the one he'd been showing earlier.

"I never said I wanted to be big boss." A lie if I ever heard one. "And even if I did, you know I won't fight a female. I appreciate the offer, but it isn't necessary. There's no reason you can't handle the boss-work—as long as you do it my way.''

"Your way!" I burst out, vocalized frustration mixing with total confusion. "Why does everything have to be *your* way? And how the hell am I supposed to direct an operation while trotting along in your shadow?"

"You'll figure something out," he said with a lot of assurance and a widening grin, reaching a hand to my hair again. "You're good at that kind of thing. And why shouldn't I want everything done my way? You don't seem to think there's anything wrong with the attitude when it's you doing the wanting."

"Would you have done this if you didn't have what to get even for?" I asked straight out, knocking his hand away again. "And don't hedge. I want a straight answer."

"Probably not," he admitted without hesitation, then made the statement more positive. "Definitely not. I don't usually take advantage of other people's bad luck—unless they've earned it. Would you like to try denying that you've earned it?"

"What good would it do me?" I asked in disgust, gesturing my opinion of such a waste of time. "The game is supposed to teach you to watch your backside at all times, which in turn helps to keep you alive. If you ignore the lesson and get mad instead, you're the one who loses out. Would you like to deny you're more alert now than before we started the trip?"

"I don't need to be beaten over the head to learn to be alert," he snorted with a ridicule I had half expected, leaning down to one elbow on the ice blue cover. "And especially not by the woman I'm enjoying in bed. If no one ever taught you how unfair it is taking advantage in a situation like that, you're about to finally learn the lesson. And now that we've got that out of the way, I'd like to know what your choice is."

I stared at him in silence for a minute, and if looks could

kill I would have had a body to dispose of. His grin returned, tempting me to tell him what to do with himself and then try Xanadu on my own, but the assignment was too important. If the only way I could get it done was his way, I'd have to do it his way.

"My choice," I echoed, still staring at his grin. "If I really did have a choice, you wouldn't be enjoying yourself so much. But I really do think you're entitled to fair warning, Val: I don't like being hustled, and I usually make a point of getting even. That doesn't bother you, does it?"

"As long as you're giving me fair warning, of course not," he said laughing softly. "I'll just return the favor with my own warning: if I don't like the way you get even, *you* won't like what happens to you. Are you ready for the ground rules of our new association?"

He was still enjoying himself so much that I could have cheerfully loosened his teeth, but I didn't have that option. I shifted on the ice blue bed cover in frustration, trying to ignore all the roiling inside me, then grabbed a fistful of the silk and nodded reluctantly.

"Sure you're ready." He laughed, looking at the expression on my face. "Someone would think you were bracing yourself for the onset of torture. Just how painful do you expect behaving yourself is going to be?"

"With your definition of it?" I asked with a grimace. "Very. Just get on with it."

"There's isn't much to get on with," he answered with a shrug, then leaned back off his eblow to tuck his hands behind his head. "If there's something that has to be done, you'll tell me about it and I'll decide which of us does it. If I decide there's something that has to be done, you'll do it without argument. That's simple enough, isn't it?"

"Simple's the right word," I muttered, feeling an enor-

mous urge to put my face in my hands and have hysterics.
"And you expect that to work."

"Of course it will work." He grinned. "Now it's your
turn. Let's hear what we do first."

"First we check out the Station," I said with a sigh,
stretching out flat on my back on the bed so I didn't have to
look at him. "As soon as we know for sure that Radman has
left for the planet, we take ourselves after him."

"You think he might still be on the Station?" Val asked,
surprised. "The possibility hadn't occurred to me. How do
we find out if he is or not? And what do we do if he is?"

"The general computer registration will tell us if he's still
on the Station," I answered, muffling a yawn. "Most people
keep their Station accommodations if they won't be on the
planet very long, and the computer lists them as non-resident
when they take a shuttle. If it turns out he's still on the
Station, I take care of him and you talk real fast to keep
Station security from shooting me down."

"You think they'll catch you?" he asked, and this time he
sounded bothered. A second later his face was above mine,
his eyes staring down at me. "I thought you were good
enough to get it done without anyone knowing who it was."

"On the planet, sure," I said, finding nodding difficult
while lying flat on my back with him hanging over me. "I
might even have managed it here on the Station—if I hadn't
been declared a minor. I wasn't kidding about the kind of
surveillance I'll be under, and I don't think I'll be able to lure
Radman to one of the Station's null areas. If he's still here,
I'll just have to wipe him and hope the security people stop to
ask a few questions before burning me down. They sure as
hell won't use stunners on someone caught in the act of
'cold-blooded murder.' "

"I don't like the sound of that." Val frowned, the look in
his eyes showing that he was contemplating possibilities. "If

he's here on the Station, we'll have to think of something else. I'm all for getting rid of Radman, but not if you have to go with him."

"That's one of the risks I get paid to take," I said, briefly wondering why he was looking angry. "And don't even think about making any personnel substitutions in the executing of that warrant. Down on Xanadu you're as likely to get away with it as I am, but Stations are Federation territory and you're not authorized to execute a death warrant here. Even if the security force didn't shoot you down, the Federation would take care of it for them. They don't like having people issuing and executing their own death warrants."

"We'll have to worry about that if the question comes up," he said, looking vexed. "We'll check those computer files first thing tomorrow, after we have a decent dinner and a good night's sleep. If he's gone the way I hope he is, we'll follow as soon as we can get a shuttle reservation."

"I prefer checking the files now," I said, starting to sit up on the bed. "We've wasted enough time. . . ."

"That a little more won't matter," he said, pushing me back down with one hand. "Right now I think you can use a nap, so you won't be yawning and falling asleep over dinner. This 'day' is going to be a lot longer than standard before it's finally over. I say you'll take a nap and then dress for dinner. What do you say?"

"You claim you don't like that kind of language," I countered moving against the slight pressure of his hand. "Let me up."

"I asked what you say, Jenny," he repeated, his voice softer than mine had been, his eyes staring down into mine. I was being forced to do things his way, and the look in his eyes said I didn't get mine until he got his. I really did want to give him his, but I still had that damned assignment to consider. I stirred under his hand again, hating the way he was looking at me, then turned my eyes away from his.

"Yes, uncle Val," I got out, nearly choking on the words, so furious I could have killed with a big smile on my face. "Whatever you say, uncle Val. Anything you like."

"*Anything* I like?" he repeated in a very satisfied murmur, his hand coming to my face, his own face moving closer. "I think I like the sound of that."

"Don't like it too much," I said, turning my eyes back to him, but making no effort to free myself. "If I have to be seventeen, that's much too young to get involved with a man your age. Just be glad you have your own bedroom—you'll be needing it."

He stared down at me in silence for a minute, the look in his eyes pushing at me to see how determined I was to stick with what I'd said. If I hadn't been so furious he probably would have been able to make me back down the way he'd done much too often in the recent past, but strong anger has always been able to overcome the more delicate emotions in me. I met his gaze with a look of my own, the sort of look people had been known to grow very uncomfortable under, but all it did for him was recall his grin as he shook his head.

"I *can't* have it both ways, can I?" he asked, not me but himself. "If you didn't need to learn a little restraint so badly I would not consider depriving myself, but since you do need to learn the lesson I'll just have to wait. It's a good thing you stayed with Bellna's appearance; I've always found brown hair and eyes the hardest to resist. Have a good nap."

His hand moved from my face to gently brush aside some of my hair, and then he was gone from the bed and heading for the door out of the room. I twisted around to watch him go, waited until he'd closed the door behind him, then took a strand of my hair to chew on. After two months of living with him, it bothered the hell out of me that I still didn't know where he was coming from. Another man in his position would have pressed his advantage and forced me to do anything he was in the mood for, but not Val. If he had forced himself on me, I would have been a hell of a lot happier; I could have filed him away in the proper niche then, and once the assingment was taken care of could have happily broken him up into small pieces. But he hadn't forced himself on me, hadn't even tried to talk me out of the decision I'd made, and suddenly, stupidly, I was regretting that decision. For the first time in many years I felt bewildered and somehow vulnerable, as though everything I had learned to protect myself with was suddenly negated. I put my fingers to my eyes and rubbed hard, then got up to get out of my jump-suit and retrieve the pillow I'd thrown. Maybe the idea of a nap wasn't so stupid after all; if I were asleep, at least the thoughts would stop rampaging around in my head. I took the pillow, lay down with my arms wrapped around it, then determinedly closed my eyes.

CHAPTER 6

The idea of a nap turned out to be terrible. My dreams were filled with unending arguments with people who insisted on believing I was a tiny child, and the fact that everyone towered over me only helped to convince them they were right. I woke up just as the maddening frustration was about to make me strike out blindly in all directions, then sat for a few minutes with my head in my hands, forcing myself to separate dream happenings from real ones. Even after I knew which way was up the depression hung on with claws and fangs, setting me growling as I climbed out of bed and headed for the shower. If nothing else, I had to get rid of that growl; in that mood, I would have been unreasonably danger-ous to those around me even if I'd been surrounded by nothing but the spirits of Faraway.

A hot shower and leisurely air-drying took care of the growl, but stopping in front of the bathroom's mirrored wall reinforced the depression almost to the point of tears. Sure the face I had gotten from Bellna was devastatingly beautiful, and sure that face and the long red hair matched well with my body; that didn't change the fact that that face was a young

girl's face, and that body registered just as young on a
biodetector. And what had Val meant, saying it was a good
thing I didn't still have brown hair and eyes? All he could see
was the Bellna overlay; why wasn't he thinking about that
alone? Everything about that simple assignment was starting
to twist out of its track, up to and including my thinking. It
was up to a certain reflected redhead to set it all straight, but I
watched the pretty young girl in the mirror chewing an end of
her hair, and realized she hadn't the faintest idea of where to
start.

I sat down on the blue bathroom carpeting for a while,
facing away from the mirror wall, and slowly, slowly, fought
my way back to a proper perspective. The idea of being
declared a minor had thrown me, and Val's messing around
hadn't helped; but I was starting to come back from the shock
to my normal way of thinking. Since the minority nonsense
had to be put up with until the assignment was finished, all I
had to do was finish it quick and then I'd be in the clear.
After all, it wasn't as if I really was seventeen, so what was
the big deal if everyone did get the wrong idea? That was
what I'd been counting on their doing, back when I first
thought about whether or not to keep the face, wasn't it? I
leaned my right shoulder harder against the black and pale-
blue-tiled wall, suddenly understanding that I would have
begun coping with the problem a lot sooner if Val hadn't
been there to take advantage of the situation. It almost seemed
as if he were deliberately trying to push me off balance, as if
he had more in mind than simply getting even. What else he
could be after I couldn't imagine, but a shrug dismissed the
thought as I climbed to my feet. Val was determined not to
get to work until the new Station day started, but he was
determined about a lot of things. By the time he realized that
going to the dinner dining room could also be called casing
the joint, it would already be done.

Putting on makeup or trying to—almost brought back the depression; the Bellna-face was so young and innocent that nothing but the gentlest highlighting was possible. Anything more would have looked ridiculously out of place, like a three-year-old girl wearing her mother's high-heeled shoes. I didn't realize how much the incident annoyed me until I went to my luggage for something to wear, and found myself digging around for one particular outfit. It was something Kate Newman, another agent, had talked me into buying, and when I finally found it I understood what my subconscious was up to. The thing was a pale, shimmering electric blue body suit, slit in front from the tight, high collar down to the navel, and so close-fitting that it would look painted on. It was also long-sleeved, with very thin, almost invisible ties at two points across the long front diamond to keep it from gaping awkwardly open when I sat. It was not an outfit a child would wear, and would be a statement of my position that my inner self seemed to require. I stared at it in silence for a minute, trying to decide how wise my inner self was being, then said to hell with it and reached for the silver high-heeled sandals and small bag that went with the outfit.

Once I was dressed I added a silver pendant and earrings, brushed my hair, then examined the total effect in the mirror wall. If the suit had been even a shade deeper in color it would have gone badly with my hair, but as it was the bright, cascading red added to the overall picture. I turned a little in front of the mirror, the cynical side of my nature sounding cat-calls in ridicule, the rest of me just short of grinning evilly. I'd had to be talked into buying that outfit because I don't believe in waving candy under the noses of babies and then refusing to let them have it, but right then I was more interested in soul-satisfaction than in fair play. I looked at myself over one shoulder as I tugged gently at a sleeve cuff, ran a smoothing hand down a shimmering hip, then turned away from the mirror and sauntered toward the door to the sitting room.

When I walked out of my bedroom, Val was standing behind one of the white couches of the sitting room and in front of the bar, carefully examining what he was pouring into his glass. He didn't look around at the sound of my door opening, but he proved he knew I was there.

"You certainly took long enough getting ready," he said in a distracted voice, watching the level of the liquid in his glass rise no more than an inch despite the fact that he continued to pour from the bottle he held. "What in the name of the Mother of All Life *is* this stuff?"

"That's called ambrosia," I supplied, amused at his reaction of incredulity. "It's a graduated intoxicant, set for the one-inch level of a glass like that. If you pour the first inch you find it light and only faintly intoxicating, something you could drink all night and barely feel. The next inch makes it more potent and the following inches even more so, until you reach the point where one sip is enough to keep you drunk for a week. I don't know how long you've been pouring, but if that bottle was full when you started, you'd better pour some over into another glass before tasting it."

"It *was* full," he muttered, righting the bottle and then putting it aside for the second glass I'd suggested. He poured over the first inch, snorted with delight as the second inch began darkening the pale rose of the first, then put aside the initial overpouring so that he could sip carefully at the couple of inches in the second glass. At that point I could see he was wearing a formal comp-suit of gray and black, no indication of discomfort about him at the full ruffles at wrists, throat and shirt front. He sipped at the ambrosia, his brows rising in surprised approval, and then he began to turn more fully toward me.

"This is really good," he approved, looking at the rose-colored fire-water that cost more than some people earned in a standard month. "I thought it was just a silly toy, but it's really—"

His words stopped so abruptly I thought he might have suddenly died, but there was nothing dead about the look in the eyes that had just come to me. That look burned into me where I stood, a raging black fire that actually sent him forward a step or two until the couch back woke him up by slamming into his legs. He stopped then, not too happy about having to do it, continued to stare briefly, then finished off the ambrosia in one swallow.

"I can see there are some things worth waiting for," he said at last, back in control of himself despite the still-smoldering black fire he hadn't been entirely able to put out. "I can't complain because you did warn me, but you're still not being very fair. I wasn't expecting to be hit below the belt, so to speak."

His grin was faint but still definitely there, something I didn't understand any more than I understood what he was talking about.

"What do you mean, I warned you?" I asked with a frown I could feel, beginning to make my way over to the bar where he stood. "What was I supposed to have warned you about?"

"You warned me you would get even for my taking advantage of your problem," he reminded me, watching as I took another glass and poured over about an inch and a half of the ambrosia he'd put into the first glass. "I thought I was on guard against anything you might do, but there are some things no man can guard against."

I turned back to him to see that his eyes were still on me, and from that close the look in them was very unsettling. The civilized gentleman looking down at me was aroused by what I had momentarily forgotten I was wearing; if the primal

hunter behind his eyes managed to get control away from
him, I'd have a fight on my hands.

"I don't believe in getting even that way," I told him,
sipping at my drink. "I'm not silly enough to believe that
you'll be doing without just because I kicked you out of *my*
bed, so what would be the point in wiggling my backside in
your face and then laughing? When the time comes for me to
get even, you won't be smiling."

"I see," he said, sounding as though he didn't believe a
word I was saying. "You put that thing on just to have
something to wear. It never occurred to you that with you
wearing something like that to dinner, they could serve me
roast asteroid dust and I would never notice. If this isn't
getting even, I don't know what is."

"Just stick around and you'll find out all about it," I
assured him, swallowing a grin at the plaintive note he'd put
in his voice, at the same time stepping back from the hand
that had begun moving toward my waist. I would have been
an imbecile to let him touch me, especially since there were
things that needed doing. "I'm ready to go if you are."

"I was ready to go about three seconds after I first saw
you," he said with a theatrical sigh as he put his empty glass
back on the bar. "If you're talking about dinner, though, I
suppose we might as well get on with it. We can finish
discussing getting even later, when we get back here."

In a pig's eye, I thought as I put my glass next to his, then
let him head us both to the door out of the suite with a hand
in my back. I knew how he discussed things, and wasn't
about to let him make me change my mind about sleeping
arrangements. I needed that assignment to be over as soon as
possible, and letting him distract me wouldn't get it done.

We took the elevator up to the main floor of the Station,
but I didn't let Val head us immediately toward the dinner
dining room. I pleaded an unexpected need for the ladies'

room that stood not far from the elevator bank, got his gallant and amused permission to take all the time I needed, then went inside with an innocent smile he would not understand till later on. There were half a dozen other women using the larger facilities, all of whom looked at me with the widest range of expressions I had ever seen; I hadn't the time or interest to do more than ignore them as I appropriated and locked a private stall. There wasn't room for much in the small silver bag I carried, but the computer tap I'd brought didn't take much room, and was disguised as a cigarette case. The master files I had to check were on the opposite side of the wall I stood next to in that ladies' room; waiting to do it the next Station day would have been a waste of time.

Getting through their security lock-out could have been a life-time project—if I didn't already have their password and keys. The Station people would not have enjoyed knowing I had them, so I made sure to tap directly into the memory file without activating any of their terminals. My tap acted as the terminal, with the information forming in the air above it, a running list that continued on without the need for tabbing. I could have put a direct inquiry in about Radman instead of wasting time going through the alphabet, but all too often those lists are tapped, and I didn't want anyone knowing who I was looking for. The name Richard Radman appeared in its turn, the non-resident designation showing right after it, and as soon as the next complete page formed itself in the air, I deactivated the tap, put it away, then got myself out of there. There was no way the Station computer could have kept me from tapping in, but that didn't mean it had also refrained from signaling all sorts of alarms.

Val smiled at me when I came through the door, an encouraging sign in view of my recent illicit activities. If there had been any hullabaloo yet, he wouldn't have looked so unconcerned.

"Well, that wasn't bad at all," he said with a grin as he walked up to me, pretending to look me over. "And I can't tell if there's actually been an improvement, or if it's just seeing you come back that makes this corridor brighter."

"You must really be desperate," I remarked, keeping my voice as low as his had been as I looked up at him. "A line like that can't have any justification *but* desperation, and that doesn't make any sense. Haven't you noticed how every female in sight is looking at you? If you felt up to it, you could even get away with handing out numbers."

He grinned deeply in acknowledgment of the truth in what I'd said, but he didn't even bother glancing at the women and girls passing us in the corridor or standing at the various game machines the wide corridor held. Xanadu Station had a lot more people than Faraway had had, and most of the women were staring at Val openly, hunger and interest and availability clear in the stares. A single nod would have brought more than half of them to him, and that despite the fact that very few of them weren't with men of their own.

"I don't see you accepting the invitations of all those men," he countered instead, gesturing very slightly with his head. "If they keep that up much longer, everyone in the Station will be covered in drool. If you're not showing any interest in them, why should I feel any differently about their female counterparts?"

His comment about the men startled me, but one glance around showed that he was right. If the women were ready to drop at Val's feet, the men were too busy gawking at me to notice. I could see I had made a mistake wearing that outfit after all; for two agents on an assignment that required a large degree of privacy, we were being noticed by more than three-quarters of the people in the Station.

"I like to take my time making a choice," I told Val, giving him a small, faintly amused smile. "And I'm also not coming up with desperation lines. If you're waiting for me to go first, I'll let you know as soon as I've made a decision.''

"You do that," he agreed, losing his grin as he wrapped my right arm around his left and began heading us toward the dining room. "And I'll let you know whether or not your choice meets with my approval. If it doesn't, you might want to consider desperation lines of your own."

I hadn't understood his amusement until that very minute, but once I did I would have pulled my hand and my arm away from him if he hadn't been holding on tight against exactly that kind of move. The bastard had as much as admitted that he was going to keep me celibate with his authority as my "guardian," probably until I couldn't take it any longer and had to go to him for what I needed. He didn't yet know me well enough to know I would go up in flames before I did that, but he would sure as hell find it out. I closed my hand on his arm into a fist, deliberately crumpling his sleeve, and kept my eyes on where we were going.

The dinner dining room wasn't very far up the corridor, and was, of course, adjusted to major continent planetary time, as was the rest of the Station. People staying in the Station waiting for their liner to wherever they were going didn't find it necessary to adjust whatever schedule they were following, but those going down to the planet found it easier doing the adjusting before they hit dirt. If it turned out that their destination planetside was half a world away from the designated major continent they'd have to adjust again, but more people went major than minor, so setting up alternate schedules was too much of a pain.

The maitre d' greeted us with a smile then led the way to a table, taking us through a good portion of the elegant room. Lace and crystal and soft music and expensive wines set the mood of a formal dinner dining room, enhancing the splendor of the formal occasions.

Val played gentleman by holding my chair for me at the cozy table we were shown to, then sat down opposite me. A large number of eyes were on us again, male and female both, and that added to the overall annoyance I was feeling— until I caught a glimpse of the squad of security men going by out in the corridor. They were moving somewhat slowly and glancing at hand meters, and none of them looked at all happy. With my tap deactivated they had no way of tracing me through it, and that upset them. They would eventually consider the single computer null point in the area—the ladies' room—but I hoped by then I would be gone from the Station.

"See anything that interests you, Jennifer?" Val asked in a distracted tone, clearly referring to the menu he was looking at, a second copy of which sat quietly in front of me. The menus on Xanadu Station were like the ones on the planet, fully holographic and smell-equipped, saving the diner from having to ask questions about any dish he was unfamiliar with. There was even a small tasting square next to each exotic main dish, and Val had made use of a couple of them.

"I'm not very hungry," I answered, ignoring the menu. "As a matter of fact, I'm thinking about going straight back to the suite."

"You can think about it all you like," he came back, throwing me a glance as the majority of his attention stayed on the menu. "I let you get away with not eating anything earlier, but you won't be skipping two meals. We have things to do tomorrow, and you'll need your strength."

He let his eyes rest on me longer that time, reminding the unreasonable half of the partnership that there was a job to do. I refrained from laughing in his face, then shook my head.

"Making shuttle reservations doesn't call for too much

strength," I said, looking casually around the dining room. "Our friend has already left, so we go down after him."

"How could you possibly know that?" my partner demanded in a soft hiss, his black eyes suddenly looking annoyed. "You haven't been out of my sight long enough to do *anything* on your own!"

"How long do you think it takes?" I asked with amusement for his annoyance, enjoying it the way he had enjoyed mine. "Couldn't you see it in the brighter glow of the corridor? Or were you too busy with other, more interesting thoughts?"

"So you did it then," he nodded, sitting back in his leather armchair, looking at me through lidded eyes. "And he's definitely gone off the Station?"

"No question," I agreed. "Just remember to be curious about the squads of security people you see prowling this area when we leave here. If you're not, they'll think you're guilty of something."

"I am guilty of something," he answered, still obviously annoyed. "I'm continually guilty of considering you like other women. Maybe if I really work at it, I'll learn better. What do you want to eat?"

"I told you, I don't want anything," I said, leaning back in my own chair, my eyes still on him. "Hunger is well known for cutting down on the sexual urge, you see, and that should save you some trouble. If I don't want any men, you won't have the bother of passing on my choice."

"You're too considerate for words," he said, his tone dry. "Although I can't tell you how much I appreciate your offer, I'm afraid we'll have to forget about it for now. You've been a busy little girl, and busy little girls need nourishment to keep them going. Unless you've decided not to be any busier."

I stiffened in my chair at the threat, furious all over again at the way he was forcing me to do things his way, but there was nothing I could do to stop it. He was more than capable of leaving me on the Station and going after Radman alone, just as he was hinting he would if I didn't listen to him. I didn't realize I was sending a kill-stare again until I saw him grin, and that got me even more.

"You just wait!" I hissed through my teeth. "You have your fun now, but one day soon it'll be my turn, and then you'll learn the real meaning of fun! If I do nothing else in this life, I will do that!"

"I've always admired dedication and purpose," he commented, the grin still there as he went back to checking the menu. "Now let's see what we can find to strengthen those two admirable qualities. If you're a good girl, I might even let you get a dessert."

He seemed to have no trouble ignoring the way I was staring at him, so I gave it up and switched my stare to the delicate and intricate pattern of the Ilian lace cloth on our table. With Ilian lace no two patterns ever came out the same, and I tried concentrating on that fascinating bit of information to take my mind off what my emotions were doing. I was coldly furious and hopping mad and a dozen and a half other things including outraged—but I was also beginning to be very faintly intimidated. I hated the feeling even more than I hated what Val was doing to me, but I could no more stop it than I could stop *him*. A bad precedent had been set on Tildor when Val had pushed me around as Fallan, with Bellna doing the intimidated part. Since then I hadn't been able to think about our time in the Paldovar Village without feeling strange, and it occurred to me that maybe Dameron's people hadn't removed Bellna's *persona* from me as thoroughly as they'd believed. If that was true there was *really* nothing that could be done about it, with the possible exception of brooding. I turned to one side in my chair and folded a leg under me, then spent some time thinking about brooding.

I hadn't used the two chances I'd been given to make a food choice of my own, so I wasn't given a third. When Val closed his menu a robot waiter glided up to our table, and in another minute it had been given an order for two tru-steaks with all the trimmings. It was also given our drink order, which consisted of two inches of ambrosia for Val and "something very mild" for the "young lady." I flatly refused to look at him after that, not to mention refusing to respond to his attempts at light conversation. No man had ever dared treat me that way before, and especially not with that "no arguments" look in his eyes.

When our "drinks" came I ignored mine, which turned out to be a damned good thing. If I'd been sipping happily and listening politely to Val's supposedly disarming chatter, I would have missed the approach of someone I hadn't expected to see. The man was of medium height and somewhat on the thin side, and I knew that thick-lipped face as soon as I saw it. John Little was one of Radman's stooges, a spotter who usually traveled with Radman and stayed on the lookout for salable merchandise. For some reason Radman had left him in the Station and had gone down to Xanadu alone, and now Little was coming over to *us*. He stopped at Val's elbow, waited for his target to notice him, then came up with a greasy smile.

"Excuse me," he said with the sort of cultured tones and practiced charm that usually broke the ice for him with anyone he approached. "I saw you from across the room, and feel certain that we've met before. I travel so often I must know half the people in the Federation. My name is John Little—do you remember me?"

He put his hand out for Val to take, another ploy that was designed to breed flattered awe and instant friendship, but he had apparently never tried the routine on someone like Val before. Without any sign of hesitation Val rose easily from his chair, took the hand offered him, and looked down at a very startled con man.

"Valdon Carter," he acknowledged, pretending not to see the way Little flinched at the mashing of his hand. "I'm sorry to disappoint you, Mr. Little, but I'm certain we've never met before. I have an excellent memory for faces and names, and yours just aren't there. Good evening."

If Little hadn't been nursing crushed fingers, he probably would have gotten around the abrupt dismissal Val handed him. He backed off with uncharacteristic fluster as Val sat down again, then turned and headed back where he'd come from. I didn't make the mistake of staring openly at him at any point, especially not after his hasty retreat, but I couldn't help but find the attempted contact fascinating to consider.

"You did that just right, Jennifer," Val said as soon as Little was out of hearing range, amusement in his voice. "Keep it up, and that dessert is yours."

"Did what just right?" I asked, forgetting in the distraction of my thoughts that I wasn't talking to him. "I didn't say or do a thing."

"Exactly," he came back. "You obviously remembered that the option of approval or disapproval is mine, and left the situation to me to handle. I hope the next one uses more imagination in his approach, but at that he's lucky he didn't try going around me directly to you. I wouldn't have been as pleasant as I was."

"Pleasant," I echoed, amused myself, finally understanding what he was talking about. "You thought he came prowling by because he was on the make for *me*? I'm sure he noticed everything about me, but only on a professional level. John Little's tastes don't run to my type; if it was a personal call, he was more interested in you."

Val's eyes darkened as he struggled against outrage and indignation.

"I don't understand why you're so upset," I added, watching him fight his way back to control with a minimum of outward sign of the struggle. "If you're still as desperate as you seemed to be a little while ago, it's the perfect opportunity. Don't forget, he came to you, so he isn't likely to turn you down when you make a suggestion."

"I thought you understood my own tastes run to softness," he said at last, and there was the distinct hint of a growl left in his voice. "And how the hell would you know what that man prefers? If he was wearing a sign on his chest, I must have missed it."

"It's too bad you feel that way, 'uncle' Val," I murmured, suddenly trying to control outrage of my own. "Unfortunately for your tender sensibilities, John Little isn't a subject we can ignore."

Val opened his mouth to say something, argument-wise if his expression meant anything, but the robot waiter had trundled up to our table with the food that had been ordered, cutting off all relevant conversation. We sat there in silence while the table between us was filled with dishes, but once the little robot was out of pick-up range, Val leaned an elbow on the table.

"If I hadn't been caught by surprise, I would have noticed sooner that you weren't guessing about a stranger," he said, his eyes now more intent than angry. "Who is he?"

"A friend of a friend of ours," I answered, pointedly not glancing around. "But this isn't the place to discuss it. We'll go back to our suite."

"You're forgetting something," Val said, interrupting the gathering-together-to-leave process I was starting. "We'll finish our meal, and *then* we'll go back to the suite. Little Jennifer needs her nourishment."

I looked at him sharply, my lips parting to argue, but that damned "no" was so strong in his eyes that I threw my purse back on the table without saying a word. He was determined to make me listen to him, and to say I was furious would just be indicating the inadequacy of spoken language to communicate with accuracy.

Despite an excellent kitchen, that had to be one of the worst meals I'd ever had. The leather armchair I sat in grew more uncomfortable every time something else was added to my plate, and at least one sample of everything that had been put down ended up there. I didn't want any of it no matter how long it had been since I'd last eaten, but Val couldn't have cared less. He callously served me everything, then kept those eyes on me while I tried picking at it—which he refused to allow. I ended up swallowing most of it down in tasteless lumps, so upset that nothing of this universe would have appealed to me. I hated being under seventeen and having to listen to Val, and I was even beginning to hate him.

When torture time was finally over, I was nearly sick to my stomach. I was glad to hear there would be no dessert—until I was told it was being withheld because I'd been a bad girl by teasing my uncle Val. At that point I was tempted to throw up everything he'd forced on me, right there in the middle of the dining room, and I would have if I hadn't been so anxious to get the hell out of there. I knew it was absurd, but it felt as though everyone in the room could tell how humiliated I felt, and was laughing over it and at me. Look at the little girl all dressed up and pretending to be a woman, their amusement seemed to say, the amusement I could feel even though I looked only straight ahead as Val guided me out of the place. I wasn't pretending to do everything he told me to, I was being forced into really doing it, and the difference between the two states was so vast it was well-nigh indefinable.

"Is something wrong?" I heard Val's voice say, and looked up to see that he wasn't talking to me. The five security men moving around near the elevator bank were the targets of his curiosity, and the captain who turned to him gave no indication that he knew the curiosity was as phony as my supposed biological age.

"There was a report that some children were using these elevators as a playground, sir," the captain lied smoothly, looking Val right in the eye. "A few of our guests were disturbed, so we've been sent to see if we can find out who they were. We'd like to ask their parents to watch them a little more closely."

Val nodded as though everything had been made perfectly clear and his curiosity had now been satisfied, but his play-acting annoyed me. He didn't really know what he was doing, and I suddenly had the urge to prove it to him.

"They assigned a captain of security to look for a bunch of kids?" I asked before the captain could turn away or Val could hustle me into the waiting elevator car. "What did they do, play the game of execution for real?"

I was also tempted to mention the constant computer surveillance—which would have made guesswork about anybody messing with the elevators unnecessary—but the general public didn't know how tight surveillance was on orbital stations, and I was just annoyed, not looking to get myself noticed. For the last, though, I'd forgotten again what I was wearing. The security captain, a broad, attractive man, noticed me anyway, and a faint grin lit his features.

"Nothing but the best of service for guests on Xanadu Station, Miss," he drawled, letting his eyes move over me slowly. "Children who presume are asking to be punished, and I may have to question you later to see if you know anything about the problem. I'm sure I can count on your cooperation."

"Of course you can, Captain," I purred, smiling slowly to let him know he'd have all the cooperation he wanted. He really was a very attractive man, but I'd forgotten there was a fly in the ointment I'd planned on using to grease the new friendship.

"We'll both be glad to cooperate, Captain," Val put in so smoothly he sounded more amused than annoyed. "If you happen to call after my niece's bedtime, I'll be glad to answer any questions you might have alone. We've only been on the Station a matter of hours, and girls my niece's age need their rest."

"Girls your niece's age?" the captain asked Val blankly, his grin gone completely. "What age is she?"

"Not yet seventeen," Val answered, ignoring the furious look I turned on him. "I know she seems older, especially in that outfit, but her age was confirmed at the time we registered."

"You shouldn't let her wear clothes like that," the security man growled, looking me over again in an entirely different way. "If she smiles like that at the wrong man at the wrong time, you could find yourself filing rape charges on her behalf. If I were you, I'd do something to make sure that doesn't happen."

"You're absolutely right, Captain," Val said hastily, deliberately interrupting the way I began to assure that jerk of a security man that I could damn well take care of myself no matter what I was wearing or who I smiled at. "I'll see to it first thing in the morning. Good night."

With his hand wrapped tight around my arm I was forced into the elevator car, and a few minutes later we were walking into our suite. As soon as Val closed the door behind us, I rounded on him in a fury.

"That was a hell of a lousy thing to do to me, and I won't forget it!" I snapped, throwing my purse away from me hard enough to break something if it hit the wrong way. "You just wait until *you* find something you'd like to take to bed! She'll be gone so fast it'll make your eyes water! In this business there's supposed to be courtesy between partners, partner, and courtesy means not cramping your partner's style even if you think you have something to get even for! You don't screw somebody out of a good time when that could be the last good time they'll ever have! In case it's slipped your mind, we're not here partnering for laughs!''

I turned away from the sober, quiet way he was looking at me, more raw over the stupid stunt he had pulled than I'd been when he'd only threatened it, and his next words didn't help much.

"You said we'd talk about Little when we got back to the suite,'' he reminded me in calmer tones than I'd been using. "What does Little have to do with Radman?''

"Is that all you've got to say?'' I demanded, whirling back to face him, outraged. "Back to business, and to hell with everything else that's happened? Well, why not? You're not one of us, and you never will be. Little works for Radman in the capacity of flesh expert, someone who knows immediately and almost instinctively which bodies will and won't sell. The decision isn't as easy as most people think it is, so he collects a nice piece of change for his efforts. I don't know why Radman didn't take him down to Xanadu or leave him behind altogether at their headquarters; Little sure as hell can't ply his trade in this Station.''

"Why not?'' Val asked, opening his jacket before sitting. "For the same reason that you can't operate here?''

"In his case, computer surveillance doesn't mean a thing,'' I denied with a head shake. "The only thing a computer scan would show him doing is looking, a pastime 98 percent of the people in this Station indulge in. When it comes time to go for the target, it's handled by professionals in *that* field, ones who know when and where to hit. No, Little can't operate here because the Management on Xanadu doesn't want anything like that going on in this Station. Rich people avoid places that aren't safe, and the Management doesn't want Xanadu and its Station avoided. That's why their security is so tight: to protect their clientele. Radman has no choice but to go along with it; Xanadu's one of his biggest customers.''

"Then why did Little come over to us?" Val asked, frowning at the same puzzle that had been bothering me. "If they can't do any kidnapping in this Station, why did he try to get to know us?"

"They may be thinking of sending a team to follow us after we leave here." I shrugged, starting to pace around. I wasn't in the mood to sit down, not with everything I had on my mind. "What happens to people after they leave is not the Management's concern, and Xanadu isn't the only market Radman has. He doesn't have to worry about being embarrassed by selling the Management slaves who used to be clients. I'd just like to know if he has anything else on mind—or if he has any intentions of joining Radman on Xanadu. Following Little would be a hell of a lot easier than sniffing along a cold and probably guarded trail."

"You sound like you have something in mind," Val observed, watching me where my pacing had taken me, about two feet from where he sat. "Something to make him take off so that we can follow?"

"Not exactly," I said, partially distracted by consideration of all the possibilities my mind was developing. "If we make him take off, there's no guarantee he'll take off in Radman's direction. If we let him join the party, though, he'll very likely use the opportunity to let the boss confirm the wisdom of his choice."

"What do you mean, let him join the party?" Val asked, suspicion suddenly lighting in his eyes. "You intend asking him to come along with us?"

"No, you're the one who'll do the asking," I came back, staring down at the agitation he was trying to keep under control. "It would be out of character and probably a waste of time if I tried it, even if he swung that way. You're supposed to be the head of this expedition, so the invitation has to come from you. What's the matter, partner? You afraid he'll catch you in a weak moment and rape you?"

The idea of Little, half Val's size, forcing Val to do anything at all was ludicrous, just as ridiculous as the trapped expression on Val's face. The need to have Little join us came strictly from the situation as it stood, but it suddenly struck me how funny it was. Val didn't want to have anything to do with Little any more than I wanted to be a minor, but neither of us could do a thing to change the situation.

"Come to think of it, you might have a problem at that," I drawled, folding my arms as I looked down at him. "You're the one who'll be making the opening move, and you can't get huffy and walk away no matter what suggestions he makes to you. In fact, you might even have to go along with some of them. But at least that will solve your other desperation problem."

I made no attempt to hide my amusement, just as he had made no attempt on his own part earlier, but equal opportunity wasn't Val's style. Without any warning he moved as fast as he had on Tildor, coming up out of that chair and grabbing my arms with such speed that he caught me asleep at the switch. Once he had pulled me to him he let himself fall back into the chair which, of course, ended me up in his lap. No more than seconds passed before I started to struggle, but then those hands closed on me.

Much as I would have enjoyed it after being pulled into his lap like that, killing him had to be out. There was no arguing against the fact that I needed him to get the assignment done, not to mention how upset the Council would be if they found out I'd permanently punched the ticket of the authorized representative of another star-faring humanoid race. But just

because I couldn't do it the right way doesn't mean I simply
gave up without a struggle. I'm not built to give up without a
struggle, and being grabbed like that triggered my urge toward
self-protection. I managed to get an elbow into him as
we landed back in the chair, hoping to loosen his grip enough
to let me pull free again, but no such luck. He ignored the
force of the blow, and then his arms were around me with his
hands clamped to my wrists.

"Of all the desperate problems I have, you're the biggest," he grunted, forcing my left shoulder up against his
chest as he tightened his right arm around me, trying to get
me to stop pulling against his hands and kicking. "You don't
seem to believe me when I promise you something, and that's
not the way to make this partnership work. In order to rely on
what I say, you have to know my word is good. I told you
what would happen if you teased me about Little again."

"Val, stop it!" I yelled, starting to get desperate. I couldn't
pull my wrists free, he had hooked one leg over both of mine
to keep me from kicking out, and he had already done the
same thing to me once before—or twice before, if you counted
that brief episode at the beginning of our trip together. I
couldn't believe he would do something that mindless—and
knew without the shadow of a doubt that that was exactly
what he intended.

"You could have stopped it yourself simply by making an
effort to behave," he said, sounding so damned calm that I
really began to worry. "If I tell you I don't care for something, the information's supposed to tell you to let it alone,
not that it's perfectly all right to continue to ride me."

"But it's just fine if *you* ride *me*!" I came back, a little
mad moving in with the worry. "You were fast enough
taking advantage of *me* because of this assignment, but now
that something's come up that makes *you* uncomfortable, it's a
case of hands-off, don't touch. You can but I can't."

"Damned right you can't," he agreed, but much too dryly. "No other woman alive would have the incredibly bad judgment to do to me what you've done—and then expect to get away with it. There's not one of them who wouldn't know better— and be sure she watched her step. Well? Which way are we going to do it?"

I'd been getting a good view of the gold carpeting from the position he was holding me in despite the way my hair was hanging down, but staring at it wasn't bringing me any ideas on how to get out of that mess. I didn't particularly like what he was asking me to do, but that part of it made no difference; I still would have had a problem even if I'd really wanted to do things his way.

"Looks like you've given me another choice that's no choice at all," I said at last, very aware of his hand on my backside, but still helpless to change the answer. "I've made it a practice never to give into blackmail, Val, not unless something really important is at stake. The assignment may be that important, but my delicate sensibilities aren't. If you feel the need to beat me you go right ahead, but no one forces me to give my word on anything, and that's the way it has to be."

I said my piece and shut up, and then it was Val's turn to consider in silence. His grip on my wrists hadn't loosened, he hadn't moved his leg, and his hand hadn't left my prettily covered behind, but I suddenly had very high hopes. I hadn't told him anything but the strictest truth, but my subconscious had obviously been working overtime to set up a con. Val might be feeling self-righteous and justified, but he clearly considered himself a man of honor. Would a man of honor punish a woman for standing by her convictions? Could he? My subconscious was betting he couldn't, which was why it had made me phrase my refusal the way it had. I hoped to hell it was right.

After a minute or two the thigh under my stomach shifted, and I thought I heard a sigh.

"I see you really do think more about the assignment than you do about yourself," Val commented, his tone blessedly neutral. "And you have principles, too. Are you sure there's nothing I can say that will make you change your mind?"

"Nothing," I confirmed, trying to sound both unwavering and martyr-like at the same time.

"I'm glad to see there's hope for you after all," he said, his tone noticeably warmer. "You can't be taught to be principled, that's something you are or you aren't, but you *can* be taught proper values. Treating people the right way is a value, and one you'll be much better off for learning. Then you can apply your principles to the right thing."

"Val," I began slowly and unbelievingly, "You don't mean you're still going to—Ow! Stop it! You can't do this to me!"

"Sure I can," he answered, giving my seat another hard whack. "I can't force you to make a promise that goes against your principles, but that doesn't mean I have to let you do whatever you please to me. You were right when you said I wasn't one of your group, Diana, and you may have been right when you said I never would be. First I'm going to have to see something to make me want to be, and so far I haven't."

That big hand came down hard on my seat again and then again, giving me the best motivation there is for breaking free, but motivation is useless when that's all you have. I pulled again at his hand around my wrist, found I still couldn't get loose, then fought hard against the wave of intimidation that rolled over me. It didn't matter how he could do it, he *was* doing it, punishing me just the way he'd said he would. No one had *ever* done that to me before, and I knew without doubt that it wasn't my role character he was reacting to, it was *me*. I swallowed down a yelp as he really began reaching me, and then there was only one question left: how long would he keep it up?

My question was answered when my wrists and legs were freed, and the answer turned out to be both not too long and much, much, too long. I don't think he spanked me as long as he had on Tildor, but it had been long enough and hard enough to bring an ache to my bottom and tears to my eyes. I ignored the tears as I pushed myself to my feet, damned if I would cry in front of him no matter what he did to me, and made sure not to look at him even when he immediately followed me erect—until he took my hand.

"What are you doing?" I tried to demand when he began leading me through the sitting room, but there wasn't enough snap in the question to offend an ant. No matter how hard I had tried to fight against it he had managed to intimidate me, and even though I hated the feeling there was nothing I could do about it. I wasn't up to fighting him or even challenging him on a non-physical level, and the worst part about it was that I was sure he knew it.

"I'm putting you to bed," he answered, not even glancing back at me. "You had a hard day today, and we have things to do tomorrow."

"But, Val, that's *your* room," I protested as I was led across the threshold into a melon and silver copy of the other bedroom and the door was closed behind me. "You said you wouldn't . . ."

"I should never have said anything like that," he interrupted, dropping my hand as soon as I stood next to the big bed and immediately started getting out of his suit and ruffles. "You were right about my not understanding the position we were in, about how unfair it is to keep someone from a good time when that might be the last good time they'll

ever have. I don't want to be done out of my last good time,
and I don't think you should be either. Get out of your
clothes, Diana.''

"I don't want to get out of my clothes," I mumbled,
unable to take my eyes off him. He wasn't wearing anything
under the suit and shirt, and my breath caught. "If you force
me into that bed it'll be nothing but rape, and I won't sit still
for rape."

"I hope you won't *lie* still for it either," he said with
something of a grin, leaving his clothes where he dropped
them to come and stand in front of me, looking down into my
eyes. "If you didn't want to be raped you shouldn't have
worn an outfit like that, a glittering, irresistible second skin.
I'm not made out of lifeless metal, Diana, and you should
know that by now. If you won't come to my bed voluntarily
I'll carry you there and toss you in, but this is one night I
won't take no for an answer."

"But you can't!" I all but begged, silently cursing the way
he was making me feel. "Not after what you just did to me.
It isn't fair!"

"I know I have you at an unfair advantage right now," he
said very softly with a gentle smile, reaching out an equally
gentle hand to smooth my hair before putting the arm around
me. "If it had been any other night I would have put you to
bed in your own room, but tonight I can't do it. I'd intended
honoring your choice and finding someone else to sleep with,
but you made that impossible. You're responsible for the way
I feel, so you're the one who has to do something about it.
Take your shoes off."

He had changed his order from clothes to shoes because he
was already seeing to my body suit, both hands working
carefully but quickly as he slid it down off my shoulders and
arms to my waist. I closed my eyes with a shudder as he

chuckled, knowing he was chuckling at the sight of my hardened nipples. I couldn't ever remember being as aroused as I was then, or as confused. I wanted to turn and walk away from him, slamming the door as I left, but I couldn't move. It was as though I'd been fed a zombie drug, and couldn't refuse him no matter what he ordered me to do. I didn't want him to take me to bed, not the way I was still aching, but I wasn't being given any say in the matter. He pushed the suit down over my hips to my ankles, crouched to slip off the silver sandals while I held onto his shoulder, and then the suit was gone and thrown away.

"Val, don't, *please*," I whispered as he picked me up and began putting us both into the bed, my hands involuntarily going to his impossibly broad shoulders. "You don't know what you're doing to me. You *can't* know."

"Tell me what I'm doing to you, Diana," he murmured, settling me down beside him with his arms around me. "Is it anything like what you do to me when I touch the softness of your skin?"

"No, don't, don't," I begged as he raised himself above me, separating my legs with his knees, still holding me in his arms. He'd been ready even before he'd taken his clothes off, and I couldn't stop the tears that were running down my cheeks.

"You know I won't hurt you, Diana," he said softly as he kissed my face, the words nearly a soothing chant, his desire finding and entering me even as he spoke. I cried out almost with fear as he took complete possession of me, his hand stroking my hair, his lips touching my throat. "You also know you want me as much as I want you, only you're too stubborn to admit it."

His own words ended then as his lips took mine, but that was all that ended or stopped. His body kept thrusting into mine, demanding a response that I couldn't refuse, over-whelming me so completely that I thought I might faint. He had made me horribly vulnerable and then had taken me to his bed, and I knew the tears of fear continued even after coherent thought abandoned me completely.

CHAPTER 7

"It's all right. Diana, wake up. It's all right."

I heard the words for some time before they got through to me. The first thing I became aware of was Val's arms around me, the second that I was shivering violently. The dream was still enough with me so that I knew why I was shivering like that, but I wasn't up to stopping it yet.

"Diana, can you hear me?" Val persisted, his voice disturbed as he held me tight to his chest. "Try to wake up."

"Am . . . up," I managed through clenched teeth, burying my face in his chest and starting to try for control. "Give me . . . a minute."

He made a sound of agreement and began stroking my hair, trying to calm something he didn't understand. Val and I were still in his bed with the cover over us instead of beneath us, and I should have felt cozy and comfortable with his arms around me. That was a hell of a time for the shakes to get me so badly, but it wasn't hard to understand why it had happened.

"You seem to be coming out of it now," Val said after considerably more than the minute I'd asked for. I was still holding tight to him and breathing as though I'd been going uphill for hours, but I was finally making some headway in pulling myself back. "That must have been some bad dream."

I shuddered at the memory of it and put my face into his chest again, but I didn't lose the control I'd gained back. It wasn't the first time I'd had that dream and I should have been used to it after so many repetitions, but even pretending to be blasé didn't dull the edge of the memory. It had to have been my mindless thoughts of the night before, that had triggered it, dragging me back to that time on Circlonet. I'd infiltrated a secret, fanatical terrorist organization that was headquartered on that backwater world and was doing fine discovering the leaders of the group—until word came through to those leaders that there was a fly in the soup. They separated out the last dozen people to join the organization— which included me—and took us one by one to be questioned. Truth drugs are notoriously unreliable against those people you most want to make talk, so they fell back on a very old method of questioning which consisted of stringing us up by the wrists and letting a heavy whip do the asking for them. I was the third newest and therefore the third to be questioned, and I hate to admit how close I came to telling them everything they wanted to hear. The pain in my arms and wrists from supporting my weight, the trembling fear I was showing that wasn't entirely acting—and then the agony of my back being torn open, the blood flowing, the flesh parting, the unbelieving shock even as I screamed and screamed and screamed. —The fourth victim turned out to be a snoopsheet newsie who had wormed his way into the organization for an exclusive story, and he broke almost as soon as they first began stroking him. He thought admitting the truth would make them stop hurting him even though it would also get him thrown out before he had the rest of his story, but he was wrong on both counts. They did stop whipping him, but only until they had brought the first three of us back in. We three had been badly and unnecessarily hurt because of him, and it was only just if we were allowed to watch him being whipped to death. The newsie had forgotten it was fanatics he was dealing with, and that was the last mistake he ever made. Toward the end, watching him had almost been worse than getting it myself. . . .

"That's much better," Val said, raising my face in the dimness to look down at me. "The trembling is gone, and your muscles have finally relaxed. Want to tell me about it now?"

"There's nothing to tell," I said with a shrug, noticing how gentle his touch was. "Dreams like that are an occupational hazard, something that goes along with the territory. What time is it?"

"Not too early to get up, but I don't want you doing that yet," he answered, tightening his arm around me to keep me from sitting up. "After something like that, you need a few minutes to pull yourself together—not to mention the ordeal you went through last night."

"You're as funny as a terminal illness," I told his idiotic grin, then pushed his hand away from my face. "If you ever again try telling me you don't believe in rape, I'll call you a liar to your face."

"Rape means forcing yourself on someone who is unwilling," he countered, the shadowy grin still there.

"Oh, you were looking for *unwillingness*," I said in tones of great revelation, ignoring the rest of his nonsense.

"My definition of unwilling includes bodily reactions," he said, then bent his head to quickly kiss my breast. "Right now I'd classify you as unwilling, and your body supports the contention; last night was another story. You seemed to be afraid of something at the same time, but that something wasn't me. What were you afraid of, Diana?"

"I was afraid that something unacceptable would happen because of the disadvantage you had me at," I answered without taking my eyes from the dark gaze looking down at me. "Happily, nothing of the sort happened, and now I'd like to get up."

"If nothing happened, why are you in such a hurry?" he asked in a murmur, lowering his head to my breast again. "Say, look at this! I think your unwillingness is changing its mind."

He was lying to my right with his left arm around me, me on my back, him on his side, that stupid grin above me and widened now. When his right leg moved over both of mine, I didn't need a formal posting of his intentions to know what he was up to; I just knew I couldn't let him do it. Val was starting to get the wrong ideas about me, and that was something that had to be stopped fast. As his head bent down toward me a third time, what I could see of his eyes in the dimness filled with confidence, I quickly snapped the back of my right hand against his nose, catching him sharply and just in the right way. He yelped and pulled back fast, both of his hands going to his face, and I was able to roll out of the bed and to my feet.

"If you'll notice, that time I used words first," I said to the anger looking at me over cupped hands, tears of pain filming the eyes. "If you're starting to feel put-upon, consider that my thank-you for last night. I know you earned a lot more, but all I can manage right now is a down-payment. Expect the balance later."

I turned my back on him and strolled out of his room, crossed the sitting room, and made it back to my own bedroom before I began cursing under my breath. We had a job to do and he was nothing but my partner, and it didn't matter how good he was in bed! It also didn't matter what *he* thought, *I* was the one running the assignment! No softheadedness over him, and no softheadedness *from* him! The assignment was what counted, and I'd see that it got done! I stopped my furious pacing in mid-stride, tried to get back control over myself, then said to hell with it and went to take a shower.

Showers don't always do the trick, but by the time that one was over I'd spent a considerable amount of time thinking, and was more than ready to get on with that assignment. My most important decision was to stay away from Val, and also make sure he stayed away from me. If he was starting to come down with infatuation, it was my job to cure him, not catch the same symptoms. The Special Agent who got involved was a damned fool, and if I hadn't learned that over the years I deserved whatever I got. I took one last look at myself in the mirror to check the jumpsuit and deck shoes I wore, then went out into the sitting room.

"Good timing," Val said when he saw me, looking up from the couch he was sitting on. "I only just got out here myself."

"I hope it's a preview of future timing," I said with a nod, ignoring what had happened earlier just the way he was doing. "We've got a lot on the schedule today and you'll be doing most of it, so we'd better get with it. The first order of business will be that reservation on the Xanadu shuttle."

"And the second?" he asked, watching me sit on the couch not far from him. He looked more resigned than rebellious, but there was a faint glint of hope in with the resignation.

"The second has to be Little," I said, heartlessly crushing the spark of hope. "Pick him up, get buddy-buddy, then let him know we're going down to Xanadu. Pay close attention to what his reaction to that is; if he jumps for joy, we'll have to watch our step."

"If he jumps for joy, he better not do it in my direction," my partner grumbled, running one hand through his hair. "If it was you and a female Little, you'd probably think of a way around the need.''

"Why would I waste the time?'' I asked, getting up again for a cup of coffee from the wall server. "If Little was female and gave me the come-hither sign, I'd smile and go thither. It would hardly be the first time, and if that was the worst my job ever called for, I'd go through life with a big grin on my face. That sort of loving has a lot going for it.''

"Like what?'' Val demanded, his eyes on me as I came back with the cup, his outrage stronger than the day before, then he waved a hand in dismissal. "Never mind, I don't want to know. You're probably just stringing me anyway, to sell me on what you think has to be done, but you're wasting your breath. Buddy-buddy is as far as I'm willing to go with Little, and nothing you can say will make me change my mind.''

"There's something you'll have to go into a little more intimately than that,'' I said, paying a lot of attention to the coffee I was sipping. "When the time seems just right, you'll have to let him know I'm for sale.''

"You're—what?'' Val said, freezing in the middle of brushing at the dark green slacks beneath his yellow shirt, his eyes coming up to stare at me. "Are you out of your mind?''

"No, I'm just covering all the bases,'' I explained, using the coffee to keep myself from smiling at his new outrage. "You'll make it clear that I'm *not* for sale to the Pleasure Sphere, only to private customers, and that should guarantee a meet with Radman. If he wants to know why you won't sell to the Pleasure Sphere, tell him you know you can get a better price in a private sale, and don't let him talk you out of it. When I get down there, I don't want to find myself belonging to them.''

"You'd rather be a one-man slave,'' he said with a nod,

then snorted with ridicule. "I think that whacking you got last night rattled your brains."

"And just in case, don't let Little pay for anything that involves us on Xanadu," I went on, ignoring what he'd said. "If we go down as his guests and he suddenly yanks his backing, they won't give us the time to establish a line of credit of our own. Looking the way we do, we'll be arrested for vagrancy so fast you'll get a chill in the wind generated, and then we'll be on our way to the Pleasure Sphere to work out our sentences. Maybe *you'd* enjoy serving their women patrons, but I'm hardly likely to be as crazy about the men."

"They'd never try making *me* a slave," he said with another snort, then grinned at the idea. "I'm not built the way you are, and I'm not soft and cuddly and easy to make squirm. It's the little girls they want, not someone like me."

"Guess again, pal," I said with an evil leer, not about to let him get away with garbage like that. "Most women don't want something soft, they want something big and hard as a rock. They'd drug you if they had to, and after that you'd use a knothole in a fence if nothing better was available. Would you like an estimate of how much they'd charge just to let some fat, slobbering matron run her hands over your chest and shoulders? To go down below belly level they'd charge even more, and by then you'd be begging her to drop her girdle and bend over. If you want to bet on it, we can put the stakes to one side until you get a chance to see how it works with your own two eyes. I wouldn't want you to think I was stringing you."

"If you ever gave up stringing me, you'd have trouble holding up your end of a conversation between us," he growled, nothing left of his recent amusement. "And no matter how you try to distract me from the point, I still don't like your idea. What if someone offers me an amount I can't refuse? Do I just take it with a polite thank-you?"

"Certainly," I agreed with a grin. "You accept the highest bid, then arrange to turn me over to my new owner as soon as we get back to the Station. They'll know how unwise it is to get the Mangement involved, so they'll be glad to wait. Once we're back here the assignment will be over, so I'll be able to take care of the problem myself."

"Like hell you will," he said in a flat, no-arguments tone, those eyes cold as dark seas in winter. "If I have to make the deal, I also get to break it. And I still can't see any real reason why it has to be made in the first place. Why can't we simply be two of the people going down to the Pleasure Sphere?"

"Val, you don't really know what goes on in the Pleasure Sphere, and I'm supposed to be less than seventeen years old," I said with a sigh of exasperation. "Use your imagination to fill in some of the gaps, and then tell me how many of the people down there will be bringing along teenagers to indulge in it. Do you expect me to find Radman in the middle of their kiddy park? Don't you think your potential customers will know how well-primed I'll be after going through some of the Sphere's specials? That'll be your reason for taking me along, so that I'll have some idea what to do when I find myself in my new circumstances. The Sphere gives almost the best preparatory training there is."

"Almost the best, huh?" he said with no change of expression. "Who gives the best?"

"The Adepts of Saccarion," I answered without hesitation. "But they'll only train you if you convince them that you're joining them permanently, and they're not interested in words of sincerity. Or you can find yourself a renegade Adept, the way I did."

"Well, there you are," he said, gesturing with one hand as he moved to get more comfortable on the couch. "You don't need any more preparation. You happened to meet a renegade Adept, and she taught you all you need to know.''

"He," I corrected with so much satisfaction that those eyes came back to me. "The Adept was male, and you don't just 'happen' to run into one. And you also don't get trained overnight. You mention anything like that, and you'll blow this whole deal. If I were Adept-trained, I'd be worth more as permanent rent-out than you could possibly get in a single sale, and they'll all know it. If you're that determined to screw this up, Val, let me know and I'll take it from here alone."

"You can't do it alone," he came back, those eyes still mightily displeased. "If I don't get you down to Xanadu, you have no way of getting there."

"Legally," I qualified. "You'd be surprised how many illegal options I have, but the risks involved are too high to consider if there's any choice in the matter. If I have no choice, though, it becomes the only game in town."

"And you'll play the game no matter what you have to go through to do it," he summed up, definitely unhappy with me. "It looks like I'm the one with no choice this time, and I don't like it any more than you did. This clever idea of yours is going to cause trouble."

I watched him grow vexed, knowing the idea had already caused trouble.

"All right," I compromised, taking another taste of my coffee. "Suppose we change the clever idea just a little, to make it easier for you to live with. Don't come right out and say I'm for sale, just hint at it when the need arises. If it'll make you feel better to hesitate dramatically over such immoral behavior, go ahead and do it. You don't know what Xanadu's regulars are like, and we don't need more trouble than we already have."

"You can say that again," he agreed with a snort, looking

considerably happier. "If I'm wishy-washy enough about committing to it all the way, I might not even have a deal to break when we get back. What's *your* attitude supposed to be about this whole thing?"

"I haven't completely decided yet," I answered, getting up a second. I wasn't crazy about the sort of agreement I'd gotten out of him, but it would have to do. "I won't know anything about your horrible plans, of course, but I can't decide just how innocent I ought to be. Pretending you don't know things when you do is dangerous, especially when a slip is so easy to see. You just make sure to be interested in everything female coming past you *but* me."

"Am I supposed to be blind?" he asked, watching me sit back down. "If I'm—excuse the expression—into females, why would I miss going after one like you?"

"Don't you have *any* imagination?" I complained with a sigh. "If you have your eye on me along with everyone else, why would you be thinking of selling me? And if you're not thinking of selling me, Little might decide to stay with the kidnap squad, instead of taking you to Radman for an offer to be made. If Radman's offer hits you the wrong way, you're big enough to do the same to Radman, which would abruptly shorten Little's life span. It's simple logic, Val, so it shouldn't be beyond you. If anyone asks, tell them little girls, no matter how pretty, turn you off. Lots of men feel like that, at least the normal ones, so lie a little and pretend that you do, too."

"Why do I have the feeling I've just been insulted?" he asked the empty air, then brought his eyes back to me. "Am I mistaken, or did you just call me something other than normal?"

"I called an interest in a very young girl something other than normal," I said very sweetly to the look in his eyes. "If you don't fall into that category, it can't have been an insult toward you."

"That's true," he said with a judicious nod. "In point of fact, little girls *don't* turn me on, not the way big girls do, especially certain big girls. When I don't have to fight to stay undamaged, that is."

"Yes, that kind of fight would certainly be a turn-off," I agreed. "I guess it's a good thing uncle Val has no real interest in little Jennifer."

"Okay, okay, I got the point," he grumbled with one hand up. "Little Jennifer could dance naked in front of uncle Val, and all he'd do is yawn. Is there anything else I have to know?"

"One of the most important things has to be that if you run into trouble and I'm not around to help, call the Management," I answered with a frown. "Clients are protected on that world, so that's your best and only out. There must be more, but my mind is too eager to get started; it's not letting me think about what everyone knows except you. I'll try to think about it while you're making the reservations, but we'll have to come up with an emergency code for talking about things like that when we're where we might be overheard."

"We already have a code that no one will be able to break," he came back with sudden inspiration, pointing a finger at me. "The trade language Dameron gave you. Can we get away with calling it a private family language?"

"I don't see why not," I said slowly, liking the idea as soon as I heard it. "If anyone says anything about never having heard of such a thing, we turn very surprised over their lack of knowledge. Almost everyone *we* know has a family language, handed down through the generations to all branches of the family. We just won't give them any translations of any part of it, to make sure no one feeds it into a language computer. That was really good thinking, Val."

"Thanks," he said with a grin for the pat on the back I'd

given him, standing up as I got to my feet. "Are we ready to go now?"

"I don't know how ready we are, but that's what we're doing," I agreed with a nod, walking over to return my coffee cup to the recess I'd gotten it from. "We still have some time for me to remember whatever it is I'm missing, but I wish . . ."

I let it trail off because we did have the time, but I still felt vaguely annoyed. The term, "properly thorough briefing" had taken on new meaning with Val around, but I couldn't let that distract me from everything else that had to be considered. My partner and I moved together toward the door, then left the suite.

We stopped for a quick breakfast, and that was when Val "just happened" to bring up the subject of my wardrobe; since the same thought had already occurred to me, I hadn't been able to argue very convincingly. As that security man had pointed out the night before, my clothes were geared to a full-grown woman, not to a young girl, and something had to be done about them. It would be stupid to give anyone on Xanadu food for thought which just might be digested after I had taken care of Radman; it was an unnecessary risk which could result in my having to produce the death warrant, and there was no telling how Xanadu's Management would react to it. Oh, they were legally bound to honor the Council's instrument just the way any other Federation planet was, but that didn't mean they couldn't give me one hell of a rough time before they did. No, the wardrobe problem had to be taken care of; I just didn't like the way Val intended doing it.

We went to the shuttle reservations desk first, waited for the couple in front of us to finish their business, then found out that the earliest reservation we could get was for late that afternoon. Val was pleasant about it and accepted the added delay without strain, but I had to pretend to total indifference to keep from snarling and kicking that thirty-foot, low-chaired counter into its constituent plastic parts. All of the delays and stupid little problems were starting to give me bad vibes about that assignment, and I had to firmly remind myself that imagination didn't usually affect an assignment one way or the other. If it was handled right it came out right, and vibes had nothing to do with it.

After the reservations desk, Val took me shopping. As soon as I saw the shop-front I knew he'd been checking Station listings again, and any hopes I'd had about the experience turning out bearable went right down the tubes. The place was called "Pretty Little Miss," and I immediately regretted all the breakfast I'd eaten; nausea does not sit well on top of a full stomach.

"If you keep hanging back, people will start to notice," Val muttered at me in the trade language that was our secret code, glancing at the passersby who were passing us where we stood in the corridor, just outside the shop. "Get inside, and right now."

I glanced up to see that no-arguments look in his eyes, sighed in defeat, then went ahead and pushed through the door into the shop, he coming along right behind me. I heard nothing in the way of a gasp out of him once we had crossed the threshold, but that was likely due to the way he was consciously refraining from reacting to things that were new to him but usual to everyone else. The shop's decor was one, huge vu-cast window, wrap-around without sharp corners, the door we had entered by the only break in an otherwise perfect little glade. The sun shone down through the overhead leaves, nicely bright but not glaring, the "fresh" canned air was full of woodsy perfume, and the carpeting under our feet was make-believe grass. Once the door had closed behind us we could hear faint but cheerful birdsong, faint stirrings of the "foliage" around us working hard to add to the overall attempt at true outdoors. It was impossible to tell what planet the scene had been recorded on despite the vaguely green sky, but one thing was as clear as the gently flowered projection around us: if we bought anything in that place, we'd pay through the nose.

"Good morning, and may I help you?" came a pleasant, throaty female voice, causing us to turn toward one of the larger "trees" in our vicinity. There was a barely noticeable hesitation where that tree fit in with the rest of the scenery, and that had to be where the woman had come from. In her late twenties or early thirties, she stood in front of the tree with her hands clasped in front of her, the half-skirt, half-pants outfit she wore showing her excellent taste, her really beautiful face smiling in sincere greeting. My partner—who was having such trouble getting interested in other women—stirred in interest as soon as those black eyes touched her, and I had to swallow down a laugh of true amusement.

"I'd like to see some appropriate outfits for my niece," Val answered easily with a smile of his own for the woman, an action which caused her to shift her stance immediately from neutral yet friendly to posing and interested, with the woman most likely unaware that she'd done it.

"May I ask what you mean by appropriate, sir?" she said, coming forward to stand closer to us. "Do you have a specific occasion in mind?"

"I have all occasions in mind," Val said, gesturing slightly in my direction. "My sister let her do her own clothes shopping, and everything she has is years too old for her. I'm more than tired of having to tell every other man who looks at her how old she really is, so I'm here to see if I can get some clothing to do the telling for me. Do you think you can help me?"

"I'm sure of it, sir," she said, then gave me a professionally estimating up-and-down.

"If that jumpsuit is indicative of the rest of her wardrobe, I'm afraid you're right," she told Val without looking at him, a very attractive frown making up her stare at me. "It's of excellent quality and shows very good taste, but despite the way it fits it's obviously too old for her. How old is she?"

"Not yet seventeen," Val answered, making sure not even to glance in my direction.

"My goodness," the woman said with a startled blink, looking at me considerably more closely. "Her height and degree of development are really misleading, aren't they? Not to mention that long red hair. Well, I'm sure we can achieve the effect you're looking for, sir. Do you have any style preferences in mind, dear?"

"Sure I do," I answered, both awed and stunned that I'd finally been addressed. "My preferences run to what I already have. As far as I'm concerned, this is a complete waste of time."

"Just ignore her," Val advised the slightly embarrassed woman, sticking with the line we'd agreed on. I had no idea what current teen-age styles were, and wouldn't have known even if I hadn't just come back from an extended tour of the outer provinces, so to speak. That was one situation where Val could admit ignorance but I couldn't, so we'd decided to finesse the problem.

"Just ignore her," Val told the woman with another smile, one that unfortunately added to her fluster. "Since she's not prepared to cooperate in the slightest, we'll have to make the choices for her. You'll show me what you think is appropriate, and I'll tell you whether it's what I had in mind."

"But, sir," what if she won't wear what you choose for her?" the woman objected. "Once the outfits are cut to her size, the shop won't be able to take them back. I—I won't be able to give you any sort of a refund."

"Don't worry about whether or not she'll wear them," Val

said, then deliberately moved his eyes to me. "She may not want to, but she'll wear them."

I made sure to drop my eyes at the look I was getting, carrying through with the sullen-and-rebellious-but-obedient bit we were pulling, but not before I saw the expression on the woman's face. She'd actually flinched at the way Val was looking at me, and suddenly she wasn't posing for him any longer.

"I'll get seats for us, and then we can look at what's available, sir," she said, professionally. "Just a moment, please."

She turned away from us with a nod of her head, and moved toward the tree she'd appeared near; once she had disappeared behind it, I looked over at Val.

"Pretend I'm complaining and trying to whine you into changing your mind," I told him in the trade language, using the apporpriate tone for what I was supposedly saying. "While you're ignoring my protests, make a note somewhere to tone it down and keep it toned down. If that woman wasn't too cultured and svelte to have hysterics, you would have had her cringing and sobbing against the wall. Wishy-washy, weak-willed men like you aren't supposed to be able to do that to women."

"Damn it, you're right," he growled, then immediately changed his tone to what might be described as firm petulance. "While I'm telling you that you'd better obey me and cut out the nonsense, I'll also tell you that the slip is mainly your fault. You've ignored me for so long now, I've almost forgotten how other women react to me. If you don't show proper fear every now and again, how am I supposed to remember?"

"Very funny," I answered with proper sullenness instead, then stamped my foot and turned my back on him. "I'll remember to scream later. Meanwhile, get that amused look out of your eyes. You're not supposed to be having that much fun."

He grunted in a non-committal way that could have been an uncaring dismissal of whatever threat his little niece had thrown at him, and then we waited in silence until the woman came back. When she did she was followed by a brawny type swinging in two cloud chairs, and she herself carried a small, padded stool. In another minute or so we were all comfortably seated—with the woman's stool next to *my* chair—and then the fashion show began.

When it was all over and we'd left the shop, I was tempted to start feeling depressed again. The woman had advised Val and he'd made his selections, but I was ready to swear that the age they'd been trying for was more like ten or eleven than seventeen. The choices Val had made were absolutely ridiculous, and I was only waiting to get back to our suite before I told him what to do with them—which did *not* include any wearing.

"Oh, I do beg your pardon," said an abrupt, apologetic voice just as we were jostled a little from behind. "The fault is entirely mine, and I hope you'll— Well, hello there again."

After the first three or four words I hadn't needed to look around to know who it was, but I still joined Val in turning toward the one who had "accidentally" jostled us. John Little stood there with an urbane smile on his face, oozing friendliness toward Val—but with the faintest hint of wariness in his eyes. It looked like he was prepared to cut and run if Val took offense, but my partner wasn't taking anything but his medicine—like a good little scout.

"Mr.—Little, wasn't it?" Val said with a friendly smile of his own—and his own hint of wariness—as he extended his hand. "How are you this morning?"

"Just fine, Mr. Carter, just fine." Little beamed, flinching only a little over the handshake. "It's good to finally run into a friendly face on a strange Station—and please do accept my apologies for having done that in the most literal sense. Have you breakfasted yet?''

"Yes, we have," Val said, still sticking with open and friendly. "We've just finished some shopping for my niece here, and were heading back to our suite. By the way, this is my niece, Jennifer Kent. Jennifer, Mr. John Little."

"How do you do, Jennifer," Little said to me with polite, uninterested friendliness, without offering his hand. I had told Val that Radman's assistant would be more interested in him than me and although I hadn't really been lying, the whole truth was that Little swung both ways, depending on mood and circumstance. His coolness had to be calculated then, possibly to make my ''uncle'' believe that he had no designs on his pretty, young niece. That meant he would open up more completely if I were elsewhere, leaving him a clear field to get buddy-buddy with Val.

"I do great—at home," I answered with as little interest as he had shown, deliberately not looking at Val. "Why I let myself be talked into this trip, I'll never know. Uncle Val's ideas of fun are too archaic for words."

"Now, Jenny, you know I've been trying to entertain you," Val said with mild reproof in his voice, showing nothing of the look that had done such a thorough job of rattling the woman in the shop. "If nothing else, the idea of our going down to Xanadu and the Pleasure Sphere should excite you."

"Big deal," I said with no enthusiasm whatsoever, pretending not to see the brief burst of exultation in Little's eyes. "All they do in the Pleasure Sphere is have sex, every minute of the day and night. If I wanted sex I didn't have to come here for it, I have enough partners back home. And there'd also be something *interesting* to do besides that."

"My dear girl, only amateurs provide 'just' sex," Little

told me with an indulgent, superior smirk, glancing at Val to share the amusement with him. "The Management of the Pleasure Sphere is far from amateurish, which means you have a rare treat before you. The vast majority of young ladies your age are never given the opportunity to so indulge themselves. You should be grateful to your uncle for his generosity."

I glanced at Val as though I would have said something nasty to that but didn't care to go quite that far, then let my very evident skepticism say what I wasn't putting into words: the whole scene was a drag, and I had no intentions of believing what I'd been told. Uncaring boredom with the universe as a whole wasn't an untypical reaction of the age group I supposedly belonged to, and it had the benefit of being an acceptable out in case I slipped and forgot to be impressed by something I'd supposedly never seen before.

"My niece doesn't consider me generous, Mr. Little," Val put in in that same mild way, but with a hint of sternness. "My sister has indulged her shamefully, continually allowing her to do just as she pleased, and now has given her over into my care more or less permanently so that she might run off to one of these frontier planets leaving no responsibilities behind her. That I brought Jennifer along on this trip when I might just as easily have left her behind apparently means nothing, except that she now begins to understand that I refuse to be disobeyed and ignored in the way her mother allowed. You *have* learned that lesson, haven't you, Jenny?"

I sent him a look of pure hate, but felt more like grinning and congratulating him. The line he'd come up with was perfect, and also gave me the exit excuse I needed.

"I've told you before that my name is Jennifer," I hissed with the flush of embarrassment reddening my cheeks. "And if you aren't ready to go back to the suite, I am."

I turned and stalked away without paying the least attention to a chuckling Little, and let my mad carry me all the way back to our suite. Once inside I indulged the urge to grin, especially when Val didn't show up right behind me. He and Little had gone off somewhere to strengthen their new friendship, finally getting that assignment off the ground the right way.

Not knowing how long I would have to wait, I walked into the middle of the sitting room, thought about the various entertainments the suite offered, then shook my head and went into my bedroom. Now that something was actually being accomplished and it was only a matter of time before I got my own hand in the batter, the impatience I'd been feeling was back to a level I could live with easily. There was no telling what we'd get into once we hit dirt on Xanadu, so it was time I noticed that I hadn't had much sleep the last couple of days—or enough sleep free from footsie-playing and nightmares. I stretched hard when I stopped next to my bed, opened my expensive and tastefully fashioned jumpsuit after kicking off my deck shoes, then climbed happily bare between the ice-blue covers.

I came slowly awake when my appetite stirred for the third or fourth time, something it hadn't done in quite a while. I'd eaten breakfast that morning only because Val had threatened to send me to the baby-sitting service for a while if I didn't, and he'd had that look in his eyes that said he'd do it just for the hell of it if I refused. Now that there was the prospect of action ahead of me my appetite was starting to get interested again, and it felt like I'd slept through lunch. I turned my head on the pillow to peer up at the headboard, and sure enough, Station lunch time was behind me. I knew I'd have to get up soon to see about the problem, but the bed was comfortable and I was still half asleep. I snuggled down under the covers, rubbed my face against the smooth, cool pillowcase, felt my eyes closing—then sat up fast at the sound of glass shattering somewhere in the sitting room. I didn't know what the hell was going on, but I no longer felt sleepy.

I eased open my bedroom door without making noise doing it, but I needn't have bothered. The only one in the sitting room was Val, and all he was doing was what the room called for. One of the white and gold walls had a splotch of liquid streaming down it, with a small pile of broken glass lying at the base of the wall, but there was no true indication of how the splotch and broken pieces had gotten there. One of the deep, comfortable light-gold chairs was helping Val do his sitting, and when I stepped into the room he looked over at me.

"I didn't mean to wake you up," he said very quietly, more—subdued, I guess you would call it—than I'd ever thought he could be. "We still have plenty of time before we have to be at the shuttle, so if you need more sleep, go ahead and take it."

"I was just lying there and thinking about getting up anyway," I answered with a headshake, making an effort to keep a frown off my face as I took the chair opposite his. "How did it go?"

"My good pal John will be going down on the shuttle with us," he said, sounding and looking the least bit—distracted. "Since he's been to the Pleasure Sphere before and I haven't, he insists on playing guide. He now knows how unhappy I am about being saddled with a teen-aged pampered princess— how it cramps my style—but doesn't know yet what I hope to do to get rid of her. Once we get to know each other a little better I'll let him in on my plans, but not until then. We also got our sexual preferences established, and since anything is fine with me as long as it's female, he's decided to do it my way for the time we're together. He doesn't mind in the least, and we ought to have a lot of fun."

"Val, what's wrong?" I asked, really disturbed at the
tonelessness in his voice as he finished his report. By rights
he should have been chewing me out for not telling him
that Little was a switch-hitter instead of the one-track I'd
described him as; rather than that he was just sitting quietly in
his chair, his yellow shirt and dark green pants more rumpled
than sharp-looking, his face expressionless, his body oddly
tense. "Val, tell me what happened."

"John Little wasn't the only one I got to know better," he
answered, looking as though he were forcing the words out.
"For the first time in my life, I also got a really good look at
myself. If you're not going back to bed, put some clothes
on."

I glanced down at myself to realize that I'd come into the
sitting room in the same thing I'd slept in—which is to say,
nothing but skin, but what difference did that make? We were
in the middle of something a lot more important than clothing
or the lack of it.

"I'll get dressed as soon as we finish this conversation,"
I said, gesturing aside his comment. "What did you mean
you . . ."

"You get dressed, or this conversation *is* finished," he
interrupted with a growl, looking at me in the weirdest way.
"As a matter of fact, I want you to haul out a couple of those
weapons you have in your trunk and start carrying them. Do
it now."

I opened my mouth to argue with him, closed it again in
exasperation, then got out of the chair to go back to my
bedroom. It took about five seconds to get into my jumpsuit
and smooth closed the staytab, then I headed back into the
sitting room.

"Okay, now I'm dressed," I stated as I reclaimed my
chair. "I've protected your modesty, and now you're damned

well going to tell me what's going on. What the hell did
Little do to you?"

"It wasn't Little, and you didn't have the time to get those
weapons I mentioned," he came back, only a very small
portion of the tension gone out of him. "You get in there and
get them, or I'll . . ."

"No, Val!" I interrupted sharply, standing up to walk closer
to his chair. "In case you've forgotten, I'm still leader of this
assignment, and if there's any threatening to be done, I'm the
one who'll do it. If it bothers you that I'm not armed, don't
worry your pretty head about it. I *am* armed, and as soon as the
attack comes I'll prove it. Now what the hell is eating you?"

He looked up at me where I stood above him, his exposed
and vulnerable soul staring out of his eyes, and then he
looked away again.

"I was only thinking of your safety," he said in a faint
voice. "I know now that I can't be trusted, not even by
myself. Mother of Life, how could I have done it?"

He buried his face in his hands and leaned so far forward
that I thought he would topple out of the chair; there's no
question about how close he came. He rocked forward and back,
so tormented that I wanted to take him in my arms and hold
him as tight as my strength allowed, but when I put my hand to
his shoulder he pulled away, either denying himself comfort or
afraid to accept it. I have a fairly vivid imagination, but it was
impossible for me to come up with what he might conceivably
have done to tear him apart so. There was only one thing
I could think of to get me the answers I couldn't pry out any
other way, so I went back to my room a second time to get it.

It didn't take very long to get my kit, which meant Val was
in the same place when I stopped next to him again. I opened
the kit and slid out one of the miniature pressure hypos, filled
it from the vial of Easy, then emptied it again into his arm,
right through his shirt sleeve. The hiss of the hypo was too

low to break through his upset, so I just replaced the instrument in its bands and went back to my chair to wait for the drug to take effect. Easy earns its nickname by building up a thick, soft wall between you and your emotions, taking the importance out of everything, relieving stress from whatever source. With enough Easy in you, you could even help cut your own head off without worrying about it; the project would be too unimportant to get excited over.

It took a good three or four minutes, but finally Val's body relaxed enough to let him sit back in his chair. I got out of my own chair and walked over to him, perched on his left chair arm, then smoothed his black hair back the way he so often did with me.

"Tell me what you and Little did, Val," I suggested softly as his eyes came to me. "Where did you go after I left you?"

"We went for some coffee and conversation," he answered without hesitation, still looking up at me. "I told him how hard it was for a gentleman of leisure to be tied down with an unwanted responsibility like a young girl, but my older sister was in charge of our parents' estate and would have cut me off from the money if I'd refused. You know, the story you made up for me to use."

"I remember the story," I said with a nod of approval. "Is that all you did? Just drink coffee and talk?"

"No," he said in the same direct but dreamy way. "After he sympathized with me we talked about sex, and then he suggested we go somewhere to get the bad taste of being crowded by a woman out of my mouth. He said he knew just the experience to do it, and we'd both have fun."

"Experience," I repeated, suddenly suspicious. "Val—did he take you to the Exotic Rooms?"

"Yes," he answered, not a flicker of upset in the black gaze resting easily on me. "We went to the Exotic Rooms, and I did what Ringer suggested for any time I was caught in a situation where I would be expected to know what was going on, but didn't. I told John I was in the mood to pretend I'd never been there before, and that I'd taken to pretending that with a lot of things, just to make them interesting again. He liked the idea of leading a novice around, and joined the 'game' by taking over completely.''

"He would," I muttered, blessing Ringer *in absentia* for coming up with such a useful out. It fit in well with the "I couldn't care less" attitude I'd had to come up with, and would probably be very effective for the cover we were then using. "What sort of experience did he arrange for the two of you?"

"It was for the four of us," Val corrected with no emphasis on any part of the statement. "He picked out two very pretty girls as our escorts, then had us taken to a private room. A completely hairless girl served us all odd-tasting drinks, we drank until we fell asleep, and then we were someplace else and other people.''

He stirred very faintly in the chair then and almost looked away from me, a reaction that made me wonder what his constitution was like. The drug shouldn't have let him feel anything, but then I realized he probably still had Exotic Rooms drugs in his system, too. I'd have to neutralize all of it, the Easy included, but I needed some more answers first.

"Tell me what those other people did," I said, hoping that if I put it impersonally, he'd be able to accept it and talk about it in the same way. Happily I hit the right combination; he sat still in the chair again, and didn't try to look away.

"The two men were desert bandits on a world I didn't know," my partner said, his gaze turning inward. "The two pretty girls were a King's daughters, and the bandits led their men in attack against the caravan that was taking them somewhere. The bandits killed all of the caravan guards, and then we found the two girls, who had been trying to hide from us.

John took one and I took the other, we threw them across our saddles, then we carried them back to our camp. My little redhead was terrified, but she and her sister still expected to be ransomed back to their father with nothing else happening to them. John and I dragged them into his tent by the hair, forced them to strip in front of us and all of our men, then he and I raped them. They were both virgins and both hysterical, but we did it anyway. And then the dream went away and the four of us were back in the room we'd been drinking in, and I took the girl lying next to me and—did it again. She screamed and begged me not to, but I still raped her.''

His breath was coming the least bit faster and his eyes had dropped to belt level, and all I could do for a minute was sit there and stare at him. It's been contended that most men, no matter how polite and easy to get along with they were normally, deep-down inside enjoyed the thought of taking women by force. Quite a lot of Exotic Rooms experiences were based on that contention, and very few people saw anything wrong in it. As long as a man didn't go around excercising his preference with women who wanted no part of the deal, no one had the right to tell him his preferences were wrong. From my own experiences with Val I knew he'd been conditioned against using force, but his basic nature and the way he'd begun acting with me should have kept him from being as bothered as he obviously was. I was clearly missing something, but I didn't know how to get at it.

"I can see there was something involved in that that you didn't like," I said slowly, trying not to push too hard. "When you and the girl were on the desert world, did you hurt her?"

"No," he answered with a faint headshake, looking up at me again. "I only raped her. I wanted to rape her and it felt good. But it wasn't me doing it, it was that stranger, and everyone said he was doing the right thing. But then we came back.''

His gaze flickered at that, at the thought of coming back, and that was the help I needed.

"And once you came back it *was* you," I said with as much understanding in my voice as I could manage. "But you didn't hurt her then, did you?"

"Of course I did," he said with what I swear was the ghost of indignation in his voice. "I looked at her where she lay next to me on the carpeting and she shook her head, trying to beg me not to do anything to her. I knew she didn't want to be taken but I did it anyway, and what's more, I enjoyed it. A part of me tried to tell me she didn't belong to me, but I didn't listen to that part. It just felt good and right until John and I had finished the lunch we were brought, and then I was able to understand what I really was and how right all those women were not to trust me. That's when I left John and came back here. If I'd had anywhere else to go, I wouldn't have come back.''

He was speaking almost matter-of-factly again, the confession behind him, the brutal truth laid out for the universe to see. I cursed under my breath at the way I'd blundered, but how the hell could I have told him everything about the Federation in a handful of days? I'd missed something important and he'd been caught by it—and then I remembered how I'd accused him that morning, which had to have made it worse—

I got my kit again, refilled the hypo with paneutrol, then gave him the dose and sat back on the chair arm, waiting for it to take effect. When his eyes started blinking and he took a deep breath, I knew it was time.

"You should be just about clear now," I said, drawing a sharper gaze than I'd been getting up till then. "Is all the fog cleaned out, or do you need another couple of minutes?"

"What have you been giving me?" he asked with definite annoyance, running a hand through his hair as he shifted an inch or so away from me. "And get back to your own chair, I don't like being crowded."

"Tough," I answered without the least compassion, ready for the stare that quickly turned in my direction. "Why should I worry about how comfortable a heartless rapist is? And that *is* what you are, isn't it?"

"You don't sound very convinced," he said, an odd flicker coming to those eyes. "Are you waiting to be grabbed and jumped before you'll believe it?"

"I'm waiting to explain to you about Exotic Rooms drugs," I came back flatly. "Are you ready to listen with an open mind, or do I need to get another glass of water first?"

His eyes went briefly startled as he remembered our time together on the ship, and then he lost some of the intensity he'd been building toward again.

"If you're trying to say you know something I don't, you won't have to twist my arm to make me listen," he said, not quite up to finding humor in the situation. "I'd like to hear that the whole thing was just a bad dream, but I know it wasn't."

"Do you think you can get it through your thick head that you don't know one damned thing?" I asked, not bothering to hide my impatience. "The truth of the matter is that it *was* a dream, every bit of it including the time you woke up back in the room. That's part of what the drugs are supposed to do when you're escorted: carrying the dream over into the real world for a while."

"I don't understand," he said, looking horribly confused. "I know I was awake when we got back to that room, so how could it still have been a dream? Dreams stop when you wake up."

"Not if they're being helped along by drugs, they don't,"

I said "The four of you started out 'drinking' together,
something that tasted strange. That was the drug, of course,
the one that let you all enter the experience together. Then
they ended the experience to make it carry over into reality,
and let your escort earn her pay. Experiences always carry
over anyway, but when there's no escort involved they add
some sort of sleepy stuff, to cut you down in time to keep
things from getting out of hand with anyone who might be
waiting for you in your room. You'll never go after a stranger
because of an Exotic Rooms experience, but if you're traveling with someone you could have a problem. Or she could.
The point I'm trying to make is that your great revelation
t'warn't no such thing. The girl cringed back from you
because of the experience carry-over and because it's her job;
you ignored her pretend terror because of the drug; once you
negated the after-effects a little with food, you came back to
yourself enough to see what you'd one with critical eyes,
but weren't back far enough to understand it was the drug
rather than you. If you didn't spend so much time feeling
guilty about the chicken reactions of other people, you never
would have come apart over a stupid little experience. And I
was awfully glad to hear that you'd already eaten. Now how
about being a good little rapist and ordering something for me
before I fall over from starvation."

I got up from the arm of the chair and started to take the kit
back to my bedroom, but I didn't get more than three steps
before a big hand was on my arm, stopping me. I didn't
know what he wanted this time, but he didn't leave me in the
dark long.

"You're really angry," he said, and although he still
sounded confused, he also sounded calm and back in control.
"Why are you so angry with me?"

"I'm not angry at you," I said, keeping my eyes on the

door to my bedroom. "As a matter of fact, it has nothing to do with you. Are you going to order lunch for me or not?"

"It has to have something to do with me," he persisted, ignoring the question I'd asked. "You weren't angry, when we first started talking, and you weren't angry when you were questioning me. I couldn't keep from answering your questions, but nothing stopped me from noticing things. It seemed to start when you brought me out of that muddled sea of confusion and began explaining the facts of life. If you aren't angry at *me*, what *are* you angry at?"

"I told you it was nothing!" I snapped, pulling my arm out of his grip. "We've got an assignment to see to, and it's about time we started seeing to it. I've got things to do and so do you, so . . ."

"No," he interrupted very quietly, and then his hand was on my arm again, this time pulling me around to face him. I didn't want to face him and tried to pull away again, but would have had to use a kick to get both of his hands unpeeled from where they held me. For some stupid reason I felt like trembling, and I had no interest at all in looking up at him.

"You're not by any chance—angry at yourself?" he asked with that same damned calm, probably looking down at me. "You can't think that what happened to me was *your* fault? Diana, you weren't even there."

"I noticed that, too," I answered, looking at the fourth button of his pretty yellow shirt. "If I hadn't been so clever about getting out of the way, though, I would have been. And would have been around to explain about how Exotic Rooms work, the way I should have before this. Considering where we're going you should have been told all about Exotic Rooms, but I wasn't bright enough to think of it. It just goes to show you what happens when you rely on a partner to watch your back: you end up getting it in the neck. If you'd prefer forgetting about the lunch, I'll understand.''

For what seemed like the fiftieth time I tried turning away from him, but he still wasn't having any. His breath came out in a long, deep sigh, and then he pulled me up against him so that he could put his arms around me.

''I really do wish you would learn to apologize like other people,'' he said, and damned if there wasn't a faint chuckle in his voice. ''It would make life so much easier for both of us. If you don't apologize to me for something that isn't your fault, how can I play the big-hearted hero and forgive you?''

''Like hell it wasn't my fault,'' I muttered into his chest, raising my left hand to toy with one of his buttons. ''If you'd known what to expect from the experience, it wouldn't have strung you out like that. I'm the one who's supposed to be making sure you don't get caught, so what do I do when I'm really needed? I take a nap.''

''Diana, you're not responsible for my basic nature, or the way I was raised, or the—chicken way people react to me,'' he disagreed without the chuckle, one hand stroking my hair. ''I was taught to treat women gently and never use my size and strength to force them into anything they didn't want to do, even if the growling hunger inside me had to go unfed. I never saw anything wrong in going along with that and always did go along with it, even though I felt hurt and somehow disgruntled when women first began acting as if they didn't believe I would keep my word. I was very young, then, and very touchy about my 'honor,' but as the years went by I couldn't help wondering if all those women knew something about me that I didn't know myself. The ones who didn't shy away told me that I was very different from other men they'd tried, but they never said different in what way. When I found myself raping a woman and actually enjoying it, I felt as though I'd betrayed everything I believed in, everything I'd ever been taught, proving how right all those women were not to trust me. All the explanations in the world wouldn't have prepared me for facing something like that while still drugged, so why shouldn't you have taken a nap instead of wasting oceans of breath? The explanation couldn't have done me any good until I was free of the drug and could think clearly again.''

''Do you plan on making a career out of excusing the lousy things I do to you?'' I asked, finally looking up at him. ''You get mad at the jokes, but the seriously damaging things you just laugh off. Are you a card-carrying masochist, or just into amateur pain? And if that emotional upheaval was so inevitable that a warning wouldn't have done anything to head it off, why didn't it happen when you raped *me*?''

''It didn't happen because I didn't rape you,'' he said with a grin, pushing some hair back from my face. ''You were so ready for me that I would have been blind to miss it, and you gave me your permission a long time ago. If it had been any other woman that off-balance I wouldn't have been able to go against my up-bringing by taking advantage of her, but you're not like other women. You're so different that everyday rules don't apply to you, mine or anyone else's, and I knew that once I got around the mad you were feeling you would respond to me the way you always do. You did respond to me, and so strongly that you almost overwhelmed me, so if there was any rape involved, I wasn't the one guilty of it. Isn't forcing yourself on someone rape?''

''But I didn't!'' I protested, knowing he was teasing me, but finding his argument too close to the reason I hadn't wanted to buy that outfit in the first place. ''I didn't deliberately put it on to force you into anything! It just—happened.''

''Just like that,'' he said with another nod that rejected the whole idea. ''You didn't once glance in the mirror after getting dressed, so you had no idea what you looked like.

And since you know you're not built very well, you didn't have to spend any time wondering how you would affect everyone. I guess you're right about it just happening. I'll order up some lunch for you now."

He turned away from me and headed for the phone, leaving me standing there like a dummy with nothing to say. My mind fluttered around for a minute trying to find a counter to his contention that didn't seem to exist, and then it found something else that gave me a small jolt. I knew Val wasn't seriously insisting that I'd raped him, and he knew I knew it. The whole point to the silliness had been to make me forget how I'd been feeling, to give me something else to think about besides what my negligence had made him go through. If he'd known what to expect he could have taken it in stride, and that was the bottom line even if he refused to admit it. I watched him using the phone with only a trace of his original awkwardness, then turned away to reclaim the chair I'd been using. I was taking him into a dangerous situation because I had no choice in the matter, but there was something I did have a choice about. Val could either be my active partner or simply along for the ride, and if he was just along for the ride the situation would not be nearly so dangerous for him. Since I owed him more than one I would handle it that way, keeping him out of trouble even if it meant more work for me. For someone who was just visiting he'd been hurt enough, and as he turned off the phone I promised myself that it would not happen again.

CHAPTER 8

"Stop fidgeting," Val said to me in a low voice as we moved into the docking area. "You're supposed to be seventeen, not seven."

"It's too bad you didn't remember that when you were buying these clothes," I almost snarled, keeping my voice as low as his only with an effort. "You had no right forcing me into wearing them."

"I didn't buy them so you could leave them behind," he came back, able to keep the grin off his face but not out of his eyes. "You look just the way we agreed you should, so forget about it."

"Forget about it," I muttered, then shut up before I started a real fight with him. We'd spent the last few hours with me dredging up everything I could remember hearing about Xanadu and the Pleasure Sphere, during which time my new clothes had been delivered. We both ignored them until business was taken care of, but then Val had started getting stubborn about seeing how wrong the clothes were. He refused to let me try finding something among my own things to use instead of the new stuff, and there was no arguing with that babysitting service threat. The idea of leaving me behind really appealed to him, and the more he thought about it, the more he liked it. I couldn't afford to be left behind, not with that service having the help of the Station computer in keeping their charges where they belonged; it would take me too long to get around the surveillance and follow him down. That meant I had to do things his way, even if it made me feel like a prize fool.

"Well, Val, right on time I see," a voice called, and I looked up to see John Little walking toward us from the shuttle lock we were heading toward. "In just a little while we'll be on Xanadu, and then I can start introducing you to the Pleasure Sphere."

"I'm looking forward to it, John," Val answered with a sly look, and then the two of them laughed that dirty laugh that some men loved to share. "I don't expect to find myself bored."

"You have my word that you won't be," Little promised, and then he turned his attention to me. "Nor will you be, Jenny. And please allow me to say how lovely you look."

His smirk was enough to get him belted under normal circumstances, and I wasn't far from being willing to call those circumstances normal. I was wearing almost the same shade of blue I'd been wearing the night before, but this time it was on what the woman in the shop had called a sailor dress. The thing came high in front to hide all traces of cleavage, moved up across my shoulders and above cap sleeves to halfway down my back in what was laughingly called a collar, fit across my hips with no strain whatsoever, and continued on down to no more than an inch or so above my knees. A very nondescript pair of flat shoes came along with the dress, as did a pair of white gloves, a straw-like white hat, and a small blue purse on a white chain. I looked about as lovely as I felt, and Little knew it.

"My name is Jennifer," I told him coldly with as much scorn as I could stuff into my tone. "You make a good friend for uncle Val, Mr. Little. Remembering my name seems to be beyond him, too. And I'm sure that anything capable of keeping *your* attention must be absolutely captivating, so why would you think I was worried about being bored?"

"That's enough, Jenny," Val put in in a hard voice, but happily nothing like the one he'd used in the clothing shop. Little was staring at me through the smirk he hadn't allowed to disappear, and there was nothing friendly in the observing, only calculating. "Mr. Little *is* a friend of mine, and I won't have you using him as a target for your tongue. I'm sure there are places even on Xanadu where hairbrushes can be bought."

"Hairbrushes?" Little echoed, looking over at Val. "You're supposed to buy her a hairbrush?"

"I'm considering it," Val answered, giving me that impatient, petulant look. "Not to used *by* her, but *on* her. By me. If she doesn't behave herself."

Little found Val's threat amusing enough to chuckle at, especially when I called a blush up into my cheeks and looked away in silent fury. I had the feeling that Val was trying to warn me not to antagonize a twisted creep like Little, but I knew the man better than Val did. Little was not a normal AC-DC; he had sex with other men not because he liked it, but because he hated women that much. When he involved himself with women, it was always in a way that brought pain and terror to them, the only way he could ever enjoy women. No matter what I did or didn't do, I would never be winning any popularity contests where Little was the judge, so I had decided to use the situation to my own advantage. Little already knew "Jenny" wasn't too crazy about her "uncle Val"; if I lumped him in along with Val, he would not wonder why I wasn't around much once we got to the Pleasure Sphere. I intended making a point of avoiding them but watching from the sidelines, waiting for the time Little guided Val right up to Radman. At the first opportunity after the meeting broke up Radman would be mine, and then Val and I could both forget Little and just get ourselves out of there.

The shuttle docked right on time, took on its load, then headed back to Xanadu with all of us aboard, me at the port, Little on the aisle, Val between us. I spent most of the trip down listening to a commentary of the wonders of Xanadu through a set of headphones, but gave it up when I nearly laughed aloud at hearing the Pleasure Sphere described as "a naughty delight for those daring enough to taste forbidden fruit." The section just outside the Pleasure Sphere was reserved for everyone's aunt Hattie and uncle Bill, who were looking for a "naughty delight"; the workers there wore peek-a-boo costumes, pretended to be hotter than hell, and spent most of their time publicly propositioning people who never made love with the lights on. That plus a few simple games kept the ordinary man-and-woman-on-the-street happy as sin. The real Pleasure Sphere was not for the ordinary.

Val and Little carried on a low-voiced conversation until we grounded at Rainbow, the planet's major port, then we and the others with us filed out into the late afternoon sunshine and down the ramp to the circle of reception tables being set up around the shuttle. Xanadu's patrons were never put out to the extent of having to walk anywhere unnecessarily, and the non-homogeneous shuttle group had to be separated into its component parts before anything else could be done. The four major continents were each represented by about 85 degrees of arc and brightly colored banners, the first depicting sunshine and sand, the second green water and a boat, the third a forest with mountains and snow in the background, and the fourth a fun ride in front of a roulette wheel. There were, of course, sub-sections covering specifics under

these general headings, and most of the people debarking had
no difficulty in finding the section that applied to them. The
section we wanted was dull and quiet in comparison, but the
large black P on a background of lilac said something the
others didn't, at least as far as the dozen people heading for it
were concerned. Strangely enough our group was quieter than
any of the others, and that made me stop and think for a
minute; considering what they were going toward, maybe it
wasn't that strange after all.

Val and Little registered with one of the people under the
black P, and then we were directed to a waiting vehicle that
consisted of cushioned comfort chairs and quiet, efficient
people taking and serving drink orders. The vehicle was open
on all sides but the top and was large enough to hold forty or
fifty people, and once we were seated I was actually brought
the glass of wine I'd asked for. Val was pretending he didn't
know what I was doing, covering himself in case anyone
called him on the point, I supposed, but I appreciated the
thoughtfulness. Looking around casually is a lot easier when
you can pretend to be doing it as a fill-in between swallows.

In another twenty minutes the shuttle was empty and everyone going our way was already aboard the vehicle, so the
show was promptly put on the road. The port was large but
very uninteresting, with big, modern buildings decorating its
outer edges but nothing else to look at. The vehicle started
smoothly with only a preliminary hum, to be sure not to spill
the drinks, I guessed. Hors d'oeuvres consisting of finger
sandwiches and pastries were brought around by the drink
servers, so I helped myself to a small cake of the 1000 calorie
variety and ate it fast, as though ashamed to have anyone
catch me being young enough to do something like that. Val
was still not noticing what I was doing as far as Little was
concerned, but I caught a glimpse of amusement in his eyes
showing that he hadn't missed the gesture; after all the des-

serts he'd made that I'd eaten, I was sure he knew I hadn't taken the cake just to strengthen my characterization.

Once we left the area of the port, we found ourselves all alone on a well-paved highway that threaded through pleasantly cool forest with birds singing in the trees. For my purposes the forest was as useful as the port had been, so I was far from disappointed when the highway began skirting a large lake and a dock appeared in the near distance. There was a vessel tied up at the dock that was as strange-looking a water vehicle as the land vehicle we then rode, but I couldn't see all of it from our position on the highway. The front of it seemed open but sectioned off, and beyond that there were parts that looked to be entirely closed, but our angle of approach kept me from being certain.

"You should like that boat, Jenny," Little's voice came, showing my interest in our destination had been noticed. "The crew are all employees of the Management, but the servants are slaves. You can order them to do anything you please, and no one will mind."

"But slavery isn't legal," I said, turning my head to send him a frown where he sat. I could see from the amusement in his eyes that I'd given him the answer he'd expected—which was the reason I'd said it in the first place.

"On Xanadu, slavery is completely legal," he informed me, a faint, cruel smile just curving his lips. "If you commit a crime or step out of line in some other way, you will most likely be sentenced to slavery to work out whatever punishment you've been given. If I were you, I would be very, very careful not to step out of line."

"What do you mean?" I asked, not liking his smile one little bit. "I don't have to worry about something like that. I'm here as a guest, and everyone knows guests are protected."

"Your uncle Val is here as a guest," he corrected with a lot of satisfaction, sipping lazily at his drink. "As a minor, your classification is something else entirely and not clearly defined. If you bring yourself to the attention of the Management, they may just decide you deserve to be taught some manners. Allow me to assure you that you would make a most desirable slave, my dear, and I would be certain to see that I was one of the first men you were sent to serve."

"So you'd better be very careful of your behavior, little girl," Val put in with a greasy smirk while I stared wordlessly at Little. "If you antagonize anyone here who happens to be in a position of even moderate power, you could find yourself facing something a lot worse than having a hairbrush applied to your backside. Not that John couldn't see to it that that was done as well."

A glance showed me that above the smirk Val's eyes were filled with warning, underscoring the speech he'd made. Something more must have passed between him and Little, but I couldn't help keeping my stare directly on Little himself. His threat had sounded as though he might have something specific in mind to tie me up, and I couldn't afford to get involved in something like that. I hadn't expected my obnoxious act to push him that far that fast, but Little wasn't straight enough to be judged easily or predicted with any sort of precision. I had to backpedal if I could, and hope it would do the trick.

"I want to go back to the orbital station," I said in a voice shaky with shock, letting my eyes go appropriately wide. "Please let me go back, uncle Val."

"Too late, Jenny." Val laughed lightly, his characterization enjoying the spot his snobbish niece had been put on. "We're here and we're staying here, until *I* decide it's time to leave. Until then we'll be watching to see how well you behave yourself, and if we don't like what we see, you won't like what happens."

They both laughed at the appalled expression I showed

them, then went back to their private conversation, leaving me to sink back in my chair in a thoroughly cowed manner. Inside I was cursing at that "we'll both be watching you" phrase Val had used, and it didn't matter whether he was just being creative in character or was warning me that Little had plans he couldn't cancel out. I couldn't afford to be watched, not by someone who would love to turn me in to the Management, but avoiding it would probably turn out to be easier said than done.

In another few minutes our vehicle slid to a smooth stop in front of the pretty white dock the water vessel was tied up to, and we were all able to see how much bigger the thing looked up close. The center section *was* enclosed and both ends were partitioned but open, and the bright colors it was painted brought a festive feeling to everyone but the little girl who had been badly frightened by the two grown men she was traveling with. Little Jenny tried hanging back when everyone began leaving the vehicle, presumably to ride it back to the shuttle port and from there get a shuttle to the Station, but her uncle and his friend made very sure she was with them when they began the short walk to the boarding ramp. I let my shoulders slump and a frightened look peer out of my eyes, but made sure not to mention that I'd never intended being left behind. People on Xanadu weren't simply allowed to board a shuttle any time they pleased, not with all the slaves the planet boasted. If you didn't have a properly made departure reservation you attracted official attention, and on top of that I had no intentions of leaving—until I got what I'd come for.

Each group boarding was met by a smiling attendant, females for the men, males for the women. If the group consisted of two and they were one male and one female, the dominant half of the partnership was catered to, whichever it happened to be. The operation was carried off so smoothly I was sure they'd been tipped by those working the land vehicle, which would have been the smart way to handle it. A tall, well-made brunette came forward as soon as we reached the top of the ramp, and her smile was mostly for Val.

"If you'll come this way, gentlemen, I'll show you to your accommodations," she said as she moved to the left, away from the ramp. "We'll be casting off as soon as everyone from the bus is aboard, and you might like to rest before dinner. Cocktails will be served at sundown, the meal itself at full dark. If you need anything before then—or afterward, for that matter—just press the white contact beside your door. The Management wishes you a pleasant stay."

"Thank you," Val answered, looking the girl over carefully but only with the intensity of his role. After his comment about being partial to dark hair and eyes, I'd been briefly worried at seeing our beautiful guide; if he'd turned those hunters eyes on her it could have been all over for us, but apparently he had more control of himself than that. He watched her behind moving under the flowered sarong she wore as she led us up a wooden corridor between what seemed to be the accommodations she'd mentioned, but the look in his black eyes never sharpened, not even when she stopped in front of a door on our left.

"This one is yours, Mr. Little," she said, opening the door as she smiled at him. "The next one is yours, Mr. Carter, and the last is for the young lady. I'll see each of you inside, and then leave you to your rest."

"I think I would prefer having my niece between Mr. Little and myself," Val told her, stopping her just as she was starting for what was supposed to be his door. "Being on Xanadu and heading for the Pleasure Sphere is beginning to frighten her, but being between the two of us ought to be reassuring."

"Certainly, sir," the girl answered immediately, coming

up with another smile. "The accommodations are yours to arrange as you like, most especially as they'll only be for this one evening. Please follow me."

Val sent Little a satisfied look as he and I followed the woman, but Little hadn't seemed quite as satisfied. The last glimpse I had of him was an attempt at smiling approvingly at Val, but an angry frustration was fighting hard to flare out of his eyes. Something had just happened that I didn't understand, but there was no immediate way of finding out what it was.

When the girl opened the next door down the line and gestured me inside, I stepped past her to find that the open, partitioned part of the vessel was what was used as cabins. The entire far wall of the area was gone, showing that we were just casting off from the dock and beginning to move, slowly pulling away from the bank and heading toward the middle of the lake. I stopped in the middle of the cabin to stare in professional dismay at the countryside moving past, and the woman came over to put her hand on my back.

"Don't be frightened, dear, there's a force field there to keep you from falling overboard," she said in a gentle, unamused way. "It lets air and light through, but it won't let a human body past it. Would you like me to walk over there with you so you can see that for yourself?"

I gave her a half-hearted smile and shook my head, which brought me another reassuring pat and smile before she left to get Val settled in. I followed her to the door and closed it behind her, then turned back into the cabin to look around. The area was no more than twelve by ten and made entirely of a dark, polished wood like the corridor, with a single bunk along the wall the door was in, a piece of colored cloth hanging on a peg set in the wall to the right, and what had to be communicating doors in both left and right walls. There wasn't a sign of my luggage or Val's, and there wasn't even a chair to sit down on. I sat down on what proved to be an unbelievably comfortable bunk. There was nothing to do but wait to see what happened next, and there was no telling how long that would take.

What happened next came about ten minutes later, after I had put my cigarette out on the cabin floor and was taking that ridiculous hat off. The white gloves were already thrown down next to the purse on my bunk, and I was seriously considering letting the dress follow the rest when a sound came at the right-hand door, the one leading to Val's cabin. I got up from the bunk and slid back the latch holding the door closed, and Val opened it then gestured me into his cabin. I stepped through the doorway, but when I tried to close it behind me, Val shook his head.

"Leave it open," he said very softly in the trade language, our secret, unbreakable code. "I have a feeling Little knows his way past these latches, and I don't want him wondering what we're talking about."

"What *are* we talking about?" I asked in the same language, relieved at the lack of tingling in the round white earrings I was wearing. That meant our conversation hadn't triggered any listening devices, which probably meant we weren't being monitored in any other way either. "Is the conversation going to include the reason we played swap with the sleeping arrangements?"

"Among other things," he nodded, keeping one eye on what he could see of my cabin through the opened door. "First I want to know if you're all right. You looked badly shaken before, but now you seem calmer."

He took most of his attention away from my cabin to look me over carefully, just as though he were searching for tears or something. I found it very hard to believe he was serious, but was very much afraid that he was.

"Hey, Val, remember me?" I said, waving a hand to get

his attention. "This is your intrepid partner you're looking at, the one who can look shaken at the drop of a sneer. You're not going to start believing what I say and do again, are you? All that happened was that I changed my line of attack because of Little's reaction to the first version; I'm not frightened, I'm not upset, and I'm sure as hell not in need of comforting. I also won't be any of the above even if I hang sniveling on your sleeve and coat. Do you think you can remember that?"

"I'm not sure I can," he came back, a peculiar look mixed in with a tinge of embarrassment. "Don't you know how real it looks, when you do things like that? You weren't pretending to be frightened earlier, you *were* frightened, and even Little believed it. Staying in character to gloat was one of the hardest things I've ever done; what I wanted to do was put you behind me, then smear Little all over the landscape. If you have to do it, can't you tone it down a little?"

"You mean, make it unbelievable?" I asked, trying to be as gentle as possible in response to the plaintive note in his voice. "Val, I've been doing this a long time, and I've always had an aptitude for it, so it's not surprising that it looks real to you. It's supposed to look real, otherwise I'm wasting my time. You have to make yourself understand that no matter how real it looks outside, inside it's just another gag I'm pulling, on you and everyone else. Inside I'm laughing at everyone who believes me, and you don't want to be laughed at, do you? Isn't it better to be in on the gag than taken in?"

"That was a good try, but it's not helping," he said with a sigh, rubbing the back of his neck with one hand as he looked down at me ruefully. "Every time you wilt under Little's stare, I get the urge to wrap my hands around his throat and squeeze. I'll try to stay in character the way I've been doing, but the longer this goes on, the harder it will be. If you want to go back to the Station and wait for Radman to show up there, I'll get started making the arrangements."

"Going back to the Station is out," I growled. "This whole thing is so stupid. Look, can't we agree that if I really need your help I'll ask for it? In this language, so there won't be any chance of confusion? If I don't start yelling in the trade language, I'm still putting on an act and everything's fine. How does that sound?"

"It helps," he agreed with only a trace of enthusiasm, then he grinned faintly. "Most women would *want* to be protected from something like Little, but you're still running counter to the breed. Just don't run so far counter that you close your eyes and walk blindly into whatever he puts in your way. If you do, yelling probably won't help."

"What has he been telling you?" I asked with a frown, finally understanding why Val was being so reflexively protective. "I know he didn't like my high and mighty act, but backing down should have helped at least a little. He was certainly gloating hard enough."

"That's because he enjoys seeing fear in women," Val said with disgust thick in his voice and eyes, his attention back on my cabin. "When you treated him as less than a bug, you made a permanent enemy of him, and nothing you do now can change that. He's been trying to talk me into selling you to the Pleasure Sphere."

"Before or after you told him selling me was what you had in mind?" I asked, making sure none of the chill I felt reached a place where Val could see it. My partner still didn't know how far things could be taken in the Pleasure Sphere, and considering his protective reflex, I wanted to keep it that way.

"Before," came the answer, and those eyes still kept themselves away from mine. "Selling you was his idea, one that scared me but still brought a certain amount of interest. I told him that even if I did sell you it would have to be a private buyer, but he's still pushing for the Sphere. A private buyer would probably not give you everything you deserve, he insists.''

I described Little's personal habits briefly but colorfully, then turned away from Val to walk to the open side of his cabin. We were out in the middle of the lake now, and the fiery red of the setting sun was playing over the ripples our transportation was making.

''Whatever you do, don't even pretend to agree to that,'' I said after a minute, feeling the fresh lake breeze tickle through my hair and over my face. ''If he's keeping after you, he's probably prepared to record any sort of agreement he can drag out of you, and once he has that they'll come after me at light speed. Stick to the private buyer line, and there won't be a problem.''

''I'm glad you think so,'' he said from behind me, and somehow I had the feeling he was looking at me. ''According to my friend John, no matter whom I sell you to, I first have to have you appraised. You know, to find out what your potentials are. He's been trying to get me to agree to having it done tomorrow, when we get where we're going. That's why I switched cabins with you; if we were right next door to each other, he would have been at me non-stop. I was hoping having to go a distance through the corridor would keep him away for a while, at least while he's still pretending to be interested only because of our 'friendship.' He thinks I did it so that the two of us can keep an eye on you more easily.''

''I wish to hell we didn't need him to lead us to Radman,'' I muttered, then turned away from the lake view to find that I'd been right about being stared at. Val was not happy in the least, and I didn't have to tell him he had company in that. ''Your friend is right, so you can stop avoiding him and start agreeing. Tell him you do want me appraised after all.''

"Diana, you're out of your mind," he said harshly, those black eyes flaring at me. "If Little wants it done, you can bet there'll be nothing but unpleasantness in it for you. Do you expect me to just stand by and watch them do whatever they please to you?"

"That's exactly what I expect," I came back just as harshly. "It's part of the job, and that's what we're here for, to do a job. If you can't remember that, you're useless to me, and worse than useless. And how many times do you have to be told that my name is Jennifer? Are you *trying* to get me killed or taken?"

His eyes showed hurt before he turned them away from me, and that told me he didn't realize I'd slapped at him on purpose. I had to do something to make him shed that protectiveness, or we were both going to be in it hip-deep.

"Being appraised isn't as bad as you think it is," I told the stiffened back facing me. "It's humiliating and degrading, but not painful. Some of the people who come here send themselves through it, others get sent through by the people they're traveling with, as a joke. It's main purpose is to measure the physical potential of the individual being appraised, to see if they've reached full sexual maturity or could use some additional development. Little may want the report to turn over to Radman if the need arises to bring his boss into it."

"And everything that brings you closer to Radman is worth whatever you have to pay for it," he said very flatly, turning back to face me with a look in his eyes to match the tone. "I know how dedicated you've told me you are, *Jennifer*, but I can't help wondering if in this case the dedication runs a little stronger than usual. It looks to me as though you might be crossing the line between dedication and obsession."

"If you want to know if I'm personally out for Radman's blood, the answer is yes," I told him without any bush-beating, making no effort to avoid his gaze. "If I hadn't been given the assignment I probably would have come after him anyway, which is why Ringer got that death warrant back into effect so fast. He knows me well enough to know what I'll do, but he also knows I can handle it. Professionally. If this was purely a personal hunt I *would* pull back and pick a better time and place, but it's not. When it's business you don't always get to pick your spot and minute; this is business, so we stay with it. Do you understand?"

"The way you mean it, yes." He nodded, expressionless but not soothed. "In all other definitions of the phrase, I don't even begin to understand. What's supposed to happen after you've been 'appraised'?"

"We go deeper into the Sphere no matter what Little suggests," I said, sighing. "He must have approached us originally with the idea of spotting us for his own organization, then got side-tracked when I 'insulted' him. If we get him close enough to where his boss is, we may force him into forgetting his own plans and going through with the original one."

"Which would get you sold to a small organization rather than a big one," he summed up, still expressionless. "What I don't understand is how Little can suggest selling you to the Sphere, and you confirming it can be done. Didn't you say Pleasure Sphere customers are protected?"

"From each other," I clarified, shifting my weight where I stood and wishing there was a chair to sit down on. "The Sphere won't let its clientele do what it pleases to others like them, since they're all paying customers. What you have to remember is that Little wasn't stretching things too far when he said my 'age' puts me in a different classification from other guests. Even if I become a confirmed Sphere enthusiast during this visit, a number of years have to pass before I can come back on my own, and I have to have the bucks as well

as the desire to do it. What money I have now might be from
a trust; at what age do I get control over that trust? How good
are the administrators of the trust? What happens if there's
nothing left when I get my hands on it, or if I turn out to hate
the visit? There are too many variables involved for the
Sphere to clearly classify me as part of their clientele. You're
my guardian and you're picking up the tab this time, don't
forget; coming here at all marks you as a wastrel, so neither
one of us might have the wherewithal to make any further
visits. If they buy me their profit is guaranteed right now, and
that would be tempting for them—if you were to offer them
the deal. If you don't that's another story entirely, and I don't
think they'd give in to the temptation and come after me on
their own."

"You don't *think* they would," he repeated, back to a
flattened tone and stare. "I'm glad you can reassure me with
such positive statements. If you couldn't, I might have thought
about worrying."

"People who spend their time worrying never get anything
else done," I told him, unable to keep the sourness out of my
own tone. "If you want to waste time like that that's your
business, but I'd rather be doing something constructive—
like making sure they don't get too interested in me. Which
means I have to adjust my character."

"And how do you plan on doing that?" he asked, ignoring
the rest of what I'd said. "An established character is usually
difficult to change."

"I'm just going to have to reveal my 'true' character," I
said, shifting in place again. "Some time during the meal,
find an excuse to leave Little and me alone. I'll take care of
the rest. Now, is there anything else we have to talk about? If
not, I'm going back to my cabin to sit down for a while."

"There's nothing more to discuss, but we have an exchange to make," he said, turning away from me to walk to

the wall near our communicating door. There was a bright piece of flowered cloth hanging there, something like the cloth hanging in my own cabin, and he took it down and held it out to me. "This is what you'll be wearing to dinner tonight, just this and nothing else. My outfit is hanging on your wall."

"Looks like they go for informal dinners on this vessel," I observed, taking the rectangle of yellow and brown cloth with a small amount of surprise. "How do you know I'm supposed to wear this, and what if I don't want to? Or, more specifically, what if someone with a whole lot of money and pull doesn't want to?"

"That girl who led us here told me about it," he answered, watching me examine the cloth. "And anyone who tries refusing to wear one will be stripped forcibly and stuffed into it. She didn't put it quite that bluntly, but the message still came through loud and clear. We all signed contracts when we got off the shuttle, I was told, and this sort of thing is enforceable under the contract."

"I guess you could call it breaking the ice the most direct way," I said, shrugging at his implied question. "A lot of people shuck their inhibitions with their clothes, but if you left them to do it on their own, they'd take forever at it. This way it's like jumping into really cold water; once the initial shock is over, you can settle down and start enjoying the swim."

"This is one swim I don't expect to enjoy," he said, still looking down at me. "No matter how many times I jump in. You'd better watch your step with these people very carefully. If I see you taking unnecessary chances, I'll come down on you myself. I don't like unpleasant surprises like being told about sudden, fatal accidents."

"If anyone tries telling you I'm dead, insist on seeing the body," I advised him, making the decision to ignore his jittering. "If there are no marks on me, I'm not dead, I'm drugged, so grab the carcass and run like hell. Other than that, play it cool and loose."

His glance of annoyance told me how well he liked my answer, but he didn't say anything aloud as he followed me back to my cabin to claim the blue-and-red-flowered cloth that was his dinner outfit. It was really getting closer to sundown, and we had to dress for cocktails and dinner.

More accurately, it was necessary to *un*dress for cocktails and dinner. I stripped off that stupid dress and the underwear I'd been forced to put on under it, then wrapped myself in the length of cloth before getting comfortable on the bunk again. Val had given the open wall of my cabin an unhappy look once the cloth that was his was in his hand, and then he had gone back to his own cabin and closed the door with very little enthusiasm. It occurred to me then that he and most of the others would feel as if they were stripping in public when they changed, even though we were out in the middle of the lake and there didn't seem to be anyone watching from the bank. The open wall had to be another inhibition-relaxer, and led me to wonder how many more of them there would be. It looked like Little had been right when he'd said the trip would not be dull.

The fiery red sun was already down behind the darkening trees on shore when a tap came at my door, and then it was opened by the dark-haired woman who had been our guide. I'd noticed immediately that the doors had no locks—and with nothing movable in the cabin there was no way at all to bar them—but it would have been out of character not to be startled by the abrupt entrance. I quickly turned my attention from the scenery to the intruder, sitting up at the same time, and got another friendly, soothing smile for my efforts.

"My, how pretty you look," she said, briefly examining the yellow and brown cloth I wore. She wore the same cloth the same way I did, wrapped one and a half times around and tucked in under the left arm, but hers looked a little more fitted than mine did. Not that mine looked all that bad. Even without a mirror I could tell that the thin cloth was clinging to me, hugging my curves all the way down to the middle of my thighs. Being shorter than I was hers came down a little lower, but not so much that it really made a difference.

"Thanks," I responded with a brief smile of appreciation for her encouragement as I got to my feet. "Is it time to go?"

"I've already called Mr. Little," she answered with a nod, stepping back to give me room to get out into the corridor. "Once your uncle is with us, I'll show you all to the dining area."

She turned away then and headed for the door to Val's cabin, and when I pulled my own door closed and looked to the right, I found Little's eyes on me. Radman's lieutenant leaned against the dark wood of the corridor wall with one shoulder, his arms folded casually across his chest, his thin body bare except for the blue-and-red-flowered cloth wrapped around his hips. He wore it wrap-style rather than loincloth style, and it came down longer on his thighs than mine did on me. His eyes were already on me when I turned to see him, and although he didn't move or change his pose at all, I could feel the rushing around inside his head as he automatically began assessing my value on the current market. His eyes touched mine in a very businesslike way, possibly looking for the fear I'd shown him earlier, but that particular line of attack had become inadvisable to continue. I returned his stare very briefly, a fatal calm in the look rather than empty challenge, then turned my attention toward the plain, polished-wood wall directly in front of me.

A minute later the dark-haired girl stepped back from Val's cabin door to give him access to the corridor, and the look in her eyes showed how hard she was struggling to keep from

being visibly impressed. Val wore the same strip of cloth
Little had on and had wrapped it in the same way, but where
Little was of average height and slender of build, Val wasn't.
The cloth that was long on Little nearly had trouble covering
Val well enough, and the massive chest above it—not to
mention the broad shoulders and strongly muscled arms—
turned my partner into something to make a woman lick her
lips. I glanced at him with no outward sign of interest whatsoever as he came toward me, but the dark-haired woman
who trailed along behind him couldn't say the same.

"John, this is intolerable," Val complained to Little as he
passed me with the same sort of glance I had given him.
"Don't they know people came in different sizes? I feel the
next thing to naked in this rig, and it isn't fair."

"I don't think you'll mind for long, Val," Little said with
an amused chuckle, quickly pulling himself out of the fixa-
tion he'd had on his good buddy. That stare had been half
professional assessment and half personal interest, but he'd
let it go before Val might notice it. "There's a reason for
dressing us all this way, and you'll be compensated for any
inconveniences you might suffer. The Management won't let
you continue feeling put-upon."

"Are you sure you won't tell me what to expect?" Val
asked in the same half-petulant tone he'd been using, looking
down at Little in near annoyance. "Anticipation of delights
adds to one's pleasure, you know."

"And anticipation of unknown delights adds to it even
more," Little countered with another chuckle, then looked at
the dark-haired woman. "You came to guide us, I believe?"

"Yes, sir," the woman answered, sliding carefully past
Val to recapture the lead position of our little party. "Right
this way, please."

She headed back toward the spot we'd boarded, moving
slowly so as not to get too far ahead of us. Little and Val

stood aside to let me go ahead of them, but there was nothing gentlemanly in the double gesture, at least as far as Little was concerned. He wanted me to know I was being watched carefully, probably in an attempt to dig for the fear again. I hated to disappoint him, but knowing how Val would react to my playacting had forced me to a complete revamping of my previous plans. I glanced at Little as I passed him, with the new me just beginning to peek out, and followed our dark-haired guide without comment. When I got Little alone during the meal, he would understand completely about my change of character.

The smooth, clean boards of the vessel's deck were not very difficult to walk on bare-footed, and even if they had been we didn't have very far to go. Our boarding point was all closed up when we passed it, no more than a pretty little colored lantern marking the spot, and then we were moving into the center of the vessel, where there were already more than the dozen people we had come aboard with. Most of them were standing around admiring the spectacular sunset, and with the gorgeousness all around me it took a bit of effort to remember that this was the enclosed part of the ship. The large, roomy section had to be almost all vu-cast window, or at least the two supposedly open sides did. We followed our guide into the center of the area, feeling a gentle lake breeze caress us, smelling the clean, fresh air all around, and then we were being directed toward a man. He was a surprisingly big man in his early thirties, almost Val's size, in fact, but instead of black hair and eyes his were light brown, his face square and strong with an easy arrogance, his big body well muscled and clearly in top physical condition. His cloth wrap didn't fit any more easily than Val's did, but the look in his eyes said he was no more than amused by it. He sipped slowly from the glass of wine he held, his eyes moving around the large room, but when we all stopped in front of him, his complete attention was ours.

"Mr. John Little, Mr. Valdon Carter, may I present Greg Rich, your host for this voyage," the dark-haired woman said, standing just a little behind the big man while he bowed slightly in a somewhat sardonic fashion to the men he'd been introduced to. "If there's anything about this voyage that disturbs you in the least, you have only to speak to him about it and he'll have it taken care of."

"Immediately," the man called Greg Rich added, obviously meaning it despite the amusement in his eyes. "We'd like this little voyage to be a pleasant beginning for you, so if you come across anything you don't like, don't worry about saying so. We expect to have the impossible asked of us, and we also expect to be able to supply it."

"Then how about something decent to wear," Val said immediately, bringing a flash of surprise to Little's eyes. Most people wouldn't have had the nerve to complain to Greg Rich about something the big man obviously approved of, but Val wasn't any more like most people than I was. I felt sure it would have been more in character for him to keep quiet—as Little's surprise seemed to indicate—but all Rich did was grin faintly.

"Giving you something else to wear would not be impossible, but it would be impractical," he said with no hint of apology whatsoever, his eyes surreptitiously measuring my partner. "I know how you feel about this silly little outfit, but the Management believes that the sooner we get people to relax, the sooner we can give them what they came here for, and one of the methods of quick relaxation they picked is these sarongs. Being in it may bother you now, but in a little while you'll forget you even have it on, you have my word on that. Talla, see that the gentlemen are supplied with whatever they'd like to drink, and then show them the sunset."

The dark-haired woman smiled and gestured Little and Val after her toward a mobile bar that was being tended by another sarong-clad, attractive female, and with Little's help Val was convinced to go along. Both of them seemed to have forgotten about me, but when I tried to follow after them I found a big hand on my arm.

"For some reason, you seem to have been excluded from the introductions," Greg Rich said to me, his light brown eyes looking at me with a directness that not many men were up to. "I'll have to remember to speak to Talla about her absentmindedness. Would you like to tell me who you are?"

"I'm Jennifer Kent," I supplied, meeting his gaze with what I hoped was an appropriate curiosity. "I'm here with my uncle Val and his friend Mr. Little. Are you the one representing the Management here?"

"Among others," he nodded, his amusement increasing. "Would you be impressed to know that those others all report to me?"

"Why would I be impressed?" I asked with a shrug. "Unless you own the whole shebang, you report to someone, too. And even if you do own it, you probably have stockholders to report to. Having to answer to other people isn't particularly impressive."

"That's very true," he agreed with a widening grin, looking down at me with increased interest. "I have a feeling I've been misinterpreting something about you. How old are you, Jennifer?"

"I'm almost seventeen," I said with a heavy sigh designed to show exasperation. "I know being that age in this place is just short of illegal, but I'm tired of hearing about it, and it shouldn't be for much longer. Every time I get a lecture about what I can and can't do, I age a little more. Before you know it, I'll be ready to retire."

"I'm not about to let you age *that* fast." He laughed,

taking another sip of his drink. "You're much too attractive at the age you currently are, and I have news for the people who have been lecturing you: on Xanadu, there's *nothing* you can't do—especially if you do it with me. Suppose we start by getting you a drink."

His hand came to the middle of my back, and then I was being guided to another mobile bar, one being tended by a very handsome male in a male sarong. He accepted my request for two inches of ambrosia without blinking an eye, and my new friend Greg Rich didn't make a sound either. He just stood looking down at me as though he were examining me in detail, which led me to wonder just how much interest he was developing in me. It was probably nothing more than the urge for some bed time, in which case I could simply indulge his curiosity and then forget about him; in the unlikely event that my luck had turned so sour that he was interested in more than a simple roll in the hay, it would definitely be a problem. I had enough problems without adding new ones, but the big man wasn't likely to leave the choice about his doings to me. I accepted my drink with a friendly smile for the attractive young male doing the bartending, trying to be obvious enough about my interest to send Greg Rich looking elsewhere, but the vessel's Management rep was too sure about his own power to attract to be bothered even a little.

"I'm sorry to disappoint you, but he's already been reserved for the evening," he told me as I tasted my drink, his eyes laughing at me. "Won't I do for an adequate replacement, or do I make you nervous?"

"I'm not really used to men so much older than me," I told him with a candor he seemed to be expecting, hoping it would be just that easy to get rid of him. "If I have my choice, I'd rather have someone his age."

"Being rejected in my old age is hard for me," he said

with a grin he couldn't keep back, reaching out to touch my chest just above the sarong with one finger. "You're made for men rather than boys, but I'll make a deal with you. Spend this one evening with me, and then if you still feel you'd be happier with someone your own age, I'll see to it that that's exactly what you get for the rest of your visit. How does that sound?"

"I guess it'll be okay," I agreed with only a little reluctance, more relieved than I cared to show. It *was* only a taste the man was interested in, and once we got where we were going, I'd be rid of him. "Do you need to take vitamins or something first?"

He was sipping at his drink when I asked my question, and he started laughing so abruptly he nearly choked.

"No, I don't need vitamins or something first," he managed to gasp out after a minute, shaking his head and chuckling. "Old men of thirty-one are sometimes able to do without them, and I think this is one of those times. If I find myself able to perform at all after an evening of your complimentary observations. Don't you know it isn't nice to doubt a man who has asked you to go to bed with him?"

"I was never really asked before," I said with a shrug, seeing I could give up on the ploy of trying to make him question himself. "There was always a party to go to, and once the party really got rolling, it usually just happened. What did you mean about the bartender being reserved? Do you mean he already has a date?"

"I meant one of our guests reserved him," was the answer, those eyes watching me closely. "He happens to be one of the slaves we have aboard to see to our guests. Did you want to try a slave?"

"Not particularly," I answered in turn, but made sure to sneak another look at the man who was serving an older woman a drink with the same sort of smile he'd given me. "I don't think I like the idea of slaves, and I certainly don't like the idea that somebody could do the same thing to me. He doesn't look like a slave."

"Because he's not wearing chains and rags?" Greg Rich asked with renewed amusement, drawing my eyes back to him. "That doesn't mean he isn't a slave, you know. Not all slaves are kept in chains and rags. Your uncle seemed somewhat interested in Talla, and if he decides later that she's the one he wants, she'll have to serve him even if she doesn't care to. That's because she's a slave, too, which you may not have realized. Will *he* have to take vitamins or anything if he takes her to his cabin?"

"I have no idea what he takes or doesn't take," I told the veiled but deep interest looking down at me, making sure to draw back into myself just a little. "My uncle doesn't like me very much, and I couldn't care less what he does. And if he does decide to take Talla to his cabin, I feel sorry for her even if she is a slave."

"Why?" was the next question, very gently put. "Isn't your uncle able to live up to his looks in bed? Is that the reason you're so uninterested in older men?"

"I don't know what my uncle is like in bed, and wouldn't want to try finding out even if he asked me," I came back with calculated stiffness, closing up even more under that light-brown scrutiny. "I told you that he doesn't like me, and I don't mind saying the same about him."

I took a good swallow of my ambrosia as if I were trying to end the discussion, but in strictest truth I couldn't have been happier that the point had been raised. Being able to lay an official basis for avoiding my traveling companions in the future was a break I hadn't expected, but I wasn't in the habit of passing on any good fortune coming my way. Greg Rich would be filing a report at the end of that voyage, and if that report showed a reason for the wandering I intended doing, that wandering might very well be ignored by the next Management rep I came across. There was no guarantee it would work out that way, of course, but it was certainly something worth trying for.

"If your uncle can't see how much there is to like about you, he's a fool," my new friend assured me in a firm, friendly voice, raising his free hand to touch my face. "Why don't we just go look at the sunset, and forget all about him?"

I gave him a half-smile and a nod, showing I was willing to be diverted to topics more interesting than my uncle, and we both turned toward the wall that showed a view of the shore we had left, the shore behind which the sun was setting. I'd thrown a quick glance behind me before turning all the way, wondering why my jailers hadn't come back to claim me, and had gotten something of an answer. Val, I'd seen, was just about knee deep in beautiful women, some carrying trays of snacks, some standing empty-handed, all most likely slaves trying to interest him in reserving them for the evening. That he was the most attractive man in the room wasn't hard to see, and even if he'd been crazy enough to walk away from his admirers to find out what I was doing, he had a role to protect. He was stuck with the need to inspect a bevy of beautiful girls as though he were really interested in them, and Little was silently watching him look them over. I gazed at the beautiful red and purple and pink sunset with Greg Rich, thought about how tough certain assignments were for poor, overwhelmed agents like Val, and would have laughed out loud if I could have possibly gotten away with it.

In another few minutes all the guests aboard were in the area watching the sunset, and Greg Rich turned briefly away from me to be introduced to the last of the arrivals. He'd been keeping up an easy conversation during almost the entire time we'd stood there, and I welcomed the short period of quiet to think about the interesting suspicion that had begun creeping up on me. I took a sip of my drink, swallowed it carefully, then closed my eyes as though I were enjoying the lake breeze, but in reality I was monitoring my reactions to what was going on around me. I'd known almost from the first swallow that the ambrosia was spiked, but I hadn't been able to figure out with what. By itself the drink wasn't really doing anything to me, but once I closed my eyes I could feel the urge toward utter relaxation and heightened physical awareness, most likely keyed by that "breeze" that was blowing in off the vu-cast walls. Most of the people who had come in just short of blushing at their abbreviated costumes were no longer aware of embarrassment of any sort, and a large number of them were standing very close to the nearest member of the opposite sex, in most instances one of the slaves. That told me what the rest of the evening was destined to be like, but not at what rate it was supposed to progress.

I sighed as I opened my eyes and took another sip of my drink, briefly wondering what life would be like without all the complications I always seemed to be running into. I didn't know what the Pleasure Sphere people were using to hype up their guests, but I did know that although I was aware of the goings-on, it would not be affecting me the way it did everyone else. Special Agents are conditioned to resist as many coercions as humanly possible, and as mild a concoction as was working on me right then didn't stand much of a chance to do what it was designed to do. I was able to know something was trying to affect me and also know in general what it was supposed to do, but that left open the questions of how strongly I should be affected and how quickly I was supposed to reach the end of the line. I was going to have to fake what everybody else was really feeling, and wouldn't that be fun without answers to the specifics!

The Lord of Luck came to my rescue in the form of Greg

Rich, who reappeared at my side to put an arm around my shoulders. Until then he hadn't really touched me at all, and the sure, decisive gesture told me he wasn't simply testing to see if the little girl would pull away from him in discomfort. He was expecting the possessive hand slowly stroking my bare arm to be accepted and responded to, which dictated what my reaction had to be. I glanced up at him with a lazy smile and snuggled just a little against him, then continued with sunset-watching and drink-sipping.

By the time the pretty colors were faded from the sky and the gaily decorated lanterns had come on along with the soft music, the food was beginning to be brought out and our seating arrangements were being explained. No tables and chairs were brought into the wide area, which was to be expected from the costumes we'd been provided with. Instead of the restraints of formal dining we were given wide mats and cushions, two to a mat and the food placed on the floor in front of the couple on the mat. Big wooden platters held the food, but eating utensils were also conspicuous by their absence, leaving nothing but fingers with which to dig in. The very relaxed crowd was delighted by this innovation; and any time anyone's glass got emptied, it was quickly refilled.

I'd more than half expected that Greg Rich would find a dim corner for us to share a mat in, so I found myself surprised when he guided me over to a place where three mats were being arranged around floor space adequate to hold platters enough for six. A glance at the rest of the room showed that no one was being allowed to sit in a shadowy corner, and no couple was being left to sit alone. Six was the smallest number of any group, and one batch even had twelve. People were laughing and talking softly, old friends and new acquaintances alike, and just as we reached our mat the other four of our little set reached theirs. One couple was Val and the dark-haired Talla, she trembling softly and almost afraid to look up at him, and the other was John Little and a friend. It didn't bother anybody that Little's friend was male, not even the male slave he had chosen, especially since they weren't the only ones in the room to be part of a unisex couple. As long as everyone formed half of a required pair, no one made any further demands, comments or distinctions.

"Where were you?" Val's voice came, and I looked up to see that he was talking to me, disapproval distinct in his eyes and tone. "I expected you to be right behind me, but when I looked you weren't. Did I give you permission to wander away?"

"I'm afraid the fault is mine," Greg Rich interrupted smoothly before I could say anything, his arm tightening the least bit around me. I had stiffened in an automatic way at the supposed criticism, but apparently the slip was acceptable even in the presence of whatever we'd been given in our drinks. "I kept your niece from following you, Mr. Carter, so whatever blame there is must fall on my head. I can see our food is on its way to us, so I suggest we all get comfortable now."

The woman Talla began trying to get Val's attention as Greg Rich turned his own attention to showing me which mat was ours, but she didn't have immediate success. Val spent a few seconds staring at the big Management rep before turning his attention to the woman he'd chosen, and I sincerely hoped no one but me had caught the look in his eyes. As I sat down on the soft, yellow mat next to my escort for the evening I firmly kept myself from wondering about that look, but that doesn't mean I didn't worry a little. It had been so much like Val's hunter look that it had startled me, but there had also been one of readiness to answer a challenge before Val regained petulance, and that readiness hadn't been any part of the character he'd adopted. I didn't bother asking myself in what way he thought he was being challenged, because I

didn't really want to know. If I had been smart enough to
tackle that assignment alone, the question would never have
come up.

Once we were all settled on the mats the food was put in
front of us, and playtime began in earnest. It was pointed out
to me by Greg—"Call me Greg; or you'll start making me
feel ancient again"—that we could share the food much more
easily if I sat in his lap and we fed each other, so that's what
I did. I didn't mention how ridiculous I felt sitting in a man's
lap even if he *was* almost Val's size, and he didn't suggest
that we talk about the first thing to come up; we spent our
time stuffing food in each other's mouths, and if that had
been a different time and place the silliness would have been
a lot of fun. The music changed slowly to a rhythm with a
throbbing beat in it, and when we became aware of it, we
began exchanging a few sticky kisses in between bites. That
turned out to be funny instead of sexy—stickiness and chewing tend to do that to kissing—but that just made it even more
fun. We laughed and ate and had our glasses refilled, and had
just as good a time as everyone else in the room.

Or, almost everyone else in the room. After we'd washed
in the large bowls brought around by the serving slaves and
had dried on the towels they carried, Greg and I tried another
kiss and discovered that it was no longer funny. His arms
held me tight to his chest and his lips were definitely becoming demanding, and I didn't have to work too hard reminding
myself that my resistance to him was supposed to be just
about all washed away by the drinks-and-breeze arrangement.
Greg Rich was a very attractive man, one who was looking
for nothing but a brief good time, and that combination raised
his interest level for me. I returned his kiss with more youthful
enthusiasm than skill, something that seemed to amuse him,
and then he was pushing me to my feet and following me

erect. It was time to go elsewhere and get comfortable it seemed, and I wasn't in any way reluctant.

When I stopped to stretch and look around the room, I discovered that more than half of those who had been with us during the meal were no longer there. Four of five couples had decided that the walk to a cabin would waste too much time, and were going at it right there on their mats. John Little was also being worked on by his slave, his eyes closed at the pleasure he was being given, and then I ran into the stare of the only one in sight who didn't seem to be part of the general good time.

"And where do you think *you're* going?" came the flat question which went so well with the stare, both coming from my beloved partner. I stared at him like an idiot, totally beyond understanding what he was doing, those black eyes unrelentingly on me despite Talla's attempt to bring his attention back to her, and for the second time Greg Rich came to my rescue.

"She's coming with me," he told Val, the professional pleasantness in his voice beginning to be strained around the edges as he looked down at my "uncle." "If you're worried that something will happen to her while you're occupied with Talla, you can set your mind at rest. I'll see that she's looked after."

"Is that all you intend doing with her?" Val asked with all the pettiness of his characterization, pushing Talla away so that he could stand up to face us. "Just looking after her? Or is that 'happening' I'm not supposed to worry about included in the looking after?"

"She's too young to have a slave assigned to her," Greg came back with more calm than Val was showing. "A slave would take advantage of her lack of experience, as you know since the matter was explained to you. I'll see that she has just as good a time as you do, which is, after all, the reason she's here and one of the reasons I am. You don't have any objections to that, do you, Mr. Carter?''

"Of course he has no objections," John Little interrupted, shoving his slave out of the way as he climbed hastily to his feet. "There's no reason for you to object, Val, so tell the man you don't mind."

"I didn't bring her here to be spread by every heavy breather to come by," Val muttered, but he was clearly backing down in the face of Little's obvious but unexplained fear. He had looked away from Greg Rich's penetrating gaze as though he were afraid of the Management rep, and to my critical eye he hadn't done it as convincingly as he should have. I could see he hadn't wanted to back down, but happily Greg Rich saw nothing but the end result.

"What *did* you bring her here for, Mr. Carter?" he asked very softly with only a hint of triumph in his eyes, the picture of a man who was used to being deferred to. "If you didn't expect her to be given pleasure, what did you expect?"

"That's my business," Val muttered, glancing at him while ignoring Little's very low words of urging. "She's my niece, and what I do with her is my business."

"Only under certain conditions, Mr. Carter," Greg Rich answered as he put a hand in the middle of my back. "The Management tends to be rather strict about the actions of their guests under all other conditions. Ask your friend Mr. Little to explain what I mean—before you run into trouble you weren't expecting. I wish you an enjoyable evening."

The hand in my back then moved me out of confrontation position before anything else could be said, the body attached to the arm following along beside me as we headed toward the exit, stage left. The thought was a stranger one than usual for me, but that's exactly how I felt, as though I were wandering around a stage after having missed all my cues. I now knew what Val had been trying to tell me with the odd

routine he'd started, but I didn't know what to make of it.
The Management didn't want me using their slaves was the
message, probably given to Val while I was being shown the
sunset, but the real reason behind the decision was a mystery.
And what had Little been whispering to Val, and why had
Radman's lieutenant been so afraid? And now that Val had
put himself close to the top of Greg's shit list because of the
need to pass on information to me, how was I going to get
him off it again?

I spent so much time letting all those fascinating questions
fight each other back and forth in my mind, that before I
knew it a door was being opened in front of me and I was
being guided into my cabin. The room glowed with a soft,
pearly pink radiance that must have made the vessel look like
a mirage ship from shore, but I wasn't given much time to
admire the prettiness.

"You've been awfully quiet the last few minutes," Greg
said as he closed the door, drawing my attention to him.
"You weren't upset by what your uncle said, were you?"

"That all depends on which part of what he said you're
referring to," I answered, deciding I'd better decoy him away
from thoughts about my "uncle." "And as a matter of fact,
it was more what you said that really reached me. I may be
young, Mr. Rich, but I'm not entirely stupid. It was nice of
you to walk me back here, but I don't need to be done any
favors. I'm sure you have 'experienced' women waiting for
you, and there's no real reason to keep them waiting."

I turned away from him and walked toward the open wall
of my cabin, hoping my injured-dignity speech bought me
more than the solitude I'd pretended to ask for. I needed to
know what was going on around there, but demanding the
answers would have gotten me nowhere. I stopped a foot
away from the invisible force field and stared out over the
darkened water, holding myself around against the stiffened

lake breeze, and a minute later two wide, warm palms were moving down my upper arms.

"I'm devastated that you found me out," he said in a half-amused murmur, letting his hands slide slowly down my arms until he was holding me around. "Now you know that the only reason I'm here is to do you a favor and perform my job. Sometimes duty can be hell, but I'm strong enough to take it without flinching."

"You expect me to believe you *want* to be here?" I demanded, but with the tremor in my voice that his arms would have produced if I really had been less than seventeen. "You asked me if I wanted to try a slave, all the time knowing I wouldn't be allowed to even if I did. And you told me I could *have* a slave closer to my own age if I wanted one, and that was an out and out lie."

"It wasn't a lie, Jennifer," he said very gently, the amusement gone from his voice as his arms tightened around me. "I could hear in your voice that you didn't really want a slave, and I discovered that that pleased me. I wanted you to want *me*, and I didn't want your uncle interfering. He was the one I lied to, not you, and I intend using the rest of this evening proving what I say. Come tomorrow morning, you won't want anyone *but* me."

"I don't understand," I said shakily, turning in his arms to look up at him, very much afraid that I *did* understand. "After all the beautiful, experienced women you've had, you can't be interested in *me!* I know what I look like and I know how I affect men, but you're different. You're *used* to looks like mine."

"Used to them and just short of tired of them," he agreed with a wry smile, raising one hand to stroke my hair. "I also never expected to be attracted to a child half my age, but if there's one thing I've learned in this job, it's to not waste time fighting natural urges. After the first five minutes with you I knew I wanted you, and also became determined to make you want me. There's something about you that makes you different from any other female I've ever met, and if I have to use every ounce of authority I have on this world to protect you from that uncle of yours, I'll do it."

"To protect me?" I repeated, and this time the shakiness was all too real. "What do I have to be protected from?"

"I'm not sure yet," he answered, the smile turning to a frown. "I'm convinced he brought you here with a specific purpose in mind, and his being in the company of John Little makes me even more certain. Little isn't the sort to be friendly with, not if you're looking for nothing but a good time, but this isn't something you have to worry about. Little knows exactly how much power I have, and he won't take the chance of crossing me. If things go the way I want them to, your uncle will get the same message and back off permanently."

"I see," I muttered, and it sure as hell was no lie. Rather than being in danger of enslavement on that world, I had acquired a champion who was determined to see to it that nothing unpleasant happened to me—which meant that he would be watching me closely to make sure that no one took advantage of me. It also probably meant that he was ready to turn thumbs-down on Val at the first sign of game-playing on my "uncle's" part, and that was just ducky. I now knew why Little had been so frightened, and I couldn't really blame him. Greg had officially classified me as a guest, and if he and Val tried doing anything unpleasant to another guest, my protector would make sure the Management found out about it—and that would be it for Val and John Little. At that point I wasn't even sure if Little would take the chance of introducing Val to Radman, which would make every effort I'd made until then one big wasted effort.

"I think you're doubting me again," Greg said, and his

hand came to my chin to raise my face. I'd looked down and away from him without realizing it, and that wasn't something he wanted. "I told you you had nothing to worry about, and I meant it. Now I'd like to see how much *I* have to worry about."

"How much *you* have to worry about?" I repeated, beginning to feel like an echo. "What are you talking about?"

"I've never been captured by a woman before," he said, and the amusement was back stronger than it had been. "I'd like to find out how tight the chains are—and just how strongly I'll be held. If I manage to break loose—which *could* happen—we'll still be friends, but we just won't be any more than that. Are you ready to help me find out?"

I gave him a shy smile and a nod, but I really felt like laughing out loud in relief. Greg Rich was catering to his infatuation in the hopes of negating it, and that was just fine with me. As soon as he had his taste of innocence his curiosity would be satisfied, and then he'd be able to wave a fond farewell to the young girl who had momentarily tickled his fancy. Val and I would be able to continue along the trail to Radman, and all of us but Radman would live happily ever after.

"Well, if you're ready and I'm ready, then let's get to it," he said, letting me go so that he could take my hand. He led me over to the wide, comfortable bunk, sat down on it, then pulled me into his lap.

"You certainly are a big girl," he said, touching his lips to my shoulder as he reached across to tug loose the tucked-in end of my sarong. "Is everyone in your family as large as you and your uncle?"

"Some are bigger," I answered with a half-muffled squirm, making no attempt to help him or reach for his own sarong. I would have to spend our time together letting him do all the work, responding innocently, and not giving him half of what he had surely grown used to having; that way the novelty would wear off faster, and we would suddenly become "just friends." It was a shame to waste the time with a man like him, but there was nothing else I could do.

"Bigger maybe, but certainly not better made," he murmured, letting the cloth fall away from me before running a hand over my left breast and down to my belly. "You look nothing but curved and girl-soft, but there's real muscle here under this silky skin. I like seeing a woman who takes care of her body."

"I exercise a lot," I murmured back, putting my arms around his neck before starting to kiss his face softly. I hadn't expected him to be that observant, and my excellent physical condition was another topic it would be best to avoid.

"So do I," he said with a soft chuckle, then twisted around to move me off his lap and onto the bunk before putting himself next to me. "I exercise as often as I can, and especially in horizontal positions. Let's see how well we exercise together."

His lips came to me with a strength he hadn't shown earlier, his hands touching my body everywhere, and I suddenly knew I was going to have a problem. He was built so much like Val that my body was all ready to respond to him the way it did to Val, and I couldn't allow that to happen. I wanted to discourage Greg Rich, not encourage him, and to accomplish that I'd have to stay completely alert rather than relax and enjoy myself. As I was drawn into his arms and up against his body, I suddenly had the feeling that I would have preferred a different set of arms, but that was stupid and entirely beside the point. I had no choice about who would be holding me right then, and even if I did there was nothing wrong with the man beside me. All he was looking for was a good time, which was better than involvement any day.

CHAPTER 9

The morning sun had been shining brightly off the lake for a while before Greg began stirring, a satisfied feel to his muttering and movement. I lay quietly and regulated my breathing as though I were still asleep, but I was too disgusted with myself for sleep to really have a chance at me. Although the night had been a disaster as far as I was concerned, I was hoping hard that the man next to me would consider it another kind of disaster and separate himself from me as fast as humanly possible. There was always the chance that I had misinterpreted his reactions during the night and had gotten away with it after all, but the chance was on the same order as the possibility of taking off by flapping your arms hard enough. I could have said it was all Val's fault, but establishing a scapegoat didn't do a damned thing to change the situation.

"Pretty little girl, you have given me one hell of a night," came the words I hadn't at all wanted to hear, whispered softly as a big hand touched my right arm the same way. I lay facing the wall on my left side, Greg cozily close behind me, and I couldn't help closing my eyes in defeat. I hadn't been

223

able to keep from reacting to him the night before, not since he reminded me of Val, and although I hadn't used anything Adept-taught, I also hadn't been the inexperienced innocent I'd wanted him to see. I didn't know how deep a hole I'd dug myself, but I was bound to find out in the very near future.

"Jennifer, are you anywhere near awake?" Greg asked in a slightly louder murmur, his lips coming to my shoulder and neck, his right hand reaching around to caress. "I have to leave soon, and I don't want to go without saying a proper good-bye."

I'd prefer a final one, I thought as I pretended to stir partly awake, and then moaned low without any pretense at all. Greg wasn't as accomplished as Val when it came to raising a female's thermostat, but he was far from clumsy and was unknowingly reaching me through that stupid conditioning my time with Val had developed. I could have pretended disinterest if Greg hadn't been in a position to check for himself, but he was and he did, so I couldn't. He turned me to my back and kissed his way down from my neck to my breasts, all the while keeping his well-educated fingers busy, and the normally strong self-control I come equipped with suddenly became missing in action. I held to his shoulder and back, desperately searching for a way to get him away from me without getting physical or obvious, and unexpectedly found a possibility when my eyes fell on the open wall of the cabin.

When I'd looked that way I had expected to see the open water of the lake middle with solid ground a good distance away, but saw instead a floating city very close around us. Pastel colored buildings and walkways rode solidly on wide, stable pontoons not forty feet away, and between us and them were various-sized boats making a leisurely way in the same direction we were going. The occupants of the boats were looking at our vessel with less curiosity than faint amuse-

ment, some of them frankly staring, and it came to me that
"Jennifer" should by then be free of the drink-breeze grip of
the night before.

"Greg, there are people looking at us!" I gasped, squirming against the arm that held me still for his attentions.
"You've got to let me go so I can find my clothes!"

"Of course people are looking at us," he answered in a
distracted murmur, tightening his hold to keep me from slipping away. "This is the Pleasure Sphere, remember? Some
people get pleasure from doing, others from looking. And
you can't have your clothes, at least not until after the
preliminaries. Now stop squirming around until I'm in a
position to enjoy it."

His lips and tongue hadn't just been forming words during
his short speech, and I hadn't been able to keep from closing
my eyes against the sensations coursing through me. It turned
out that closing my eyes was the wrong thing to do just then;
before I could try any other stall, he was around third base
and sliding into home.

"No, don't," I moaned, finding it impossible to either
keep him from thrusting deep or keep the words inside.
"Greg, you can't."

"Stop worrying about being watched," he chuckled in
amusement, his hands smoothing my hair back as his hips
began working, happily misinterpreting my blurted protests.
"Before you leave here you'll be completely used to it, and
this first time won't be a really good session. I have to be
through and back on duty before we dock."

He put his lips on mine, then, ending all further conversation, and turned his attention to getting through. It didn't
bother him that I was at least able to do nothing more than
follow along; right then he was more interested in simply
using a female than in finding fancy response. He used me to
his complete satisfaction, taking only enough time to be sure

I had some satisfaction of my own, and then he was gone, standing up from the bunk to retrieve his wrap-around from the deck.

"You'll wear your sarong until the preliminaries are over, and then you'll be given your clothes back," he told me as he wrapped the cloth around his middle, a soft smile on his face as he looked down at me. "Right after that you'll find me showing up again, since I've decided to exercise one of the privileges of my rank. Talla will be by in a short while to show you and the others to the sanitary facilities, and then you'll be given something to eat. Just relax and take it as it comes, and I'll see you later."

He winked at me before turning away toward the door, and once he was gone I just sat there on the bunk with the sheet held modestly in front of me, working hard to keep the disgust I felt off my face. I'd done a good job complicating things, and right then couldn't see any way to uncomplicate them. I'd have to wait and see how bad it would be, and then try to think of something to shake myself loose.

I retrieved my own sarong from the floor and wrapped it around myself without giving the staring individuals in the small boats anything to look at, noticing in passing that the clothing I'd worn onto the vessel was gone. The security in the Pleasure Sphere was even tighter than I'd expected, and I was glad I'd kept my earrings on. There would be nothing odd to be found in them if anyone but a member of my department began fooling with them, but that would ruin the bug detectors in them in a permanent way. A casual electronics check would find them inert and leave them usable, so I hoped that's all that would be done. I touched one of the tiny buttons casually as I sat back on the bunk to wait for Talla, and felt the soundless beep that told me the bug detector was still working.

I was expecting the arrival of the pretty woman-slave at

any time, so the sound of the latch sliding back on the communicating door between Val's cabin and mine didn't surprise me. I'd thought he still had Talla with him, but when the door opened he walked in alone.

"Generally speaking, I'm here to check on my property," Val said in the Absari trade language, his tone bored and slightly annoyed. "Specifically speaking, I'm here to check on my partner. Are you all right? He didn't do anything to hurt you, did he?"

"Generally speaking, I'm resenting your insufferable attitude," I responded with the necessary stiffness, glancing toward the small-boat watchers still looking us over. "Specifically speaking, I'm doing lousy. Instead of turning him off the way I'd planned, I now have a new boyfriend."

"How did that happen?" he asked with a frown I was sure was real, the annoyance growing noticeably thicker in his voice. "I thought you knew how to handle men."

"I do," I told him, letting my tone go momentarily dry. "Why do you think I have a new boyfriend? I'll try to get rid of him as soon as possible, but until I do you'll have to watch your step. He's not very fond of you."

"The feeling is mutual," my trusty partner assured me, the look in his eyes hardening as he stared at me. "Why didn't you refuse to get involved with him?"

"You're under the impression I had a choice?" I asked, having some trouble keeping the sarcasm out of my voice. "If I had met him in my own *persona*, I could have either given him a friendly welcome or sent him on his way, whichever I liked. As a little girl with a big, bad uncle, I was in no position to tell the knight in shining armor to get lost. He's decided to protect me from you, you know."

"Bully for him," he answered sourly, leaning one hand against my cabin wall. "Where I come from, men who want to protect women don't do it in bed. Are you sure he didn't hurt you?''

"With his level of skill, if he ever hurt a woman it would have to be on purpose," I told him with a shake of my head, briefly wondering if dear old Greg ever did get into anything like that. "Hurting an inexperienced young female the first time you take her to bed would be crude, and my new friend is definitely not crude. If he switches tactics, it won't be for a while yet."

"I love the way you keep reassuring me," he came back, still sounding and looking annoyed. "How fast do you think you can get rid of him?"

"Depends on how things go." I shrugged in answer, grinning privately. "If I have to suffer playing footsie with him for another couple of days before he gets distracted, well, the job has to come first, you know. Have you told your buddy about your change of heart in the question of having me appraised?"

"Yes, and he was delighted," Val answered with even more of a frown, leaning off the wall he'd had a hand against. "We'll be making the arrangements as soon as we're off this boat. What do you mean, if you have to 'suffer' for a couple of days? You can't possibly mean you *enjoy* having sex with that—conscienceless user?"

We were interrupted by the opening of my cabin door. Talla stepped in with a friendly smile for me and a shy one for Val, and that was the end of our conversation. Which was probably a good thing. I was immediately tempted to ask Val how he could possibly have enjoyed himself with a *slave*— something he obviously had from the warm look he and Talla exchanged—and it wasn't likely my partner would have appreciated the question.

Talla collected Little, who had already been called, and then led the three of us back toward the area we'd had dinner in the night before. Val's good buddy was so pleased to see me he was almost civil, a pleasantness brought about by the thought of my upcoming appraisal, no doubt, and I suddenly remembered I hadn't shown him my altered character. As we walked along I tried to decide if there was enough time right then, but the decision was taken away from me.

"I must admit I was rather surprised a few moments ago, Jenny," Little said to me in his oily way, falling back to walk next to me while Val brought up the rear. "I had expected to see you leave your cabin with Mr. Rich rather than your uncle, as my own friend and his stayed until the last possible minute. Can it be Mr. Rich wasn't quite as pleased as he had expected to be?"

The thought that I'd lost my powerful protector really tickled Little, an attitude that brought me the urge to sneer in his face, but there's more than one way to rub someone's nose in the distasteful.

"He said he had to be back on duty." I shrugged, totally uncaring about the whole thing. "But he also said he'd see me later."

"My dear girl, *later* he'll be gone with this boat, back to the pick-up point for the next group of guests," Little told me with vicious condescension, delight glowing in his eyes. "Perhaps I would do well changing my mind about requesting you, should you ever be made a slave. Your efforts must be devastatingly unsatisfying."

"I don't care about anybody else any more than they care about me," I said with another shrug, giving him the line I had intended giving him the night before. "My mother never cared about me, and even gave me away to uncle Val. I thought for a while he might be different, but all he wants to do is get rid of me the way my mother did. I don't care if Greg doesn't want me any more than anybody else, I never

expected him to. If they try to make me a slave, I won't do
it.''

I glanced at the faint frown line that had developed between Little's brows, seeing nothing showing in the way of
suspicion, then turned away from him at Talla's gesture and
went to the part of the wall she'd indicated. The entire area
was enclosed this morning, and some of the other people who
had been led into it were looking around wondering where the
extra two walls had come from. The night before the wall in
front of me had been blank and had stayed blank, but right
then the polished wood slid aside as soon as I was in front of
it.

The sliding panel let me into a cozy little bathroom area,
complete with orange carpeting, yellow lounge, and red dressing table and chair. I couldn't keep from wincing at the color
combination as the panel closed again behind me, but that
didn't stop me from heading straight for the facilities and
using them. After that I stripped off the sarong and my
earrings, and stepped into the shower, and once the water was
running I could take a couple of minutes to think.

Little had seemed surprised at my lack of fear, but not
surprised to the extent of being suspicious, and that's what
I'd been trying for. It was perfectly logical for a child who
was rejected by everyone around her to in turn reject everyone else, and that despite the initial fear she'd shown in shock
over a newly threatening situation. If I couldn't show fear
without taking the risk of having Val blow both our covers
I'd have to show indifference instead, and now that the
indifference had been justified it ought to work. I'd expected
more in the way of a reaction from Little than the frown I'd
gotten, but he probably needed time to adjust to the new
situation he'd been hit with. Once he adjusted, he might have
to be watched.

I soaked for a time in the shower before washing, then

relaxed while the air jets dried me. When I left the shower stall it was to find a fresh, neatly folded sarong lying on the spot I'd dropped the old one, but my earrings were apparently untouched. I wrapped the clean but identical sarong around me and carried the earrings to the dressing table, brushed my hair for a couple of minutes, then casually replaced the earrings. The silent beep telling me they were still operational almost made me smile; it seemed there were going to be benefits after all to being young and innocent-looking. The Sphere's security people were apparently giving me an automatic pass, which would hopefully turn out to be one of the bigger mistakes they'd ever made.

The dressing table had cosmetics of nearly every description, liquid, solid and invisible skin cover, eye shadow and accenter, lid liner and lash enhancer, lip and cheek rouge and paler, permanent, semi-permanent and temporary. There was also sparkle and decals and paint and brushes for original art work, and every bit of it suited the coloring of a redhead, which was very thoughtful and thorough of my hosts. It said the room had been prepared just for me, even though it had been decorated with a color scheme designed to hurry me out as soon as possible. Not wanting any of the make-up I felt ready to be hurried out, but then I had a thought. Kids who felt unwanted very often did things to *make* themselves unwanted, as though justifying the attitude of those around them. Make-up would make the face I wore then look cheap and used instead of fresh and innocent, and that might just be the key to sending Greg Rich on his way. Since I had clear justification for it in any event, it was certainly worth a shot.

With the decision made I got to it, and in a way it was a lot of fun. I had never been one to enjoy heavy make-up, but deliberately putting on a mask is another matter entirely. My skin was already light but I lightened it further, making it look dead instead of alive. Next came very dark brow pencil,

shadow and eye liner, then very bright lip-gloss, leaving me
to sit and stare at my reflection for a minute, trying to decide
if I ought to use rouge. I already looked terrible but cheek-
bone coloring should add to it, so I tried it and it did. I didn't
even look as wholesome as your average joy girl, and that
gave me even more of a kick than the painting up in general.
I surveyed the results one last time, decided I was satisfied,
and so took myself from the dressing table and the room.

Val and Little were already back in the large area when I
came out and headed toward them, and the way they both did
a double-take was really funny. Little looked startled, but Val
was struck absolutely speechless for a minute, and then he
became scandalized.

"What the hell have you done to yourself?" he demanded,
stepping forward to stare down at me. "You look like a
walking ad for the two-credit special."

"Why should you care how I look?" I came back with
muttered belligerency, trying to remind him what his attitude
was supposed to be. He really didn't like what I'd done to
myself, and was reacting outraged when he should have been
scornful.

"What you look like reflects on me," he answered at
once, doing a good job of covering up, the flicker in his black
eyes showing he'd picked up on the goof. "I don't care to
have people looking at you like that and then looking at me.
Take it off at once."

"I don't have to take it off," I told the black-eyed sternness coming down at me, trying to send him a "back off"
stare. "Greg said I could do anything I pleased, and this is it.
He told me I'm as much of a guest as you are."

Mentioning Greg had made Val stop and think the way I'd
wanted him to, but the sudden frustration in his eyes said he
didn't want to back off. I could see he didn't know what I
was up to and didn't even particularly care if I'd done what I

had with a purpose in mind; he didn't like it and wanted it changed. His narrowmindedness narrowed his eyes as well, but before he could say anything, another voice interrupted.

"This isn't exactly what I had in mind when I said anything," Greg put in as he came up, flinching theatrically when I turned my face to look at him. "I appreciate your efforts in trying to pretty up for me, but I have a much better idea."

He took my arm and guided me away, ignoring Little's impressed surprise and Val's silent anger in the same way he was ignoring my feeble protests. I let him drag me away, but I was mad enough to curse for five minutes straight in as many languages, because it was suddenly clear that Greg had been watching me play dress-up with the make-up, and had really moved to get to me before I left the vessel. That the bathroom had turned out to be less private than guests were led to believe wasn't the point that bothered me; I hadn't expected any privacy on that world, so being watched in the bathroom didn't come as a crushing shock. What got to me was that my instincts had been right, and if I'd been able to disembark looking like payday Patty, Greg Rich probably would have faded back into the landscape, to save face if nothing else. The main thing that had kept that from happening had been Val's failure to stay in character, delaying me long enough for Greg to catch up to me. I'd have to remember to thank Val for that bit of help—him and his narrowmindedness together.

I wasn't given more than a few steps worth of time to think my furious thoughts; Greg headed me right back to the bathroom I'd come out of, and before I knew it I was inside again, but this time with company. The hand on my arm steered me straight over to the wide sink to the left of the sliding panel, and the mirrored wall behind it fed us our reflections when we stepped in front of it.

"Now let's get that mask washed off," Greg said briskly as he studied my reflection with half-veiled amusement. "I like my women natural-looking, and right now you look anything but. If I have to sit through breakfast staring at that, I'll starve from lack of appetite."

"I don't want to wash it off," I told his own reflection, immediately deciding to play stubborn. Having fun in bed is all well and good, but most men don't consider having to deal with a balky teenager fun. If I could get him annoyed enough, he'd walk away and forget the whole thing. "I put this make-up on because *I* wanted it on, and I don't want it off. If you don't like the way I look you can just go back with this boat the way you're supposed to, and then you won't be bothered. If you stay, you'll have to stay with me looking like *this*."

"Which you don't expect me to do under any circumstances because of what Little told you," he said, anger showing briefly in his eyes. "No one cares about you so you don't care about anyone, and you're ready to prove it. Well, I think I'll do a little proving of my own."

His big hand came to the back of my neck, I was bent forward over the sink, and despite my squawks of protest the soaped water was turned on and quickly slathered over my face. It was no surprise that he knew I'd used the water-soluble stuff instead of the permanent kind that had to be taken off with a special solvent, but something else *had* been a surprise, and a nasty shock as well. He had talked about my conversation with Little, and he hadn't been guessing; he'd *known* what had been said, and that meant he'd listened in, but my earrings hadn't warned me. That in turn meant their eavesdropping equipment was a good deal more sophisticated than I had expected it to be, and my bug-warning earrings were absolutely useless. And I'd thought they hadn't bothered checking because of procedural sloppiness!

Greg Rich ignored my yowling and struggling and did a thorough job of face-washing, then pulled a towel out of the sink-counter slot and stuffed it at me. I wiped the rinse-water away fast so that I could glare at him properly, but when I lowered the towel I found a wide grin meeting my glare.

"You have no idea how much better that is," he said with a chuckle for the outrage in my expression, folding thick forearms over a broad chest as he looked down at me. "Hurry up and finish drying, and we'll go and get some breakfast."

"What makes you think I *want* to have breakfast with you?" I demanded, deciding to see if I could get rid of him by walking away in a huff. "You had no right doing that to me, and I don't like being treated like a baby! Why don't you go and have breakfast with somebody you like just as she is?"

"That's exactly what I'm going to do," he answered, his grin softened into a smile. "I don't know what it is about you, Jennifer, but every time I see you with your uncle and that Little character, I get the urge to stand in front of you. I've never felt like that about a female before, and I've decided I like the high it gives me. You're having breakfast with me because *I* want you to have breakfast with me, and if you're not dry and ready to go in the next thirty seconds I'll take your sarong away and make you go to breakfast in that towel. Then everyone will be able to see what a lucky man I am."

His smile had grown into a grin, but that didn't mean he was kidding. The towel he'd given me was about eighteen inches square, just fine for drying a face or hands, not so fine for using as a sarong substitute. As a nudist I couldn't have cared less, but Jennifer wasn't a nudist and she was the one he was talking to. I produced a blush that set him chuckling again, then resignedly went ahead and did as I'd been told.

Val and Little were no longer outside the door when we came out, and Greg seemed to be expecting their absence. He took my right arm and wrapped it around his left, then led me to the vessel's exit amid a thin stream of other departing guests. The gangway to the dock was softly carpeted, a beautiful, blue-skied day was just starting above us, and the sleek, clean, floating outdoor restaurant we were docked near was designed to lift the spirits, but none of it was able to do much to lighten my mood. A soft, warm breeze fluttered my hair as we stepped onto the smooth, easy-on-the-feet flooring of our landing, and happily Greg was too busy pointing things out to me to notice that I was holding my expression neutral to keep it from going sour.

After Greg's speech in the bathroom, it had finally come through to me that I'd been operating under a set of mistaken beliefs. I'd thought the attraction I held for Greg was entirely physical, but physical actually had very little to do with it. From what he'd said, he'd played the gallant hero for a young, helpless female for the first time in his life, and he'd discovered that he enjoyed being protective. Working on Xanadu he couldn't have had much opportunity before I came along; after all, not many young, helpless female-types show up there as guests. He must have had buried and suppressed sympathies for the slaves around him, but hadn't been able to externalize them until he met me. It helped that poor, little Jennifer was exceptionally pretty and somewhat talented in bed, but I'd been considering that the major motivating factor involved, and it wasn't. Which brought up the fascinating question: how long would it take for the man to get bored with heroing? He was watching every move I made and listening to every word; how was I supposed to get around that to reach Radman? I didn't know the answers to those questions, and what was worse, didn't even know how to find out.

Val and Little were already seated at a table among the others from our vessel, food and drink in front of them, a servant hovering nearby in case they wanted or needed anything else. There were quite a few servants around, and every one of them was dressed in less than the guests they served, which is to say, nothing at all. They may well have all been slaves, but not necessarily so; lots of people are willing to work without clothing if they're paid well enough, and pay wasn't a problem in the Pleasure Sphere. Greg nodded pleasantly to Val as we passed within ten feet of my partner's table, then led me to a table of our own.

"I think we'll find this meal more pleasant if we share it only with each other," he said as he seated me with my back to Val and Little, then went around to sit opposite to me. "Are you hungry?"

"I suppose so," I answered with very little enthusiasm, wondering how you turned off a man who was determined to protect you. "Is this really the Pleasure Sphere everyone's always talking about? It doesn't look like that much to me."

"That's because this is only the gateway to the Sphere," he answered with a smile, gesturing over one of the servants with the food. "The real Sphere begins once you go through the gateway, which will happen this afternoon after you've passed your physical. I think we'll manage to impress even someone with your refined tastes."

"Physicals?" I echoed, having forgotten about that aspect of Sphere regulations. "What kind of physicals do you have to pass? And what happens if you don't pass?"

"If you don't pass, you'll be thrown to the carnivores in the arena," he said with heavy, phony menace, then chuckled at his little joke. "Don't worry, little girl, you'll pass, and if you don't, I won't either. Whatever happens will happen to both of us, so we'll be able to keep each other company. The physicals are more of a weeding-out process, to make sure you don't leave with anything you didn't bring. Those who have picked something up in their travels are guided through the Sphere in a slightly different direction, but they don't miss out on anything, and aren't restrained in any way, except by being kept apart from other guests. Some of them leave here without even knowing they were separated out.''

He flashed me a quick grin, then gave all his attention to the food that was being put on the table between us, totally untouched by the sickening implications of what he'd just said. If a guest came to the Pleasure Sphere and was found to have venereal disease, he or she was not turned away. As long as they could pay for their fun time they were given whatever they wanted—by slaves who had no choice but to become infected. That was bad enough in itself, but I had the feeling most of the infected slaves weren't put through one of the cures afterward; after all, why bother when they would just be infected again the next time? I poured myself a cup of coffee and took a cigarette from the dispenser on the table, wondering about Talla and the rest of the slaves from the vessel that had brought us. They all had to have started with a clean bill of health, but what would be done with them if they served a guest who was later found to be infected? Would they be given one of the cures—or would they be sent to serve in the areas that catered to the contaminated? Did they know what they had been set up for and accept the situation as unavoidable, or did they find out only afterward, when their bodies showed them the shocking truth? It was impossible to imagine living like that; my mind flatly refused to consider the possibility; even as an alternative to death.

"You aren't feeling chilly, are you, Jennifer?" Greg asked, drawing my eyes to him over my coffee cup rim. "I thought I saw you shiver, but the sun and air are too warm to cause that.''

"No, I'm not chilly," I answered, using sips of the hot

coffee to melt the remains inside me of the lie I'd told. "How can you stuff your face like that so early in the morning?"

"A good breakfast makes all the rest of the day go right," he answered with a grin, secure in the knowledge that he had nothing to worry about even if he *had* picked up something from me. The cure would be his for the taking any time he wanted it; that was one of the benefits in being a member of the ruling class. On Xanadu the Management ruled, and I was beginning to understand just how tight the fist was that they ruled with.

A lot less time was spent on breakfast than had been spent on dinner the night before, and by the time we were through eating most of the tables around us were empty. I finished the last of my coffee and stood up to join Greg, who was already on his feet and waiting to put an arm around my shoulders.

"The physical won't take long, and after they're finished with you we'll go some place to have fun until lunch," he told me, letting his palm slide up and down my arm. "After lunch we'll be ferried over to the far bank, and then you can decide which part of the Sphere you want to see first. It's been a couple of years since the last time I took the tour, so I'm looking forward to it."

He was leading me across the open eating area as he spoke, toward a pink door I'd seen the departing women guests going through, and when we reached it we stopped. Val and Little had gone through the light blue door to the left of the pink one some time earlier, and it had looked as though Radman's assistant had had to really struggle to keep Val from stopping at the table Greg and I were eating at. My partner hadn't actually done anything out of character, but he'd come close enough to make me sweat on the inside, and I'd breathed silently in relief once he and Little had disappeared through the door. It was obvious something was eating on Val, but since I was doing a lot better than we'd thought I would, I couldn't imagine what it was.

Greg pressed his lips to mine as his hand patted my back-side, and then I was being urged through the pink doorway into a featureless hall that led off to the right. With the near-silent hiss of the door closing behind me my only company I started up the hall, impatient to get through their requirements and make an opportunity for a few private words with Val. He had to know about the surveillance we were under, and I had to know what was bothering him. That he didn't like Greg Rich was no excuse for unprofessional behavior, and that was something I would make *him* know.

After twenty feet of light-peach blankness the hall turned to the left, to a dark green waiting area about twelve feet square. The farther end of the waiting area held four closed doors with a small but expensive desk standing guard in front of them, and someone who was probably the desk's user was right then guiding a wide-bottomed, sarong-clad figure through the second door on the left. The one doing the guiding was female, and she wore a standard nurse's uniform with small, matching white cap; when the door closed behind the portly woman she'd been guiding, she turned back to her desk and sat down behind it.

"Just make yourself comfortable in one of the chairs, young lady," she said to me with the quickest, most dismiss-ing glance I'd ever seen, her eyes and hands busy with the array of buttons and screens on the desk in front of her. "I'll let you know as soon as they're ready for you."

The two other women in the waiting area had already made themselves comfortable in chairs, so I ignored the supposed nurse's tone and did likewise. Just as I was sitting down the woman in white got to her feet again, gestured deferentially to the guest sitting not far from me, and guided her to the third door from the left. That left the woman across the room as my sole waiting companion, and the way her light eyes moved over me said I'd be better off waiting alone.

No more than five minutes passed before the second woman was conducted to the extreme righthand door, and then it was me and the nurse and the otherwise empty waiting room. I was just shifting in my chair when my summons came, and predictably it was the extreme left-hand door I was directed toward.

Inside was one of the most efficient crews I'd ever run into, both in speed and thoroughness. Four nurses and two doctors, mixed half and half male and female, met me three steps inside the door, and went into their routine with overpowering dexterity. My sarong was replaced with a paper wrap practically in one motion, and then I was hustled to an examining table in the midst of tons of sophisticated-looking equipment. Once I was on the table bodily fluids samples were taken, including a small amount of blood from one finger. The crew worked so fast doing so many different things at the same time that I barely knew what was being done to me, but that doesn't mean it was all over in five minutes. It was closer to an hour before they were through with me, and by then they had to know the exact condition of every cell in my body. They'd even used a biological detector on me, something I don't think I was supposed to have noticed in the general flood of efficient investigations, and I wondered briefly why they'd tried camouflaging that particular point. How sinister could checking my age be?

I was still considering the point when they turned me loose, all but a single blond-haired female who urged me off the table and aimed me toward a door in the wall opposite to that through which I had entered.

"Just go through that door now, dear," she said, nodding toward the exit in question. "The people out there will direct you farther."

"You mean they'll give me my clothes back?" I asked, resettling that paper wrap around me. "I was told I could have my clothes back after the physical."

"I'm sure they'll do everything that has to be done," she said with a neutral smile, opening the door. "Right now we have another guest coming in after you, so if you don't mind?"

Without waiting to find out if I minded or not she just about pushed me through the door, closing it fast behind me. I kept myself from tripping on the bottom of the paper wrap, muttered a few opinions about her personal habits under my breath, then turned around—to see the "they" who were waiting to do everything that had to be done.

"Excellent physical condition and entirely clean, Alec," the bigger of the two men commented, glancing through the papers he held. "Also undeniably less than seventeen standard years of age."

"Which means the request for appraisal is entirely understandable," the second said, his light eyes moving slowly over me. Both of them were blonds, and both of them were wearing black uniforms with lilac Pleasure Sphere patches on the left breast, marking them as Management personnel. I'd temporarily forgotten about the appraisal business, but the way the second blond was looking at me would have brought it all back even without his having spoken of it.

"Which also means we can dispense with that wrapping paper," the first one said, and his attention was no longer on the report he held. "Just let it drop to the floor, little girl. We want to see the rest of what we'll be working with."

I parted my lips to say something innocent and filled with lack of understanding, but a sudden, faint blurriness interrupted the intention, then chased it away altogether. I could feel my body briefly attempt a struggle against the blurriness and what was behind it, but the try was a washout; my vision cleared as suddenly as it had blurred, and most of the thoughts in my head disappeared with the distortion.

"I'll be damned," the one called Alec said as he moved nearer to peer at me more closely. "Look at that, Gil. She's reacting to it already."

"With the dosage they used on her, I'm not surprised," Gil, the taller one, answered, coming up to the right even as he checked again through the papers he held. "The residue in her blood from last night's dosing was so low that her body must have neutralized the infusion almost as quickly as it was introduced. With the appraisal ahead of her, they wanted to make sure the same didn't happen again. She's got enough trystisil in her to turn a Fendian arena-beast shy and smiling."

As the two men had been talking one of the doors behind them had opened, and a third man had entered. He was husky and wearing the same black uniform with lilac Pleasure Sphere patch on it, but he was dark-haired and somehow didn't seem to fit the uniform as well. Peripheral vision kept his face indistinct until he had moved up to stand behind and between the two blonds, and then my crawling blood stopped dead in its sluggish track.

"I hope you understand just how irregular this is, Mr. Radman," the taller blond Gil said to the dark-haired newcomer, a certain nervousness in his voice. "Clients aren't usually allowed in here during an appraisal."

"I know that, Gil, and I hope my appreciation was enough to let you and Alec understand how grateful I am," Radman answered in a rumble with his eyes burning into me, his tongue all but licking his lips. "I happened to be talking with a friend of mine who told me about her, and when I heard she was scheduled for appraisal, I just hopped on back. All I want to do is look and touch a little, no harm done. Once that trystisil wears off she won't remember anything anyway, and we've all been special friends a long time. No one will mind.''

The blond Gil chuckled in agreement, Alec also smiling faintly, but Radman was wrong; someone in that room did mind. At the first sight of him I'd tried fighting harder against the drug that already had me in its grip, the drug that had already taken most of my volition, but it was still no good. Even though my target was right in front of me, all I could do was stand there—remembering what he'd done the last time he'd been that close to me.

"She sure is a looker," Radman went on, stepping between the two other men to get so close that I could smell his bad breath. "Let's see what the rest of her is like."

His hands went to the paper wrap I was still holding closed around me, and if I could have snarled or shivered or screamed, it might not have been so bad. I wanted to do all of that and a lot more, but all the trystisil let me do was watch calmly as he tore the paper wrap just below where my fists were closed on it. My thoughts were growing more and more vague; if they hadn't been vague, they would have been frantic.

"Well, now, will you look at that," Alec murmured, Gil's stare and Radman's drool saying the same thing. Radman had let the paper wrap fall to the floor at my feet, and the weight of their eyes on me was almost more than I could stand.

"You two sure have a sweet job," Radman rumbled, his voice so thick it could have been spread on bread, his gaze all but consuming me. "After this, I just may apply for it myself."

"They don't usually look like that," Gil put in with an odd, faint smile, watching as Radman reached out deliberately to touch me. His hand moved between my thighs and began caressing me, and all I wanted to do was close my eyes and shudder.

"You know, I just thought of a way for you boys to earn a

little more gratitude," Radman said suddenly, his eyes glittering. "You can even monitor her during it, and I won't mind at all. Since she won't remember anything that happens, there might as well be more for her not to remember."

No, please, not again, I immediately begged in my mind, aching with the need to escape the hand that touched me in so sickeningly possessive a way, horrified that my body did nothing to try to stop it all. Radman had raped me before putting me aboard that crippled ship, and now he wanted to do it again.

"I don't think we ought to go quite that far," Alec said with a frown for the back of Radman's head, glancing at Gil. "Looking and touching are one thing, but to stick it to her—I think we'd all better remember that technically she's a guest."

"Technically she's a minor, and her uncle is the guest," Gil disagreed immediately, his eyes still locked to me. "As long as we don't do it to him, there shouldn't be any trouble. Mr. Radman's stay here will be much more pleasurable, you and I will have his gratitude, and after he's through we can even—monitor her again a couple of times."

"Come on, Gil," Alec said with a good deal of exasperation while Radman grinned slowly. "You don't mean she's got *your* interest, too? Aren't there enough slaves around here for you?"

"That's just the point," Gil murmured, raising his head a bit with a faint smile showing. "She isn't a slave that anyone can have. She's . . ."

A sudden knocking interrupted whatever he was about to say, a knocking that paled his face and immediately pulled Radman away from me. The burly slaver hurried to the far left of the room and opened a wall cabinet to rummage around in, and as soon as his face was no longer visible, Alec moved to the door that had been knocked on and opened it.

"What the hell is going on here?" Greg Rich demanded as

he came through the door, leaving it to Alec to swing it closed again behind him. He had exchanged his sarong for a lilac shirt and black pants and shoes, a small Pleasure Sphere insignia on the left side of his shirt. "What are you Appraisal men doing here, Alec?"

"We're doing our jobs, Greg," the smaller man answered, staring at the newcomer in surprise. "This kid's uncle requested appraisal, and we were assigned to see to it. What are *you* doing here?"

"I thought I was here to pick up my date," the big, brown-haired man said with a growl, fury looking out of his eyes. "That bastard was looking for a way to screw this up, and I'll bet he thinks he found one. How about taking my authorization for a cancel, Gil?"

"We can't do that, Greg," the taller blond said with a shake of his head, looking frustrated and annoyed. "The man has a right to ask for appraisal for his niece, and since she's a minor, he's the only one who can cancel. You know what would happen if we accepted your authorization and he squawked."

"Damn him," the big man muttered, one hand rubbing his face as frustration glared out of his eyes. "Yeah, I know what would happen, even better than you. Okay, you've got to go through with it, but how about hurrying it up a little? I had plans to fill the time until departure."

"We'd be glad to hurry it up," Gil said in a suddenly persuasive voice, moving toward Greg to put a hand on his shoulder. "Why don't you go back to your office or apartment, and wait there until it's finished? As soon as it is, I'll give you a call and you can come right over."

"I'm already over, so don't go out of your way," Greg said, moving his arm to get Gil's hand off his shoulder. "How long do you expect it to take you to put her through her paces?"

"The situational alone will take better than an hour," Gil answered with the frustration back, clearly wishing he could just order Greg out. "And that doesn't count any of the rest of it. You know we're also supposed to check to see what sort of a slave she'd make if she tests out sensual enough, and just looking at her takes all the if out of the question. Don't you think you'd be better off going back . . ."

"No," Greg interrupted without waiting to hear the rest of it, his brown eyes cold. "You know that with one like her nothing but the situational will give you any real information, so why screw around with the rest of it? Why are you stalling, Gil?"

"I'm not stalling!" Gil came back sharply, his eyes flickering briefly to Alec, who stood silent behind Greg. "It just doesn't happen to be proper procedure! The routine still gives us information, even if it isn't complete! But if you insist we go directly to the situational . . ."

"That's exactly what I do insist on," Greg interrupted again, his tone entirely uncompromising. "You can blame the loss of the additional information on me."

"And don't think I won't," Gil came back, a thinly veiled hatred in his voice, and then he turned from Greg to stalk over to me. "Come with me, little girl. We've got to get on with it as fast as we can. There's someone here waiting for you who can't wait to get *in* with it."

He put his hand out to me, clearly expecting me to take it, and although I didn't want to, I dropped the crumpled ball of paper I had in my left hand and reached out to the bigger hand being offered to me. There was no way I could have refused, and none of them seemed to expect anything else. Alec went to a door in the wall to the right and opened it, then stood aside while Gil led me through.

The room beyond the doorway was very dim, just short of being dark. Straight ahead I could see the outline of a small, raised circular platform, but instead of going to it I was led to the left, to what looked like an examining table surrounded by machinery. As we moved forward gentle lighting came on; I was given a low stool to step on to reach the table, and then was directed to lie down on the soft, pliable skinlike surface of the thing.

"This part of the operation is mostly mine," Alec said, coming over to the table to look down at me where I lay. "The first thing we have to do is get these electrodes and sensors attached to you."

"What are they all for?" Greg asked, sounding friendlier as he stepped closer to stand behind Alec's right shoulder, watching the blond man reach for something behind my head. "Don't electrodes and sensors do the same thing?"

"Not in this equipment," Alec answered cheerfully, pulling out thin wires from the place behind my head. "The electrodes deal with brain output, the sensors with bodily reactions—and both of them are capable of directing and controlling their respective areas as well as recording data. We rely on suggestion a good deal with our subjects, but suggestion alone doesn't do what we want it to."

While he spoke, he was attaching the tiny pad-endings of the thin wires to my face and head, pressing them gently into place where they clung without adhesive. I was aware of everything being done to me but none of it seemed to matter any longer, none of it had meaning that had to be thought about or worried over. The table I lay on was very soft and comfortable, I was scarcely aware of the wires being attached to me, and the fourth figure that hung back near the door we'd come through barely made me want to shiver.

"Now for the sensors," Alec said, moving a short distance to his right along the table I lay on. "Raise your eyes to the ceiling, Jennifer, and don't move unless you feel something that forces you to move."

I raised my eyes to the plain, pale yellow ceiling as directed, but the first sensation that came didn't cause me to move. Alec—or someone—was closing thick, soft straps over my wrists where they lay on the table at my sides, and although something very faint inside me wanted to fight against being tied down that way, none of the rest of me felt the same.

"Do you expect her to try to escape?" Greg's voice came, amused. "And do you expect the rest of us to be too weak and helpless to stop her if she does try?"

"The restraints are mainly for the situational," Gil's voice broke in, sounding faintly distracted. "Are you ready, Alec?"

"Starting right now," Alec acknowledged, also sounding distracted, and then something touched my breasts. First the right nipple and then the left developed the sensation of being held between gently caressing fingers, and I couldn't keep from moving somewhat as the fingers continued caressing.

"Good Lord, will you look at these readings," Gil said, his voice uneven. "Sensual isn't the word for her. She must respond to a man with everything in her! You won't see something like this in more than one woman in a hundred hundred thousand!"

"And with only two sensors in place," Alec pointed out, still sounding distracted. "No wonder Greg is in such a hurry. A very large portion of this part of her nature must come through during her times of full consciousness."

"Making her the next thing to Primal Woman," Gil added with barely concealed frustration. "It would take a lot of man to hold the interest of one like her, especially once she enters her peak sexual years. Lucky for you you're around now instead of then, Greg; she's still young so she tolerates you. Once she matures, though—all you'd be good for then would be to help pass some otherwise empty time."

"As I recall it, my rating is still higher than yours, Gil,"

Greg came back, his tone very carefully controlled for evenness. "And I've already proved I can reach her where she lives and give her something to remember. I tend to doubt you'd be able to do half that."

"How about leaving the cattiness to the girls, you two," Alec put in, nevertheless sounding faintly amused. "None of us could hold the permanent attention of a female like this, and I don't know that I'd want to be a man who could. Considering how inadequate other females would be for him, her male counterpart would be a walking mountain of frustration until he found her—*if* he found her. If he didn't, he'd never have—this."

Without leaving my breasts those caressing hands spread to stroke my neck and thighs, the touch on my neck more like feather-light kisses. My body had begun to burn with the demand born in my blood, setting me to moving on the very soft skin beneath my back, a mindless, unswallowable moan forcing its way from my throat. I needed something from a very specific someone, someone who wasn't there.

"While continuing to keep your eyes on the ceiling, Jennifer, picture the most attractive man you've ever seen," Alec said, his voice coming from right beside my ear even though I knew he stood toward the feet end of my table. "This man will be kneeling above you, and if you're a good girl, he'll give you what you need."

He appeared above me just the way Alec had said, the black eyes under black hair looking down at me as I continued to stare up at the ceiling. I wanted to raise my hands to the broadness of his shoulders and lean into the caressing of his fingers on my breasts, but something held my wrists to the table and I couldn't free them. He grinned at my helplessness and leaned down to kiss my throat, his clear intention to take his time, but he should have known better by then than to try that garbage with me.

"What happened?" Gil's voice came, sounding puzzled. "She's starting to turn off."

"I must have somehow miscued her," Alec said, his voice again coming from where he stood. "I'll get her back to where she was, and then we'll put her straight into the situational. Jennifer," and his voice had shifted back to being near my ear, "there is no longer anyone above you, no longer anyone for you to picture. Close your eyes and simply feel the sensations being given your body."

My annoyance disappeared with the figure above me, and when I closed my eyes it was to feel the caressing all over again, this time spreading to the very center of my being. Gentle, demanding fingers now moved between my thighs, and the moaning I did was louder and more deeply felt than what I'd done before. I moved against the sensations, trying to escape them, pulling at the straps holding my wrists in place, and gentle laughter sounded in my ear.

"You seem very much in need, girl, but that's to be expected," a voice said through the laughter. "In the place where you will soon find yourself, female slaves are kept in constant need so that they will always please the men who use them. You will have been a slave long enough to have learned how to keep yourself alive through obedience, but you have never given up the dream of finding something more in your captivity—and someone more. You are, at the current time, unaware of it, but those things you seek are just before you."

The voice droned so insistently that I began to feel myself going away from the table and the dim room, away to a place a small part of me didn't want to go. That small part fought to stay where I was, struggled with all the strength left to it, but that strength was useless against the voice that continued.

"Sink down deeper and deeper, and picture in your mind's eye the hall you now traverse, the hall of the palace in which you serve as a slave," the voice said, taking me over completely. "The columns tower above you as you walk, carrying your small burden, and the guards who stand beside the columns let their eyes touch you as you pass them. . . ."

CHAPTER 10

The hall was long and cold and silent, stretching in its marble grandeur far ahead of me as well as above and all around. I walked the marble equally as silently in my bare feet, attempting to keep a shiver from touching my half-naked body, knowing a shiver might well spill the contents of the bowl I carried. The contents were nothing to anyone not a slave, merely a thick meat stew, yet if I were to spill it I would be well beaten. I had walked that hall many times in my slavery in that place, and yet its ability to cause me to wish to shiver had never abated.

Perhaps the eyes of the guardsmen had a deal to do with the way that hall affected me, I thought as I continued on, seeking to make myself as small and nearly invisible as possible. They stood before the countless, towering columns lining the hall, their red and gold trappings marking them out clearly from the milk-white and pale blue and gray of the marble, their large bodies unmoving save for the shift of their eyes. Those eyes ever shifted to me in inspection, observing the manner in which it continued to disturb me to be bare-breasted, despite the length of time I had been slave, despite the slave nectar spilled down my throat and the slave salve spread upon my private parts each morning. In some manner they knew I feared them as well as desired them, and this brought them amusement.

"Slave." The single word brought me quickly to a halt, before a guardsman who stood no post and who was therefore free to address me. A leader of fifty he was, perhaps inspecting those of his command who stood their watches, one who had momentarily turned from his men to the inspection of a slave. I stood before him with head down, and yet was I able to feel the weight of his eyes as they touched the long red hair streaming down my back, the bare, full breasts which thrust out before me, the tiny bit of gold skirting which circled my hips and barely covered my privacy, the thin, golden bracelets which held my wrists and marked me as a slave. Despite my earlier resolve I began trembling as I stood before him, and his amusement came forth in low laughter.

"You are indeed an excellent choice for the task, slave," he said, his left hand moving from the hilt of his sword to my chin. My face was raised so that I must look him in the eyes, and I found his gaze as sky-colored as mine. "You carry a bowl meant for the prisoner, do you not?"

"Yes, master," I whispered, knowing that although there were many prisoners, the guard leader referred to the newest, the one who was prisoned in the palace itself rather than below it. It was rumored among the slaves that the Duke dared not harm him, yet was the reason for this unknown.

"When you offer the bowl, do not fail to offer yourself as well," he said, continuing to hold my gaze with his. "What number of times have you given service this day?"

"Four times, master, only four," I replied with a whimper I could not restrain, aflame from the meaningless touch of his finger to my chin. "Allow me to serve you as well, master, and I will bring you great pleasure. A slave asks only to serve you!''

''Another use and you would claw through the bars of the prisoner's cage,'' the guard leader said with a snort of derision, releasing my chin and refusing me, all at once. ''You will first deliver his bowl of stew, and then we will see what further use you will have. See that he desires you.''

''Yes, master,'' I whispered in answer, backing a step before turning from him and continuing on my way. The eyes of the silent, unmoving guardsmen followed me with their usual amusement, knowing I feared their ability to refuse me as greatly as I desired their use. I was a slave and was given no choice save to fear them and desire them, and this they knew as well.

Some distance down the hall, to the left, stood a wide door with three guardsmen before it. These guardsmen held more than a merely decorative post, therefore were they more alert than amused at my approach. After a moment I was allowed within the door, yet not before they had each of them touched me and spoken of having me serve them when their duty was done. I stood just within the chamber door after it had been closed behind me, trembling from the touch of those I had been made to desire so greatly, unhearing and unseeing in my misery till what occurred in the chamber intruded itself.

The chamber itself was large and well-appointed, with polished darkwood lining its walls, torches glowing brightly in its unwindowed dimensions, expensively woven carpeting covering portions of its marble floors, silk-covered furniture arranged here and there. In the very center of the chamber stood a large metal cage, and within the cage sat the one who was called the prisoner. Large was this man, larger than any guardsman of the palace, clad in the sort of mid-thigh-length tunic worn by them, yet in a blue rather than in guardsman red. Brown of hair and eye was he, and much did it seem that

he should also be clad in the golden armor and weaponry of
the guardsmen, yet he was not. About his wrists were wide
golden bands, much the same as those about my wrists
although larger, their presence proclaiming him slave as clearly
as mine proclaimed the same of me. About his throat was
another band of gold, a golden chain leading from it to
be bolted to the floor of his cage, and clearly had he been
well-beaten at the time of his capture. At the moment I
looked toward him he merely sat within the bars of confinement, yet the two slaves before his cage were not equally
silent.

". . . must say how pleasing it is to see a slave who is not
female, sister," said one, moving her body before the prisoner who stared wordlessly upon her. "And yet, what of the
service he must perform? How is he to please the guardsmen
he is given to?"

"The guardsmen will take pleasure from him in the only
way they might," said the second.

"Which is a great pity," said the first, raising her arms
behind her head so that her breasts might thrust out even
farther. "I am hot enough to serve a dozen men, yet must
look elsewhere for a man to pleasure. There are none here
save a *slave*."

Both then laughed in great delight at the manner in which
the prisoner snarled and attempted to reach through the bars
of his cage to them, for they stood well enough back that
they were beyond his reach. They stood a moment longer
laughing at his futile grasping before turning from him, gathered together the cloths and other cleaning things they had
used upon the chamber, then left through the door by which I
had entered. When I saw the door pulled to I looked again
upon the prisoner, and this time found his eyes upon me.

"Have you, too, come to torment me?" he demanded, the
chain leading to his throat taut from the kneeling position he

yet remained in. He crouched with one larger fist wrapped about a bar of his cage, and truly did he seem prepared to spring, as though he were some beast restrained against his bestiality.

"I have come only to bring you this stew," I replied, pacing forward slowly till I stood where the two slaves had stood. "Unlike others, I would not torment a slave like myself with that which he may not have."

"Then you are the sole denizen of this place who feels so," he growled in answer, his brown eyes hard upon me, and then he sat where previously he had crouched. "Bring the stew closer, girl. I will not pounce upon you and steal that which has been denied me."

"Were it possible for you to have me through those bars, there would be no question of theft to the matter," I said very softly, stepping forward to put the bowl in his reach. "As I am a slave, it would not be possible for me to refuse you."

"Surely a slave such as you is permitted to refuse a slave such as I have been declared," he said, taking the bowl through the bars though his eyes remained upon me. "Those two before you seemed to have little difficulty in merely flaunting themselves."

"They are cleaning and serving slaves," I said, settling to my heels beside the cage and lowering my eyes before his gaze. "They are prepared to a lesser extent than slaves such as I, who are meant for no other thing than to serve masters. With each master I serve my need to serve grows stronger, so that I am able to bring great pleasure to many men each day. I serve till I fall senseless from the effort, and while I lay senseless my body is tended. When I awaken with the morning sun, I am again prepared to serve."

"And again and again," he said, swallowing and chewing at the stew, though taking little notice of it. "You are set to giving service without end, and I am able to find no end to lack of service. We seem an oddly matched pair, you and I. For what reason have they had you bring me this sustenance?''

"I was to offer myself to you with the stew," I replied, my hushed voice refusing to remain tremorless, my eyes unable to rise above his wide, strong hands on the bowl. "I know not how you were to accept or reject the offer, but I was to cause you to desire me."

"You have succeeded," he said, putting aside the bowl he had emptied so quickly. "It seems to me, however, that you have not attempted my seduction with the ardor which was intended. I would know why you disobeyed—and what might become of you because of it."

"I cannot find it within me to—seek advantage over one who—is caught by the same bonds which hold me," I whispered, finding it impossible to quiet the turmoil which whirled me about. "When they learn I have disobeyed I will be punished, and yet—it will not be the first punishment I have been given."

"You sacrifice yourself for a stranger in need," he observed quietly, an odd tone to his voice. "There are few who would do such a thing for one unable to return the boon, yet you need not fear. You have succeeded in all you were sent to do, and that despite my own resolve to the contrary. You need not fear punishment."

I raised my eyes to his when his great hand came gently to my face—then gasped in startlement and backed to the bars of his cage when the chamber door was suddenly thrust open. The leader of fifty appeared with three guardsmen in his wake, and all strode insolently toward the cage of the prisoner.

"His Grace sends you greetings, Your Highness," said the leader of fifty when he stood no more than two paces before the cage, his eyes and tone as insolent as his stride had been. "Are your accommodations to your liking? Your meals adequately and artistically prepared? The needs of your body seen to by our slaves?''

''Most certainly, leader,'' replied the prisoner, his tone having turned to a drawl despite the sharp anger in his eyes. ''A cage is ever my first choice in accommodations, I rarely eat meat more often than once in two days, and I often go without tasting female delights which are presented me. Please convey to the Duke my thanks for his hospitality.''

''The Duke will be gladdened by the thanks of Prince Gamoy, youngest son of our lord King,'' said the leader, offering a mock bow to the prisoner. ''Perhaps Your Highness will consider granting the Duke an audience, during which time he might discuss certain pressing questions he would like to put to you.''

''I, too, have questions which are pressing,'' said the prisoner, his tone calm with the anger remaining beneath. ''For what reason have I been treated in this manner, and what has become of my men? For what reason were we fallen upon without warning at our appearance? For what conceivable reason . . .''

''Your Highness, please,'' interrupted the leader with one hand raised, this time taken with mock dismay. ''Did we not ask the reason for your presence before offering our hospitality? Did we not request the location of your father's forces with due courtesy? Did we not inquire politely concerning the thoughts of your father in connection with the Duke? What more would you have had of us?''

''I would have had belief concerning my replies,'' said the prisoner, his voice now cold as mountainous heights. ''My men and I sought temporary shelter after our hunting trip, I have never asked my father's thoughts upon the Duke, and our forces are deployed in whatever manner our generals have seen fit to deploy them. What occurs here in the Duke's realm, that he seeks so ardently to discover my father's thoughts and doings?''

''What occurs here or does not occur is none of your concern, Your Highness,'' returned the leader, his voice exquisitely polite despite the slapping insult of his words and the smirk of a smile he wore. ''I shall see to it that a truly adequate meal is brought you, and also offer you the immediate use of this slave. Too, new accommodations will be prepared, so that you may quickly be transferred to them.''

''In just so off-hand a manner?'' demanded the prisoner, his brown eyes narrowing. ''For no other reason than it now pleases you to provide such things?''

''Our reason for providing such things will be more than adequate, Your Highness,'' said the leader, his smirk somewhat widened. ''After you have filled your belly and filled this slave, you will speak a time with the Duke and give him the answers he requests from you. Should he be pleased with your answers, your new accommodations will be an apartment filled with all the slaves you care to demand. Should the Duke find himself disappointed with your replies, however, your new accommodations will be a cell in our dungeons, handily near the precincts of our torturer. The choice, of course, will be solely yours.''

Again a mock bow was sent toward the prisoner, and then the leader gestured to the guardsman who stood to his right. The guardsman came forward, dragged me to my feet by one arm, then took me to the side of the cage where another guardsman stood with a key in his hand. The key saw to the unlocking of the cage, I was thrust inside, and then the cage was relocked, which was the thing the leader had been awaiting. He turned without further word or look, led his three to the chamber door, and departed as quickly as he had come.

''Twisted tool of a twisted master!'' spat the prisoner in a low growl, his gaze hard upon the door which had given the

leader exit, his great hands closed into fists. His anger frightened me a good deal, causing me to stand trembling beside
the back wall of the cage, and then the prisoner's eyes came
to me. "Heard you the insolence of the fool?" he demanded,
turning somewhat toward me. "Are you able to credit such
ravings?"

"He spoke lies," I whispered, sinking to my knees,
trembling even more greatly. "No matter the words you give
the Duke, he will not release you. He has often boasted that
never has he released a slave already enslaved, and also that
never will he do so. You will be a slave for as long as you are
allowed to live."

"And such a fate disturbs you, I see," he said, for some
reason faintly amused at the observation. "I have been given
a slave whose loss I should not find myself able to countenance, and will therefore speak the words the Duke lusts
after, so they believe. My well known and more than often
propensity for fine foods and finer females is meant to coerce
me into complying with the wishes of my captors, and the
slave I am given speaks truth rather than flattering lies. Have
you no knowledge of who your masters are, slave?"

"My masters are yours, and this I do indeed regret deeply,"
I replied, lowering my gaze. "When free my position was not
yours, yet am I able to feel your loss as my own."

"A loss you may now in some degree assuage," he said
with great gentleness, causing me to look up again. "You
have been put in this cage to give me pleasure, therefore
would I have you come to me before you are again removed."

"You—wish me to serve you?" I whispered, disbelieving
the possibility that fate might have turned so kind. "You—
will not refuse me so that you might withstand their im-
portunities?"

"I am able to withstand a great deal when once I have had
my fill of pleasure." He laughed, raising gold-braceleted arms

to me. "Do you mean to force me to do no more than look upon you?"

From the moment I had first seen the prisoner, my desire for him had been great even above the forced urgings of my body. Gladly and willingly did I wish to give myself to him, and now he had indicated he desired me as well. I put my palms to the cold metal of the cage floor before my knees, crawled quickly to where he sat, then gasped with the heat rushing through me when he folded me in his arms. So broad was his chest, so strong his arms, so demanding his lips and caressing hands! I melted to him in complete helplessness, and his chuckle indicated he was well aware of my state.

"It has never before been my pleasure to have so hot a slave," he murmured after a time, holding me to his chest with one arm the while his free hand caressed my privacy with eager anticipation. "Am I now your master, slave?"

"We both of us serve the same master," I gasped out, attempting to touch him in every way I might. "I am the slave of another, yet I am yours to use in any manner you wish, a thing I give thanks for with every fiber of my being."

"And yet you will not see me as your master," he said, the amusement continuing. "You must be taught, I think, that to wear the golden bands of a slave does not make one a slave."

His touch upon me changed then, and so abruptly complete was his command over my womanhood that speech was lost to me, breath was lost, and nearly did consciousness join them. I had believed I knew the meaning of need earlier; the true meaning of the state was now brought home to me, and all save mewling proved beyond my ability. I clutched at the man who held me, my breasts pressed to the cloth covering his chest, my lips parted wide in disbelief, my eyes as wide and staring.

"I am the master of any woman I use, be she slave or

freed," he murmured, putting his lips to my hair. "Who is your master, pretty slave?"

"You, master, you, master!" I whispered helplessly, able to speak no other thing than the truth. "Please, master, have me now!"

"And so I shall," he said with a laugh, putting me to my back upon the cold metal of the cage floor. "See that you greet my entrance with proper abandon."

Had it been necessary to lie still or give up my life, I would not have survived the following moments. He entered me with a thrust of metal, and thereafter all thought and volition were lost to me. He used me till my own raging need was nearly gone, spent a short time rekindling it, then put me to my hands and knees. Just as he was again entering me a number of slaves arrived with many platters of food, yet he continued to use me despite their giggling amusement. That I was still unable to resist him amused them even more, for they were serving slaves and only prepared against the possibility of a master unexpectedly desiring them. I was made to serve completely and acknowledge the prisoner as my master, and when I was at last allowed to lie belly down at the end of the service, I knew I had once again spoken the truth. Never before had I been used as the prisoner had used me, and truly had it been fitting that I call him master.

The prisoner accepted the food brought him by taking it through the bars of his cage, and once the serving slaves had gone he insisted that I share the bounty given him. Half of the meat and vegetables and breads were eaten by him, and then the balance of the serving was given to me. It had been so long since the last time I had eaten such food that I was able to do no more than taste it, which the prisoner saw yet made no comment upon. When he was done with all he wished to eat he stretched hugely, then looked upon me with bright brown eyes.

"I have just proven to myself that a tasty wench is more toothsome than a tasty meal," he said, reaching forth to touch his palm to my face. "You are by far the best I have ever enjoyed, and I shall not allow you to stray from my side. Are you prepared for our escape?"

"Escape?" I echoed in shock, trembling more from the earlier words he had spoken. He would not allow me to stray from his side! Never had I expected to hear such a thing, and the thrill which coursed through me was nearly unbearable.

"Yes, escape," he agreed with a chuckle and a grin, reaching into his blue tunic from underneath. "They will soon come for me for that discussion with the Duke, and it would be wise to be gone before that even if it were not time for the thing according to my own schedule. Remain close behind me and make no sound, yet be prepared to aid me should I require your aid."

His hand then drew forth two keys from his tunic, keys which had been sewn beneath the cloth, keys which were clearly for the collar about his neck and the door of his cage. I watched in silence as he unlocked the collar and then moved to the door, keeping my questions unspoken as I had been bidden to do. Where could those keys have come from? What schedule might he be speaking of? And what aid might I conceivably be able to give such a man?

In another moment the cage door stood open and the prisoner was able to step out, therefore did I hurry to follow as I had been told to do. I surely expected him to move then to the door leading out into the hall, yet there was a smaller, less imposing door in the back of the chamber which immediately became his objective. He moved quickly and quietly to it, listened briefly, then turned to look down at me.

"There is supposed to be no more than a single guardsman beyond this door," he whispered very low, barely breathing the words. "The guardsman is also purportedly one who considers his own comfort and pleasure before duty. If you were to go out there and beg to serve him, he would soon be too deeply immersed to perceive my departure. Are you willing to aid me in such a manner?''

''I would aid you in whatever manner you required to effect your escape,'' I returned in a similar whisper, warmed beyond words that he had asked rather than command. ''Your freedom is as precious to me as it surely is to you.''

''I expected no other reply from you,'' he whispered again with a gentle smile, briefly touching my face. ''My freedom, however, will also mean the freedom of others as well. Take yourself through the door quickly now.''

I stepped to the door as rapidly as the urgency in his tone commanded, opened it, and slipped through, even more thrilled than I had earlier been. Freedom for others, he had said, when I had thought the priceless state forever beyond me. It was also my own freedom I strove for, and although I would have done the thing for him alone, the action now had other, fuller meaning.

Beyond the door, in a dim, narrow back hall, indeed stood only a single guardsman, the sole living thing to be seen even to the many cross-corridors visible. He turned quickly with hand to hilt when I emerged from the chamber, yet relaxed the pose and looked closely upon me when he saw I was no other thing than a slave.

''Master, I beg to serve you,'' I breathed, moving near to him so that I might look up into his eyes. ''I have served no more than four masters this day, and the prisoner will not have me. I am in very great need, and abjectly beg to serve you.''

''That fool in the cage refused to have you?'' the guardsman asked with brows raised in question, his light eyes scornful. ''Clearly he has lost either his sight or his manhood, and yet I must also refuse you. I am on duty, and may not now use a slave."

"Master, just a brief use, I beg you," I wheedled, touching his breastplate with my bare nipples. My flesh showed him clearly that I was indeed in need of use, a state the prisoner's use had intensified. "There are none about to see us, and none need know. I will give you pleasure the likes of which you have not often had. Please, master!"

"You beg with great attractiveness, young slave," he replied, his interest and amusement quite evident. "Perhaps a brief use, with none the wiser . . ."

"Oh, yes, master, thank you, master," I babbled, truly relieved that he would see to me. My need to serve had grown so great that it was well-nigh crippling, nearly overriding my true purpose in approaching him. I moved to the right of the door, to the nearest, darkened cross-corridor, half drawing him with me, half being eagerly followed.

Within the darkened corridor I was pulled roughly against the chestplate of the guardsman, a fist tightened in my hair, and then my lips were his, to be taken brutally and with much lust. I moaned at the delay forced upon me, causing him to laugh softly, and then I was turned with my back to him and thrown to my hands and knees. The prisoner had also used me in such a position, yet his use had brought pleasure to me as well as to himself. This guardsman began forcing himself into me in a manner which would bring release to him alone, and although I begged and pleaded in whispers, I was made to accept him and give him the pleasure he demanded. I sobbed soundlessly with the increase in need he brought me the while he laughed well at the jest he perpetrated, and when he was done I was made to reawaken him so that I, too, might be seen to. His use was jarring and brutal, completely selfish, and yet I wept in his arms and gave him unending thanks for the gift of his manhood.

When he was at last done with me, the guardsman returned
to his post the while I lay briefly upon the stone of the floor,
drinking in the sensation of satiety. Not long would the
sensation remain with me, most especially after all the use I
had had, and yet for the moment I felt replete. It came to me
then that I had heard no sound of departure from the chamber
in which the prisoner had stood, nor had the guardsman
raised a hue and cry. The prisoner had made good his escape
then, and would soon be returned to those who were not
enemy to him. The thought warmed me, and enabled me to
rise to my feet and accept the thought of my soon-to-return
need without tears.

The guardsman who had taken so great an amount of use
from me failed even to look upon me as I slunk past him,
seeking the cross corridor which would take me to the
guardsmen's barracks. In no more than half a dozen steps I
was again beset by need, one which would require a great
deal of seeing to till unconsciousness freed me from it. In the
barracks I would be allowed to give the service my preparation forced me to want desperately to give, and although the
pain would also come to me there, I could not refuse.

The third cross corridor led me to the main corridor, and
from there I hurried toward the guardsmen's barracks, the
eyes of those whose posts I passed following me with amusement. They knew well enough that I hurried to beg to serve
those who were off duty, and perhaps were remembering the
times I had served them as well. The thought upset me as
greatly as it ever did, and I hurried along with head down—
until the sounds of battle startled me out of miserable
self-contemplation.

The change from normal peace and silence to raging battle
occurred so quickly that I was not alone in startled disbelief.
Many of the guardsmen began shouting shocked demands,
yet the fighting had burned forward to include them before

any might speak answers to their demands. I trembled against one wall of the corridor, separated from the melee by the pillar I stood behind, shocked to see that the guardsmen battled other guardsmen like themselves, only ones in the colors of the King. Blue and silver fought red and gold, and although the shouting and clash of swords and screams of mortal fear were enough to deafen and daze, it soon became clear that the silver and blue was prevailing.

Nearly all of those in red and gold were either down or attempting to flee when a strong contingent of fresh red and gold guardsmen appeared, and these were led by the Duke himself. Their shouts of defiance and challenge drew back many of their fellows who had thought to flee in despair, and again the two forces came together in savage intent to wipe each other out. Through vision dampened by fear and tears I saw the prisoner, silver accoutrements glowing brightly, sword rising and falling without hesitation, forcing his way through the knots of battle toward the Duke. The leader of fifty appeared before him, engaged him with a sneer, then quickly fell before his superior skill. All about them other red and gold defenders were falling, unable to stand against the ravening silver and blue tide, and then the prisoner stood before the Duke. Less than a dozen strokes were exchanged before the Duke was disarmed, and then, with the prisoner's point at his enemy's throat, all those remaining of the red and gold were made to throw down their arms in surrender. The Duke himself was forced to his knees by those in blue and silver, and the prisoner looked down upon him with deep, cold anger.

"And so shall all traitors be dealt with," he said, with grim satisfaction. "I will know immediately the place of my brother's confinement, and you have only to pray that he has not been harmed. You were a fool to take him captive, for your machinations against our father the king were mere suspicion till then. Had you not acted the fool, you would undoubtedly still be free to plot your plots of futility. Where is he?''

''In my dungeons!'' snarled the Duke, fury and fear doing battle in his weak-featured face. ''Would that he were in the halls of hell, and you beside him!''

''You will soon have your own place there,'' said the prisoner in answer, and then he looked to one in blue and silver who stood beside him. ''Have the Duke lead you to the place where my brother is, and give him that place once my brother is freed. His journey to my father's justice may then be arranged at our leisure.''

''At once, my Prince,'' acknowledged the one in blue and silver, and then the Duke was dragged erect and forced up the corridor. His guardsmen were also forced in the same direction, and in a matter of moments only those in blue and silver remained to inhabit the corridor. The prisoner cleaned and resheathed his sword, ordered his guardsmen to posts along the corridor, then turned and came toward me. I had not thought he had seen me where I hid behind the pillar, yet he had done just that thing.

''Pretty slave, you remain unharmed,'' he said, delight in his tone and eyes as he looked down at me. ''I give thanks that this is so, for I have not been able to free my thoughts of you.''

''And I give thanks that your freedom has been restored to you,'' I replied, trembling as I looked up into the strong brown of his eyes. My body burned and screamed for easing, yet the guardsmen who would have seen to me were no longer able to take the use of a slave, and there was in truth only one who I then desired to serve.

''The need again burns within you,'' he said of a sudden, raising one palm to my breast. ''Undoubtedly due to the use you were given by the one who was to have guarded my avenue of escape. We will see to you at once, and then we must speak of the thing foremost in my mind.''

He took my arm and conducted me within one of the small, dimly lit easing rooms to be found behind the line of pillars, those rooms that were often used by guardsmen and slaves before the former stood to their posts. He put me gently to the furs before removing his sword and armor, and then he was upon and within me, giving me the vigor I had so great a need of. He used me and used me, seeing to a great need of his own, and when he finally withdrew I was once again sated and filled with deep happiness.

''And now we may talk,'' he said, lying beside me and looking down fondly at the foolish glow he must surely have been able to see upon me. ''I am free, my brother is free, and soon the Duke will be freed from the burden of his life. For the aid you gave me, the laws of my father prescribe freedom for you as well.''

Freedom! The thought filled me with such unbelieving joy that tears swam in my eyes, and I took the broad hand that touched my cheek and covered it with kisses.

''The thought of freedom pleases you,'' he said, and oddly enough a small portion of the warmth was gone from his tone. ''Should you ask for freedom you may have it, yet I would have you ask for another thing.''

I looked again to his face in confusion so vast my head whirled, unable to understand what words he spoke. Had he not said he would not allow me to leave his side? How might such a thing be if I were a slave?

''You must know that I have recently been married,'' he said, sending the pain of a sword through my heart. ''The nuptials were arranged between my father and hers, a king who has no sons of his own. At his death I will become king over his people, and my sons after me. His daughter the princess is exceedingly fair, yet I have already used her enough to know that she cannot satisfy me. She has refused to come to my bed more often than two or three times in each day, and calls my appetites unnatural. My appetites, I know, are greater than those of other men, yet I see nothing unnatural in them, merely I find difficulty in having them satisfied. You, pretty slave, are the first to satisfy those appetites with yourself alone."

I attempted to speak then, to remind him that the root of my great need lay in the preparation I was put through each morning, yet he halted my words with his palm to my mouth.

"Hush, child, I know what you would say," he scolded very gently, with just a hint of sternness. "You believe I desire you for the slave needs put upon you, and this is not so. The very sight of you sends flames all through me, so high that I have never known their like with any other woman. To see you is to want you, and I see you even when others stand before me in your place."

His hand left my mouth to caress my hair, and the smile he gave me healed the wound in my heart.

"I find I cannot countenance the thought of losing you," he said, bringing his other hand to my hair as well. "If you ask for freedom it will be given you, and yet you must know that I cannot keep a free woman beside me. If you remain a slave, *my* slave, your place will be in my apartments in the palace I share with my lady wife, and none will even consider commenting upon the matter. The preparation given you each morning will be less harsh than that given you now, only enough to see that you are able to serve me without difficulty, and freedom will be yours in all other things. You will need to serve only myself—and perhaps a friend or two with whom I share all things—and my brothers, of course, when they visit—and in such a way we may share our lives and the love we feel. I wish only to have you as my own, yet the decision must come from you. I love you; will you pledge yourself as slave to me?"

I stared at him in speechlessness, achingly torn, horribly uncertain. His hands caressed my hair and face, his lips touched me lightly and lovingly, and I was painfully indecisive. He felt the same love for me that I felt for him; never had I expected to find such a man, and he would be my love and my life—if I were to pledge myself slave to him. My desire for him was so great that I trembled between his hands, burning from the already-returning needs of my body, the tears flowing from my eyes in a stream of pain. I had to have him, I would die if I could not have him, and yet—

"I cannot," I whispered, the words torn from my flesh as though by the teeth of a predator. "My freedom was taken—never would I have given it up of myself. I love you—yet freedom is as precious as life itself. I would give my life for you—but to face forever as a slave—!"

"As *my* slave, beloved," he murmured, lowering one hand to caress me where he had already proven himself my master. "Freedom is such a foolish, little thing to stand between us, so pitifully useless a thing to choose over our love. Already I feel as though I could taste you again, and the need rises within you as well. Make the proper choice and we may love again, dearest slave child, tell me you will be mine."

"No," I wept, closing my eyes against the command in his gaze, the demand in his fingers, the weakness of my flesh. I wanted so much to make us one, and yet— "No," I sobbed, and the words grew louder and louder. "No, no, no, no, no, no. . . !"

"No!" I screamed, fighting against the straps holding my wrists down, so sick to my stomach I thought I would mess all over myself. "No, stop it, no!"

"Calm down, Jennifer, it's all over," a soothing voice

came immediately from right next to my ear while hands smoothed down my sweat-soaked hair. "Just take it easy."

"What's wrong with her?" a voice demanded, a voice that was close to outrage. "What the hell did you two do to her?"

"We proved you can scratch her from the possible slave list," another voice said, a third voice. "No matter how high her rating in sensuality is, there isn't anything about slavery that turns her on. If we hadn't been stimulating her artificially all during the situational, she would have turned off and stayed that way. Even the ultimate force play didn't budge her, and not many female types turn thumbs down on that, I can tell you."

"What ultimate force play?" the second voice demanded again, but less belligerently. "What kind of a situational did you put her in?"

"You heard me setting the stage for her," the other voice answered. "She found herself a slave in a palace, a slave whose main function was to give use to the men of that palace. She had no hope for freedom until she was given to a captive prince, who used her and talked to her, then decided he wanted her permanently. She had already fallen in love with him, and when he had broken free and brought his fighters back to take over the palace, he told her that he wanted her."

"Then why did she get so wild?" the other voice asked, sounding confused. "If she loved him, why wasn't she jumping for joy?"

"Because he told her wanted her as a slave," the answer came. "He told her he loved her, that she was entitled to be freed, but he wanted her to choose to be his slave. She was as much in love with him as it's possible to be—but she still refused to be his slave."

"I see," the other voice said, sounding impressed. "You set her up to be crazy about him, and then he asks her to be his slave. If I'd had a chance to put money on it, I would have bet on her going along with anything he asked.''

"Most of them do," was the agreement. "The only usual exceptions are women who've had men lie to them in the past, but she should be too young to have that in her background. As pretty as she is, though, she must have had it handed to her a couple of times even before other girls knew what men were all about. Give me a hand, will you? We've got to bring her all the way out of it.''

"Sure," the other voice answered, and then there were tugs on the straps around my wrists. I didn't know what was happening, but I did know I couldn't do as he'd asked. I wouldn't do as he'd asked, and I kept shaking my head and saying so.

"Come on, Jennifer, and sit up now," another soothing voice said in my ear, the voice that had done the explaining to the other voice. "It's all over and you're fine, but you have to sit up now and open your eyes.''

I let the hands help me into sitting, then opened my eyes to find a dimmer light all around. I blinked, still shaking my head a little, and then I saw him. Brown-haired and brown-eyed, seriously concerned, he stared at me the way he'd been doing earlier, and the trembling came back and brought tears to my eyes.

"No," I whispered, cringing back against the other arms supporting me, trying to escape his stare. "Please, I can't, don't you understand that? I can't.''

"Jennifer, what's the matter?" he asked, frowning as he stepped closer and put a hand out to me. "Why are you crying?''

"Don't touch me!" I begged, shivering and edging back even farther. "You're just like all the rest, not giving a damn about me, just what you can get out of me! Leave me alone, do you hear me, just leave me alone!''

"What the hell is going on here?" a new voice demanded as *he* frowned more deeply and reached out again to touch me. He and the others all turned fast to the new voice, and the man left the doorway to move farther into the light. He was very big, black-haired and black-eyed, and so angry he looked just about ready to strike out at everyone in reach.

"Who the hell are *you*?" one of the blond men demanded in turn, the one standing near a bank of machinery. "Who told you you could come in here?"

"I'm Valdon Carter, and I don't need anyone to tell me anything," the big man came back, the words coming out almost in a growl. "What are you doing to my niece?"

"We're appraising her," the same blond man said, a faint tremor now audible in his voice. "If you're her uncle you're the one who asked for it, so what are you complaining about?"

"I'm complaining about the fact that nobody mentioned she'd be terror-stricken," the big man said in the same near-growl, sending his hard, black-eyed stare from one man to the next until he saw *him*. "And what the hell is *he* doing here? Is he supposed to be a regular member of your appraisal team?"

"No, he's not a regular member of our team," the blond man holding me said when the other remained silent. "But he *is* a high-ranking member of the middle-Management, and therefore is entitled to . . ."

"Nothing," the big man interrupted in a very flat voice, his eyes still on *him*. "I don't care how big a wheel he is, when it comes to my niece he has no right to anything, and especially not to horning in where he doesn't belong. Get a blanket."

"But she's not all the way out of it yet," the man holding me protested. "You can't just. . . ."

"Get a blanket!" the big man interrupted again, his voice

growing even colder. "She's my niece, and I can 'just' do anything I damned well please. Now, move!"

"Just calm down, Mr. Carter," *he* said in a smooth, persuasive voice as the blond man near the machinery hesitated very briefly then bent to a nearby cabinet. "If you didn't know what appraisal entailed, you shouldn't have asked to have your niece put through it. Any of our staff could have told you what was involved, but you don't seem to have made the effort to find out. Now you're angry and looking for someone to take it out on, but it seems to me . . ."

"You seem to think I'm interested in your opinion, Mr. Rich," the big man cut in again, his tone unchanged, his eyes even colder. "Unlike those you seem to be used to dealing with, I find nothing about you of interest. From now on, stay away from my niece."

He took the blanket the blond man was holding out to him, opened it as he came toward me, then put it around me. I was still trembling and crying and wasn't sure if I could trust him, but there had been a shadow in the back of the room that wasn't there any longer, and I seemed to have some sort of memory of the black-haired man from somewhere that was a good-feeling memory. When he wrapped me in the blanket and lifted me off the table into his arms I put my own arms tight around his neck and my head to his shoulder, and his hold on me tightened in a comforting way. Without another word he turned and took me out of that place, and I felt so safe that before we had gone more than a dozen steps I was already asleep.

CHAPTER 11

"Of all the stupid, bird-brained, *mindless* things to do, that has to be the prize-winner!" I snarled in the trade language, glaring at my so-called partner. "How could you do it?"

"It was easy," he answered mildly, popping another grape into his mouth, his feet comfortably propped up on the table in front of his chair. "I didn't like that appraisal idea to begin with, and when time passed and you didn't show up, I decided to do a little investigating. I'm still attuned to you, so finding where they had you wasn't hard, and neither was getting you out. I thought you said there would be nothing to it. What I walked in on didn't look like nothing. What did they do to you?"

His voice had grown harder by the time he got to his question and those dark black eyes were on me, no longer mild. I knew most of the growl inside him wasn't for me, but it still made me uncomfortable.

"Never mind what *they* did," I came back, shifting around on the wide, beautiful bed I sat in. "Let's talk about what *you* did. You blew your characterization, and there's no way

to unblow it. How does it feel to screw up the very first
assignment you're given?''

"I didn't screw anything up," he answered with a
headshake, the least bit annoyed. "I'm the only one who has
the right to mistreat my niece, and I let them know it. There
was nothing more to it than that."

"Nothing more to it?" I almost screeched, seriously considering the idea of killing him. "You practically offered
Greg Rich his choice of weapons! Or if not with weapons,
barehanded with no holds barred! That's your idea of nothing?"

"I don't like the man," he said with a grimace, taking his
feet down so he could stand and come over to sit next to me
on the bed. "Why were you cowering away from him when I
came in? What did he do to you?"

"*He* didn't do anything," I answered with a grimace like
the one he'd shown, deciding to get his morbid curiosity
satisfied. "I wasn't supposed to be able to remember anything that happened, but despite the heavy jolt of trystisil, I
still have it all. It didn't mean much until I came out of the
fog completely a little while ago, but I do remember it. My
best guess is that Greg threw his weight around a little too
hard with one of those techs, the one standing near the master
board, the one named Gil. Gil got huffy, then apparently
decided to get even with Greg by making him the model for
the main male role in the situational they set me into. When I
opened my eyes and saw Greg, all I could understand was
that he was still after me to make the decision he wanted. I
didn't know how long I could hold out against him if he kept
at me, so I was terrified."

I couldn't stop shuddering then, or raging in anger at how
terribly that slave I'd been had been taken advantage of. I
could still feel the echoes of the love I'd felt for that prisoner,
that slime who would ask a woman in love with him to give
up something more precious than life to accommodate his

convenience. I felt horribly betrayed, and knowing it hadn't been real did nothing to ease the feeling. And I also remembered something else that doubled the shudder.

"What was he after you for?" Val asked, his hand on my shoulder very gentle despite the too-soft tone in his voice. I looked up to see his eyes, and couldn't understand the expression in them.

"We have something to think about more important than that," I told him. "Before Greg got there I had another visitor, one who showed up right after the trystisil got its claws in me, someone who must have been sent for. He was there right in front of me, Val, and I couldn't move."

"Not—" Val began, and then his hand was tightening on my shoulder. "What was he doing here? And what did he do to you?"

"He didn't have a chance to do much of anything," I answered, noticing that my own hands were not quite as steady as I'd thought they were. "What he would have done is another story, but Greg barged in and broke up the party. As for what he was doing here, that's obvious: your good buddy called him."

"But why?" Val demanded. "Why would he call him? What kind of twisted game are they playing?"

"I wish I knew," I said with a sigh, stirring uncomfortably in the tightened grip on my shoulder, an action which at least made him ease up a little. "Whatever it is, we'll have to keep going along with it until I can face that garbage without any trystisil in me. Maybe we'll get lucky and find out he's still here."

"I'd be willing to bet against it," Val said with suddenly deeper vexation, his expression telling me he'd had an unpleasant memory. "When I was on my way to that place to find you, some sort of flying vehicle passed overhead, making everyone around me look up. One woman wondered aloud who the VIP was; as far as she knew, flying vehicles aren't allowed in this area. The man with her said it didn't much matter who it was; the thing was leaving, not coming in for a landing. If that wasn't our target, the coincidence would be too much.''

"And if flying vehicles aren't allowed, then we can't follow as fast as he can lead," I summed up, folding my legs in front of me with a growl of frustration. "After being that close—! All we can do now is keep going with your friend. I don't have to wonder if he got whatever approval he was looking for; if he's still hanging around, it's only because another meeting's been scheduled."

"As long as *I'm* there next time," Val said, his eyes directly on me again. "And speaking of meetings, you still haven't told me what Rich was after you for."

"Val, I told you it wasn't him," I said with as much exasperation as I felt, suddenly aware again of the hand on my shoulder. "What's more to the point is that your denying it doesn't change the fact that you *did* blow your role. You weren't supposed to care about me; barging in and dragging me out of there, especially the way you did it, was completely out of character. If you care enough about someone to challenge Sphere officials for them, you don't sell them to the highest bidder—which is what you're supposedly up to with me, remember?"

"Well, I can always say I changed my mind." He shrugged. "Since I can see I'd better keep a closer eye on you, I can claim I didn't realize what good stuff I had right in front of me until that Rich character tried moving in on it. If I turn out to be lecherous instead of weak-willed, who'll know the difference?"

"I'll know," I told him in sub-zero tones, reaching up to purposely and finally move his hand from my shoulder. "Let's try saying instead that you didn't want your merchan-

dise damaged before you could turn it over, and you were
afraid Greg Rich would swing a deal before you could. And I
want this feud between the two of you stopped right now."

"No problem in that." He shrugged again, looking at me in
that strange way a second time. "As long as he stays away
from you the way I told him to, there won't be any call for
feuding."

"Now, look, Val," I began, really getting hot. "You can't
just . . ."

"But I *can* just," he interrupted, pointing a finger at me.
"You seem to have forgotten that it's *uncle* Val, and that
what I say goes. From what I've seen of this place so
far—not to mention the sort of visitors you get—you'll have
enough problems doing what you have to without getting any
further involved with someone like Rich. You'll stop encouraging him, and he'll stop coming around."

"Encouraging him?" I choked, absolutely furious. "What
do you mean, encouraging him? And you can't just brush him
off and expect him to stay brushed off! He's a . . ."

"I don't care what he is," my sweet partner interrupted
again, that "no" clear in his eyes. "You're all finished
playing around with him. It's almost time for us to be moving
on, so you'd better get up and get dressed."

"Now, you wait just a minute!" I growled, but I was
already talking to his back. He had gotten up from the bed
and was heading toward the door outside, and then the door
was closing behind him.

I sat for a minute just staring at that closed door in disbelief,
then sank back down against the pillows. I was more than
willing to believe I was still dreaming, but things like that
didn't happen in dreams, only in nightmares. My brand-new,
totally inexperienced partner had not only just ignored a
direct order from the assignment leader, he had also turned
around and issued an order of his own that he intended seeing

obeyed! It looked like being in a position to run things had
gone to Val's head even above the point of getting even; he
was really beginning to believe he could tell me what to do! I
had no intentions of listening to him, of course, even if it
were my choice about whether or not to see Greg again, but
his attitude was more than a pain. Sure as sin, there would be
more trouble over it than he was anticipating.

The room I sat in was pretty, but my mind jumped back to
Radman again, so I took Val's "suggestion" and got up to
get dressed. In the middle of all the melon ruffles and lace
was my luggage, since that was the room I'd been assigned to
for the post-physical-exam period. Val had brought me there
and put me into the bed, and I'd slept until only a few
minutes earlier, when my system had finally been able to
break loose from the trystisil. On top of the single, small
trunk I'd brought from the Station lay a squarish brown dress
with fluffs and a full skirt, obviously another "suggestion"
from my "uncle." He'd been wearing white slacks and a
lemon-yellow shirt, but he wanted me, completely covered
and in a dark, sweaty dress at that. I threw the thing onto the
floor and opened the trunk, then pulled out a white shorts
outfit I'd brought along, something of *mine* that any female
of any age could wear, provided she had the figure for it.
Once I had the outfit on my figure and had added white deck
shoes, I repacked the brown monstrosity and reset the trunk
lock before closing it up again. Giving Val access to my
wardrobe had been a mistake, but at least it was partly
correctable.

Val was outside waiting for me, but not directly outside the
door. The room I left was one of a string that circled an
umbrellaed lounge area, and Val was at a table with John
Little, the two of them sipping something tall and cool. When
I walked up to their table and took the third chair, Val's eyes
stayed on me until I was seated.

"That isn't what I took out for you to wear," he commented after a long minute, his tone unexpectedly unargumentative. "Didn't you like my choice?"

"As a matter of fact, I didn't," I answered with restrained surprise, only glancing at the naked servant who was putting a glass of tall and cool whatever in front of me. "It's much too hot here for a dress like that."

"Too hot for a summer dress," Val answered with a small smile, glancing at Little as if he were sharing an inside joke, and then he showed a faint grin. "Well, it so happens *I* prefer your choice, too. I like the way you say, 'thank you for saving me.' "

"You expect me to thank you for pulling me out of something you got me into in the first place?" I asked with all the sarcasm I was capable of, just short of laughing in his face. "If you do, you're dreaming. I didn't put this outfit on for *you*."

" 'Methinks the lady doth protest too much'," Little quoted as he sipped at his drink, the amusement still in his eyes. "Appraisal bares one's true nature, Jenny, and I saw the way you were holding your uncle around when he carried you away from it. Are you sure you aren't the least bit curious as to what it would be like to go through the Sphere partnered with him? You've learned what other men are capable of; are you sure you don't want to know what *he* can do? And are you completely sure you don't secretly *like* what he's *been* doing to you?"

I stared at Little open-mouthed, finally understanding the line Val must have handed Radman's assistant. My "uncle," after finally noticing the largesse under his nose for so long, had also discovered that his little niece had a crush on him. She wasn't about to admit that crush, of course, but why shouldn't he use their presence on Xanadu to take advantage of the situation? It had to be something like that for Little to

get such a kick out of it, but there was no reason for me to go
along with it.

"You're both crazy for even suggesting something like
that," I told them, getting stiffly to my feet. "If you think
I'm going to stay here and listen to any more of it,
you're . . ."

"Jennifer," Val interrupted, his voice low but his tone
somewhat—implacable. "Sit down and drink your drink, and
behave yourself. You're not going anywhere until departure
time, and then you'll be going with us. If you try disobeying
me, I'll punish you."

Those black eyes stared up at me, telling me I had no
choice, telling me his threat wasn't simply window-dressing.
He'd told Little I secretly enjoyed being roughed up by him,
and to prove the point he'd do whatever he had to in the way
of "punishing." Come hell or high water he'd go with his
own decision, and I didn't have to wonder what his "punishment" would consist of; he got his own back from females in
only one way, and there was nothing I could do to stop him
or escape him. I was a minor, he was my legal guardian, and
I couldn't even simply pick up and walk away. I now had a
reason for going along with him, but once that assignment
was over . . . I sat down again without a word, letting
him see the fury in my eyes, but all that did was make him and
his friend chuckle again.

"Quite a decision, wasn't it, Jenny?" Little drawled, leaning back from the table to let me see more easily the ridicule
in his eyes. "But have no fear, my girl. I'm sure your uncle
will find any number of opportunities to punish you in the
following days. You haven't really lost out on anything that
would give you pleasure."

I couldn't help giving him an infuriated glance, which
amused him even more. Val was amused too, but for entirely

different reasons. I wasn't amused at all, but nobody gave a damn.

After a short wait we three and the other people around us were led to large, sybaritically furnished barges, the sort with wide, soft cushions, striped awnings, and naked slaves with feather fans almost as tall as they were. Drinks were again available, soft, cool, alcoholic, or any combination of the above, along with snacks, cakes, ices, fruits, breads, you name it. Soft music came from four naked slave musicians, and everyone seemed delighted with the arrangements—again with one exception. When I picked a large, blue cushion to lie down on, I didn't get to do more than make myself comfortable under the awning before I had company on the cushion. Val lay down behind me and put an arm around my waist, and I wasn't permitted to either push the arm away or squirm loose from the spread-fingered hold. I was laughingly ordered to lie still and enjoy the cool breeze playing around us, but what I really did was make sure my eyes would be wide open for an opportunity to leave Val behind. He'd shown me the benefits in working with a partner, all right, which underlined my wisdom in usually working alone.

The barges took us across the lake to the opposite side we'd started from, then went downcurrent a considerable distance until they reached a long, festively decorated docking. The weather continued beautiful and the crowd continued happy, but everyone was more than simply happy. The drinks had been subtly added to again, and no one was finding fault or feeling bored with anything, especially with the extra slaves sent out to meet us. Laughing, naked females surrounded the men and their grinning male equivalents appeared around the women, and that way we were separated and led to individual pavilions.

At first Val had been reluctant to be separated from me, but whatever had been in our drinks convinced him quickly enough that the female slaves were worth his attention for a while. Little had been led away by a couple of pretty boys, and an interesting all-male specimen had attached himself to me, taking my hand to direct me while his eyes moved over every inch of me. I discovered I didn't mind his attaching himself to me in the least, and by that understood the drug had a tenuous hold on me as well. As long as I was aware of it and therefore had the option of going along with it or not, there was nothing to get excited about, but I couldn't help wondering what the drug was and what purpose it had. If it was reaching me it had to be powerful, and I didn't think the Management would use something that powerful just to turn their clients happy.

The pavilion I was led to was powder blue and white, large and square and deliciously secret-looking, as though all sorts of forbidden pleasures might be found in it. I knew that strange an idea had to be caused by the drug working on me, and the first words spoken to me by the slave holding my hand confirmed the guess and added to it.

"Inside these cloth walls I'm yours completely, mistress," he murmured, his light eyes looking down at me as he held aside the cloth draping the entrance. "I'll do whatever you order me to do, give you pleasure or take it from you, anything you like. All you have to do is command me."

I walked past him into the pavilion without answering, in the process pulling my hand loose from his, most of my attention on the room I entered. Blue and white silks hung on the walls, white furs lay scattered on the floor with blue cushions, and the other rooms of the pavilion were closed off from that one by more drapes. Pleasantly low lighting came from some invisible source, the air was cool and comfortable as though conditioned, and small tables of dark wood held wine flasks and glasses and small assortments of food to be nibbled on. I heard the naked male slave enter the pavilion behind me and resettle the drape over the entrance, making the room complete in its attractiveness, but I was beginning to feel an impatience that the drug couldn't overcome. Fun is fun, but all that messing around wasn't doing a damned thing to bring me closer to Radman.

"How long do we stay in *this* place?" I asked the slave without turning to face him, wondering if I could justify taking the chance of grabbing Little and drugging him. He had to know where Radman was, and if I could get the location out of him I could see about moving on ahead of this group inching its way into the Sphere. The sooner that assignment was over the sooner I could get back to a normal life—and *away* from slaves anxious to please.

"If you're really as bored as you sound, I must be losing my appeal," another voice answered for the slave, an amused voice I recognized. "Don't tell me you're going into tri-v withdrawal?"

The voice was Greg Rich's, and I turned slowly to see the Management rep standing just beyond a draping to the right. He had to have been waiting in another room of the pavilion, and had shown himself only after I had entered. The male slave who had led me there was on his knees with head bowed, a definite nervousness and purposefully obvious subservience in his manner due to the presence of one of his true masters. The sight of his slavish posture sickened me, but I didn't realize how much of my opinion was visible until the amusement left Greg's face.

"You really *don't* like slaves, do you?" he asked, true puzzlement in the question. "Most people jump at the chance to lord it over them, taking to slave-enjoyment the way they take to breathing pure, sweet air. What makes you dislike it so?"

"I suppose I have a better imagination than other people," I answered with only a brief hesitation. "I'd hate being a slave, so I don't like seeing people who *are* slaves. What are you doing here?''

"You mean, after I was ordered to stay away from you?'' he asked, again amused. "It so happens *I* wouldn't make much of a slave either, especially when it comes to taking orders. And I wanted to find out if you were all right.''

"Why shouldn't I be all right?'' I asked, suddenly finding the pavilion too airless and enclosed. "Uncle Val yelled at me about not seeing you again, but he didn't do anything beyond yelling. Why should anything be wrong?''

"Jennifer, I can't tell you what happened, but take my word that something *is* wrong,'' he answered soberly, beginning to move slowly toward me. "A louse named Gil tried to ruin things between us, and don't think I haven't reported him for it, but—that doesn't change what he did. Even if you don't remember what happened, I'd like a chance to make it up to you. Will you give me that chance?''

"I don't know what you're talking about,'' I answered, finding that I had to turn away from his brown-eyed stare. I wasn't supposed to remember anything that had happened while I had been under the influence of the trystisil, but feeling uneasy in his presence without knowing why was only to be expected. The fact that I *did* remember, all of it, was giving me something of a hard time, and I had to see if I could get rid of him.

"I'm talking about the fact that part of you believes I want you as a slave,'' he said from right behind me, and his voice had softened. "You don't need to know *why* you believe that, but I give you my word it isn't so. I *don't* want you as a slave, Jennifer—but I do want you.''

"Greg, please give me a little time alone to think about this,'' I began, the palms of my hands moist, my eyes locked to the blue and white silks on the pavilion wall in front of me, my fingers uselessly pulling at one another. Having him around was dangerous in more ways than one, and if I could get him to walk away, even temporarily . . .

"Time spent alone won't do it, Jennifer," he denied immediately, and then his palms were stroking my bare arms. "If I don't show you how wrong you are right now, there will never be a later. Don't you want there to be a later—as well as a right now?"

I discovered that my eyes had closed at the first touch of his hands, and my heart was pounding so hard the slave must have heard it on the other side of the pavilion. I *did* remember the appraisal, all of it, including how much in love I had been with Greg in the situational. Telling myself the love wasn't real didn't help; no love was real or lasted very long, but that didn't stop it from tearing you up inside for as long as it held on. I didn't want to go through that again, I *didn't*, but he had said he didn't want me as a slave, and then his hands were turning me around so that his arms could hold me, and it felt so good I nearly moaned with the pain. I might have been able to control myself if not for the latest drug I'd been fed, but with that pulling at my strings of judgment, all I could do was let my own arms steal around him.

"That's much better," he said with a chuckle, letting his hands move all over the back of me. "I was regretting the time together we were done out of earlier, but I think it may well prove for the best after all. I think you're more ready for me now than you were then."

Ready was too pale a word for what I was feeling, and even though I struggled against it, I couldn't make it stop. He removed my arms from around his waist and picked me up, chuckling again when I transferred my hold to around his neck, then carried me back toward the room he'd come out of.

"Bring two glasses of wine," he told the slave as we passed him, and then we were behind the draping and into the

other room. Done all in silver and gray, it was the most
sensually obvious bedroom I'd ever seen. The bed was a low,
wide square right in the center of the room, the light was
flickering candlelight, and the mirrors threw back numberless
images at us amidst the fur and silk decorations. Greg wasn't
carrying me quite as easily as Val did, but he still managed to
get us to the barely raised platform that was the bed and put
us both down on it.

It was no more than a minute's work getting me out of my
shorts outfit and deck shoes, so I was as naked as the slave
when he brought the wine Greg had asked for. Greg was just
stripping down to his shorts when the slave appeared next to
the bed, but all he did was throw him a glance while he
stripped the rest of the way. I lay flat on my back in the
middle of the silver fur that was the bed's cover, so badly in
need I couldn't keep from moving around, but some small
part of me still remembered the role I was supposed to be
playing.

"Greg, send him away," I asked, looking up at the light
eyes staring down at me. "You know I don't like to be
watched like that."

"Jennifer, you've got to get over those provincial atti-
tudes," I was informed with a grin that brought a faint smile
to the slave as well, and then Greg was lying beside me, to
my left, no longer hampered by clothing. "What harm does
being watched do you?"

"I just don't like it," I answered lamely, glancing again at
the smiling slave before turning on my side to Greg. "I
thought you were anxious to make love to me."

"I am," he answered with a wider grin, then slid a hand
between my thighs so fast that I gasped and tried to push it
away. "And you, it seems, are anxious to have me make love
to you. Does it bother you so much to be watched that you'd
refuse to let me touch you if the slave stayed?"

"Greg, please!" I whispered, growing even more frantic as the flames began roaring high and consuming me. "Please send him away!"

"But, Jennifer, what will we do without wine?" he murmured, lowering his head to my breast. I was already so far gone that that nearly finished me, and with a sob I threw my arms around him, begging for what I needed so desperately, not giving a damn if the entire planet was watching. Greg laughed and took me in his arms, and the flames rose up to claim us both. It was somehow not quite long enough before it was over, but by then the slave was gone. Greg lay beside me sipping from the glass he'd been given while I tried to push aside wide, unformed thoughts of vague dissatisfaction, and he smiled when my eyes finally came to his face.

"You were better than ever, sweetheart," he assured me, reaching above my head to retrieve the other glass of wine from where it stood on the floor. "Being watched wasn't quite as terrible as you thought it would be, was it?"

"No," I conceded in a small voice, making sure I blushed a little and looked briefly away from him. The slave had stayed through the entire performance, getting a lot of fun out of watching what Greg had done to me. I was really raw over being put on display like that, but I found myself wanting to blame the slave instead of Greg. Love, even artificial love, tends to turn people stupid, but I wasn't so stupid that I didn't refuse the wine with a shake of my head. If I gave the drug a chance to flush out of my system, I might be able to do something about the rest of it.

"Now that you know there's nothing wrong with watching, maybe you'd like to do a little of it," he said, returning the glass I'd refused before sipping at his own. "I owe your uncle a little something, and tonight would be the perfect time to pay up on it. If you like, you can join me."

"What do you intend doing to him?" I asked, suddenly

more alert than I had been. I attended only to Greg, but I couldn't let him hurt Val.

"I intend doctoring the placement testing he'll be going through tonight," Greg answered, his chuckle somewhat on the rough side. "Everyone coming into the Sphere gets filtered through this placement camp, the night's stopover being used to find out what they really want. They're drugged and then put through a series of experiences, and the drug makes them react honestly. Some women talk endlessly about equality and superiority, demanding their rights to do as they please, but what they really want is to be captured and enslaved and raped without mercy. Some men shout about how strong men have to be, how they can never let women get the upper hand, but they'd love to be shouted down, whipped hard and long, and then be made to kiss a woman's feet. After the testing we know what direction to send them in, and that way they get the most out of their visit and usually decide to come back again. Somehow, I doubt your uncle will want to come back again."

"But what are you going to do to him?" I insisted, getting up on one elbow to look at him more directly.

"I told you, I'm going to change his testing experiences," Greg said with more of a grin, reaching over to touch a finger to the tip of my breast. "In the routine sequence he would start out being captured and enslaved by a female, would be given the chance to escape and take the female captive in turn, and then, if the second part of the sequence was completed, be given the chance to free the female and share pleasure with her without forcing it on her or having it forced on him. Some people get the most pleasure out of sharing instead of taking or being forced to give, and we take that into account, but there are other things to be taken into account as well. Different people have different tastes, and we have sequences to cover it all, but those sequences can be modified. What do you think would happen if your uncle was 'accidently' put through the forced slave sequence alone, for example?''

"He'd really flip out," I answered slowly, finding something ugly in his grin of delight. "But what will happen if he complains? If he gets put through something like that he'll know it was you, and he might complain."

"I've already thought of that," he said with even more of a grin. "If his complaint was passed on I'd really be in it, but I've already seen to it that it won't be passed on. And tomorrow, once he comes out of it, I'll let him know that there have been occasions when guests have had terrible accidents or have disappeared entirely. It usually turned out that rogue slaves were responsible for those awful happenings and the slaves were tracked down and then harshly punished, but the punishment came too late to be of any help to the unfortunate victims. I think he'll be smart enough to take the hint and let it lie after that, not to mention keeping his hands off what other people have expressed an interest in. But enough about him; let's talk about the zone I'm going to be taking you through.''

He began describing something called the orange zone then, a place that appeared to be one non-stop party, but I was listening with only partial attention. I didn't like the sound of what he intended doing to Val, but I couldn't very well say so, and as long as his plans didn't include anything really harmful I'd have to go along with them. I didn't want to believe Greg would hurt Val, and after a couple of minutes I'd convinced myself he was only looking to even the score a little. That made me feel considerably better, so much better that I could listen to his descriptions of what we'd be doing together with as much anticipatory eagerness as he was showing. After that he put his glass aside and took me in his arms again, and the way I felt almost made his lovemaking something I'd been looking for all my life—if it had been more satisfying. For some reason the inner me was expecting more from him, and when it didn't come it was more than disappointing.

We stopped for a quick snack before getting dressed, then left the pavilion in the slave's keeping and went outside. It wasn't long past sundown but the camp was oddly quiet, as though everyone had turned in early to get a good night's sleep. Greg put his arm around me against the cool of the night, and led the way through and around the silent pavilions to a pavilion that was four times the size of the others, was colored in what the lights around it showed to be lilac and black, and which had two men in Sphere uniform standing in front of it. The two men nodded to Greg as they stepped aside, and we went on in through the hanging drape.

Inside was brisk efficiency, with the entire interior partitioned off into small cubicles which held very sophisticated equipment, people either sitting in front of that equipment or hurrying from place to place. Our destination lay at the back of the pavilion, which we reached by moving along the aisle stretching between the cubicles, no one paying any particular attention to us until we got to where we were going. Inside that cubicle the man at the equipment looked up, then flashed Greg a quick grin.

"You're in time to watch the last of his fun," the man said, gesturing toward the screen in front of him. "He's as high as a kite, and has been going through those slaves like a bull through a herd of cows. It's too bad you missed the rest of his performance. I've picked up more pointers than I knew there were."

"Never mind how good you think he is," Greg said with a snort of dismissal, not even glancing at the screen. "I've got something to change in this program, and I want you to set it up now. When the projectors go on, I want it all ready."

The man at the screen raised his eyebrows, but still got up and went to a different piece of equipment with Greg, and began listening to Greg's low-voiced explanation. Since I knew what he was talking about I could afford to let my attention wander, and where it wandered was to the screen. The picture was somewhat small but extremely sharp, and what it showed was something I'd never seen unemotionally before: my partner using his talents on a woman. Right then the woman under him was crying out hysterically, but with pleasure rather than fear or pain. He rode her like a master equestrian, his grip gentle but unbreakable, his assurance complete, his ability at pace-changing demonstrated without effort. The woman screamed and then wept, helpless to do anything but give him his due, helpless to do anything but continue on at his command. She looked as played out as the two others who lay limp in pick-up range, but the man who had made them that way wasn't yet through taking his pleasure.

I stood and watched Val until he finally let it end, impressed in spite of myself and more than a little curious. The three slaves he'd chosen were all brown-haired, and I didn't understand why they all looked so exhausted. He hadn't used the third nearly as long as he usually used me, and *I* had never ended up that exhausted. Overwhelmed and very impressed, sure, but not exhausted. I didn't know what was wrong with the girl, but the question left my mind as soon as Val lay down on the bed next to her. His eyes closed and he seemed to fall immediately asleep, and the two other slaves stirred where they lay on the floor and began to get to their feet.

"Why the hell are they taking their time?" Greg demanded, showing he was looking over my shoulder at the screen. "They're supposed to get the contacts on him as soon as he conks out."

"You can't blame them if he was too much for them," the

tech said with a chuckle, coming back to reclaim his seat. "They don't often find themselves serving a stallion like that, and they aren't used to it. I don't think it's hard figuring out what *he* really likes; if he was putting on an act, he wouldn't have used all three of them."

"But we're not here to guess, are we?" Greg said with grim satisfaction, watching the two slaves on the screen pull out a bunch of contacts from under the bed and begin to attach them to their victim. "We need to see with our own eyes how he reacts to a given set of circumstances—like the standard sequences we just set up. How long until the projectors go on?"

"Loads of time," the tech answered in distraction, playing his board like the delicate instrument it was. "Minute and a half at least. And the last contact is just—about—set. Nothing to do now but wait."

The tech sounded very satisfied at that, but it was obviously meant to apply only to Greg and me. He himself continued to touch his board in a definite rhythm, and the two slaves on the screen had left Val and were pulling and tugging the third slave off the bed she'd been lying on. It seemed to be important to them to get her off the bed, and just as they managed to tumble her to the floor, the screen began to flicker.

"They're lucky their timing's so good," the tech commented with a chuckle, nodding toward the fading image of the three slaves. "Another five seconds and she would have been in the sequence with him."

"Which she would have really regretted once this was all over," Greg said with a hard edge to his voice. "I don't want him having a single out not provided by us."

"What's happening?" I asked, feeling a chill move over me at Greg's tone. His worldly, easy-going attitude was just about all gone, and I didn't like what was left behind.

"The projectors are reaching through the contacts to him," Greg answered, absently putting an arm around me. "He'll be drawn into the sequence that way, and he'll also color the sequence with his reactions. We'll be seeing the composite on the screen, just as though we were there in the sequence and watching it. Of course, if he wasn't hooked up, there'd be no sequence to see; it can't be run without a central subject."

I nodded briefly in understanding, and I *did* understand. We would see how Val really felt about what was being done to him, and everything that happened would be based on that. He would not be able to control what was being done, but his reactions to it would be strictly his.

The image on the screen continued to flicker for a few seconds, and then it settled down to show a bedroom, but a terribly frilly, feminine bedroom. Lace and ruffles hung all around in a dozen shades of yellow, on the windows, on the walls, on the wide bed, on the delicate dressing table. Gold cushions were thrown around on the ruffles and lace, cuddly dolls sat neatly arranged on some of the cushions, and looking at the scene gave the viewer the impression that the air was filled with flower perfume. Everything was neat and pretty and just where it belonged, and then a door opened to admit two figures. One was black-haired and black-eyed and really large, and the other was red-haired and even larger. Both figures were male and the black-haired one was impressive, but the redhead was absolutely awe-inspiring: he was as much bigger than the black-haired one as Val was bigger than me. The redheaded mountain had a giant hand around Val's arm, and didn't turn him loose until they both stood in the middle of the room.

"From now on, this boudoir is yours," the redhead said with a gesture at the room, watching as Val rubbed his arm where it had been held. "Be sure to keep it perfectly in order, or you'll find yourself well punished. Now give me those rags."

"Rags?" Val echoed, looking down at the white shirt and slacks he wore. "These aren't rags, they're perfectly good clothes."

"You weren't asked for your opinion, boy," the redhead answered with impatience, snapping his fingers. "Give them here and be quick about it."

"If you can wear them, so can I," Val answered, glancing at the same whites on the redhead before turning away to look around the room. "And I don't like this—'boudoir.' Why can't I have a normal room?"

"You young ones are so much alike you make me tired," the giant grumbled, completely put out. "You know nothing, not even how to behave properly, but you think you know it all. Well, before I'm through with you you *will* know it all, and it's time for your first lesson."

Val turned back to him fast at that, the look on his face showing he intended defending himself against whatever came, but there's a saying about the best laid plans. The giant came up to him, took him by the arms and lifted him off the floor, then put him down on his back on the pretty yellow carpeting. Val fought and struggled to get loose, but the giant knelt across him and began undressing him, ignoring his struggles the way he usually ignored mine.

When the giant had Val stripped he took the whites and got to his feet, then grinned down at his furious victim.

"If you learn to behave yourself you'll be given something else to wear, boy, but you'll have to earn that something else," he said. "In the meantime we'll just enjoy the sight of that pretty body of yours, and hope you don't learn to be too good too fast."

Val's fury increased as he climbed to his feet, but all the giant did was chuckle at the sight. He'd already proven Val couldn't hurt him, and didn't mind throwing the fact in Val's face. He stared at Val for another few seconds, just about daring him to try something else, then turned away to walk to another door and open it.

"The boy is here and ready for you, Highness," he said to someone out of sight. "Do you wish to see him?"

"Oh, indeed I do," came the laughing answer, clearly a female voice. "I've been waiting for him to be brought."

The giant stepped back from the doorway and opened the door wider, and Val's jaw dropped at sight of the woman who strode through. She was nearly as tall as the giant, which meant she towered over Val, but she was very, very thin. She had no hips to speak of and her breasts were little more than bumps, and her see-through gown hung on her like flesh on a long-dead corpse. She had very long blond hair and a very long, thin face with no make-up on it at all, not that makeup would have helped. The most it could have done was cover up what was there. She stopped in front of Val and looked him over with a crooked-toothed grin, then turned her head to the giant.

"He's as pretty as you promised he would be, but I thought you said he was ready." She giggled, putting one hand on a nonexistent hip. "If that's as ready as he can get, I think he's still too young."

"He's a boy and therefore shy, Highness," the giant said with a glance toward two carbon copies of himself who had come into the room behind the woman. "A boy's shyness must be overcome with coaxing. May we prepare him for you?"

"Oh, yes, please do." The woman giggled, looking down at Val again, but he was no longer looking up at her. All his attention was on the three monsters who were walking toward him, and if he didn't pale, he came pretty damned close. He began backing away from their advance, the look on his face determined, but I could have told him how much determination means in the face of greater strength and/or numbers. They caught him before he could launch himself through the glass of the double window, let him waste most of his strength fighting uselessly against their strength, and then they got down to cases. They all laughed and chatted among themselves as they "prepared" him, and from their comments it suddenly came to me that the woman wasn't the only one who would be using him. That didn't sound like any standard capture sequence to me, and I had to find out what was going on. I turned my head to Greg, and put a hand on his chest.

"Greg, something's gone wrong," I said, trying not to sound worried. "Shouldn't that sequence. . . ."

"Nothing's gone wrong," he interrupted me with warm assurance, squeezing me gently with the arm around me. "You're too softhearted is all, but I took care of it. This will be a sequence he'll never forget."

The look on his face was downright feral, and I didn't have to wonder if he'd relent and change his mind; if he did, it would only be to make things worse. It looked like he wanted to hurt Val in a way that was worse than physical, and all because Val had tried to keep him away from me. It didn't seem to matter to Greg that I was ignoring Val and seeing him anyway; he wasn't about to forgive the fact that Val had dared to tell him what to do. When Greg was the good guy trying to protect the poor little girl from her mean old uncle everything had been fine and acceptable, even being put down by Val. As soon as Val changed to the one doing the protecting, though, Greg had slid into what seemed to be an old groove, a getting-even-at-any-price groove. I'd been right when I'd told Val not to mess with Greg, but Val hadn't listened any more than he ever did. It would serve him right if I left him to take his medicine, but as far as I was concerned, the punishment was too extreme for the crime.

Greg and the tech were completely intent on the screen, where the four giants were playing with their new toy, just about licking their lips. I could see I didn't have much time, but I wasn't completely sure I could stop the fun and games. If the equipment behind us was what I thought it was we were home free, but if it wasn't . . .

Borrowing trouble never pays, so I pushed my doubts aside and concentrated on slipping away from the arm around me. Earlier Greg had tightened his hold in order to reassure me, but the doings on the screen were holding him so attentively that his grip had loosened, giving me the chance to turn out of the circle of his arm. Rather than noticing I was gone he reclaimed his arm and stepped closer to the screen, and one glance showed me why he was so rapt. The giants were getting ready to give Val a chance to work off the problem they'd given him; they were going to make a Val sandwich, one that set them all drooling, and the look in my partner's eyes was so close to madness that I couldn't stand it. I turned away from the screen fast, ran silently to the machinery against the pavilion wall, then started looking for what *had* to be there.

I don't know whether the Lord of Luck was in my corner or Val's, but there was no doubt he was there somewhere. The equipment used by the Sphere was adapted but standard, the sort that was built to be handled by the numbers. I was no expert but I did know how to turn it on and off, processes made purposefully simple by the manufacturers of the equipment. Number-one switch disconnected all outside contacts, number-two switch stopped the program, and number-three switch purged the program entirely, and that's the way the switches were meant to be closed, one, two and then three. As I hit the first switch I wondered how many people knew what I did, but it wasn't something to wonder about long; as I hit the second and third switches simultaneously, I knew there would soon be lots of people sharing the secret.

The first switch immediately cut the contact with Val, but the exclamations of protest from Greg and the tech were hardly out of their mouths before the fireworks started. The machinery was doing some protesting of its own over the simultaneous closing of the second and third switches by beginning to short out in pretty blue crackles and static, a thing the manufacturers warned would happen if those switches weren't closed one at a time. The shorts grew more violent as they spread through the machinery, smoke began rising in dark, angry wisps, and backing away from it all brought me smack into Greg.

"You stupid little fool, what have you done?" he demanded in a shout, pulling me around by one arm to face him. "Don't you know you've ruined everything?"

His handsome face was twisted with fury and livid with rage, and somehow I didn't think he was talking about the machinery I'd trashed. It hurt to see him so angry with me, hurt more than I'd expected it to, but I'd already noticed that love turns people stupid.

"Greg, let me make it up to you." I tried with some difficulty, really wanting him to know I was sincere. "Let's forget about this and go back to my pavilion, and then we can . . ."

The slap cut my words off the direct way, sending me staggering to my right, and then he had me by the arms again, and was pulling me back to face him.

"I almost had him and you want me to forget about it?" he growled, digging his fingers into my arms as he shook me like a rag doll. "You don't have to worry about making it up to me, Jennifer. I'll take care of making it up to myself, you wait and see if I don't."

He pushed me hard as he let me go, sending me down to the floor of the pavilion, and by the time I was able to sit up and turn back, he was gone from sight. The tech was busy with a smother extinguisher, putting out the handful of small fires that had started, and the people who had come crowding into the small room didn't pay the least attention to me as I got to my feet and made my way out of the place. I looked around to see if I could spot some sign of Greg in the darkness but he had disappeared completely, and the cool wind of the night had stiffened considerably. I shivered in the thin, foolish little shorts outfit I was wearing, then began looking around for Val's pavilion.

With the help of a guest list and directions from one of the Sphere people patrolling the camp, I eventually found Val's pavilion. The three slaves were gone, their job over and done with, and Val lay on the low, square bed, tossing in semi-consciousness and struggling to come out of it. I removed the contacts from him, lessening his struggles considerably, and then decided against bringing him awake the way I'd originally intended doing. Whatever sleep he'd be able to get would not be wasted, and I could bring him up to date in the morning as easily as right then. I straightened to standing, looked around at the silver and gray bedroom with appended mirrors, then went back out to the front room of the pavilion.

My body ached a little when I lowered it to the carpeting, but it wasn't anything worth paying attention to. What took more of my attention was the memory of how angry Greg had been, and how well that anger fit in with the same sort of anger I'd had to face in the past. They all started out attracted and pleased, but then came the time I did something that had to be done and all the attraction and pleasure disappeared. They never wanted to understand, never *could* understand, and just because what I felt for Greg wasn't real didn't mean it hurt any less. I'd given up getting involved in that sort of thing a long time ago, and it didn't help that this time I'd been forced into it without wanting any part of it. Curling up on carpeting is never better than curling up in the arms of a man you feel something deep for. It's only safer.

"D—Jennifer, what happened?" a blurry voice demanded from behind me, and then I heard the sound of a body sitting down. "What are you doing here?"

"Just making sure there was no burnout on this end," I told him in the trade language without turning. "Did that sequence get ended before things went too far?"

"Damn—I remember now," he said the same way, and a faint sound came as though he were running a hand through his hair. "That woman and those monsters— They were just about to— How the hell did *you* know about it?"

"You may not have noticed, but I have a knack for being in the right place at the right time," I answered, moving my head around on my arm. "In case you're interested, this isn't over yet. Greg was faintly annoyed that his present to you wasn't delivered in its entirety, and has promised to make another stab at it in the near future. Whatever that turns out to be, though, you can bet he won't make the mistake of telling me about it beforehand again."

"So you were the one who stopped it," he said, his voice both stronger and softer as his hand came gently to my arm. "And I can see how faint his annoyance was by these marks on you. How badly did he hurt you?"

"Don't be silly," I said with an odd smile only I knew about. "Haven't you learned yet that nothing can hurt me? Too uncaring and too unfeeling—remember?"

"Too thickheaded is more like it," he growled, suddenly less pleased than he had been. "If you'd listened to me and stayed away from him, you wouldn't be sporting that set of bruises now. If I ever catch you near him again, I'll put you on a leash."

"Aren't you forgetting something?" I asked, turning to my back to frown at him where he sat, almost on top of me. "If I hadn't been there you'd be sandwich meat now, complete with mustard and relish. I don't know how partnerships work where you come from, but around here we usually try to keep things like that from happening to our partners. You would have preferred if I'd simply stood to one side and just watched?"

"If it meant keeping yourself from getting hurt, yes," he answered, the faint flush on his skin doing nothing to detract from the steel-like insistence in his black eyes. "I'm supposed to be here to keep things like that from happening to you, not to be the cause of their happening. And he hit you too, didn't he?"

"Yes, he hit me," I answered, ignoring the very gentle fingers that carefully touched my cheek. "Absolutely the first to ever lay a glove on me. Most of the men I meet on assignments bow and kiss my hand. Don't you think you're being ridiculous?"

"No, I don't," he answered in a very flat way, then climbed slowly to his feet. "What I am being, though, is exhausted. Let's get to bed and catch what sleep we can."

"*We* prefer sleeping right here," I told the hand outstretched to me, more than disgusted with his nonsense. "Sleep is something I need too, and I'll do a better job of it if I work at it alone. Besides, don't you think you've had enough females in that bed for one night?"

His skin went flushed again, darker than before, and unbelievably those eyes avoided mine. I'd just been trying to be my usual sarcastic self, but Val was embarrassed! It had clearly only just come to him that everything he'd done in that pavilion had been watched, and for some reason the idea upset him.

"That wasn't what I meant, but you might be right at

that,'' he muttered, rubbing his face with one hand as he
continued to look away from me. "I'll get you a pillow and a
cover.''

He took himself out of the room, was back in a minute
with the pillow and a fur cover, then disappeared again and
stayed disappeared. I got myself comfortable and settled down
to sleep, but a last, strange thought came to me before I
drifted off. I didn't know how I knew it, but I would have
sworn that Val's embarrassment stemmed not from his actual
doing, but from the fact that I knew about it. Why it should
bother him to have me know about something like that was
beyond me, but there was no doubt that it did bother him. Val
was strange all right, in some ways stranger even than the
members of the non-humanoid races I knew, but there was
nothing I could do right then to change him. Once the assignment was over, though . . .

CHAPTER 12

"Now, people, we're ready to go," the amiable young man announced to the lessened crowd around him, his handsome face smiling attractively at everyone. "The ladies will leave first, and in a short while the men will follow. You may go anywhere you please in the white zone, but remember to stay in the white zone only. If you wander into another color zone, you'll find yourself in a different proposition, one you probably won't care for. You men should be especially careful of that."

The men looked at each other with grins and chuckling, understanding the point without needing explanations. Everyone there knew what was happening, and the best thing I could come up with about the situation was that we were finally beginning to move on deeper into the Sphere.

Slaves had come to wake us that morning, and the fact that one male slave accompanied the three females said that my location wasn't a surprise to whoever was in charge. I wasn't in the mood for what he was offering and said so, but wasn't given the option of refusal in the matter of bathing and dressing. We were up to the costumed part of the tour, and it was taken for granted that not many people would know everything there was to know about the clothing brought by the slaves. I gave in without more than a token protest and let myself be dressed, then went to have breakfast with Val.

The costume brought to me was more than modest, a long-skirted light pink dress with very wide skirt, high neck and long sleeves, delicate lace clustered around throat, hem and wrists. Val appeared in red leggings, black boots, dark brown tunic-vest, and light pink shirt, complete with swordbelt and sword and sheathed dagger; we spent a minute looking each other over before sitting down to the meal the slaves had brought. I'd been told I didn't have to worry much about the dress, but should avoid moving too abruptly or putting undue pressure on seams. The dress was designed to rip when attacked in the proper way, and underwear was, needless to say, not included in the outfit. Being given that particular information wasn't terribly surprising, but I couldn't help wondering if Val's stuff was set to do the same thing.

"You're looking well rested this morning, Jennifer," Val said smoothly and in character as he seated me at the table that had been set up in his front room. "Our schedule has been arranged for us, and we should both enjoy it."

"What are we scheduled for, uncle Val?" I asked, and the wariness I showed wasn't acting. Val had a definite twinkle of amusement in his eye, and I'd learned to be wary at the very least when it came to things he considered funny.

"We're scheduled for a ride through the countryside before lunch," he told me, sitting down at the table and starting to uncover dishes. "It seems the Management has decided that I would be happiest if I were allowed to pursue the gentler sex and bend them to my will, so that's what I'll be doing. You, of course, will be the member of the gentler sex that I pursue and bend."

"I don't understand," I protested, trying to sound young

and confused instead of old enough and cynical enough to tell him what to do with his pursuit and bending. "What has a ride through the countryside got to do with . . ."

"The ride won't simply be a ride," he interrupted as though not at all interested in what I had to say. "You, as the pursued, will be a young woman who is willfully running away from the protection of her family to avoid the need to obey them. I, as the pursuer, will be an outlaw who finds the trail of the young woman and decides to avail himself of the bounty so fortuitously placed in his grasp. I will take you captive, ignore your pleas for freedom, and happily work my will upon you."

"And what if I don't want to have your will worked on me?" I asked, showing as much of my mad as was safe. "What if I want to do something else?"

"As your uncle, I'm entitled to make your choice for you, sweetheart," he told me with amused patience and a wolfish grin. "Your choice turned out to be doing it my way, so we don't have to go into it any further. Just make sure you stay in the white zone when you start running. There are other zones around here you'd like a lot less, where all women found in it are made slaves and badly abused, some dominated by men, some dominated by other women. There are also all-male zones where women would be very unwelcome, and you especially don't want to end up there. Just eat your breakfast, and then we'll get started."

"I don't want to get started," I said through my teeth, seriously considering throwing all those dishes of food he was uncovering at him. "And I don't want any breakfast if I have to have it with you! I'm going back to my own pavilion."

"You don't have a pavilion any more," he answered, half ignoring me as he began piling my plate with food. "Just the way I won't have one any more once we finish this food. We have to be moving on to the next place that's waiting for us, and the next thing to be done—and the place where we'll rejoin John Little. He sent me a message saying he'll be going through a different zone, but we'll meet again farther in toward the center. Now, pick up that fork and start eating.''

The look he shot me then was supposed to be stern and commanding, but I could tell he was watching for a reaction to the information he'd just given me. I didn't try to hide the fact that I found it just as interesting as he did, or at least I didn't try to hide it from him. For the benefit of the slaves and any viewing equipment they might have gotten working again, I pouted, snarled, glared and huffed, then dug into the food I had suddenly developed an appetite for.

The day around us was pretty even at that early hour of the morning, and most of the men in the crowd were walking back and forth inhaling the fresh air and touching the hilts of their swords, as eager and excited as a bunch of kids waiting to start their first mixed but unchaperoned picnic. Most of the women in the group were young and pretty, sending the men teasing, insolent glances while we waited for the mounts to be brought up. That teasing majority consisted of slaves, of course, and the men had been cautioned to run down only the woman whose dress matched the color of his shirt. Some very few of the women were going through with male companions, and mix-ups wouldn't have been appreciated by either member of those couples.

When the mounts were brought up, there was a delay in departure until all of the guests present had a chance to examine them. Rather than supplying live animals which would give trouble to the inexperienced rider, the Sphere provided very cleverly made robots in the form of four-footed kiddie cars, capable of being managed by anyone with an I.Q. above 20. The things were large enough to accommodate any of us comfortably, came in stripes and plaids and solid colors, seemed to be made of hide and hair, and even moved their heads as if they were alive. The reins on them were jeweled leather, and they were only partly for show; the mounts' forward movement was controlled by foot pedals installed in the stirrups of the wide, soft-leather saddles; press down with either set of toes and the thing rolled rather than walked forward, moving up to a good clip depending on how long you pressed. If you wanted to slow or stop you pulled on the reins, again the length of pulling time determining whether you simply slowed or stopped completely. The mount was not only well balanced to avoid its going over, it even had a computer brain to keep it from doing something that *might* cause it to fall over. It was as foolproof as high technology and lengthy experience with damned fools could make it, and those in the group looked forward even more to getting started.

The mount assigned to me turned out to be white, an occurrence that set some of the men chuckling as one of the male slaves helped me into the saddle. The skirt of my dress was wide enough to let me sit astride, and I didn't notice the snickering group with their eyes on me until one said something to the others that set them laughing, then was answered by another, "She won't be for long if she makes a habit of riding *that* way. Getting caught might come too late."

They all laughed again and sent brief glances toward Val, who was deep enough into his role to chuckle indulgently while sending me a dirty grin. If I'd had even a hair less self-control I would have dismounted again and practiced some forms on all of them, but that wasn't the time or place to act like a beginner. I sent Val a glance that had a solemn promise in it, turned away from the lot of them, and toed my mount into motion out of there.

It was an odd feeling to be rolling over the grass instead of trotting or galloping, but there was no denying my kiddy car was easier and more comfortable to ride than some of the

mounts I'd had in the past. I headed away from the area of
pavilions behind and among some of the other women, our
direction also taking us away from the river, the open country
running into modest forest once we had gone a short distance.
As soon as we were out of sight of the pavilions the girls who
were slaves each picked a separate direction, and five minutes
later I was riding alone.

I continued on through the wide, bright forest, beginning to
enjoy the day and the ride in spite of myself. The Pleasure
Sphere, just like the rest of Xanadu, was carefully weather-
controlled, which guaranteed that no one would have their
pleasure spoiled by day after day of rain or cold or something
else inimical. I usually preferred natural weather, but riding
under wide green trees bathed in golden sunshine, breathing
in air like perfume, and hearing the birdsong all around,
didn't let me be overly critical.

Despite the way I was enjoying the ride, I didn't hesitate to
toe my mount up to top speed and keep it there. It would not
be too long before the men came riding after us, and if I
could possibly manage it I was going to ride all the way to
our lunch stop before Val caught up with me. That pursuit
game was great entertainment for the men, but there was a
reason why most of the women involved were slaves; once a
man sets out to literally hunt a woman down, something
happens inside him and he's no longer the nice, harmless guy
who bought you a drink the day before. He becomes something else entirely, something unpleasant. I didn't expect the
same thing to happen to Val, but he was having too good a
time at my expense and I didn't see any reason to give him
more of it.

The forest changed back to open grassland, and I still
didn't see any signs of anyone else. When I reached a rise in
the ground I spotted a few tall poles in the distance to my
left, white pennons standing out motionless from their tops,

probably announced the beginning or end of the white zone, depending on how you looked at it. If I'd known for sure what was in the adjoining zone I might have gone that way, but only the men had been given that information and Val hadn't indulged any urges to share it with me. I moved in annoyance on my saddle, pulling at the pink skirt under me to make it more comfortable, but it really didn't help much. Riding in skirts was stupid, but I supposed attacking a woman in pants wasn't as easy or entertaining.

I'd been riding almost an hour when one of my occasional checks behind showed a lone figure, some distance off but rolling right in my direction. I didn't have any doubts as to who it could be, but jamming my toes into the stirrups didn't get me any more speed. It came to me then that the men must have been given some way of finding their matching females, and also that their mounts were probably set to roll faster than those of the women. Playing the games that unfairly made me mad, even though it wasn't anything completely unexpected. The men were the ones paying to have a good time, so weighting the game in their favor was only a matter of course. If I hadn't been one of the ones being pursued, I wouldn't have thought about it twice.

But I was one of the ones being pursued, and playing sitting duck has never been my favorite pastime. There was the beginning of a stand of stone ahead and to my right, a jumble of rocks and boulders that almost seemed dropped there to break up the monotony of the landscape. I turned my mount in that direction and continued on at top speed, determined not to give up without a struggle.

By the time I reached the rocks the rider behind me was a lot closer, and was now recognizably Val. I had turned to check on his progress any number of times, but not once had he tried signaling me to stop, just as though he wasn't about to change the rules of the game. If he had signaled me we would have been partners again instead of pursuer and pursued, and I didn't think he was ready to go that way yet. He was getting a kick out of chasing me down, but not the sort of kick *I* would have enjoyed giving him.

I turned my mount in among the rocks and boulders, doing nothing to slacken my speed, but the computer brain in the kiddy car didn't agree with my decision and automatically slowed me down to keep me from piling up because of a badly placed piece of rubble. I cursed with frustration and nearly put my toes through the stirrups, but my speed kept going down instead of up, my mount no more than picking its way between two twenty-foot monoliths. I passed the slabs of rock, searching hard for the break I'd been hoping for when I'd entered that place, and suddenly a large form leaped up behind me, put a hand around my waist, and pulled the reins out of my quavering fingers. I'd had an instant to see that it was Greg jumping up behind me to ride double, dressed the way Val was, and the startlement quickly gave way to something a lot colder.

"You'd better watch that language, young lady," he said with mock sternness as he began guiding my mount around the monolith on the right. "If I hear it again, I'll have to punish you. But at that, you've done me a favor. I expected to have to ride out after you, not have you come in here to me."

"Greg, what are you doing?" I asked unsteadily, seeing with surprise that behind the rock there were three male slaves waiting with four mounts, the men also dressed in the costumes Greg and Val wore. I knew immediately that the three were slaves; they were too good-looking and well made to be guests; what I didn't know was what they were doing there, riding with Greg. I thought I knew well enough what *he* had in mind, in general if not specifically.

"What I'm doing is capturing a runaway female I intend having some fun with," he answered in amusement, stopping my mount in front of the slaves, then gesturing to two of them. "I'm going to have a lot of fun with my captive, Jennifer, right after I have even more fun with the man following her."

He put both arms around me then lifted me toward the two reaching slaves, and all I could do was struggle a little as they got me on my feet between them. Greg slid down off my mount and let the third slave lead it away, then moved closer to stop in front of me. I looked up at him with what must have looked like vulnerability, and he grinned suddenly and put a hand to my cheek.

"Pretty little Jennifer," he murmured, letting his fingers move gently over my cheek. "You said last night that you wanted to make it up to me for what you did. Are you still ready to make it up to me?"

"Yes," I conceded with difficulty, knowing it was a waste of time, but saying it anyway. "I am ready, Greg, so you don't have to . . ."

"Ah, but I do," he interrupted with an even stronger grin, watching as I tried to get away from the two slaves and go to him. "Your uncle has to be punished for the way he spoke to me, and you—you have to be punished for what you did last night. Are you ready to be punished?"

"Greg, please don't . . ." I began, but I was being ignored again. Both of his hands came to the front of my dress and pulled with moderate strength, and the fingers of the slaves tightened on my arms as the whole top of my dress ripped away.

"You really are very pretty, Jennifer," Greg drawled, smirking as his eyes ran intrusively over my now bare breasts. "Pretty all over. Have you any idea what it will be like to be used by three male slaves who have spent the last year or more catering to the whims of very rich, very spoiled women? In all that time they haven't been allowed to really have a woman, but now I've told them they can have you. Do you think you'll still be able to make things up to me after they're done with you?''

The fingers of the two slaves holding me automatically closed tighter on my arms again, and a glance at them formed the ice in my middle and froze it solid. The looks in their eyes held the memory of everything those men had been forced to go through so long, the memory of every pain and insult and slight and frustration they'd been made to put up with. Right next to that look was the one that said they'd soon be able to replace those memories with better, more pleasant ones, and the soft breeze fluttering around the pile of rocks touched my bare flesh and made me shiver.

"Greg, don't do this," I tried, looking up at him distressed. "I know you're angry with me, but if you give me the chance I really can make you forget about it. My uncle won't. . . ."

"Do anything but regret what he's already done," he finished for me, an absolute refusal to consider anything but what was already decided on in his tone and eyes. "And I don't think that will be long in coming. Since he's gotten so possessive about you, maybe I ought to make him watch your punishment before giving him his."

Greg chuckled in amusement, reached out to take one of my breasts in his hand, then turned to watch the faint trail around the monolith we stood behind. I could hear Val's mount picking its way through the rocks on the other side just the way he could, and the two slaves didn't let me pull away from the deliberately insulting touch.

In no time at all Val appeared, his mount rolling easily around the slab, he himself looking around in amusement while glancing down at this saddle. I was sure then that there was something that let his mount follow mine no matter where I went, but what I wasn't sure about was what to do next. I now knew what Greg had in mind for *me*, and although it wasn't likely to be pleasant it also wasn't likely to kill me or incapacitate me for long, which meant I had no real excuse for breaking my role. What he had in mind for Val was the kicker, though, the unknown that could make or break the entire assignment. It was almost certain that we were under the sort of observation we'd been under since we landed on the planet, so I had to be careful about what I did. I was sure Greg was just angry and didn't intend doing anything *too* awful to Val . . .

"Well, good morning, Mr. Carter," Greg called out to Val as soon as my partner saw us, pleasant welcome in his voice. "Lovely day for a ride, isn't it?"

"What do you think you're doing, Rich?" Val growled, his amusement gone, his mount pulled to a halt about ten or fifteen feet away from us. "I thought I told you to stay away from my niece."

"So you did, Mr. Carter, so you did," Greg agreed amiably, giving my breast a last squeeze before turning all the way to face Val. "But I'm not really here to see your niece; she'll be taken care of by the men with me. The one who actually brought me out all this way is you."

"You're not much my type, Rich," Val answered dryly, then dismounted and walked forward a few feet. "Tell your men to let her go, and then we can settle this between us."

"I don't think they'd care for the idea of letting her go just yet," Greg drawled, taking a step or two toward Val. "You see, I promised her to them after I took care of you, and I'd hate to disappoint them. How are you with your hands, Mr. Carter?"

"You intend fighting me?" Val asked, his face expressionless as he watched Greg open his swordbelt and throw it aside. Someone who didn't know him might believe he was expressionless through fear, but I could see the strong, eager anticipation in his eyes. I stirred between the two men holding me, surprised and relieved that that was all Greg had planned for Val, and the two slaves tightened their grips again.

"No, Mr. Carter, I don't intend fighting with you," Greg answered, and now there was a cold, hard edge to his voice. "I intend beating the living hell out of you, and I usually make my intentions good. Get rid of that swordbelt and step right up—if you've got the guts."

The mockery in Greg's challenge brought Val's head up in insult, the damned fool, and his hands went immediately to his swordbelt. A minute later it was open and gone, and then the two of them had closed to fighting distance with each other. Greg held his hands up in formal boxing style, and Val's loose, non-boxing stance and movement made the Management man grin.

"I'm really going to enjoy this, Mr. Carter," he gloated, beginning to circle to his left. "You, however, won't get any fun out of it at all."

With the last of his words he threw a left jab and a fast, hard right, obviously intending to catch Val flat-footed, but he should have remembered that saying about the best laid plans. The left jab didn't quite make it and the right missed by a mile, and then Greg's head snapped up and he was stumbling backward, his nose bloody from the gentle touch of Val's fist. Val didn't box, of course, but what he did do seemed to be a pretty good substitute.

"If that's your idea of enjoyment, you're in the wrong zone, Rich," Val commented, watching as Greg swiped at his bloody nose with the back of his hand. "If you're smart you'll call this off right now, and go back to where you're supposed to be."

"You bastard!" Greg snarled, glaring at his opponent. "I'll go back after I take care of you!"

His anger launched him at Val again, fists up and chin tucked in, the overconfidence gone and determination in its place. A number of lightning blows were exchanged, the sort that make you flinch at the thought of being on the receiving end of one of them, but the two big men weren't flinching. They really wanted to get at each other with their hands, but when Greg finally reached Val he didn't find the satisfaction he was looking for. I don't know much about boxing, but it looked like he set Val up for what's usually known as the "old one-two," then pulled it off. His left fist caught Val in the middle and his right followed immediately to Val's jaw, and then Val was supposed to go down. What really happened was Val grunted at the left in his stomach and moved his head a little with the force of the right, then came back and belted Greg in the face with what looked like more strength than he'd started with. I really did flinch at the power in that blow, briefly sympathizing with the stunned surprise Greg showed just before he was hit. I've mentioned before how well Val can take pain and punishment, but I don't know if I've made it clear how demoralizing that ability is for his opponent. When you hit someone with everything you've got and they just stand there grinning and getting ready to give it back, your first, very wise impulse is to turn tail and get the hell out of there. I didn't start my career as an agent with a nine rating in hand to hand, so I speak from personal experience. Greg Rich must have felt that impulse just before Val's fist reached him, but by then it was too late.

Greg staggered backward to sprawl on his back, his handsome face a bruised and bloody mess, not unconscious but too dazed to get up again. Val stood and looked at him for a minute, briefly sucking at one knuckle on the hand that had connected with Greg, then he turned away from his former opponent and started toward me, his black eyes going to the two slaves holding me. The slaves dropped my arms so fast you would have thought I'd suddenly burst into flames, and the third one over by the mounts paled and edged away from what looked like the new action that was about to start. No one was prepared to argue with that look in my partner's eyes—but Greg Rich, on the ground behind him and to the left, couldn't see it.

"Stop right there, you bastard," he slurred, leaning up on one elbow to glare his hatred at Val, one of his fists no longer empty. Val stopped and turned slowly to see the blaster the rest of us had already seen, and rather than laugh in relief, the slaves to either side of me froze in shock. What Greg was doing was clearly not on the announced agenda, and the slaves were suddenly more afraid than eager for fun.

"You really did think you were going to get away with it," Greg half-snarled, half-laughed, keeping his eyes on Val as he struggled to his knees. "I wasn't going to use this on you until I was good and ready, but I'm ready sooner than I expected to be. You can delay it a minute or two by getting down on your belly and begging, so why don't you try it? If you do it nicely enough, I might only burn your legs off."

The blaster leveled on Val was unwavering even when Greg chuckled, and my mind was racing so fast it nearly reached light speed. Anything can be stopped by words except a blaster bolt that's already on its way, I'd once thought, and even in that instance I wasn't entirely wrong. I looked around carefully as I waited for Val to say the words that would buy us some desperately needed time, but I suddenly noticed that those words weren't coming, and Greg noticed the same thing.

"Beg me, damn you, beg for your life!" he snarled, his eyes blazing as he forced himself to his feet. "Don't just stand there staring at me as if you don't give a damn what I do! Don't you care about living?"

"Life at any price turns out to be worth what you pay for

it,'' the idiot who called himself my partner answered, folding his arms as he calmly continued to hold Greg's gaze. "If I let myself fall so low that I crawled and begged, what would I do with my life even if I got it back? And if I lost it anyway, I'd have put myself through hell for nothing. You're wasting your time waiting for something that won't happen, Rich. Whether I live or die, I'll be doing it on my feet."

"Not for long, you won't," Greg growled, finality clear in every word as his hand tightened around the blaster hilt. "It's all yours, sucker, and you can't say you *didn't* beg for it."

He lifted his hand and extended the blaster just a little more, taking careful aim instead of just squeezing one off, sighting directly on a motionless, expressionless Val. With Greg Rich being so far out of reach my partner had no other real option open to him, aside from diving and trying to hit dirt, but Val didn't even try that. If he'd been alone only a misfire would have saved him, but luckily for him he wasn't alone. When it first came to me that the damned fool was going to be the way he'd been on the liner in front of those men who were going to jump on his head, I stopped looking around for a miracle and did the only thing I could. The slave to my left was too intent on the confrontation to notice when I slipped the knife out of its sheath on his hip, and also didn't notice my whispered thanks to the Lord of Luck. The weapon could have been the cheapest sticker made and would still have served its purpose as trim for a costume, but that was Xanadu, and on Xanadu things weren't done the cheap way. The shape of the sheath had led me to hope that it wasn't lying about its contents, and sure enough I got what I'd hoped for: a beautifully made bowie knife, and even more than that, one that seemed balanced properly for throwing. Greg and Val were exchanging ageless wisdom when I hefted the knife to get the feel of it, but their discussion ended too damned soon. When Greg raised his weapon and leveled it it was too late to worry any more about feel, so I took the knife by its tip, sent one last frantic appeal to the Lord of Luck, and threw with every bit of skill I could call up.

The Lord of Luck definitely had to be on Val's side. The knife wobbled sickeningly when it left my hand, convincing me that I'd also thrown away our last shot at getting out of that mess unairconditioned, but the wobble somehow equalized itself in the seconds of the knife's flight, and suddenly the hilt was standing out of Greg's chest, right where I'd wanted it to be. Greg grunted and looked down in faint surprise, raised his eyes to me with even more surprise, then tried to say something. Instead of the words coming out the blaster fell from his hand, and then he began crumpling down after it, the final glaze already in his eyes. I ignored the way he was falling and just plumped down on a bunch of stones without feeling them, then put my face in my hands and rubbed at my eyes.

"That was a nice throw," Val's voice came after a minute, sounding matter of fact. "Are you all right?"

"No, I am *not* all right!" I snarled in the Absari trade language, shaking off the gently concerned hand that had come to my shoulder. "And if I'd been stupid enough to leave things to you, I sure as *hell* wouldn't have been all right! Are you really that determined to get us killed, Val? Why the hell didn't you do what he asked and give me more than ten seconds to come up with something that counted?"

"I thought you said you understood the concept of standing on principle," he came back from his crouch beside me, ignoring the way I was glaring at him. "There are certain things I just won't do, and begging for my life is one of them. And besides that, it wasn't necessary. You didn't need more than ten seconds."

I stared at his authentically calm and easy grin for a bit longer than ten seconds, then began describing him in terms

of personal habits, probable ancestry, and anatomical varia-
tions from norm, all of the one syllable variety. His face took
on a pained expression as he straightened out of his crouch,
and then he bent down to "help" me to my feet, using the
gesture to cut into my tirade.

"You'd better turn that off and fast," he muttered to keep
his voice from traveling to the slaves, those eyes looking
straight down at me. "It would be rude and ungrateful of me
to take the woman who just saved my life and wash her
mouth out with soap, but that's what will happen if you don't
cut it out. Now, what are we going to do about these slaves?"

"You can make pickled pigs feet out of them for all I
care," I growled, yanking my arm out of his hand. "There's
no way in hell anyone observing that throw will consider it
beginner's luck, and as soon as the questions start, the game
is over. And it's too bad I didn't let you go through that
entire sequence last night after all. It might have taught you
a little prudence when it comes to dealing with me; next time
I'll see to it that you don't lose even a minute's worth.
Remember that if you're ever again in a mood for handing me
infantile threats."

My big-mouthed partner was suddenly all out of what to
say, so I turned away from him again and began walking
among the rocks and stones, trying to regain self-control. I
didn't know why I was so upset and I didn't know why I'd
been so bottom-line with Val, and I didn't know what would
happen next. It would be fantasizing to believe that our little
set-to with Greg hadn't been observed, and I wasn't looking
forward to the questioning the Management would use to find
out what was going on. Even if I told them about the death
warrant in the first five minutes they would still use questioning to verify what had been said, and then I'd be able to find
out how they'd decided to take it. They were legally bound to
honor the warrant, but what they did to Val and me for

landing with false papers before they did the honoring was the part that would bring interest to our lives. We'd be free to serve the warrant after they finished with us, if we were able to do anything as complicated as walking. . . .

I stopped still and my thoughts ground to a halt, my stare going down to what my wandering had led me to. Greg's body lay at my feet, the knife hilt still sticking out of his chest, his face too composed for the way he'd died. I crouched beside him and put my fingers to that face, that battered, bloody face that I had loved so much in the situational. He had wanted to protect me, had held me in his arms and had made love to me any number of times, and I had killed him without hesitation and without thought, buried a knife in his chest and then thanked the Lord of Luck for the accuracy of the throw. She doesn't regret what she does, Val had told Ringer, and I hadn't realized then how damning that truth was. What sort of a woman could kill a man she loved and not regret it? Wouldn't I do the same thing to anyone stupid enough to love *me*? Damned right I would, so it was a good thing nobody could or did love me. I wasn't a woman I was a Special Agent, and I couldn't afford to let anyone around me forget that.

"Come away from that," Val said, appearing next to me to lift me to my feet and walk me away, his arm around my shoulders holding me tight against him. "I thought you would be smarter than to waste concern on scum like that, Diana. If he'd had his way, you'd be entertaining those slaves right now, and most likely screaming out your pain for him to laugh at. It was something you had to do, so you did it. If it hadn't been him, it would have been me, just remember that."

He was speaking very softly and soothingly, holding me against him with one arm around me and one hand to my hair, trying to comfort what he thought he understood. The hell of it was I didn't need comforting, and perversely, that was what seemed to be upsetting me. I'd had the choice of what to be a long time ago, and I'd made my choice without regret. To start regretting it now would be as ludicrous as it would be futile.

"At least I have some good news for you," Val went on, still patting my hair. "No one saw any part of what went on between Rich and ourselves because this is a dead area, a spot never kept under observation. It was the reason Rich picked it, the slaves told me, to keep him and themselves out of trouble. They're in a panic now, believing the Management is about to find out what they were up to, and none of them can face the thought of what will happen to them then. I told them that I'll condescend to protect them if they'll swear to the story I'm going to tell, a version which won't be too far from the truth."

"And what story is that?" I asked, not bothering to move from the comfort of my position against him. I was feeling a bone-weary tiredness that would pass after a little while, but right then the strength and determination just weren't there.

"We're going to say that Rich had them ride along with him without telling them why, which puts them in the clear," Val said. "After that we're going to alter the fight a little, saying that Rich reached for his blaster while we were struggling, and I was able to put my knife into him before he could get me in his sights. I told the slaves I didn't want anyone knowing my fifteen-year-old niece had to save my life, and they bought it. They don't seem to know that a throw like the one you made isn't something every teenage female is able to do."

"It'll come to them after the shock wears off, but by then we'll hopefully be long gone," I said with a sigh, then forced myself to move off him. "I don't think we can count on having luck like this again, so you damned well better be

crazy about everyone we meet from now on. Save that mild
dislike of yours for our target.''

"Yes, ma'am, anything you say," he drawled, grinning
faintly as he let me go. "Do you want my vest before we
head out for the lunch spot?"

I looked down at the tattered rags of the top of my dress,
noticing that Val's eyes were in the same place, and made a
sour face at him.

"You were the one who was supposed to do that, but since
you didn't I can get away with covering up," I said, holding
one hand out for the vest. "As a matter of fact it might be the
best idea after all. We don't want those slaves getting the idea
of asking for me as part of their price for going along with
your story. Your role character would have no choice but to
agree.''

"Since it's my role character, I'm the one who decides
what gets agreed to," he said, slipping off the leather vest
and handing it to me. "As soon as you've got this on, get
mounted.''

He walked away from me to go back to where the slaves
were standing huddled together, giving me no chance to tell
him what I thought of him. He was still disobeying orders,
and hadn't learned a damned thing from what we'd gone
through; he would continue doing things his way, even if he
got us killed. I slipped into the vest—which was a wrap-
around for me—and resisted the urge to do a little rock
throwing on the way to my mount.

Predictably enough we made the lunch spot before anyone
else, and Val lost no time reporting the trouble he'd had to
the proper authorities. He'd left Greg's body back among the
rocks, and his indignation over the question of why he'd done
so was nearly comical. We'd decided to leave the body there
so the Management could investigate and satisfy themselves
that there was no messing around involved, but Val de-

manded to know if he was expected to worry about the body of a man who had tried to kill him. The Management reps took his misinterpretation an an indication of innocence, and hurried to smooth down his ruffled feathers. We were served a sumptuous lunch by female slaves who crawled all over him, and Greg Rich was never mentioned to either one of us again.

After lunch it was costume-changing time, and this time Val got desert gear complete with burnoose and curved sword, and I got a too-thin layer of yellow veils and silver jewelry. I was sent out first in a wheeled and curtained litter with male slaves acting the part of guards, supposedly the bride of a sultan on her way to the wedding festivities. Val followed with his own group of slaves, a khan who was the bitter enemy of the sultan, who would prevent his having the woman of his choice. They rolled up to us in pursuit, his group and my "guards" swinging their curved swords in carefully choreographed movements, and in no more than two minutes, all of my guards were disarmed and captured. The khan himself rolled up to my halted litter, dismounted slowly, then came close to raise one of the curtains.

"Well, well, what have we here?" he drawled, using the point of his sword to brush aside one of my body veils, an action that was totally unnecessary considering the transparency of those veils. "A little something to distract a man on a quiet afternoon, perhaps?"

"Don't you even *think* about touching me," I hissed, all too well aware of the attention of all those slaves. The bastard had me trapped into my role with all those witnesses around, and the amusement in his eyes said he meant to take advantage of that.

"I've already thought about it," he said with a grin, sheathing his sword before turning his head to the slave standing next to him. "Let's continue on to the place we'll be having dinner, but not at too fast a pace."

"As you say, master," the slave acknowledged with an amused chuckle, watching as Val climbed into the litter with me and carefully closed the curtain behind him. Through the thin yellow curtains I could see the slaves getting ready to move out, and then Val had his swordbelt off and was lying down next to me.

I spent the entire ride in Val's arms, the warmth of his lips on mine an almost constant thing, and when we reached the pavilions where we would spend the night I was in a strangely contented mood—until I left the litter and saw the curtains from the outside. They'd all been rolled up when I'd first gotten into the litter, so I hadn't known that they were transparent only from the inside. None of the slaves riding around the litter would have known it even if we'd spent the afternoon playing cards, only Val hadn't seen fit to mention that fact. What he had mentioned was that after that afternoon, little Jennifer should no longer be trying to keep her uncle Val's hands off her. I hadn't wanted to agree with him, but it was fairly obvious that any young, impressionable girl would have acted as I had with Val only if she were horribly in love with him. She couldn't be expected to be simply enjoying a little casual sex the way I had been doing, so I'd left the litter holding tight to his arm and looking up at him adoringly. By the time I learned the truth I was already trapped, and I was so furious it wasn't safe for Val to come near me for the rest of the evening. Another man would have worried at least a little, but all he did was grin with that stupid laughter in his black eyes.

The next three days were more of the same, with only the costumes and scenarios changing. I had to spend the time clinging to Val's arm whenever we walked together, constantly looking up at him with loving eyes, and eagerly agreeing to everything he told me to do, no matter what it was. I took one opportunity of our being alone together to tell him that I was going to kill him as soon as we were off Xanadu, but all he did was laugh and tell me he'd worry about it then.

The evening of the third day found us in a camp as large as our original camp, showing that everyone had been gathered in from the various zones. A general party was arranged in one very large pavilion, and everyone was costumed beautifully for the elegant surroundings. The crowd was in a good mood and really enjoyed the refreshments, and halfway through the evening John Little showed up at the couch Val and I were sharing, a really beautiful male slave walking along behind him.

"Well, Val, have you been enjoying yourself?" Little asked as he pulled a chair nearer our couch, leaving the slave to stand quietly behind him. "I know I have."

"I've been more than enjoying myself, John," Val answered, feeding me another salted nut. "The days have been filled with revelation and learning, haven't they, Jennifer?"

"Oh, yes, uncle Val," I said, only just able to keep from chewing off his fingers.

"Sweet little Jennifer." Little laughed, especially at the blush I didn't have to force much. "I see you've finally grown to appreciate your uncle. You've learned to obey him very nicely, and you seem much improved."

"Thank you, Mr. Little," I managed without choking, looking quickly away from the slave behind Little's chair. I'd tried to make it easier on myself by avoiding the man's ridiculous smirk, but looking at the slave was much worse. His beautiful face was expressionless, but his eyes were briefly filled with frustration and hatred and pain and weariness, likely triggered by the way Little was trying to humiliate me. He'd clearly had his own share of humiliation, that slave, and very briefly his mask had slipped.

"I've come by to resume my role as adviser, Val," Little said as a goblet was handed to him and then filled with wine. "You'll be asked later on this evening if you'd like to continue moving through your zone or go ahead deeper into the Sphere, and the answer you should give is continue on deeper. There's something in the heart of the Sphere that you just have to see."

"What's that?" Val asked, not sounding terribly enthusiastic, reaching around with his own goblet to have it refilled. Doing that he missed the way Little's slave paled, but I didn't.

"I couldn't possibly describe it," Little answered with a small laugh of amusement, only glancing in my direction. "It is, however, the best the Sphere has to offer, and I promise you you won't be disappointed. I haven't misled you so far, have I?"

"No, that's true, you haven't," Val conceded, letting me drink some wine from his goblet. "What do you say, Jennifer? Should we have a go at it?"

"I'll go wherever you do, uncle Val," I gushed, seeing the brief look of questioning in his eyes. "If Mr. Little says you'll have fun there, then. . . ."

"Then you want to share it with me," he finished in nauseating tones of fond indulgence, patting my hand. "And of course you will. It sounds fine to me, John. Onward and upward it is."

"Good," Little said with a satisfied nod, taking his goblet with him as he stood. "I'll see you in the morning, then."

He headed back toward the side of the tent he'd come from with the slave following silently in his shadow, and Val took a handful of the salted nuts and gave them to me.

"Now you feed me, sweetheart," he said, then switched to the trade language to add, "What do you think?"

"That's got to be where our target is," I conceded, putting the first nut into his mouth. "I have the feeling we're really going to have to watch our steps, though. We know they have something in mind, and this might be what he was after all along."

"Whatever that comes to," he agreed, taking a nut and feeding it to me. "Are you sure we have no choice but to walk in like blindfolded innocents? I don't like the sound of our destination, not if *he* thinks it's the best part of the Sphere."

"Come up with a workable alternative, and I'll probably go for it faster than you do," I said, looking at him as I continued to feed him. "I also have the feeling that fun time is over—for both of us."

"Only temporarily," he said around the last mouthful I'd given him, his eyes starting to develop that stubborn look. "We'll go in there, finish this thing right, then take ourselves back to the Station. Don't forget you've got a lot of getting even left to do. You're not going to let anything stand in the way of that, are you?"

"No, of course not," I told him with a small smile, then put the nuts aside and took his arm to rest my head against it. After careful consideration, being able to do that without waiting until we were alone just may have been worth all the rest of the nonsense.

CHAPTER 13

The next day was another day of travel for us, but not like
the ones so recently passed. Barely a handful of those who
had dined with us chose the trip to the heart of the Sphere,
and one or two who had wanted to choose it had been
discouraged and touted off onto something else. Val was grim
when he told me about that incident, and it didn't exactly fill
me with lighthearted joy either. Only a certain sort of people
were being allowed to continue on, and when I looked at our
fellow travelers I wondered why Val and I had been given the
go-ahead. All the others without exception, male and female
alike, had been using slaves during their previous four days,
and those slaves were very obviously the worse for it. I
thought about it for a few minutes, trying to fit the puzzle
pieces together, and then groaned silently when the light
came. Val, to those of the Sphere, was a man who had taken
his young niece and had raped her repeatedly, and had also
killed a man and shown nothing of upset at the doing. I was
just along for the ride, but the Management had obviously
decided that Val fit in perfectly, and were more than happy to
have him. I noticed how Val had taken to standing practically

on top of me right from the outset of the trip, and made sure not to mention my conclusions to him. If I had, I probably would have had him in my lap.

Our mode of transportation that day was a train that traveled without rails, each individual traveling on it having his or her own car. Our needs were seen to by another horde of slaves, and the clothing we'd been given was very old-fashioned. The men wore high-collared, uncomfortable-looking shirts with ties under severe, close-cut suits, and the women were given high-necked and long-sleeved dresses that came down to their shoe-tops. Everyone complained about the costumes, but for once our complaints were firmly denied; if we were going where the train was going, that was what we had to wear while we did it. We all grumbled but eventually had to give in, and I privately wondered why our personal luggage had been dragged along with us every step of the way. The only time we'd used our own things since landing had been the brief time after the physicals.

The train ride was, aside from the costumes, physically comfortable, but mentally it couldn't possibly have been more boring. There was absolutely nothing provided in the way of entertainment or distraction, and even requests for something to read were denied. We could sit in our chairs and stare out the windows or at each other or at the slaves, but if the sparkling conversation lagged there was nothing to bring it back to life. There was no provision for privacy in the car except in the narrow bathroom, so that meant people like Val couldn't even fill the time with their own entertainment. Despite his twisted sense of humor, my partner had proved himself to be one of those who won't perform in public unless he's drugged to the point of not knowing what he's doing. The slaves in our car kept him firmly in his own seat, which added to his grim, unhappy silence.

The slaves set up a table and served us lunch, and didn't

seem surprised when neither one of us showed much of an appetite. The day had started as pretty as the previous ones had been, but right after lunch it began to gray over. We continued on at a good pace and the overcasting continued as well, but not just with clouds. Thick mist began blanketing the ground we were crossing, and despite the warmth of the car to look outside was to shiver with an inner chill.

When John Little showed up with his slave at his heels, he did not get a warm welcome. Val had been sitting with his arm around me since the lunch things had been cleared away, and nothing I said prompted him to go back to his own seat. There was a look in his eyes that made the slaves walk very softly and stay out of his way as much as possible, but at least he had the sense to swallow it down when Little sat down opposite us.

"If this is your idea of the best there is, John, I'm going back to the zones as soon as this thing stops," he complained to his good friend. "These clothes are impossible, and I haven't even been able to relax with Jennifer. And just look at it out there!"

He waved a hand toward the window we sat near, where the ground had disappeared entirely in the mist. What trees we passed were black, and twisted and unhealthy-looking. Everything out there was gray or black, and the warmth and brightness of the sun seemed never to have touched any of it.

"It *is* rather depressing the first time you come through it," Little conceded, gazing out the window with pursed lips and almost total unconcern. "When we get where we're going you'll see how appropriate this all is, and we aren't that far from it now. Trust me, Val, you won't be disappointed."

Val grunted with very obvious doubt, but he didn't pursue his complaints any farther. He could afford to be as skeptical as he liked, but he couldn't decide firmly against the place and he knew it. Little took his eyes away from the loathsome landscape and stared at me for a while, but I pretended not to notice. There was something in it worse than what we were riding through, and I really didn't need that.

We rode on in silence for a while, and then the train began to slow down. The mist was rising even higher now, nearly covering everything inside it, but somewhere in the near distance, dark like everything else, were several unmistakable shapes. Val peered at them through the window, then turned to Little.

"Am I mistaken, or are those ships?" he asked, sounding more than a little puzzled. "Is this the Pleasure Sphere's way of showing us the exit?"

"Not at all." Little laughed, barely glancing where Val looked. "That's the heart's shuttle port, used by people who want to go directly there and don't care to waste time coming overland. Some of the regulars also come in their own ships, and bring them down here instead of paying docking fees in the Station. Almost no one who comes here simply visits for a day or two and then leaves. The place has a very special lure, Val, and just about everyone who visits it once comes back at least a second time."

Val nodded and made an attempt to look interested and anticipatory, not knowing or at least not realizing that Little was talking about a hand-picked, very select few. Of course they came back a second or third or fourth time; if they weren't the sort to enjoy what went on there, they were unlikely to have been allowed in the first time.

The train kept slowing down, and before very long it came to a complete stop. Those of us who had been cooped up so long with so little to do lost no time heading for the exit, but I noticed that the slaves who had served us hung far back and tried to make themselves invisible, possibly against the off-chance that one of us would insist they come along. John Little's slave was as pale as the mist as he followed along behind John, and he moved with a fatalistic defeat that was painful to see. He didn't have the option of fading into the woodwork, and looked about as close to tears of terror as it's possible to get. Little must have brought him along on a whim, or possibly to enjoy his terror, but whichever it was, the slave was caught.

We were helped down the train steps into the mist, and once we all stood in the wet, swirling gray the train moved on, almost silently, disappearing very quickly. It wasn't night-dark around us, only misty gray, but that misty-gray turned everything unreal and made us feel we were the only people left alive on the whole planet, if not in the entire universe. One of the other guests had brought a female slave along with him, and the girl whimpered and shook with even more terror than Little's slave. It was fairly obvious the slaves knew something we didn't—the "we" including everyone but John Little. That gem just stood quietly with a private smile on his narrow face, a smile that broadened when the guest who had brought the female slave knocked her to the ground with a casual backhanded slap to quiet her. We were all too busy looking around at nothing and wondering what would happen next to be distracted by hysterics.

We stood in the thick, clinging gray for fifteen or twenty minutes, long enough to feel abandoned and forgotten, long enough for our clothes to fill with the dampness and grow heavy and even more uncomfortable. The dress I wore had been confining but warm; it slowly grew to be confining and freezing, and Val wasn't doing much better. The material of all the clothing seemed designed to attract moisture, and then we were distracted by the exclamation of one of the guests. A small, red light had begun to glow in the mist, and even as we watched it grew and expanded to the size of a large portal. Without comment we all began to move toward it, holding the same silence we'd held the entire time we'd stood there. Casual conversation is ordinarily usual among groups doing the same thing, especially small groups; in that group not a single word had been exchanged.

We began to feel the heat as soon as we approached the redness, and by the time we were close enough to see that it really was a portal we were heading for, the heat was enough to make us sweat. The temperature rose higher and higher, forcing us to break into a run, and once we crossed the red-glowing metal threshold, panting and desperate, the torture eased off to the point where it was at least bearable. It was surprising that no one had turned and run the other way instead, considering the possibility that the heat might *not* have eased off once we were inside, and then I noticed that my automatic assumption was wrong. Although all the guests and the female slave were still with us, the pretty male slave Little had brought was nowhere to be seen.

"Welcome, travelers," a smoothly amused baritone announced, drawing our attention. "Welcome and welcome again—to the halls of hell."

The tall, very handsome man with the pointed beard chuckled at the startled reaction his announcement had drawn, but it was nothing we shouldn't have been expecting. We stood in a cavern of sorts with dark rock all about and the mists still swirling around our ankles and knees, but the lighting was red and smoldering, and the heat was still above the comfortable mark. The man greeting us was dressed in black slacks, black turtleneck shirt and black loafers, and in intricate silver medallion hung around his neck gleaming redly. He was dark-haired and dark-eyed and seemed completely at home, and when his eyes touched me as he examined each one of us in turn, I made sure to go wide-eyed and clutch fearfully at Val's arm. Val patted my hand in a preoccupied way and paid no further attention to me, clearly remembering what I'd told him forcefully enough: I was going to have to pretend to be afraid at times in that place, and as long as he didn't see me getting ready to protect myself with everything I had, he had to remember it was just an act. He had reluctantly agreed to check first before going all protective and making people wonder, but I didn't know how far I could rely on that agreement. I could just hope it would be far enough.

"Well, you seem a somewhat likely group," the man observed, still looking us over. "There are choices and decisions to be made by you, but those can wait until we get you a bit more comfortable. Just follow me."

He turned and began crossing the cavern toward its far side, and there was nothing to do but follow along as he'd all but ordered. His attitude was superior and abrasive, instilling the sort of mood in us that the Management seemed to want. We still weren't talking to each other, but now the silence was growing hostile.

We crossed the cavern and entered a side passage, and were still surrounded by rock that was lit with red. The mist only just covered the floor now, and a short way down the passage there began a series of heavy metal doors set into the rock and closed tight. The bearded man indicated a door then indicated one of us, his superior smirk adding to the annoyance he had already caused. Val was trying very hard not to look at him in that special way he had, and was succeeding only up to a point. It was a positive relief when we were shown our doors, and were able to leave the passage and the man.

Val's door was just beyond mine, but once I'd pushed open the thing and stepped inside, I could see there was no communicating between rooms. The room was carved out of the same rock the passage was formed by, and the only thing interrupting the solid expanse was another door in the opposite wall, a mate to the one I'd just used. I stepped farther into the room to see what might be behind the door, and found a pair of slaves waiting for me, one male and one female. The male quietly closed the door behind me, and the female gestured to the massage table she stood near.

"If you will allow us, mistress, we'll help you get comfortable and relaxed," she said with a forced smile, taking one small step forward. "You may also have your choice between us for your pleasure."

I glanced at the bearded male slave who stood with folded arms at the door, a smirk on his face as he looked me over, and tried not to show my annoyance. If I'd been in the mood to be appealed to, neither one of them would have made it.

"I think I'll stay with the comfort and relaxation," I told the girl, pulling the clammy skirt of my dress away from my legs. "Do you have anything dryer than this to put on?"

It turned out the girl had a towel, which the male slave held while the girl helped me out of the dress. Once I was bare the male put the towel around me from behind, then held it in place while he put his lips to my ear.

"I heard the masters talking, mistress," he murmured, positioning his hands strategically on the towel. "I've never served anyone with your sensuality rating before, but I would really like to. Lie down on the table, and I'll give you a massage better than anything *she* can give."

The "she" he was referring to was the female slave, who was busily occupied with putting aside my dress, and briefly I remembered Greg Rich's comment about the possibility of slaves taking advantage of my age. The slave behind me was telling rather than asking, but I had something of my own to tell.

"Uncle Val said I wasn't to let anyone make me do anything that wasn't my own idea," I murmured back, making no effort to pull away from him. "If they try, I'm supposed to tell him about it so he can complain."

The hands on me immediately pulled away, and I turned my head to see a suddenly very jovial male slave.

"I can tell the mistress is not in the mood for me right now," he said, laughing nervously as he backed away toward the door. "If you should change your mind, mistress, just have the slave send for me."

He completed his hasty withdrawal then, closing the door fast behind him, and I was able to take myself to the massage table without being bothered anymore. I was annoyed as hell about the slave's comment on my supposed sensuality rating, that stupidity that had come up during the appraisal. Some women may react a little more quickly and thoroughly than others, but just how quickly and thoroughly usually depends on their partner. To say one woman is purely sensual and the next inert, is to say that the men involved are laying the foundations for a great-sounding excuse. I was surprised that the slave had mentioned it at all, and just thinking about it made the relaxing I was trying to do harder.

The massage started, continued, and went on to its conclusion, and that's about the best that can be said for it. The girl was almost good, but not quite up to taking all the knots out of my muscles. When it was over she produced cool, wet cloths to wash my entire body with, then went to one of the blank stone walls, a blankness that was temporarily broken when she pressed on one part of the wall and opened a four-foot section of what looked like closet or storage area. That was the place the wet cloths had probably come from, and when the slave stepped back out she was holding something long and silvery.

"We have to get you dressed now, mistress," she said, coming toward me with a smile. "They'll be expecting you soon, and won't begin until everyone is there."

"Expecting me for what?" I asked, sitting up on the table

to get a better look at what the woman was carrying. "What won't they begin?"

"I'm not permitted to discuss that, mistress," she answered, her smile turning just slightly forced. "The masters insist on explaining matters in their own way, and it won't be much longer. Which pair of shoes would you prefer?"

The long silvery object she was carrying was a gown, and she put it down to show the wide shoebag she was holding under it. The shoebag opened easily to let her pull out two silver shoes, one a pump, the other a sling-back, both with heels high enough to make them dressy. When I indicated the sling-back she put the pump away and produced the second sling-back, then put all the shoes down and picked up the gown again. I still didn't need help getting dressed but I got it again, and once I was in the shoes she brushed my hair then opened the wall again to show me a full-length mirror. The long silver gown was slit on the sides, was long-sleeved with practically all cleavage, and was tight enough to reflect black instead of silver at certain stress points. When the slave gave me long silver earrings to go with the rest I put them on, then looked at myself again with a critical eye. I turned back and forth a couple of times, stood sideways, then came to the inevitable conclusion that no matter how long I stood there, Val would still take one look at me and push the lecherous uncle bit for all it was worth. His reaction to the last slinky outfit I'd worn was something I didn't care to remember, not when we were getting so close to what we'd come for. I could only hope the Management kept us too busy for a while for him to take advantage of the situation, at least until I did what I had to. After that I could do my own bit to make him keep his hands to himself.

The slave was beginning to get antsy over how long I was taking to admire myself, so I let her urge me away from the mirror and out the door opposite the one I'd come in by.

Outside was another carved stone corridor about five feet wide, and about ten feet to the right a second, perpendicular corridor opened up to take us away from the area of rooms. The slave led me up the twisting corridor through the roiling red mist, her ankles and mine lost to the thick, red stuff, neither one of us commenting on it. The lighting was a lighter red but still a red, and the heat was just this side of uncomfortable. They were going to a lot of trouble presenting the classic picture of hell, and much as I would have liked laughing at the effort as childish, the increasing nervousness of my slave-guide took most of the humor out of the situation.

After a couple of minutes of walking, we came around one bend in the corridor and saw a wide arch carved in the rock ahead of us, spanning the corridor and clearly acting as the entrance to a room beyond. The slave came to an abrupt stop, quickly looked away from the arch, then glanced at me with fear.

"The masters are waiting in there, mistress," she said as fast as she could, already edging back the way we'd come. "Refreshments will be served by others like myself, who have been assigned that duty. I have to get back to my own post now. I hope you have a pleasant stay."

She sketched a quick curtsey then hurried away, not once trying to meet my eyes again. If I'd been given the chance I might have told her I wanted her to go the rest of the way with me, so she'd made sure I wasn't given the chance. Sphere slaves seemed to live in perpetual terror in that place, and the attitude was beginning to get to me. I don't like people who get a kick out of terrorizing the helpless, and I've been known to show that dislike in very direct ways. I looked again at the entrance arch, then moved ahead again in a deliberate way. If they were all so tough in there, they'd be looking forward to terrorizing *me* along with the rest, and it would be a shame to disappoint them.

I walked up to the arch and through it, ready for whatever they had waiting, but the only thing waiting was about a dozen and a half people, spread out in the large room and desultorily pretending to socialize. The men were wearing all black the way the man who had greeted us had done, and the considerably fewer women were dressed the way I was, in silver, clinging gowns. Quite a few eyes came to me when I appeared, male and female alike, and then a naked male slave materialized at my elbow, carrying a silver tray of drinks.

"Will you have refreshment, mistress?" he asked in a husky voice, extending the tray as his eyes looked into mine. "I'll be glad to provide any refreshment you'd care to name."

He grinned at me insolently, just about the only slave I'd seen there who wasn't panic-stricken. Over his shoulder a familiar face caught my attention, and when I looked at it directly I was pleased to recognize, engaged in a low-voiced disagreement with John Little—Richard Radman.

"Mistress, forgive me," the male slave whispered, his insolence gone, his hands causing the tray he held to vibrate faintly. "I didn't mean to insult you. Please don't report me to the masters!"

"You didn't insult me," I told him sourly, reaching over to take one of the glasses from the tray he held. "And this is all the refreshment I'm interested in right now."

"Yes, mistress," he acknowledged with a relief that was sickening, bowing and backing away. "Thank you, mistress."

As soon as he could he turned and went elsewhere, leaving me to stand alone just inside the entrance to the room. I sipped at my drink, wondering why Val wasn't there yet, deliberately keeping my eyes away from Radman. I was somewhat curious about the reason for the slaver's being there, but I wasn't about to look my gift horse in the mouth. If Little had gotten him there for one of the reasons I'd planned, I would thank the Lord of Luck once I was off that planet. It looked like my plans were finally starting to go the way they were supposed to.

"Well, Jennifer, you look absolutely lovely," a voice said from my right, and I turned my head to see that John Little had left Radman to come over to me. "That gown becomes you more than anything else I've seen you wear."

"Thank you, Mr. Little." I pretended I didn't see the gleam in his eyes. "Do you know where uncle Val is?"

"He's likely still—dressing," Little answered with his usual greasy amusement, making sure to hesitate before the last word. "If a massage is to do what it's designed to do, it can't be rushed. Suppose I introduce you around a bit until he shows up, eh? That way he'll be here before you know it."

He took my arm without giving me a chance to refuse, and rather than balk I went along with him. The feeling that he was up to something was stronger than ever, and I wanted to know what it was. I let him direct us both to a group of three women, examining them as we approached without being obvious about it. All three of them were brown-eyed brunettes and the two younger women were pretty in a plain way, but they were too strongly built to be considered attractive, especially with the way they were holding themselves. The older woman stood square and belligerent, wearing her gown like a sack, uncomfortable and unhappy and wanting everyone to know it. She was feeling put-upon, and the two younger women reflected the emotion, their own gowns fitting better but not much. Their eyes came to me as we approached them, disapproval growing as they looked me up and down, their self-consciousness increasing when they compared the way I looked to the way they looked. John Little was wearing even more of a smirk than he usually did, and it suddenly came to me that he'd brought me over to the women for the sole purpose of making them feel lousy. If I could have walked away at that point I would have done it, but unfortunately I was already committed.

I was introduced to Margaret and her daughters, Estelle and Angela, all of us acknowledging the introductions stiffly, and in the process learned that everyone there used first names only, surnames never being mentioned. Little was sleek and urbane with the three women, laughing at them with his eyes alone, and after a couple of minutes excused us from their company. I was ready to put my foot down against being used like that again, but the next one he led me toward was Radman. The slaver looked even more square and blocky than ever, dark haired and dark eyed and a little bulgy around the middle, standing alone in his blacks with his feet in the mist. His eyes attached themselves to me even before we reached him, and John Little was just about preening himself.

"Jennifer, I'd like you to meet Richard," Little said in a tone that suggested "Richard" was no more than a casual acquaintance only recently met. "Jennifer is here with her uncle Val, Richard, and he's done quite a lot to brighten her pretty eyes. It's hard to describe how surly and bored she was before he took her in hand and taught her how to behave. She's learned that if she wants him to make her feel good, she's got to be a good little girl. Isn't that right, Jennifer?"

I gave Little the blush of embarrassment he was expecting, glared at Radman for his low rumble of laughter and tried to turn away from them both, but Little wasn't having any. His hand tightened on my arm, the grip unbreakable unless I wanted to use something fancy, his chuckle joining Radman's laughter.

"That's one of the most important lessons for a little girl to learn, John," Radman rumbled in true amusement. "If you don't behave yourself, you don't get what you need. Why don't you introduce her to James next?"

Little's amusement and satisfaction were suddenly more

forced than natural, and it took a look from Radman before
he nodded stiffly and reluctantly, then led me again away.
The man holding my arm wasn't very happy about the "suggestion" he'd been given, and that reminded me about the
quiet argument he and Radman had been having. I didn't
know what was going on, but whatever it was, Little wasn't
happy about it.

We found James seated in an intricately carved, straight-
backed chair, one of the very few chairs in the entire room, a
big, ugly hulk of a man standing behind him. James could
have been anywhere from fifty on up, but just how far up was
impossible to tell. His face looked like leather, but the creases
in it had not been made by laughter. He lifted his lean, tall
body out of the chair as we approached, and he waited,
leaning slightly on a thin cane.

"James, I would like to present Jennifer," Little said, and
his voice had a slight quiver in it. "She and her uncle arrived
with me this afternoon."

James nodded and then moved his eyes to me, and the
impact of those eyes was enough to make me try to take a
step backward. Those eyes were gray and deathly cold, and if
any eyes belonged in the precincts of hell, they were the
ones. I was stripped and knocked down and attacked by those
eyes in the seconds they moved over me, and then a faint
smile touched the leather face.

"How do you do, Jennifer," James said in a cold, raspy
voice. "I'm particularly fond of meeting young ladies as
pretty as you are. The combination of innocence and maturity
has always fascinated me."

"No one above the age of five is as innocent as you're
suggesting," I came back with a tremor in my voice that had
nothing to do with playacting. "And even above that, you're
not my type. I don't like old men."

I'd been trying to turn him off in the most direct way

possible, letting him know that his roundabout compliments were understood and entirely rejected, but he didn't get the point. His faint smile broadened a millimeter or two, and his gray eyes glittered.

"Ah, spirit," he rasped, his fingers turning the thin cane. "That makes the game even more exciting. Don't you agree, Matthew?"

"Of course, sir," the hulk behind the chair rumbled, his stone-faced expression changing not at all.

"Matthew is my bodyguard," James continued, bringing my eyes back to him. "He shares all of my—interests in life. Perhaps you and your uncle would care to be my guests after your visit here is over. I came in my own ship, and there's plenty of room for passengers. My estate on my own world has everything one could wish for."

"No," I told him flatly, feeling a chill at my backbone. "We're going home after this."

I expected some sort of argument, but those eyes merely turned flat and hooded. "A pity," he murmured, his leather-like face showing no emotion. "I would have found it most diverting. Some other time, perhaps."

He bowed very slightly from the waist, then sat down again, and Little and I were free to move on. Possibly dismissed would have been a more accurate word, but whatever word it was didn't matter to Little. He took the opportunity to get us both out of there, and for once I agreed with him completely. Anywhere in that room was better than right next to James, and I finished my drink fast and then got rid of the glass on a passing slave's tray.

We were on our way to another group of people when Val finally showed up with three more men and two women, all of them dressed in the guest motif. The other men and women headed immediately for the slaves with drink trays, but Val headed for me. The good part about that was Little's hand immediately leaving my arm; the bad part was the look in my partner's eyes as he came up to us.

"If I'd known what was waiting for me, I would have hurried," he said with a leer, reaching around to rub his hand over my behind. "You should have come to my room instead of coming here, Jenny. You don't want to be naughty and make your uncle Val do without, do you?"

"Oh, no, uncle Val," I whispered, grabbing his left arm with both of mine to get it off my backside, seriously tempted to let him know the depth of my revulsion. "I'd never want you to have to do without."

"You're such a good little girl," he said with a grin for the way I'd trapped his hand and arm, using his free hand to pat me on the head. "Let's see if we can find some place for you to be an even better little girl."

His grin widened with the knowledge that I couldn't very well refuse him as he began leading me back toward the arch, but two steps of satisfaction was all he got. One of the bearded Sphere people appeared in the arch, then walked to the center of the room.

"The time has come for your tour to begin, my friends," the man announced, looking around at the guests. "Many of you are upset and impatient, I know, but we'll soothe that away. Follow me."

Some of the guests tried to stop him and question him as he made for the far side of the room, but he ignored them and just kept going, not giving a damn that he was increasing their annoyance. The slaves in the room were standing well back away from the guests, and Val made a sound in his throat that was close to a growl.

"These people are really getting on my nerves," he muttered to me in the base language, reluctantly heading us after the bearded man. "I keep getting the urge to pick one up and smash him into a wall."

"I have the feeling they want you in that particular frame of mind," I muttered back. "See if you can get your mind off my backside long enough to figure out why."

"If you wanted my mind off your backside, you should have stayed in that other dress," he countered, but it was clear he was only paying partial attention to the banter. My comment had alerted him again to the serious side of life, and he was looking around for an answer to my question.

We and the other guests followed after the bearded man, through a doorway that led into a series of caves and caverns. The red light was redder there and the mist thicker, and we suddenly walked into a scene that was straight out of imaginative fiction. Men and women in red turtlenecks, pants and shoes with small horns pasted to their foreheads were prodding at naked, cowering men and women with sharp, three-pointed pitchforks, and the blood on the ones being prodded showed the pitchforks were for real. The naked victims were chained by the neck to the wall of the cave, and nothing they did fended off the pitchforks. Their mouths were open as though they were screaming or crying, but no sounds came through the laughter of the ones doing the prodding.

"Here's a simple choice for those whose tastes run to the simple," the bearded man said when we were all gathered in the cave. "You may be devil's helper or damned soul, whichever way your interest moves you. The lost souls start here and are softened up, so to speak, and then they're sent on to further punishment. A taste of the whip, some time on the rack, red-hot pokers, being forced to the pleasure of fiends, that sort of thing. Devils' helpers perform those chores, and also get first pick of the slaves among the lost souls. In either capacity, the time passes swiftly and pleasantly."

He sent another amused glance toward the silent victims then moved on, drawing most of us along with him. Two of the women and one of the men were staring at the two groups and licking their lips, but which part of the picture they preferred wasn't immediately apparent. Val had also been staring, but with no expression on his face, looking at the bearded male victims, and when he turned away from them to follow our guide, I breathed a sigh of relief. It had seemed at first that he would have enjoyed using one of those pitchforks, and if he'd tried I wouldn't have been able to break my role to stop him.

The next few caves showed us voiceless victims tied to whipping posts, stretched on racks, being seared by red-hot pokers, being locked in tiny cages with spear points all around, being suspended over open fires—no more than your simple, everyday, ordinary tortures. Our guide didn't even stop in any of them, and when he finally did stop, it was for something special.

"Here we have another opportunity for choice," he said, waving at the scene in front of us. "Those who are naked are again lost souls, but those in red are demons. Only a very few guests choose to be tormented here, but many choose the role of tormentor. Their victims are, for the most part, slaves."

Our guide fell silent to keep from distracting us from the scene, and it was easy to tell why most of the victims were slaves. One victim was being forced to walk on a bed of glowing hot coals, another was being prodded between a line of too-close, too-sharp knives, and another was being kept from surfacing very often in a narrow but obviously deep pool by the use of a torch in the hands of one of the demons. These victims were also screaming without sound, and when the guide turned and left the cave, Val and I weren't far behind him. Some of those with us had lingered for a longer look, but my partner and I had seen more than enough.

The rest of our tour companions were still looking around and enjoying the sights behind us, and our guide had stopped farther ahead to wait until everyone caught up to him; Val took the opportunity to make a stop of his own in the stone corridor halfway between those two points, glancing around to make sure no one was paying undue attention to us.

"I think I have an answer to your question," he murmured in the trade language. "If I don't pay attention to what I'm thinking, I experience pleasure every time I see a bearded man having something painful done to him. I'd guess that under normal circumstances, I'd choose a place in those first two sections to spend my time."

"Normal circumstances, right," I agreed, swallowing hard and fighting not to apply a death grip to his arm. My eyes had gone to where our guide had stopped, in front of a large, metal-bound wooden door, and suddenly I knew what had to be behind that door. I'd seen a report once about a certain place in the Pleasure Sphere, but the location of the place hadn't been mentioned, and I hadn't added up the clues until right then. I was sure I knew what lay behind that enigmatic door, and also knew that the last thing I wanted was to look at what it hid.

"Are you all right?" Val asked, putting his hand to my face, his eyes sober and concerned. "It's almost impossible to tell in this light, but you look pale. This place is enough to turn the stomach of a normal mass murderer. Maybe I ought to get you out of here."

"Don't worry, I'll manage to survive," I told him with a small headshake, knowing I had to continue on with it until I found out where Radman would be later—and alone. "How are *you* doing?"

"Lousy," he answered without changing expression, but something in his eyes stirred. "If I ever come across the people who started this, nothing in this universe will save them even if I have to pay for it with my own life. Sickness should be treated, not catered to, and the things who come

here are sick. Even though I know I can't do it alone, I keep
wanting to stop all this."

"Just remember you can't do it alone, or we could end up
being part of the fun," I warned him. "This is a sovereign
planet, partner, and what they do here is their own business.
If we don't like it, we can leave."

"Yeah, sure," he agreed with no agreement whatsoever,
then took us along with the strengthening trickle of people
heading toward that door. Our guide waited until everyone
was there, then gestured toward what stood behind him.

"Behind that portal lies the last of your major options," he
said, looking around with approval at all the eager faces.
"No guests are permitted to be victims here, for this is the
realm of the fiends. These victims also haven't been silenced,
so you'd better be braced for the noise. The fiends, of course,
prefer the noise to silence."

He turned away to step to the door to open it, and the first
scream rippling through sent a jagged knife across my nerve
ends. The scream had come from a man, and the terror and
pain to be heard in it defied all description. Val stiffened
beside me despite the impassive expression he'd been wearing through the previous caves, and some of our happy
chatter died at the sound. We all moved forward, some with
eyes positively shining, and followed our guide through the
doorway.

There's no way to gently or euphemistically describe what
went on in that last cave behind the wooden door. It wasn't as
bad as the report I had read; it was worse, so much worse that
every other sickening thing I'd ever before seen in my life
was relegated to the category of peccadillo. Our guide strolled
along when all I wanted to do was run, and then we came to
the place where the screaming male victim wasn't bearded. It
took me a minute to realize that John Little's pretty male
slave hadn't escaped after all, and then I really saw what was

being done to him on the surgical table he'd been strapped to. I pulled away from Val, pushed through the interested spectators who were wondering why the scene was being recorded by a wire camera, and ran ahead to the end of the area with a hand to my mouth. The end of the area wasn't far and there was a door in the wall, and I barely remember tearing through the door and slamming it behind me.

I stood outside the door and leaned against the rock wall, trembling so violently I didn't think I'd be able to stop. I'd pretended to be sick to get myself out of there, but I wasn't simply sick, I was on the verge of losing control over myself and killing every one of those scum I could get my hands on. I'd seen a lot in my years as a Special Agent, but that place outraged me more than anything else I had ever seen, anything I had ever heard of. Our fellow guests had been wondering why that scene out of all the others was being recorded, but I already knew. When it was all over the wire would be shown to the Sphere's other slaves, an object lesson to teach what happens to those who try to escape. It would not be the first such object lesson, and was undoubtedly the reason the slaves all felt such terror at this place. This was where the unlucky ones ended up, as experimental animals for the mind-sick—or as object lessons. I leaned against the rough stone wall, jamming my palms into my eyes, trying to force myself to stop shaking.

"My poor Jennifer, are you all right?" Val's voice came from beside me, right after a burst of screaming had sounded briefly with the opening of the door. He pulled me away from the wall and put his arms around me with great concern. "The poor little thing shouldn't have been shown all that," he went on, clearly to whoever was with him. "Is there some place she can rest a minute or two?"

"There's a refreshment area just ahead of us," the voice of the guide answered, heavy with amusement. "She can sit down there and have a drink, and pull herself together. You might be wise to examine some of the lighter pastimes on display there, and choose one of *them* for her instead of what you've just seen. No sense in having the hysterics of a little girl ruin your own good time.''

"I'm sure you're right," Val agreed, maintaining a pleasant tone with difficulty. "The refreshment area is that way?"

"That's right, straight ahead," the guide said. "The rest of us will be along in another minute or two."

"Fine," Val said, urging me along as he began moving. He waited until we'd taken half a dozen steps, then switched languages and added, "Fine, hell. You can't tell me this time you're all right. As soon as you stop shaking like a ship with a faulty firing chamber, I'm getting you out of here."

"No," I insisted, taking my hands away from my eyes and really making the effort to calm down. "It isn't what you think. The only thing that happened was that I nearly put us both in the soup. Never in my entire life have I been more tempted to kill in cold blood."

"Freezing blood," Val corrected, glancing down at me as we made our way toward an arch like the one on the first refreshment area. "My blood turned cold the minute we walked into this place, and went down-temperature from there. As a matter of fact, it's a good thing you ran when you did. I was seconds away from doing something like that myself, and needed the distraction. I still say we ought to get out of here right now."

"No," I repeated, filling my lungs with a deep breath. "We'll leave when we have what we came here for."

"If you aren't the stubbornest woman I've ever met, I'll eat these caves," he growled, sending me a black-eyed look that was all steel and anger. "I don't need your agreement to do it, you know. If I say we go, we go."

"As far as the assignment goes, *I* call the shots," I reminded him, meeting that look with one of my own. "If you pull me out of here before I have a chance at our target, I'll make sure my report lists the cause of failure as due to delicate sensibilities. I won't name names, of course, but the Council already knows all about my own sensibilities. It'll be a great first entry in your history file."

Those black eyes grew even sterner as he stared at me, but he didn't waste breath asking if I really would do something like that. He'd learned to know me well enough to know I wasn't above making sure there would be a permanent blot on his record if he screwed up the assignment for me. There'd be very little chance of his getting another assignment afterward, and working as an agent in the Federation seemed to be important to him. He let out some of the growl he was feeling in a soft sound deep in his throat, then dropped the subject of leaving.

The second refreshment area had a lot more seating than the first, and Val sat me down on one of the couches then gestured over a slave with a tray of glasses. I sipped at the glass of wine I was given, pretending it was soothing me, in reality being careful not to let it rekindle the flames of rage that were finally throttling down. Val finished his wine in two swallows and looked around for the slave to get another, but the slave was busy serving the rest of the guests who were just then entering the area. Instead of waiting for one of the slaves to get free from the tangle and begin circulating, he headed toward the knot of arrivals and one of the trays, too impatient to simply wait. I knew my partner wasn't pleased with me, but we all have burdens to bear in this life.

That refreshment area was even stranger than the first one, though it had the same reddish lighting and mist curling over the floor. I'd already noticed that it had more seating than the first, but it also had mirrors on the carved-rock walls and chandeliers hanging from the rough-hewn ceiling, which added more glitter than light to the room. I sipped at my drink and worked toward calming myself all the way, at the same time wondering if I ought to tell Val I'd already found Radman and the end of the assignment shouldn't be too far ahead of us. Under other circumstances I would have already told him, but I still couldn't trust his reactions. He'd been talking about getting *me* out of there, but I would have been insensitive not to know how much he wanted to get himself out as well. If I told him about Radman I couldn't put it past him to kill the slaver right there, thinking that would end the assignment and let us leave. He seemed to have the tendency to forget about the Management and what they could do to us if we were caught, and I couldn't risk a reaction like that. I looked at him where he stood with the other guests, talking to—of all people!—James and his hulking bodyguard Matthew, and knew I'd made the right decision. Radman's death warrant was mine to serve, and I'd see that it got served without Val and me being served up right behind it.

The guests spread out and sat down on the various couches and in the various chairs, talking to one another like long-lost brothers and sisters, no longer holding themselves aloof from one another. They were all soul-mates there, they'd learned, and that made all the difference in the world. I finished my wine and put the glass aside, mainly keeping myself aware of where Radman was in the room, and suddenly Val and Little were sitting down on the couch with me.

"Are you feeling any better, Jennifer?" Val asked with heavy sweetness to his concern, reaching over to lift me into his lap. "Poor little thing, you had a rough time."

"I'm feeling a little bit better, uncle Val," I conceded cautiously, wondering what he was up to. "As long as we don't have to go back to that horrible place. We don't have to go back, do we?"

"Of course you don't have to go back," he assured me

heartily and condescendingly, patting me on the behind as he pressed my head to his chest. "We'll just find something else for you to do while I'm occupied, something a little more fun. Can you start it, John?"

"Certainly, Val," Little agreed pleasantly, reaching to the buttons set into the arm of the couch to his left. He pressed one of the buttons, and a tri-v picture sprang into being right in front of us. I noticed then that others of the guests were watching something in front of where they were sitting, and remembered the guide's comment about "lighter pastimes."

"How about *that*, sweetheart?" Val asked, still rubbing his hand over my backside. "They're teaching that girl to be a perfect slave, so she'll give all the pleasure there is to the man who uses her. You want to learn how to give me all the pleasure there is, don't you?"

"Sure I do, uncle Val," I answered, wishing I could curse him out the way he deserved. The girl in the picture was being made to crawl from man to man, being taught the most abject slavery there was. If Val gave the word that's what *I* would be taught, and he wanted me to know it. He was trying to force me into saying we could leave, and didn't care how dirty he had to play to get what he wanted.

"Or maybe you'd like that, Jennifer," Little put in, gesturing toward the changed picture. "The naked woman is a guest, and the men chasing her are all true rapists, the sort who don't like giving pleasure to the woman they have sex with. You can see she's hiding in one of the buildings of that make-believe town, but hiding isn't enough. She has to get to the other side of the town before she'll be safe, and if she's caught she'll be raped, then sent back to start all over. It's like an obstacle course filled with fun."

Fun, I thought as the scene changed again, this time showing two men with two small children. The men were laughing and the children were crying, and Val's hand froze where it was on me.

"Well, that's not very interesting," Little complained, reaching over to fast-forward the action. He paused long enough to see that the next selection showed two women with whips starting to rape a man, fast-forwarded that one too, then settled back to watch a scene where a crying woman on her hands and knees was giving a ride to a big man who liked his own way of doing things. Val was quiet for a couple of minutes, his body stiff under mine, his breath almost rasping out of the chest I leaned against, and then he started all over again, this time trying twice as hard.

By the time the tri-v show was over, I wasn't in very steady shape. Val had slid his hand up the slit of my dress and had used some of his expertise on me, and with Little watching I hadn't been able to do anything but react, and in character at that. Little Jenny just couldn't resist her uncle Val, and John Little got a good laugh over the way he'd made me squirm. When Val pushed me to my feet then stood up himself, Little straightened off the couch with a chuckle.

"I'm sure you'll be glad to know we're now about to be shown to rooms, Jennifer," he said, watching the way I was trying to slow my breathing. "We've got about two hours before they serve dinner to our friendly little group, and I'm sure you'll put the time to good use. And you can also think about which of those pastimes you'd like to sample."

"I've just about decided to start her with the slave training," Val put in, taking my arm to wrap around his, also watching me closely. "If you don't like the idea, Jenny, you can try changing my mind, but I warn you now I'll be awfully hard to convince."

"Maybe that training *would* be best," Little allowed thoughtfully as we began drifting toward the door on the far side of the room with everyone else. "Once she's properly trained you'll be able to enjoy her anywhere, not just in the privacy of your own quarters. They may start out modest and shy in that program, but the trainers don't let it last for long. You'll even be able to use her to please your guests."

Val made some sort of interested answer to that, keeping the conversation going, but I'd stopped listening. My sweet partner knew how I felt about slave training, especially if it was applied to me, but what he still didn't seem to understand was how I felt about blackmail. He had an objective but so did I, and my objective was damned well going to come first.

The object of my objective, so to speak, left the refreshment room in our group, and walked with us down another carved-out corridor. At the end of the corridor the stone wall slid back to reveal an elevator car, one which easily held the dozen or so people of our part of the group. The car took us upward quickly and smoothly, finally stopping to let us out on a floor that still looked like it was carved out of rock. Doors lined both sides of the corridor-hall, and a pretty woman in a silver gown, wearing a black medallion around her neck, stepped out of a small alcove to smile at us.

"Some of you have already been shown to your rooms on this floor," she said, glancing at Radman and one or two others. "The rest of you will be shown to them now, and you can do as you like until dinner is ready. Your entire group has been assigned to this wing, and you'll be eating and relaxing together until your visit is over. Tomorrow, when you choose the program you'd like to participate in, medallions will be issued to you, showing your choice. The medallions are Sisslian silver, and are yours to keep, as a memento of your visit here. Some of our guests collect the entire set, but let me caution you: complete sets are worth a good deal more than the value of the silver, so be wary if you're approached with an offer for your medallion. If you sell it for the price of the silver alone, you're losing money. Now, if those of you who haven't yet been shown to rooms will please follow me?''

Our group split up again, and Radman gave me a last unreadable glance before heading up the hall. I made sure not to acknowledge the glance while pretending I wasn't watching him closely, and the Lord of Luck applauded my performance by giving me just what I needed. Radman stopped at a door a short way down the hall on the right, knocked once, and was admitted immediately; the female guide was handing out room assignments in the meantime, and ours turned out to be two doors closer to the elevator than Radman's but also on the right. As I watched Val unlock our door and step inside, I thanked the Lord of Luck and promised I wouldn't waste the opening he'd given me. If I couldn't reach Radman from that close a distance, I didn't deserve to reach him at all.

The room waiting for us was like a room in an old castle, the red lighting and mist-covered floor making it a haunted castle. Heavy, brocade-covered furniture and a large fireplace made the entrance room a sitting room, the lights were artificial red flames burning from wall jets, and the mirrors hung about were dark pools reflecting back nothing they saw. I expected to see cobwebs hanging from the ceiling, but a glance around as I closed the door showed clean stone walls instead. Val walked across the room to open the door there, stuck his head in, then pulled it out to look at me.

''That's a bedroom, Jennifer, and you'd better sound happy to hear it,'' he told me in the trade language: ''My friend who has been our traveling companion told me to make you squeal loud and long—and only then tell you we're being listened to. This whole apartment is bugged, so watch what you say.''

''I don't have to watch what I say,'' I answered the same way, making my tone go pleading. ''I only have to watch what I sound like. Have you been enjoying yourself, you son of a bitch?''

"Not even a little bit," he came back with a chuckle, his tone teasing. "I'm telling you right now that I can't take it here any longer, and if you don't give the go signal without prejudice by tommorrow morning, you're going to find yourself enrolled in a slave-training class. If I'll have to be spending my time giving pain to a bunch of poor, helpless bastards, you're going to be suffering at least as much."

"But that's blackmail, uncle Val, and I thought you knew how I feel about blackmail," I said in a coaxing way, as he glared at me. "You can push until you're blue in the face instead of red, and I'll still tell you what to do with yourself. I've got a job to do, and I'm going to do it."

"You can't do the job if one of us breaks and goes on a rampage," he said, trying to sound reasonable instead of irate and furious. "We'll go back upstairs and wait for our target there. If you can't operate there, we'll simply follow him to wherever he goes next. You don't have to insist on what neither of us can live with."

"No," I said, not bothering to mask the finality in my voice. "I'm the assignment leader, and I say we stick. If you take us off this planet, you do it against my direct orders. I'm not about to let that filth get the chance to contaminate anyone else, not when I'm this close to him. I have him right in my. . . ."

"You don't have him anywhere, and you know it," he interrupted, fighting to sound sleek and lecherous. "You don't know where he is any more now than you did when we first got here, but you're too stubborn to admit it. Maybe you need to be reminded how much power I have over you down here." He switched back to Basic and said, "No, Jennifer, my mind is made up. A little slave training won't hurt you, and will probably do you a world of good. Come into the bedroom, now. I want to get inside you for a while before we go to dinner.''

"You miserable, no good, gutter-crawling piece of . . ." I began, really fuming, but he cut me off again.

"But of course they'll all know what I'm doing to you," he laughed, coming closer to snap his arm around me before I could figure out just exactly what I wanted to do to him and also was able to do in that gown. "If you don't behave yourself, I'll invite some of them in next time to watch. Come along, now."

He just about dragged me into a bedroom that matched the sitting room, neither one of us about to make the struggle loud but both of us still struggling, threw me on the bed, then went through some window-dressing chatter about what he was doing to me. He forced me to the point of having to answer in kind, and then began making love to me, trying his usual tricks to get me to respond. Verbally I gave him everything he was looking for, every ooh and ahh and moan and groan, but through it all I kept every trace of expression off my face and simply stared at him, telling him to go ahead and rape me and be damned. He tried to go through with it, he really did, but in the end all he did was make the same noises I was making but the male variety, bouncing on the bed next to me and staring down. Anyone listening would have thought we were having a ball, but as balls went, that one was on the grim side.

When the sound show was over, Val turned away from me and simply lay down. We'd said everything there was to say, and at that point my telling him how close Radman was would either be totally disbelieved or believed so eagerly that he would go after him alone in the way I'd thought about earlier. Whatever was done would have to be done by me, but that was the way it was supposed to be anyway. I'd wanted to keep Val out of it; he was making sure I did exactly that.

After waiting for a few minutes for the benefit of the ears listening, I left the bed and went into the only bathroom the apartment had. I didn't have to be told that the apartment was a single, assigned to Val with me thrown in as an unimportant extra occupant. Double accommodations had two bathrooms, but I wasn't being considered a guest in my own right, not in anything that counted. I got out of my gown and shoes and earrings without letting my annoyance show, then stepped into the shower. If Val thought *he* was sick of that place, he should have tried it from my point of view.

Showering and drying didn't take long, so it was still too early to get dressed again. I thought about going back out to the bedroom until it was time to join our jolly group for the meal, then rejected the idea. I didn't want Val thinking I had changed my mind, and I didn't want to give him the chance to change it for me. The bathroom floor was nicely carpeted with no mist, so there was nothing to keep me from spending my time there. I sat down and then stretched out, trying to forget about everything.

When an hour had passed on the clock I dressed again, brushed my hair, then made my silent way out of the bathroom. I didn't want our listeners to know how long I'd been in there, and with Val supposedly asleep I had the perfect excuse for tiptoeing. Val's eyes followed me as I crossed the room toward the sitting room, but he stayed where he was, continuing to pretend to be asleep. It looked like he hadn't been able to really rest any more than I had, but as long as he didn't start in on me again it didn't much matter.

I sat in the sitting room for about fifteen minutes, and just as Val came out of the bedroom, a knock sounded on the door. He crossed the room to open it, and found that we were being called to dinner. I began to think that my time was improving, but when we followed the woman to a large private dining room on the other side of the elevator, I began thinking the Lord of Luck was at it again. Place cards were arranged on the long formal table in the center of the haunted-castle-like room, first names only, if you please, and the card directly to my right showed the name Richard. I sat down at the table with Val to my left, excitement rising in me despite the fact that Richard is a very common name and I hadn't been introduced to everyone in our group. If that was Radman who had been seated next to me, I had it made.

I waited until almost all the guests had arrived, until James came in and sat on the opposite side of the other end of the table, until the woman in silver and the bearded man in black took their places at the two ends of the table. I'd been waiting for Radman to come in and sit down, but that turned out not to be necessary. When he came in he stopped to talk to James, but by then I didn't care what he did. He was the only one not sitting down, and the only place left open was the one to my right. He must have seen to that arrangement, I realized, an unsitting spider throwing the door wide in welcome to the spider-eater disguised as a fly.

Acting as though I didn't even see Radman, I put my hands under the edge of the red tablecloth, gently scraped off a tiny piece of the colorless coating from my left ring fingernail, and took it between my thumb and forefinger. A few seconds of casual checking brought the assurance that no one was specifically looking my way, so I took the opportunity and reached past Radman's wine glass for a warmed soft roll. Opening my fingers over the glass got rid of the sliver of specially made chemical before I touched the roll, and when I brought my hand back the first step was done. Each of my fingernails is coated with a different colorless, traceless chemical, in most instances a poison, and the one I'd chosen for Radman would give him about two hours or so to enjoy his meal before it turned him completely out of focus. He'd be feeling sick enough to go to bed, and if things worked out right I'd be right behind him. I could have fed him something lethal just as easily, of course, but that wasn't the way death warrants were served. Death by poisoning can be caused by anyone or anything, even an accident, and doesn't tend to be as impressive as death by execution. The Council wanted whoever stepped into Radman's shoes to know that the same thing could happen to him if he got too far out of line, and the Council's way was how I had to play it.

Radman finally came over and took his seat, gave me what he must have considered a friendly smile, and began asking me small-talk questions about how my time in the Sphere had gone so far. I gave him unenthusiastic answers with down-in-the-mouth overtones, trying to get him to pick another victim for his conversation, but he was getting too much of a kick looking at the one he'd already picked. I wouldn't have liked the man even if I'd known nothing about him, and then he really added the icing. He took the opportunity of a slave coming over to pour wine in his glass to lean close to me, then sent his bad breath right in my face.

"Don't you worry about that class you'll be starting tomorrow, little girl," he reassured me in low tones, his hand moving under the tablecloth to touch my gown above my thighs. "I've already arranged to be there as one of the men you'll learn to please, and I really do intend to be pleased. When we sit down at this table again tomorrow night, you'll know what it's like to be screwed by a real man."

He chuckled as he gave me a final pat, then leaned away again to reach for his wine, leaving me to fight hard to keep from shuddering in disgust. I already knew what it was like to be invaded by that particular "man," and if I'd had to do it again I would have gotten sick or crazy. I watched him swallow down half his wine without even tasting it, a pig of a man with fewer manners even than an animal, walking garbage that thought it had me marked, bought and paid for. The only thing it didn't have neatly arranged was the drug in its drink, and the fact that the hunter had now become the hunted.

"Jennifer, sweetheart, are you all right?" Val's voice came suddenly from my left, his arm circling my shoulders a minute later. "You're trembling and pale-looking again just the way you were a few hours ago. Don't you feel well, little girl?"

"Not really, uncle Val," I answered in a small voice, indulging in the urge to lean closer to him and put my head against him. "I don't know what it is, but I really don't feel good."

"You probably just need some hot food in you," he murmured, tightening his arm around me and gently brushing aside some of my hair with his free hand. "We'll try it and see how it does."

I nodded obediently and just kept leaning on him, knowing he was seriously concerned but finding the out he'd given me too good to pass up. Not feeling well was a great reason for my going back to our room early, and once I was gone no one would wonder where I was. I rubbed my cheek against his shirt, glad I could do it in character, finally admitting I was glad about another thing. As soon as Val had started speaking to me, Radman had turned away to the woman on his right and had begun a conversation with her. As long as Val had his arm around me Radman's hands would be off, and that made up for a whole hell of a lot of the nonsense I'd gone through with my new partner. I remembered again the various times he hadn't taken advantage of me when he could have, a couple of hours earlier being the latest addition, and grudged the admission that it occasionally felt good to have him there.

When the dinner finally got rolling it was a lavish affair, with course after course of food and bottle after bottle of wine, all of it generous helpings, all of it indisputably the best it could possibly be. I continued to pretend I wasn't feeling well, but still managed to swallow enough food to keep me going for a while, at the same time staying away from anything stronger than water, as I intended to be working later and didn't want the edge taken off my reflexes.

Having Radman next to me put a strain on my appetite, but it did turn out to be handy; when the light sheen of sweat started covering his face and he began to tug unconsciously at his collar, I knew it was time for me to leave. The drug I'd fed him would soon begin to affect him more strongly, and I wanted to be innocently gone by then. I told Val I still wasn't feeling well and wanted to go back to our room and go to bed, and was surprisingly saved from having him insist on going with me by John Little, who sat to Val's left. He dismissed my supposed illness by telling Val it was just a reaction to the tour we'd taken that afternoon, then told him there was something special he wanted to show him in just a few minutes. Val looked at me and hesitated, then must have realized that if I'd really needed him, I would have said so in the trade language. He told me to go and get some rest, patted my cheek, and had turned back to Little even before I had pushed away from the table.

I walked the supposed stone corridor back to our room with the key Val had given me in my hand, thinking about Radman and idly wondering why Little hadn't introduced Val to him yet. Radman hadn't once so much as looked in their direction all evening, and that made me curious. Was the cold shoulder Little's idea or Radman's? Had the game Little's been playing changed, or was it deeper than we'd first supposed? If I managed to get Radman that night it would turn out not to matter, so I didn't spend much thinking time on the question;

by the next day Val and I would hopefully be on our way
back to the Station, and the slavers' plans turned to no more
than dust on a chalkboard.

I reached our door, opened it and slipped inside, then stood
thinking for a minute, annoyed by something I'd just seen.
The corridor outside was empty, but that little alcove near the
elevator the woman in silver had come out of was occupied
by three slaves, probably waiting to take care of the wants
and needs of the guests. The room I stood in wasn't far from
that alcove, and if I stepped back out into the hall for any
reason, like going to Radman's room, for instance, they'd see
me without any trouble. That was a problem I hadn't foreseen
and didn't appreciate, but there was something else to take
care of before I spent any real time thinking about it.

I moved without worrying about sound and entered the
bedroom, then went to my luggage. Pulling out a hair-fine ear
was the work of a minute, along with a shorts outfit and
canvas deck shoes. I left the clothes and shoes on the bed,
took the ear, then went back to the door to the apartment and
opened it. I'd purposefully forgotten to set the "do not
disturb" sign when I'd first come in, needing that minute to
get the ear, and that's where I set the ear, right below the
sign. With the thin, tiny bug in place, I'd know for sure when
Radman came back to his apartment.

Back in the bedroom again, I changed out of the silver
gown and sling-backs into the clothes I'd prepared, got a
button receiver from my luggage, then decided to be optimis-
tic. Among the jewelry I'd brought was a very special ring, a
large, well-set and expensive-looking ring, but it was more
than just expensive. I slipped it on my finger, put the button
receiver in my ear, then went to lie down on the bed.

Through the receiver in my ear, I could hear the low-
voiced chatter among the slaves, no words, sound only, but it
helped to off-set the feel of that bedroom while I waited. The

bed I lay on was a big four-poster, but it wasn't curtained the way it might be. The walls of the room were false stone, with a double-window breaking one of them with an exit to a balcony outside. The lighting was still red and the mist still covered the floor, and the room temperature was still up there, and I really did feel as though I waited in a room in hell. What I planned to do that night was a fitting occupation for hell, and that thought seemed to add to the faint depression I was feeling. Also, typically, the depression didn't come from the thought of doing the job, but from the thought of the possibility of not being able to do it. If I couldn't pull it off I'd be running into Radman tomorrow in a way that really would be hell.

About half an hour passed, during which time I smoked some of the cigarettes in my luggage, and then I began getting something other than slave-chatter from the receiver. Two sets of footsteps came down the hall, and one set sounded shaky.

"I hope you'll be feeling better soon, Richard," an unfamiliar female voice said. "Are you sure I can't get a doctor for you?"

"No," Radman's voice came. "If I need one, I'll call him myself. Just don't bother me now."

I listened to the footsteps, and they went the necessary two-door distance down the corridor. Nothing else was said, a knock came then the sound of a door opening and closing, and then a single set of footsteps went back the way it had come. I lay back again and gave it another half hour.

When the second half hour was over I took the button receiver out of my ear, then got up without making any sound. The receiver went back in my luggage and I went to the balcony door, also managing to open it without sound. Outside the dark was complete, but the red mist floating all around gave off a light of its own, a light that let me see that I was at least twenty stories up, but just beyond the balcony I stood on was a ledge leading in the direction I needed to go in. It wasn't a very wide ledge, but it was considerably better than no ledge at all, and would have to do; the slaves were still in the alcove and still had no one to distract them.

One leg at a time, I climbed out onto the ledge beside the window, feeling my hair being ruffled by the cool breeze coming by in gentle gusts, allowing my mind knowledge of no more than the ledge I stood on, the building I leaned against. I felt very mortal out on that ledge, but if I were going to reach Radman that ledge was the only way of doing it. In the dark and red-tinged mist I began moving slowly along the narrow walkway, away from my own balcony, getting closer to the job's end with every step I took.

I'd expected to get a break with the room between Radman's and mine, but that room had no balcony, and the window was lit, showing someone in there with his back to the window. I got past it as quickly as I could, then went on to the balcony in front of Radman's window, climbed the railing, and carefully looked inside. Radman was lying flat on the bed, and by the faint glow of one of the fake wall flames, he looked asleep. It wasn't logical for a balcony door twenty stories up to be locked, and it wasn't. I opened it with no sound at all, then stepped inside.

I stopped next to Radman where he lay on the bed and listened to his even breathing for a minute, then slipped the very special ring from my finger and gently placed the stone against his skin. The stone glowed green the way I had expected it to, but I'd still been required to check. I put the ring back on and stared down at the face of the man who had done so much to me, knowing I ought to simply finish him and then leave, but I couldn't do it. I couldn't just let him die peacefully without knowing what was happening, not even if it meant getting caught there. My whole body wanted to tremble at the sight of him, and I honestly didn't know if it was fear or rage behind the desire. I remembered the feel of his sweaty hand on my helpless flesh just before the appraisal, remembered even more strongly the way he'd forced himself into me before sealing me into a ship that had been meant to rid him of me forever, and there was no way to stop myself. I had to make him know, and then I had to make him dead.

I climbed onto the bed with him, one knee to each side of his body, straddling him as I leaned down closer to his face. His rate of breathing changed, showing that he was waking, and that was just what I wanted. I waited until his eyelids flickered, an attempt to bring me into focus, and then I put my hands to his face.

"I'm here, Radman," I whispered, watching as his eyes went startled with recognition. "You do remember inviting me, don't you?"

He stirred between my thighs and began to say something, his hands going automatically to my body, but I had no interest in whatever he wanted to say.

"Let me help you remember the invitation," I whispered, still touching his face gently with both hands. "There was you, and me, and some of your men, and a ship that had had some work done on its controls. You told me to look you up when I got back from my trip, and you laughed. This time we can laugh together."

My caressing hands moved immediately to his throat then, and neither one of us was laughing. Radman's eyes had widened in horror and he'd parted his lips to shout or scream, but my thumbs were already pressing into his throat with the weight of my body behind them, and no more than a rasping gurgle escaped him. He tried to fight me then, hands clawing at mine and groping for my eyes, his body bucking, but that didn't last more than seconds. I had a lot of years of experience and learning to call on, and causing unconsciousness isn't very hard.

It has never failed to impress me how easy it is to kill someone. Five minutes after I had first touched Radman he was dead, and I took my hands away from his body and stood up to stare down at him again. That piece of meat lying on the bed had deserved death many times over for the things he had done, but in spite of everything it hadn't given me any pleasure to end him. I was glad the job was finally done, ecstatic that he'd never again be in a condition even to think about touching me, grimly satisfied that he'd never again be able to victimize helpless children; pleasure, though, never entered into it. It was hard understanding how some people *did* feel pleasure after killing, that or enjoyment or euphoria. After killing with my hands I always noticed how easy it was, and thought briefly about the possibility of committing that easiness against an innocent by-stander, someone who didn't deserve to be ended. Although I watched myself carefully that possibility was always there, the possibility that one day I would slip and not perform an execution but commit murder. I didn't know what I would do if that ever happened, but I never let myself dwell on the question. I just shuddered briefly as I pushed it away, then went on with the job.

I shuddered briefly as I looked down at the former slaver, then got on with the job. Taking off the bio-ring a second time, I opened the band, then pressed the point of the stone into the ball of Radman's middle right finger. The gem came away with a drop of his blood which it quickly absorbed, and when the blood was absorbed, I closed the band and put it back on for the last time. There hadn't been a sound from the sitting room since I'd first come in, and I exited back onto the balcony with as little noise and fuss as there'd been in arriving.

Once I was on the ledge and inching back to my own

balcony, the easy time I'd had so far began balancing out. The man in the room between Radman's and mine turned out to be a thinker; I got a glimpse of him sitting in a chair and staring out the window before I pulled back, and knew damned well that if I went by straight up, there was no way he could miss me. Mouthing some uncomplimentary things about him, I slowly got down on my knees. In that position the ledge got even narrower, and my legs poked out over dark, empty air. I brought one hand down on the ledge in front of me, leaving the other hand to hang onto the carved stone of the wall, and very slowly, one hand then the other, one knee then the other, I edged past below the window. I kept having to lean in against the wall to keep myself from going off that ledge to the unseen ground, lots of stories below, and when I finally cleared the window I almost didn't have the nerve to stand up again. I took a couple of deep breaths and forced my hands to get a hold above me on the wall, then gingerly pulled myself to my feet. When my heartbeat slowed down I started moving again, and made it back to my own balcony without any more trouble.

Stepping silently back inside the room was the last thing that had to be done, and once it was accomplished I felt as though some giant weight had been lifted off of me. I went back to my trunk and took off and put away the shorts outfit and canvas shoes, then checked the button receiver to see if there was any indication of the party breaking up. I wanted Val to know the job was over and we could finally get out of there, but I couldn't very well go looking for him. If my "illness" suddenly disappeared and someone thought to check the timing with Radman's death, he and I could find ourselves facing a lot longer stay. I listened for sounds out in the corridor, didn't hear any, then noticed that I wasn't hearing the slaves, either. At least two of them were gone from the alcove, maybe all three, and that ought to have meant the dinner was officially over. As soon as he was through looking at whatever Little had wanted to show him, Val would be back in the apartment.

I put the receiver away again and turned from my luggage to stretch, thinking about taking another cigarette before going to bed. After we were back on the Station I was going to have to have a nice long talk with Val, and maybe one with Ringer as well. Things had happened during that assignment that I didn't care for, and we'd have to—

The thought broke off as a sound at the door to the sitting room caught my attention, but when it suddenly opened it wasn't Val coming through. Shockingly it was Matthew who was there, James's big, ugly bodyguard, and in his hand he held a slim, blinking rod. I recognized the rod as a pick-up deadener, a device that kept sound from reaching listening devices, and then Matthew pressed it to the wall by the doorway and started toward me fast. I didn't know what was going on, but that didn't stop me from leaning back and kicking him where it hurts the most, something he wasn't expecting. He grunted with the pain and went down to one knee partially bent over, and although I moved in fast through the surrealistic red light and mist to finish him off, I never got the chance. As soon as I was in reach he ducked lower and moved with totally unexpected speed to grab my legs and pull, which sent me over backward to hit my head hard on the floor. The blow dazed me for a second, and even though I tried to roll out of reach even before my head cleared, it was simply no good. A hamlike fist connected with the side of my skull, and that was definitely that.

CHAPTER 14

I woke up feeling as if my arms were being pulled out of their sockets. When I was finally able to understand which way was down I got my feet more firmly under me and did what might be described as standing, but only if you define terms rather loosely. I was dizzy and my head hurt, and I couldn't remember how I'd gotten to wherever I was, but I had the feeling I shouldn't be happy about being there. I pried my eyes farther open and tried to look around, but circumstances beyond my control kept that from being easily done. My arms had felt stretched because I was hanging from them, tied by the wrists to something wooden and high.

At that point I knew I had to make more of an effort than I'd made so far, and that pretty damned quick. I firmed up my legs under me and stood as straight as I could just then, and twisted a little to get as good a look around as possible. As far as I could see I was in a stone-walled bedroom, red-lit and mist-carpeted, and was tied to the left front post of a four-poster bed. The room looked familiar and yet not familiar, a room that was both mine and not mine. I shook my head gently, trying to think the headache into easing up, but to no avail.

I'd seen all I could of the room, so I gave some attention to what was holding me in place. When I looked up I was happy to see that my bio-ring was still on my finger, but was not as happy to see that my wrists were tied to the post at a height above the top of my head by what looked like ordinary rope. With a silent apology to my arms I tried the strength of the stuff, but it wasn't worth the effort. Ordinary rope would have given a little, but that stuff didn't budge. All it did was hang onto the carved post and cut into my skin with its fibers, the pain of it adding to the strain in my arms and shoulders. I dislike pain, and tend to fall into a foul mood when it is inflicted, I glared at the rope and pronouned an unladylike word.

"Quite right, my dear," said a voice from behind me. "You cannot get loose."

I froze where I stood, remembering that cold, emotionless voice, and then I remembered what had happened before everything turned blurry. Matthew had come into our apartment and had come at me, and I hadn't been able to put him down all the way. After the kick I'd given him I wondered what he was made of, but only briefly and in passing. What I was a lot more concerned about was the presence of James in the room, now clearly *his* room, his nearness bringing a chill to my flesh despite the ever-present warmth. I didn't know what I was in the middle of, but I did know I wanted out of it as soon as possible.

"These ropes are hurting my wrists, James," I complained in a young-girl voice, hoping I could sucker him into turning me loose. "Can't you take them off?"

"Not quite yet, child," he answered, with slight amusement. "You aren't ready yet."

"I don't understand," I said, and my little-girl voice turned shaky all by itself.

"It's quite simple," he said, coming around to the left of the post where I could see him. He still wore the blacks he'd had on earlier, and he still carried that thin cane he leaned on so slightly. "Matthew wasn't feeling very well when he brought you here, and he told me what had happened when he tried to fetch you. There aren't many *men* around who can best Matthew in a fight, yet he had to wait fifteen minutes before he was recovered sufficiently to complete his chore. Happily, the floor slaves remained occupied elsewhere." He shook his head slightly and tsked, but kept those hell-cold eyes directly on me. "That was very naughty of you, but it did show me what was necessary for your safekeeping."

"You can't get away with this," I began, feeling like a stale melodrama. "Guests aren't allowed to harm other guests, and uncle Val will . . ."

"Do nothing," he finished flatly, those eyes turning darker and colder in response to my throat. "Radman assured me that he could deliver you after you left here and that fool of a Little would take care of your uncle, but I make my own judgments as to the feasibility of a situation. I spoke to your uncle and offered him more than most men earn in a lifetime for you, and he refused me. That tells me Radman would have no better luck, and would need to have you abducted before I might have you. I dislike waiting for what I want, and I have my ship here. By tomorrow afternoon we will be on our way back to my estate, and the mystery of what happened to you can be explained by the Management."

He took a step closer to me, but the bedpost was between us. He really wasn't taking any chances.

"I would love to begin with you now, but in the interests of my own safety, I must wait awhile," he said, his death-cold eyes glittering at me. "Have a pleasant night, and let the thought amuse you that I'll be with you again in the morning."

He walked out of my area of vision, leaning on his thin cane, and a minute later I heard the door close somewhere behind me. I took all of my weight on my wrists and gave the post I was tied to a two-footed kick that would have felled one of Dameron's vairs, but the damned thing hardly quivered. I hadn't really believed it was wood just because it looked like it, but I'd had to try something. The jolly thought of what was waiting for me in the morning was enough to chill my blood.

I turned to look at the window, and it was still deep night outside. I didn't know how long I'd have to wait, but the wait wouldn't be short. Naturally I didn't waste my breath trying to yell; those apartments were soundproofed, and if the ears in the room were still in operating condition, James would never have spoken to me as he had. At least I now knew for sure why Radman had joined our group. He had clearly decided to peddle merchandise to a private buyer in the Sphere itself, most likely from Little's first reports to him and from his personal visit to the physical exam area. No wonder Little had been so afraid and had tried so hard to talk Val into selling me to the Sphere itself—if the Management had caught them trying to go private on even a semi-official guest like me, not even Radman's special status would have saved them. I forced myself to relax to wait it out. They had to untie me sometime to get me to their ship, and any slip of their part would be the last slip they made. My good luck had suddenly changed to bad, but there was no benefit in crying over it.

By the time it was full light out I was in agony. The night had stretched out impossibly long, and my arms and legs were tortured from the position I was tied in. After a couple of hours of standing and shifting from foot to foot I'd tried hanging from my wrists to give my legs a rest, but it hadn't worked too well. My arms were strained to begin with and couldn't take the weight very long, so I'd had to stand up again. After I don't know how many hours of waiting my legs were like two giant blisters, and my arms were numb. At least they were numb until I tried leaning on them, and then they burned as if they were being boiled in oil. I was in such a bad way, I was almost looking forward to James's coming back. I knew I couldn't take much more of just standing there.

Despite what I'd decided I could and couldn't take, another couple of hours passed before I heard someone at the door. I had almost passed out a few times, but hadn't been lucky enough to make it; a high pain threshold isn't always a blessing. Someone came in and closed the door behind them, and when I heard a lock click the adrenalin started pouring through my system. I managed to stand almost straight, but couldn't turn my head.

"Have you been waiting for me, my dear?" James's voice came, slowly getting nearer. "I'm sorry it's been so long, but it was all for the best. Anticipation often heightens the pleasure of an undertaking, you know. You should be ready, and I'm anxious to get started."

He came up behind me, grabbed a fistful of hair, and forced my head back. The strain it put on my arms made me gasp, and that produced a chuckle in him.

"Just about done to a turn, I think," he said while I shuddered. "We can begin any time now."

I didn't know what he was about to begin, and I didn't want to know. In desperation I lifted one of my leaden legs and kicked backward, trying to break his kneecap, but I just didn't have it in me. He grunted with the small amount of pain I'd managed to give him and stepped back, letting go of my hair.

"You will be my prize, I think, after you have been with me a while," he said, chilled and chilling delight in his voice. "Right now, you must learn what attempting to do me harm brings."

He took another step away from me, hesitating very briefly, then suddenly my back was on fire from the stroke of something he'd hit me with, something that opened my skin the way a fingernail would open cellophane. My mind went instantly terrified with the memory of that time with the whip and those terrorists and I screamed and tried to pull away, but my wrists were tied with razor-sharp rope and my arms and legs were useless. He hit me again and then again, and each time I could feel the cut going deep and I couldn't control my screaming.

"Sing to me, my pretty bird!" he gloated as he panted and laughed. "This cane will teach you the song I love best to hear! You'll sing for me many times, but the first song is always the best!"

He kept on beating me until my entire body blazed with agony, his laughter filled with such absolute delight that I wanted to curl up with my hands over my ears. I screamed until my throat closed up, and then I just hung there whimpering. He was gasping with his effort when he stopped just as suddenly as he'd started, something unexpected pulling his attention away from his delightful time. His footsteps went to the door, and through my own harsh breathing I heard what sounded like a small panel being slid aside.

"What is it, Matthew?" James panted, thick annoyance coloring his tone. "I'm busy now."

"Something has happened," Matthew's rumble came. "I think you should know about it. Radman's been found dead."

James made a noise of surprise, reclosed the panel, and I heard the lock click.

"How did that happen?" he asked as he opened the door.

There was no answer, just the sound of a scuffle, and one single blow. Something heavy fell to the floor, and a heartbeat later Matthew was next to me with a knife in his hand.

"Hang on," he said, looking up at the pseudo-rope. "I'll have you out of that in a minute." His voice sounded strange and his eyes and fingers avoided the blood running from my wrists, and I finally woke up to what was happening.

"Val," I said, but it came out a whisper. "What are you doing here like that?"

"Matthew" didn't answer, he just went at that rope with the knife. I knew it was a good knife because it was one of mine, but it took at least several minutes before the last strand parted, and when it did my legs collapsed under me as if they weren't there. Val grabbed for me and caught me, but the pain was almost too much. He lowered me as gently as possible until I was sitting on the floor in the mist, then leaned me sideways against the bed.

"Do you think you can hold out until we get to the shuttle port?" Matthew's voice asked, his eyes as hard as eyes ever got. "We're getting out of here *now*."

"No!" I whispered, trying to grab for him and causing myself more pain, pure panic flooding me at the thought of what he wanted to do and my own helplessness to keep him from it. "Go back to yourself and call the Management. Please, Val! We'll never make it any other way!"

He seemed both outraged and frustrated, and for a minute I was sure he would ignore me again, but the strengthless death-grip I had on his shirt must have made an impression on him. Suddenly his features blurred, and he was back to looking like his own self.

"You'd better know what you're doing," he growled in his own voice, putting a gentle, faintly trembling hand to my sweat-soaked forehead. "If you think I'll give any of that filth a chance at you again, you're crazy."

He straightened up from the crouch he'd been in and went
toward the sitting room, and when he passed through the
doorway I noticed James. He was lying on the floor in a
heap, his bloody cane half buried under him, his head tilted at
an odd angle. I stared at him through the burning pain
washing over me, shuddered in a way that increased that
pain, then looked away.

I must have passed out for a few minutes; the next thing I
heard was the voice of our ex-guide, sounding put out. ". . .
never allow something like that to happen here," he said.
"We have very strict rules."

"You'll see in a minute how much good your rules are."
Val's voice sounded hard and uncompromising. They came
through the doorway and the bearded man glanced at James's
body, then came over to me. He blinked at the condition of
my wrists, but when he leaned over to look at my back he
was abruptly more silent than quiet. His face came into view
again when he straightened, and the vexation of unnecessary
trouble was in his eyes—right next to the anger of vengeance
anticipated.

"It won't be much longer," he told me seeming distracted,
absently patting my arm. "The doctor is on his way." He
came back to attention and turned to the sitting room as someone came in from the hall, then called, "This way, doctor."

A man came in carrying the sort of bag doctors have
carried for centuries. He came straight toward me and followed the half-annoyed gesture of the bearded man, directing
him to my back, abruptly reaching for his bag when he saw
it. I tried to catch Val's eye, but he was staring at James's
body with no expression on his face. I wanted to tell him not
to let them put me out, but I didn't have the strength to get
the words out, and it probably wouldn't have done any good
anyway. The doctor's hypo hissed, and then the room with
everyone in it melted away.

CHAPTER 15

Waking up the next time was a good deal more comfortable. Granted, I was flat on my face in a bed that had straps pulled tight across my hips, but my torn-up wrists were bandaged and I could hear those special non-sounds that mean the unnatural quiet of a hospital. I pushed myself slowly up on my elbows, trying to figure out if I was still on Xanadu, and two strong hands took my arms and forced me flat again.

"You shouldn't have come out of that yet," a brisk female voice said from behind me. "Don't move around or you'll mess up the surroskin. It hasn't had time to bind yet."

"Where the hell am I?" I demanded, trying to see who I was talking to, too well aware of the heavy, logy feeling that meant pain killers. If I was still in the Pleasure Sphere, I'd do more than move around a little.

"You're in the hospital section of Xanadu O.S., if you must know," the female voice answered. "But you have time to worry about it later."

I craned around in time to see a hand with a pressure hypo,

but not in time to do anything about it. The hypo hissed, and I went back to dreamland.

When I finally regained consciousness, the restraints were gone and I was on my back. I was all alone in the room, so I struggled to a sitting position slowly enough to keep the tearing sensation in my back down to a minimum. Thanks to the pain killers, movement wasn't impossible, but until surroskin binds itself to you at every point, it makes you feel as though you're about to rip open. I knew from experience that it would be a good week before I was free of the sensation.

The room was about twelve by fifteen, large for a private hospital room anywhere but on a Station like Xanadu. The high bed I sat in stood off the wall at my back, and a squared, narrow, drawered table was just to the right of it. The room's door was farther down in the wall to my right, and the wall to my left had a vu-cast window like the ones in the Station's suites. The view it showed was of a snow-covered woods, white and silent in an early morning beginning, a sun just starting to rise high enough to shed some warmth. The reality of the scene was excellent, caught at just the proper angle to make you think it was really there, and the subject itself was geared to show you that bed was the best place to be just then. I ran my fingers through the tangle of my hair, then moved my gaze to the cozy table and chairs arrangement standing against the far wall. If I'd thought my legs could hold me I would have been in one of those chairs, but between the beating I'd taken and the subsequent work to repair the damage, I was in no shape to be walking around. I could almost feel the various levels of pain hovering just beyond the protective wrapping of pain killer, waiting to set me afire as soon as the wrapping faded. I tugged at the neck of the hospital gown they'd put me in, trying to loosen it as far as possible, trying to figure out what day it was. Stupid hospital gowns in stupid hospitals, where you had to launch a major campaign just to find out the standard date. I hated hospitals, hated the reason for them—and refused to let myself think about the waiting pain.

No more than a minute later, the door to the hall opened and a nurse came in carrying a tray of bandages and oddments. She was a tall woman, as solid as a nurse sometimes has to be, but still having a pleasant, obviously female figure. She had brown hair and mild brown eyes, but her eyes lost their mildness when she saw me studying her. She put the tray she'd been carrying onto a rolling table standing near the door, then approached the side of my bed.

"You *do* have a fast snapback, don't you." She frowned, looking annoyed. "You shouldn't have come out of that sedative for at least another half hour. And what are you doing sitting up? Are you trying to ruin the work that's been done on you?"

I recognized her voice as the one I'd heard the first time I'd opened my eyes, and her automatic assumption of command aroused my temper. I was really in the mood to take some of my aggression out on her, but instead of sounding off and thereby putting my foot in it, I fell back on my well-known acting abilities and started the tears going from my eyes.

"What is this place?" I sniffed as if I didn't remember waking up earlier. "And why are you yelling at me? What have I done?"

Even the gruffest of nurses are mostly good-hearted, and that one was no different from any other. She melted as if I'd poured hot water on her, and came closer to put her arm around my shoulders.

"There, there, Red, don't cry," she soothed, patting my hair and cheek. "You haven't done anything at all. You're safe in the hospital on Xanadu Station, and no one will hurt you again. I didn't mean to yell at you, it's just that your uncle has been driving me crazy since they brought you in. What in the world happened to you down there?"

It took everything I had to keep from straightening in shock, because I'd actually forgotten about Val! I didn't know what had happened after that doctor had knocked me out, but obviously Val had managed to get us back to the Station. And it looked like he was worrying about me again. Considering the fact that I knew what would happen all too shortly, it would obviously be best to distract him with other considerations.

"Uncle Val arranged for us to go down to the Pleasure Sphere," I sniffed, looking into the nurse's sympathetic face. "He said I'd have a great time learning about life, but then he let all these other people touch me and do things to me, and then he gave me to this—this—person who said he wanted to take care of me, and then—and then—" The shuddering I did at the memory of James wasn't any part of the playacting; it would take me some time to forget him.

"You poor child!" she breathed, looking shocked. "Don't you worry about another thing! I'll take care of you while you're here, and you'll be fine." Then she straightened up again. "I'll be right back. I have a few words to say to your uncle, and then we'll change those bandages on your wrists."

She stalked out with a grim look on her face, and I waited until the door had closed behind her before letting myself grin faintly. Once Val heard what the nurse had to say, he'd know I was back to being my old, lovable self and would also know that he could relax. Sitting up was getting harder and harder to maintain, so I lowered myself back down on the bed just as some sort of disturbance began outside the door. I could hear the nurse's voice shouting, but Val's voice rose above hers.

"I said I'm going in there!" he roared. "If you know what's good for you, you'll get out of my way!"

The door flew open and Val and the nurse came through

together, she trying to stay in front of him, he trying to get past her without actually knocking her down. I hadn't expected something like that, and I watched with interest, wondering who would win.

"You've done enough to that poor girl!" the nurse snapped, staying between Val and me. "If I had my way . . ."

"I am her legal guardian and I demand to see her alone for a few minutes!" Val thundered down at her. "If you find that request impossible, I'll have her discharged and moved elsewhere, but I refuse to be put off any longer!"

The nurse hesitated, then turned reluctantly to look at me.

"I'm sorry, Red, but he does have the legal right to see you," she said, as apology, then turned back to Val and finished talking to me while staring at him. "But I'll be right outside the door! If you need me for anything, just call!"

I thanked her quietly, admiring her nerve, and she marched out, walking stiff and straight. When the door had closed behind her, Val took his eyes away from it and came to stand over me. As high as the hospital bed was he stood even higher, and the look in his eyes was anything but friendly.

"Hi, Val," I greeted him, staring up at the looming mountain above me. "How are things?"

He leaned his left arm on the railing of my bed, then bent forward to put his right palm to the left of my head, flat on the bed next to me.

"Things are just lovely," he answered in a too-gentle voice, those black eyes directly on me. "I've been out there for two days worrying myself sick over you, and the next thing I know some nurse is accusing me of everything but strangling you! What the hell are you up to now?"

"Well, I had to tell her something," I muttered, squirming uncomfortably at the way he was looking at me. "It's not my fault if the facts—sort of—point to you."

"You and facts!" he snapped, still leaning over me. "That

combination just isn't possible! Just wait until you're out of that bed! When I get through with you, you'll never pull another gag on anyone as long as you live!''

"Now, Val, don't start anything foolish," I warned, not liking the hardness in his voice. "I wouldn't want to have to hurt you."

"Don't worry," he said, standing straight again but still sending that dark-eyed look toward me. "You won't. Ringer will be getting here tomorrow, and I'll be back to see you then. Right now I'm going to see if I can't find some fun around here. Rest up real well, I'm looking forward to seeing you on your feet again."

He reached for the door and disappeared through it, and seconds later that same nurse reappeared, to reclaim the tray she'd brought earlier and carry it over to me.

"Don't worry, Red, this won't hurt at all," she confided the way nurses do. "One, two, three, and I'll be all finished." She smiled a reassuring smile and got to work, cutting off the old bandages with a scissors and seeing to the medium-raw mess my wrists had been turned into. Nothing she did caused any pain, but that stemmed from the same reason I felt nothing in my back. I probably could have given her the generic name for the pain killer in me, but that wasn't the route I had chosen to travel. Ringer disliked letting the general public know where his agents were and what they were up to, and possible bad publicity aside, I couldn't help agreeing with him. Not too many people would have cried over Radman's warrant having been served, but I was in no shape to cope with anyone who did. If any of Radman's people were still close enough to hear about the Special Agent in the hospital area, they might be distraught enough to try reaching me. That side of it could be considered part of my job, but the bodies of anyone who got in their way was more than I was willing to accept. I would stay the innocent little Jenny until I got out of there, but there was one question I would have enjoyed having an advance answer to. Because of the conditioning of my job I had a fast snap-back from all drugs, pain killers included. The one they had me loaded with was bound to wear off sooner than anyone expected, and there was nothing I could say to make the time any easier. There was sure to be some warning before it wore off entirely, and all I could hope was that someone would notice before it went all the way. The decision was made, but then I insisted on dredging up a memory of what it had been like the last time I'd been beaten this badly.

"Take it easy, Red," the nurse said sharply, putting her hands on my arms. "Don't shiver like that, you'll be all right. Just lie still now and get some rest. After what you've been through, you need it."

She held onto me until the shuddering stopped, waited a minute or two to be sure I was all right, then took the old bandages she'd removed away with her. When I was alone again I turned onto my side, staring at the closed hall door and picturing Val as he'd looked when he'd stood there. He was much better off being out searching for fun than sitting beyond the door agonizing, but the hospital area had become a lonelier and emptier place. As a comparable place the Pleasure Sphere had very little going for it, but at least there I could have used my role to hold tight to his arm.

By lunchtime the next day I was finally feeling less like a decaying side of beef. If I'd told Jane—my nurse—the generic name for the pain killer in me, I would have been wrong. I'd forgotten who they thought they were dealing with, and most people don't require the strength and effectiveness of neranol. They'd used some other garbage on me, and I spent the day watching the snowy woods scene through the vu-cast window, catching glimpses of odd-looking animals, feeling the hovering pain nip and bite at me every once in a while, testing the strength of my protection, growing bolder with every successful bite. Jane had been in and out, watching me with a disturbed look in her eyes, knowing something was wrong but not knowing what. I lay in one spot on the bed, my forehead and underarms dotted with sweat, well beyond even thinking about sitting up, a sour sickness growing stronger inside me. I heard clattering noises out in the hall, noises that usually meant food was on its way, but happily nothing was brought to me.

Beyond the vu-cast window a light snowfall started, adding to whatever was on the ground, and then, unbelievably without any real warning, my defenses were gone, buried beneath wave after wave of fiery, blazing pain. My back was raw meat under the surroskin, my wrists a bloody mess under the bandages, the muscles of my arms and legs still strained from what I'd been put through, and it all came out together, rolling over me and smashing me flat to the bed. I tried not to make a sound but the screaming got itself started and kept going, and then Jane was there, grabbing for me and shouting something over her shoulder. Other faces came to view, most of them attached to hands that held onto me, and then a male face appeared, his hands holding a pressure hypo, but it had all gone on too long. Just as the protective wrapping began forming around me again, I passed out.

I couldn't have been out too long, because Jane was there wiping sweat off me when I opened my eyes. She smiled in the dimmed lighting when she saw me looking at her, and lost no time telling me that what had happened wouldn't happen again. They were now using a special drug called neranol, and would watch it closely to see when it was wearing off. I'd gotten to the point of being positive it hadn't been neranol to begin with, and Jane's confirming it made me feel considerably better. If the day ever comes that neranol

behaves the way that garbage had behaved, a lot of Federation agents will be in a lot of trouble.

I spent some time just breathing quietly, but Jane kept up a
light, one-sided conversation while she saw to it that I drank
down various thin concoctions. I drank them without argument and let her cheerful words flow around and over me
without paying any attention to them, but then a stray thought
brought to mind a chore undone. Hospitals don't like leaving
unconscious people with jewelry on them, and my bio-ring
had been gone from the time I'd first opened my eyes. Of
course, it was always possible that someone else had taken
the ring, and it was important that I find out if it was gone for
good. I waited for the first break in her monologue, then
asked if I'd had any jewelry on when I'd been brought in.
Jane hadn't known off-hand, but she'd volunteered to go and
find out, which took about a minute and a half. As soon as
she came back through the door I saw my bio-ring clutched in
her hand, but I also saw the frown on her face. She closed the
door firmly behind her and then came to stand next to the
bed.

"It could have been a lot worse for you than it was, Red,"
she told me, her large brown eyes matching her frown. "Why
didn't you say something?"

"About what?" I asked, wondering where the conversation
was going.

"About this," she answered, opening her hand to let me
see the ring. "I know a bio-ring when I see one, and I also
know who carries them. I was on the staff of a special
Federation hospital for five years before deciding to move
here."

Being helpless has a funny way of making everyone around
you seem suspect, and I'm not a particularly trusting type to
begin with. Jane's story hadn't convinced me of anything but
the fact that she knew I was an agent, and she must have seen

on my face what I was feeling. She moved her free hand to my shoulder and squeezed gently.

"The name of the hospital was Blue Skies," she said, her pretty face understanding. "You must know as well as I do how fitting the name is. Dr. Croyden was head of my service, and Dr. Madison was his superior. Ralph Madison is a tall man in his forties; Ned Croyden, short and in his thirties with a mustache. The staff calls them Mutt and Jeff, but not to their faces."

Her eyes were full of calm assurance, and in spite of myself I found the tension draining out of me. The facility wasn't called "Blue Skies" by anyone who wasn't familiar with it, and the joke about Ned and Ralph was restricted to an even greater degree. If the woman in front of me was lying, the effort she was putting into it was more than anything she might conceivably gain.

"I'm surprised you were able to take it for five years," I said at last, and she smiled and nodded in agreement with the sentiment. "Blue Skies" was set up not far from the agent-training facilities, and was the most active special hospital the Federation had.

"Five years was all I could stand," she said, handing me the bio-ring. "This place is a vacation compared to what went on over there. Have you finished your assignment yet?"

"Yes, I finished it." I smiled slightly, watching her move a chair closer to the bed and sit down. "Can't you tell just by looking?"

"Not always," she said with a laugh, and then she frowned in thought. "Hey, wait a minute," she muttered, staring into space and then bringing her eyes back to me. "Who did I chew out when I thought you were an innocent kid?"

She looked so suddenly embarrassed, that I couldn't keep from grinning.

"Val's my partner," I told her, shifting to my side to look

at her more easily. "Aside from being totally innocent of everything I hinted at, if not for him I wouldn't even be this well off. He's the one who saved what was left of my hide."

"And to think what I said to him!" She gasped, her cheeks red. "Why did you do that?"

I thought about Val out having his fun, then shrugged as well as I could.

"Val and I have a rather special relationship," I explained. "He tends to worry about me too much, and I'd rather see him mad."

"I think you're out of your mind," she pronounced, shaking her head at me. "He didn't strike me as the sort of man who would appreciate having jokes played on him. Doesn't his size bother you at all?"

"Only when he's mad at me," I answered, then closed my eyes with the deep weariness I was feeling.

"I can put you out, you know," Jane's voice came, soft with understanding but free of useless pity. "The doctor left orders for it if it became necessary."

All of my carefully nurtured instincts stirred at that, and I shook my head as I forced my eyes open again.

"No, thanks," I said, trying to grin. "I'm all right."

"The hell you are." She snorted, getting out of the chair to stand next to me. "All you agents are alike. You always have to be awake and in charge."

"It's a survival characteristic," I commented.

"I'd almost forgotten what taking care of agents was like," Jane said, her back straightening as she looked down at me. "You think you know best and you won't even consider anything else. Well, that's all right with me, as long as you remember that I'm in charge. If you're silly enough to forget it, you'll be reminded the hard way."

She took the bio-ring from my hand and put it in the drawer of the small table next to the bed, then got on about

her business. I shifted onto my back again, wondering just
how much trouble I'd have with her, but I shouldn't have
bothered wondering. Her sturdy body was in and out of the
room for the rest of that day, bringing pills for me to take,
gelatine-like mixtures for me to drink, tests that required no
cooperation on my part, and examinations that did. I tried
being as objective as possible about it, but I have a deep-
seated belief that three quarters of all things done to you in a
hospital are done just to give the staff something to occupy
them. I finally had a bad attack of lousy temper, but Jane
couldn't have cared less. She brought in a hypo filled with
sleepy stuff, and I didn't even get to see how long the
snowstorm outside the vu-cast window lasted.

When I opened my eyes again, the light in the room was
brighter than the deep night shown through the vu-cast window. Jane was nowhere to be seen—something that really
pleased me—so I grabbed the opportunity to see if I'd made
any progress in the moving around department. My whole
body felt fuzzy and almost numb, showing that the neranol
had been given to me very recently, and sitting up was no
more trouble than getting the proper muscles moving. There
was some dizziness that passed quickly, letting me raise the
back of the bed and make myself as comfortable as possible.

The peace and quiet lasted until Jane discovered I was
awake. She wore a crisp new uniform and looked well rested,
so I knew I'd probably been out the entire Station night and
part of the morning. Prying the time out of her was like
digging out ultra-secret naval plans, but when I finally had
the information I found I was right.

Not long after Jane went on her way again, the door to my
room was opened. I'd been staring at the blank light-tan walls
around me, trying to pinpoint what was so damned irritating
about them, but sight of the short, round figure in the doorway lightened my mood to the grinning point.

"A friendly face at last," I greeted him, watching Ringer frown around the room before coming all the way in and over to my bed. Despite the frown I was glad to see him, just the way I usually was.

"I didn't think I'd find you sitting up," he growled, moving those eyes over me to inspect my wrists. "Why is it that the complications you find usually turn out to be worse than the assignments?"

"Just lucky, I guess," I shrugged, in turn giving the up and down to his dark gray business suit. "Or maybe it's part of my talent. Isn't Val with you?"

"He should be along in a minute," Ringer said, opening his jacket so he could put his hands in his pockets. "I left word for him when my ship docked, and came ahead to talk to your doctor. Do you want to be moved out of here to one of our own places?"

"I'll have to think about it." I shrugged again, shaking my hair back over my shoulders. "It all depends on how long they try to keep me in bed. By the way, I've got something for you."

I began reaching over to the drawer where Jane had put my bio-ring the day before, only peripherally seeing the door open to admit Val.

"Don't stretch like that!" Ringer ordered, grabbing my arm gently before I'd moved very far. "Do you want to have another day like the one you had yesterday? I'll get it."

Val's head came up when he heard that, and he stopped short and said, "What happened yesterday?"

"How was your trip, Ringer?" I tried to interrupt, hoping he'd missed Val's question while inspecting the bio-ring. "Anything interesting happen?"

"Be quiet!" Val snapped at me, then repeated to Ringer. "What happened yesterday?" and there was no way I could stop it.

"They gave her a grade Z suppressant and it wore off too soon," Ringer said, studying Val as he put away the ring in a pocket. "Her doctor told me they had to go after her with butterfly nets, and he still doesn't understand why. Where were you that you didn't know about it?"

Val's face was a strange combination of conflicting emotions, but his eyes were hard and angry. It would have been a hell of a lot easier if the anger had been directed toward me, but I could see he was angry with himself for not being there when he might have been needed. He glanced at me quickly, almost in embarrassment, and I knew I'd have to find a way of telling him I'd gotten rid of him on purpose. He was bound to be even angrier at that, but there was nothing else I could do.

"I was—busy yesterday," he said at last, looking at Ringer with a suddenly expressionless face. "Obviously it was the wrong thing to be."

Ringer studied Val's face, but he didn't say what was going through his mind. The situation could have become considerably more awkward, but you can always trust Ringer to stick to the basics.

"I think it's time I had a report on this thing," he growled, filling the silence. "I didn't come all this way just to keep you two company."

At that point there was a brisk knock, and Jane opened the door to stick her head in.

"No more than fifteen minutes, men," she ordered, looking at Ringer and Val. "You can see her again tomorrow when she's stronger."

When Jane's head disappeared, Ringer sat down in the chair that was still near my bed and pulled out a cigarette.

"Let's make it move," he said. "We don't have much time."

"I think I ought to start," I said, and while Val came

closer to lean against a wall, I gave Ringer a rundown on all the preliminaries as well as my part of the end without going into needless detail. Val paid close attention to the doings he hadn't been around for, an odd expression flickering in his eyes when I mentioned the ledge I'd used to reach Radman. I ran it through to the end, and then it was my partner's turn.

"At dinner that night, when she said she wanted to go back to our apartment, I was reasonably certain she wasn't really ill," he said, keeping his eyes on Ringer. "I had the feeling she was up to something, but I was up to something myself with Little, and didn't want to waste the chance if I could help it. Little had something he wanted to show me, and while he was showing, I was going to try pumping him about the guests, to see if he knew too much about any of them. I didn't notice when the man who had been sitting next to Diana left, and I didn't know he was sick. Diana hadn't told me he was Radman, and she hadn't told me what she planned on doing."

Ringer's eyes came to me briefly then, no real expression on his face, his attention then on Val to keep from interrupting the narrative.

"I spent the next two or three hours with Little, but wasn't able to do much in the way of questioning," Val continued, his arms folded where he leaned against the wall, his gaze now filled with memory. "There was some sort of transmission from what he called The Arena, and more than a few of the other guests watched it with us. Naked men fought with one another bare-handed and with weapons, and in each fight only one of the combatants survived. The surviving fighter was then given a female slave to use right there where he'd fought, and the screaming of the spectators never stopped. I stayed until I was just short of kicking the walls down, then insisted on leaving.

"When I finally got back to our apartment, Diana wasn't

there. I very nearly went back out into the corridor to ask the slaves if they'd seen her, then realized I couldn't do that. For all I knew she might have been following a clue to Radman or even taking care of him, so the last thing I could do was call attention to her. There was nothing else for it but to wait, but I waited all night and she never showed up. By the time morning came and she still hadn't come back, I decided it was past time to be cautious. I made it into the corridor just in time to be rounded up with a number of the other guests who were awake, to be questioned about Richard Radman's death. They said it had happened some time during the previous evening, and that bothered me. I looked around and noticed that although Matthew was there, James was nowhere to be seen. I remembered how James had looked at her and what he'd said about her when he'd spoken to me, so when Matthew left I followed him to their apartment. I could feel that she was in there—I'm still attuned to her, you know—so I clobbered Matthew and took his place. When James opened the door, I went in and got her out.''

"My hero,'' I said, more in a murmur than aloud, and neither he nor Ringer heard it.

"I never expected the Management to handle things the way they did,'' he went on, looking frowningly confused. "I *did* expect at least a few questions about why I hadn't reported Diana missing the night before, but they never even brought the matter up. They took Matthew away somewhere, and a little while later they came for Little. He screamed and blubbered when they dragged him out of the dining room where he had been eating, and except for the slaves in that place, I've never seen a man so afraid. They must have found out from Matthew that he was involved with Radman in trying to sell Diana, and he was the only one left for them to take their mad out on. After seeing that, I spent a minute or two regretting that Diana had reached Radman after all. It would have been more fitting if he had lived to experience what he had made so many other people experience."

I had to admit I agreed with that sentiment, but Ringer didn't look like he was agreeing with anything. He hadn't said anything during the entire recital, but his eyes had drifted back to me toward the end of Val's lecture. When the last word had been said, he shook his head at me.

"What a mess," he growled, dropping his second cigarette onto the floor to grind it under his foot. "Is that your idea of a partnership? Why didn't you brief him properly instead of taking off on your own? I ought to cite you right now for stupidity like that."

"You use your definition of partnership, I use mine," I answered, barely able to shrug. "Mine might turn out to be better in the long run, so why not give it a chance?"

"I'll think about it," Ringer said grimly, answering a question I hadn't expected an answer to, while he rose from the chair. "If you hadn't forced yourself to show him how to use the telelink, I'd still be waiting for your call. You didn't follow any of the standard precautionary procedures for a two-agent operation, and it could have turned out a lot worse than it did. I'll make my report to the Council and let you know what they say tomorrow. Right now you'd better get some more rest. Come on, Valdon."

"I need company more than I need rest," I called after them as they went toward the door, trying to get rid of the faint depression that had settled on me from talking about the Sphere. "How about leaving Val here to amuse me?"

"*I'll* amuse you," Jane said from the suddenly open door, her fist on her hip as she glared around. "Out, you two men, and don't come back till tomorrow."

Ringer and Val disappeared faster than they would have at an order from the Council, and I was left with my good buddy Jane. I thought about breaking out of there, but instructions had been left by my doctor about how much sleep I was supposed to get. Since I hadn't done anything about it on my own, Jane had come in to help me out, and my thoughts about breaking out lasted about three seconds after the sound of the hypo.

CHAPTER 16

When Ringer came back alone the next day, my mood was a good deal blacker than it had been the day before. Ringer wasn't looking any too jolly himself as he reclaimed the chair near my bed, but with Jane taking advantage of the shape I was in to push me around, I couldn't muster much sympathy for him. He didn't say a word until he'd settled himself in the chair, and then those sharp, piercing eyes glared at my face.

"Why didn't you mention this thing about being a teenager again?" he growled without preamble. "Slip your mind, did it?"

I snarled wordlessly at the reminder and swallowed down what my first reactions would have made me say, and satisfied myself with throwing the plastic water glass in my hand as far as I could without crippling myself.

"That's a very touchy subject with me," I told him. "I don't like any part of it, and I've long since been fed up with being treated like a child. I want a certificate of majority here as soon as humanly possible, sooner if you think you can swing it."

"Do you," he murmured, staring at me with a strange

expression I had the feeling I'd seen before. "Well, I've already spoken to the Council about it, but I'd rather get to another of their points first. I spent some time thinking about how you handled this assignment, and I'm convinced you left Valdon out of a lot of it on purpose. The Council agrees with me, and is very disturbed about it. I passed on what he told me about wanting to take a ship from the shuttle port, and they feel he could have been killed because you didn't give him enough information to work with. Considering that they've decided to try friendly relations with Valdon's people, they are understandably upset that you might have put them in the embarrassing position of having to report his death at the first conference. They have therefore decided to cite you, but you don't get away with three months of desk duty. You will accompany Valdon during a three-month procedures course at the Agent Training Academy, and you will be returned to cadet grade and status during that time."

His voice had been stiff and official with that handing-down-a-verdict tone, and suddenly I comprehended his expression. It was the same one he'd worn when he'd taken away my knife on Faraway Station, one that said he wasn't likely to listen to anything I said to change his mind. I frowned and shook my head, not really believing he could be serious; he saw my headshake, and leaned forward in the chair to point a finger at me.

"Are you still glad you did it all yourself?" he asked, his voice now back to normal. "If you are, think again. There's more."

"What do you mean, more?" I demanded, starting to get mad. "Isn't the first of that imbecility enough? Do all of you want my blood to go with it?"

"You can keep what's left of your blood," Ringer snorted, grinning faintly. "I know you better than you think I do, and I was asked for a recommendation on this point. I discussed the minority matter with them, telling them how well you liked it, and they decided to let your conduct during the next three months have a say as to whether or not you get what you need. Until that certificate is approved, you travel as a minor and watch your step. If your step takes you out of line, no certificate.''

''The hell you say!'' I snarled, pulling the cover off me so that I could move around to face him. ''I'll be damned if I'll be blackmailed like that! I won't do it!''

''You'll do it or they'll throw you out,'' Ringer said, his voice warning as his eyes measured my anger. ''You have no idea how angry they were.''

''Let them throw me out,'' I snarled, running my hand through my hair. ''If I can't find anything else to do, I'll just go home for a few years. I won't be a teenager forever.''

Ringer didn't say anything, he just stared at me, and I felt a cold chill start around my backbone where I shouldn't have felt anything at all.

''I said, 'I won't be a teenager forever,' '' I repeated in a voice that wasn't as steady as it should have been. ''Why don't you say something? Like an agreement, for instance.''

''You know, Diana, I think I ought to feel sorry for you,'' he mused, looking at me strangely. ''And that in spite of all the grief you've given me. Valdon told me something you obviously don't know. You'll be a teenager until you go back with him to be readjusted, and if you walk out on this job you won't be going back.''

I just stared at him and shook my head back and forth, just as though it was on a wire. I couldn't believe it—I *wouldn't* believe it!

''Hang on, Diana,'' Ringer advised, his voice softer than it had been. ''There's one more thing. The Council voted to honor Valdon in his stay here with us, and granted him the rank of Agent First Class. When you two get to the facilities on Tanderon, he'll be the ranking half of the partnership."

Ringer said his piece and then waited for my reaction, but it was more than he expected—or, at the very least, different. He saw the quiet tears filling my eyes and saw, too, that the anger I'd shown was gone.

"Ringer, don't do this to me," I whispered, my breath coming in gasps. "Don't all the years we've worked together mean anything? Please don't make him senior to me, please! You don't know him, you don't know what he'll do. Please!"

I grabbed the bed's side rail to get closer to him, and he frowned and got out of the chair fast to put his hands on my arms. I moaned and cried and grabbed his shirt with both hands, all the while pleading with him, and he forced me back farther onto the bed, then pressed the nurse-call. His face looked pale and concerned over the way I was babbling, and he stabbed one-handed again and again at the nurse-call, then cursed under his breath when there was no answer to it. He put the bed down flat while muttering something soothing, saw that I wasn't trying to sit up again once he had me down flat too, and decided to take a chance. He took a lead away from the bed, watching closely to see if I was going to move, then made a dash for the door and out. I knew he'd be back in no time with professional help and I didn't want to be sedated, so I left off crying—just ragged sobs—until a nurse—not Jane—rushed in, then begged to be left alone for a while. The sympathetic woman agreed immediately, herded a still-worried Ringer out in front of her, and I was finally able to put aside the act.

Of all the damned bad luck! I stretched out flat on my back to stare up at the ceiling, wishing I had something breakable in reach. Not only had the Council decided to knock me down, they'd also opted for jumping on me with both feet. And the worst part of it was the bit about Val. Remembering the way he'd been on the Station and later on in the Sphere, I was willing to bet he'd try milking a higher rank for all it was worth. He'd made it plain that he didn't care for my sense of humor and way of doing things, and life would not lack interest with him trying to take charge again. I stirred in annoyance, knowing good old Ringer had had more than a little to say about what was to be done with me, so the worry I'd given him was no more than what he'd asked for. He and I had worked together for a long time, long enough for him to know better than to crow in front of me. I never mind someone taking his best shot, but bragging about it before it lands is asking for trouble.

A dark, snowy dawn was just beginning outside the vu-cast window, but it wasn't doing much to lighten the blue-shadowed mounds covering the forest floor. I caught a glimpse of something thin and gray moving silently between the trees, and then it was gone from view, leaving no more than dainty footprints that were already on the way to being filled. My eyes continued to stare at the scene, but my mind wandered away to consider the problem I had, examining options and possibilities, and I was so far into it that the slamming open of the door to my room took an instant to penetrate to where I was. Before I knew what was going on, I was treated to the totally unexpected presence of Val, who stopped beside my bed and reached out fast to grab my arms.

"Diana, are you all right?" he demanded harshly as his fingers dug into my arms. I was so surprised by the suddenness of it all that I couldn't hold back a gasp. The steel-like grip of his fingers hadn't really hurt me, but it was so rigid and demanding that I could almost feel it through the neranol. My gasp must have reached past the intensity he was projecting; his fingers loosened as abruptly as they'd tightened, and faint confusion filled his deep black eyes.

"I'm sorry," he said apologetically, shifting his grip to the bed rail. "I didn't mean to hurt you, but I just left Ringer and he was really shaken. He said something about hysteria and collapse, and almost had me believing I'd find you catatonic."

I have to admit Val really looked upset, but Ringer's news hadn't left me much in the way of compassion. I looked up into his face as I tucked my hands behind my head, and snorted my opinion of his comments.

"Don't look so disappointed," I advised, unable to keep the dryness from my voice. "You may have missed the catatonia, but you're just in time for the suicidal depression. I may even let you help me decide whether to cut my wrists or my throat."

If he had exploded and started shouting at me I wouldn't have been surprised, but the relieved grin that covered his face *was* a surprise. He unwrapped his fingers from around the bed rail as his grin widened, and reached out one hand to brush the hair from my eyes.

"You're all right." He chuckled, for some reason pleased with my sarcasm. "I recognize your standard courtesy of manner—and never thought I'd be glad to hear it." He took a deep breath and stretched, then looked around and spotted the chair Ringer had used. He seemed to need it, and walked over to collapse into it before looking at me again.

"You know, you never mentioned how long it takes people to heal around here," he observed, apparently no longer upset. "If we were back at the base, you'd be on your feet by now."

"You neglected to mention a few things, too," I responded, shifting over onto my side to stare at him. "I've decided that Ringer must have been putting me on. Nobody has immortality."

"Who said anything about immortality?" he asked, obviously knowing what I was talking about. "This age business is strictly in the way of being cosmetic. You're seventeen, you'll register as seventeen until you have it changed, but you haven't really been made seventeen again. Look at it this way: your heart has just so many beats natural to it from the time it was first formed. If we make your heart register like that of a seventeen-year-old, that doesn't mean we've cancelled out all of the beating it's done till then. If you were sixty when it was done, and your heart has sixty-one years of beating in it, you'd still have only one more year until it stopped, no matter what you and it looked like."

"Thanks for the lecture." I nodded, keeping my eyes on him. "It's really settled all of my problems. Now I'm free to be young and happy again."

"Poor Diana!" He laughed, stretching out comfortably in the chair. "They really gave it to you, didn't they? But from what Ringer said, you've been asking for it for a long time."

"Ringer can blow it out his— Oh, hell, never mind!" I snarled, turning away from him. "You don't know the first thing about it."

"Then why don't you try telling me about it?" he suggested from behind me, almost in annoyance. "I know it'll be a brand new approach for you, but you might manage it if you try hard enough."

I turned back and measured him for a minute, then nodded my head.

"Okay," I said slowly, sitting up straight. "I think I will. I'm in this mess now because of you, and there's no reason why both of us shouldn't know all about it. Sure, I cut you out of my operation, and I did do it on purpose. If I could have left you on the Station I would have, but that age thing kept me from doing it the right way. My original intention was to train you before letting you work with me because you do have potential, but no matter how competent you are, Val, you're still not agent caliber and never will be unless you learn to use your head in addition to other parts of your anatomy.''

"If you think you're telling me something," said Val, "you'd better think again. "Nothing you've said so far makes any sense."

"It doesn't?" I asked, warming to my subject as I continued to keep my eyes on him. "Then see how this grabs you. Certain procedures are set up for valid reasons, and assignment leadership is a perfect example of one of those. The assignment leader is usually the one on the team with more experience, knowledge, expertise, or all three, the one who gets to make all bottom-line decisions for precisely those reasons. Not only did you immediately try to take over an assignment when you had no real idea about what was going on, you also spent your time looking for ways to protect me from all those big, bad Xanadu people. If I had to guess, I'd say you still don't understand how much extra trouble we had because of those little pastimes of yours.''

"That might be because we didn't have any extra trouble," he said, stubbornly insisting on the point. "What's really bothering you is the way you had to take orders for once, instead of doing everything your own way."

"Oh, is it?" I retorted, raising my eyebrows in faint surprise I felt not at all. "Then I suppose I was imagining that little difficulty we had with Greg Rich, all because you 'didn't care for the man.' If you hadn't antagonized him to the point of challenge, I never would have had to kill him. And how about the orders I gave you on the subject of my being for sale? James told me about the talk he'd had with you, the talk during which you turned down his offer cold. If you'd followed orders he would have expected to collect me here on the Station, and most probably would not have sent his plug-ugly after me right in the Sphere. And as a final item, if you search your memory very carefully, you may remember that I made a point of telling you that if you ran into any difficulty in the Sphere and I wasn't available to consult, you were to go to the Management. I wasn't talking for the practice, but when you did run into trouble, what did you do? You went charging to the rescue and almost got us both killed. The Management is very close about what leaves the Sphere. If you had tried taking over a shuttle or ship from the port, they would have followed standard procedure, over-ridden your controls with a grabberfield the way they do with docking here in the Station, and crashed the ship in a place specifically reserved for the purpose. Am I coming through any clearer now?''

My lecture had grown downright heated, but that wasn't why Val was still staring at me.

"James was going to take you out of there," he put in, a very definite disturbance in his stare. "How did *he* plan on doing it?''

"James had his own ship, but unless he had taken some very special precautions he wouldn't have made it either," I pointed out, gesturing a dismissal. "But James wasn't very tightly wrapped anyway, so it doesn't pay to talk about it. The point is still the same. You kept overriding my orders and worrying about protecting me, and we were out-and-out lucky we lived through it.''

"Is that part of why you got rid of me a couple of days ago?" he asked, quiet now. "Ringer said you knew what would happen.''

"Sure I knew.'' I shrugged, looking briefly away from him. I was glad Ringer had told him the truth, but I was oddly disturbed over his lack of anger. "This isn't my first time in a hospital, and I didn't need you running around making things worse.''

"Making things worse,'' he echoed. "Translated, that means you knew how I would feel about standing around helplessly, watching you wrapped in the agony of pain you were suffering because of me. Because of what I did and didn't do."

"Come on, Val, let's not get melodramatic." I grew impatient as I glanced at his expressionlessness. "James may have grabbed me because you disobeyed orders, but you had nothing to do with the rest of it. If I hadn't tried hurting him when I was in no shape to hurt even so much as his feelings, it never would have happened."

"You shouldn't have had to try hurting him," he responded quietly, his big body still stretched out and relaxed in the chair, his black eyes sober with accepted guilt. "I'm sure you know as well as I do why I waited until morning to finally go looking for you. I was so damned sick to get out of that place, I kept telling myself that I could ruin everything if I tried looking for you. I'd given you a choice for the following morning, and to avoid the choice you didn't want to accept, you were tracking down Radman and finding a way to execute the warrant. When I finally came out of the dream and had to admit something had gone wrong, it was already too late. I know which part of it was my fault and which wasn't, and you can bet I won't make the same mistake again. What I don't understand is why you haven't said any of these things to Ringer and the Council. It would be bound to make a difference."

"What happens between partners on an assignment stays between *them*," I told him stiffly, folding my legs in front of me. "I don't know how they do these things where you come from, but around here we don't go crying to anyone about the problems we have. If we can't get along with the partner assigned to us, we find a different partner, which is what I intend doing. I hope you'll be happier with whomever you team with next."

"Now what are you talking about?" he demanded, sitting

up suddenly in the chair to gape at me in disbelief. "You can't refuse to be my partner! I don't want anyone else!"

"That's too bad, because I do," I said adamantly. "The only thing you seem to have gotten out of everything I just said was that you know what to blame yourself for, and to hell with all the rest of it. That perspective fits in nicely with the way the Council is looking at it, but I don't like being caught in the middle. Find somebody else to take advantage of, friend; I've already had my share."

"What do you mean, that fits in with the way the Council is looking at it?" he asked with a frown, ignoring everything else I'd said. "What does the Council have to do with this?"

"You can't possibly mean you haven't noticed that the Council has adopted you as its very own baby boy?" I said, annoyed. "Why do you think they came down on me so hard? Because I didn't stick to procedures? Hell, they go into shock when I *do* stick to procedures. The thing that's really getting them is the way you almost came to an abrupt end, which would have put *them* on the spot at the first conference with your people. They can't very well blame *you*, not while you're an 'official representative,' so they decided to get even for some past difficulties we've had by unloading it all on me. Officially I'm the goat, the one who was supposed to have been running the operation; unofficially you're scheduled for a procedures course, to make sure you don't screw up again. Since you and they think you're so perfect, I wish you all the best together; as soon as I'm out of this place, I'm going back to doing things the way I used to: alone."

I straightened my legs out again and lay down flat on the bed, moving slowly but surreptitiously. That one, stupid conversation had taken more strength out of me than an hour's worth of heavy exercise had done just a few weeks earlier, and I hated that. It would take time before I was back to being as I had been, but I had no patience for waiting.

"So you think they hit you that hard only because they needed someone to blame," Val said, suddenly standing beside the bed again to smooth back the damp hair from my forehead. "Ringer tells me they were as furious as he was to learn how close you'd come to being killed, and all because you hadn't told me what you were doing. I was wrong to let you take off on your own without keeping closer tabs on you, but you were just as wrong not to make sure you were backed up when you went to execute the warrant. The Council may have decided to adopt me, Diana, but you already belong to them. You gave them a scare, and now they're spanking you for taking unnecessary risks."

"You're crazy!" I snapped, shaking my head in annoyance against his hand. "What risks I take are my own decision, not theirs, just as it's always been! And you don't have any more to say about it than they do! Just get out of here and leave me alone."

"I can see you're hurting again so I *will* leave, but only for now," he said, looking down at me with those black, black eyes. "As far as our not being partners anymore is concerned, though, you can forget about it. If your Council is all that eager to make me feel welcome, they'll let me have any partner I want, which means you. They know as well as I do that you need someone to look after you and teach you how to behave yourself, and I'm the one who's going to do it, starting at the training facilities."

He bent suddenly and brushed my lips with his, giving me the oddest feeling, then ran gentle fingers down my cheek.

"When they let you out of here, I'll be waiting," he said softly, and I knew without doubt that he wasn't talking about looking after me or any nonsense about behaving. I was in no shape to think about what he *was* talking about, so I just watched him leave without saying a word, then rolled over onto my left side to grapple with my problems.

Val was after something, I knew that as a dead-certain fact, but what the something could be was more than I was able to imagine. Why was he so determined to be partners with me? Why did he refuse to understand that I didn't need his protection? Why did he keep harping on this garbage about teaching me to behave myself? It was almost as if he had ideas about the two of us beyond a working partnership, but that was ridiculous. Special Agents didn't *get* involved in anything beyond working partnerships, and if Val didn't know that already, he'd find it out as soon as he saw I wasn't kidding about ending ours. Being near him was too much of a distraction, not to mention the fact that he refused to follow orders. I had a job to think about, an important job, and with my life-style, one-night-stands had it all over permanent distractions.

I sighed deeply and stretched out flat again, but couldn't find a comfortable position. If Ringer ever managed to stop and think about it, he'd know I wasn't about to accept the Council's tantrum without trying to do something about it, so I had to plan my moves and act on them before Ringer was ready. I didn't know how long I'd be stuck in that hospital bed, but I'd have to see to it that the time was as short as possible. If I made my break good I'd be able to go back to Dameron's base and take care of the nuisance of being a minor, but if I didn't make it, the Council would see that my time was well filled. I shook my head in annoyance, then gave it up and tried to make myself relax. There was an ancient curse attributed to a group once called Chinese that went, "May you live in interesting times." One way or another, the next few months were going to prove to be very—interesting!

DAW

Presenting JOHN NORMAN in DAW editions . . .

DAW

DAW Books now in select format

Hardcover:

☐ **ANGEL WITH THE SWORD**
by C.J. Cherryh
0-8099-0001-7 $15.50/$20.50 in Canada

A swashbuckling adventure tale filled with breathtaking action, romance, and mystery, by the winner of two Hugo awards.

☐ **TAILCHASER'S SONG**
by Tad Williams
0-8099-0002-5 $15.50/$20.50 in Canada

A charming feline epic, this is a magical picaresque story sure to appeal to devotees of quality fantasy.

Trade Paperback

☐ **THE SILVER METAL LOVER**
by Tanith Lee
0-8099-5000-6 $6.95/$9.25 in Canada

THE SILVER METAL LOVER is a captivating science fiction story— a uniquely poignant rite of passage. ''This is quite simply the best sci-fi romance I've read in ages.''—*New York Daily News.*

NEW AMERICAN LIBRARY
P.O. Box 999, Bergenfield, New Jersey 07621

Please send me the DAW BOOKS I have checked above. I am enclosing $_____ (check or money order—no currency or C.O.D.'s). Please include the list price plus $1.50 per order to cover handling costs.

Name _____

Addres _____

City _____ State _____ Zip Code _____
Please allow at least 4 weeks for delivery